By Troy Denning

STAR WARS

CRUCIBLE

TROY DENNING

arrow books

Published by Arrow 2014

2 4 6 8 10 9 7 5 3 1

First published in Great Britain in 2013 by
Century
Random House, 20 Vauxhall Bridge Road,
London SW1V 2SA

www.starwars.com
www.randomhouse.co.uk

Addresses for companies within The Random House Group Limited can be
found at: www.randomhouse.co.uk

The Random House Group Limited Reg. No. 954009

A CIP catalogue record for this book
is available from the British Library

ISBN 9780099542933

The Random House Group Limited supports the Forest Stewardship
Council® (FSC®), the leading international forest-certification organisation.
Our books carrying the FSC label are printed on FSC®-certified paper. FSC is
the only forest-certification scheme supported by the leading environmental
organisations, including Greenpeace. Our paper procurement policy
can be found at: www.randomhouse.co.uk/environment

Printed and bound by Clays Ltd, St Ives, PLC

For Marissa Hayday
May the Force be with you on all your adventures

Acknowledgments

Many people contributed to this book in ways large and small. I would like to thank them all, especially the following: Andria Hayday, who is always the first person I turn to when I want to brainstorm or sharpen a draft. It would be impossible to overstate the value of her input. Leland Chee, Keith Clayton, Pablo Hidalgo, Erich Schoeneweiss, Scott Shannon, Frank Parisi, and Carol Roeder, for their thoughtful suggestions; Shelly Shapiro and Jennifer Heddle, for everything from their incredible patience to their insightful manuscript notes; Dave Eidoni, for his thoughts regarding Monoliths; Kathy Lord, for her attention to detail; my agent, Matt Bialer of Sanford J. Greenburger Associates, Inc.; all of the people at Lucasfilm and Del Rey who make writing *Star Wars* so much fun; and, finally, to George Lucas, for sharing the galaxy far, far away with us all.

THE STAR WARS NOVELS TIMELINE

BEFORE THE REPUBLIC
37,000-25,000 YEARS BEFORE
STAR WARS: A New Hope

c. 25,793 YEARS BEFORE *STAR WARS: A New Hope*

Dawn of the Jedi: Into the Void

OLD REPUBLIC
5000-67 YEARS BEFORE
STAR WARS: A New Hope

Lost Tribe of the Sith†
Precipice
Skyborn
Paragon
Savior
Purgatory
Sentinel

3954 YEARS BEFORE *STAR WARS: A New Hope*

The Old Republic: Revan

3650 YEARS BEFORE *STAR WARS: A New Hope*

The Old Republic: Deceived

Red Harvest

The Old Republic: Fatal Alliance

The Old Republic: Annihilation

Lost Tribe of the Sith†
Pantheon
Secrets

2975 YEARS BEFORE *STAR WARS: A New Hope*

Lost Tribe of the Sith†
Pandemonium

1032 YEARS BEFORE *STAR WARS: A New Hope*

Knight Errant

Darth Bane: Path of Destruction
Darth Bane: Rule of Two
Darth Bane: Dynasty of Evil

RISE OF THE EMPIRE
67-0 YEARS BEFORE
STAR WARS: A New Hope

67 YEARS BEFORE *STAR WARS: A New Hope*

Darth Plagueis

33 YEARS BEFORE *STAR WARS: A New Hope*

Darth Maul: Saboteur*
Cloak of Deception
Darth Maul: Shadow Hunter
Maul: Lockdown

32 YEARS BEFORE *STAR WARS: A New Hope*

STAR WARS: EPISODE I
THE PHANTOM MENACE

Rogue Planet
Outbound Flight
The Approaching Storm

22 YEARS BEFORE *STAR WARS: A New Hope*

STAR WARS: EPISODE II
ATTACK OF THE CLONES

22-19 YEARS BEFORE *STAR WARS: A New Hope*

The Clone Wars
The Clone Wars: Wild Space
The Clone Wars: No Prisoners

Clone Wars Gambit
Stealth
Siege

Republic Commando
Hard Contact
Triple Zero
True Colors
Order 66

Shatterpoint
The Cestus Deception
The Hive*
MedStar I: Battle Surgeons
MedStar II: Jedi Healer
Jedi Trial
Yoda: Dark Rendezvous
Labyrinth of Evil

*An eBook novella
† Lost Tribe of the Sith: The
  Collected Stories

THE STAR WARS NOVELS TIMELINE

Dramatis Personae

Ben Skywalker: Jedi Knight (human male)
C-3PO: protocol droid
Craitheus Qreph: industrialist (Columi male)
Dena Yus: refinery chief (female biot)
Han Solo: captain, *Millennium Falcon* (human male)
Lando Calrissian: industrialist (human male)
Leia Organa Solo: Jedi Knight (human female)
Luke Skywalker: Jedi Grand Master (human male)
Marvid Qreph: industrialist (Columi male)
Mirta Gev: Mandalorian security-force commander (human female)
Omad Kaeg: asteroid miner (human male)
R2-D2: astromech droid
Savara Raine: troubleshooter (human female)
Tahiri Veila: Jedi Knight (human female)

A long time ago in a galaxy far, far away. . . .

STAR WARS™

CRUCIBLE

One

With lowlifes of every species from three-eyed Gran to four-armed Hekto standing belly-to-bar, the Red Ronto reminded Han Solo of that cantina back on Mos Eisley—the one where he had first met Luke Skywalker and Obi-Wan Kenobi all those years ago. Smoke hung in the air so thick and green he could taste it, and the bartender was pulling drinks from a tangle of pipes and spigots more complicated than a hyperdrive unit. There was even an all-Bith band onstage—though instead of upbeat jatz, they were blasting the room with outdated smazzo.

Usually, the driving bass and stabbing wailhorn made Han think of banging coolant lines. But today he was feeling it, and why not? This trip promised to be more getaway than mission, and he was looking forward to seeing his old friend Lando Calrissian again.

"I don't like it, Han," Leia said, raising her voice over the music. "It's not like Lando to be so late."

Han turned to look across the table, where Leia sat with a half-empty drink in front of her. Wearing a gray gunner's jacket over a white flight suit, she was—as always—the classiest female in the joint . . . and, despite a few laugh lines, still the most beautiful. He thumbed a control pad on the edge of the table, and the faint yellow radiance of a tranquillity screen rose around their booth.

The screen was a rare touch of quality for a place like the Red Ronto, but one Han appreciated as the raucous music faded to a muffled booming.

"Relax," he said. "When has Lando ever missed a rendezvous?"

"My point exactly. Maybe that pirate problem is more dangerous than he thought." Leia nodded toward the entrance. "And take a look at that miner over there. His Force aura is filled with anxiety."

Han followed her gaze toward a young olive-skinned human dressed in the dust-caked safety boots and molytex jumpsuit of an asteroid miner. With a nose just crooked enough to be rakish and a T-6 blaster pistol hanging from his side, the kid was clearly no stranger to a fight. But he was not exactly streetwise, either. He was just standing there in the doorway, squinting into dark corners while he remained silhouetted against the light behind him.

"He doesn't look like much of a threat," Han said. Still, he dropped a hand to his thigh holster and undid the retention strap. As a Jedi Knight, Leia felt things through the Force that Han could not sense at all, and he had long ago learned to trust her instincts. "Probably just some crew chief looking for new hires."

The miner's gaze stopped at the Solos' booth. He flashed a brash smile, then said something to the bartender and raised three fingers.

"He's looking for us, Han," Leia said. "This must have something to do with Lando."

"Could be," Han allowed, but he hoped Leia was wrong. Missed rendezvous and strange messengers were never a good sign.

Any lingering doubt about the miner's intentions vanished when the bartender handed him a bottle of Corellian Reserve with three glasses and he started in their direction. There was something in his bold stride and cocky grin that set Han on edge.

"Whoever he is, I don't like him," Han said. "He's way too sure of himself."

Leia smiled. "He reminds me of *you* at that age," she said. "I like him already."

Han shot her a scowl meant to suggest she needed an eye exam, and then the newcomer was at their table, stepping through the tranquillity screen. He placed the glasses on the table and opened the bottle.

"I hope you don't mind," he said, pouring. "But they keep a case of Reserve on hand for Lando, and I thought you might prefer it to the usual swill around here."

"You were right," Leia said, visibly relaxing at the mention of Lando's name. "Whom shall I thank?"

The miner placed a hand on his chest. "Omad Kaeg, at your service," he said, bowing. "*Captain* Omad Kaeg, owner and operator of the *Joyous Roamer,* one of the oldest and most profitable asteroid tugs in the Rift."

Han rolled his eyes at the overblown introduction, but Leia smiled. "It's a pleasure to meet you, Captain Kaeg." She motioned at the table. "Won't you join us?"

Kaeg flashed his brash smile again. "It would be an honor."

Instead of taking a seat where Leia had indicated, Kaeg leaned across the table to set his glass in the shadows on the far side of the booth—an obvious attempt to position himself where he could watch the door. Han quickly rose and allowed Kaeg into the back of the booth. If a stranger wanted to place himself in a crossfire zone between two Solos, Han wasn't going to argue.

"So, how do you know Lando?" Han asked, resuming his seat. "And where is he?"

"I know Lando from the miners' cooperative—and, of course, I supply his asteroid refinery on Sarnus." Kaeg's gray eyes slid toward the still-empty entrance, then back again. "I think he's at the refinery now. At least, that's where he wants you to meet him."

Han scowled. "*On* Sarnus?" The planet lay hidden deep in the Chiloon Rift—one of the densest, most difficult-to-navigate nebulae in the galaxy—and its actual coordinates were a matter of debate. "How the blazes does he expect us to find it?"

"That's why Lando sent me," Kaeg said. "To help."

Kaeg's hand dropped toward his thigh pocket, causing Han to draw his blaster and aim it at the kid's belly under the table. He wasn't taking any chances.

But Kaeg was only reaching for a portable holopad projector, which he placed on the table. "Let me show you what you'll be facing."

"Why not?" Han waved at the holopad with his free hand.

Kaeg tapped a command into the controls, and a two-meter band of braided shadow appeared above the pad. Shaped like a narrow wedge, the braid appeared to be coming undone in places, with wild blue wisps dangling down toward the corrosion-pitted tabletop and even into Han's drink.

"This, of course, is a chart of the Chiloon Rift," Kaeg said.

He tapped another command, and a red dash appeared in the holomap, marking the cantina's location on Brink Station just outside the Rift. The dash quickly stretched into a line and began to coil through the tangled wisps of hot plasma that gave the Chiloon Rift its distinctive array of blue hues. Before long, it had twisted itself into a confusing snarl that ran vaguely toward the center of the nebula.

"And this is the best route to Lando's refinery on Sarnus," Kaeg said. "I've been doing my best to keep the charts accurate, but I'm afraid the last update was two standard days ago."

"Two *days*?" Han asked. With three kinds of hot plasma rolling around at near light speed, hyperspace

lanes inside the Rift tended to open and close quickly—
sometimes in *hours*. "That's the best you can do?"

"I'm sorry, but, yes," Kaeg said. "It's important to
take it slow and careful in there. If you were to leave a
hyperspace lane and punch through a plasma cloud, you
would fry every circuit on your ship—including your
navigation sensors."

"You don't say," Han said. Hitting a plasma pocket
was one of the most basic dangers of nebula running, so
it seemed to him that Kaeg was working way too hard
to make sure he knew how dangerous it was to travel
the Rift. "Thanks for the warning."

"No problem." Kaeg grinned, then let his gaze drift
back toward the cantina door. "Any friend of Lando
Calrissian's is a friend of mine."

Instead of answering, Han caught Leia's eye, then
tipped his head ever so slightly toward their tablemate.
She nodded and turned toward Kaeg. After forty years
together, he knew she would understand what he was
thinking—that something felt wrong with Kaeg's story.

"We appreciate your concern, Captain Kaeg." Leia's
tone was warm but commanding, a sure sign that she
was using the Force to encourage Kaeg to answer honestly. "But I still don't understand why Lando isn't here
himself. When he asked us to look into the pirate problem in the Rift, he was quite insistent that he would
meet us here at the Red Ronto personally."

Kaeg shrugged. "I'm sorry, but he didn't explain the
change of plans. His message only said to meet you here
and make sure you reached Sarnus." Continuing to
watch the door with one eye, he paused, then spoke in a
confidential tone. "But I don't blame you for hesitating.
This trip could be very risky, especially for someone
your age."

"Our *age*?" Han bristled. "You think we're old or
something?"

Kaeg finally looked away from the door. "Uh . . . *no*?" he replied. "It's just that, uh—well, you *do* need pretty quick reflexes in the Chiloon Rift."

"It's called *experience*, kid," Han said. "Someday, you might have some yourself . . . if you live that long."

"No offense," Kaeg said, raising his hands. "I'm just worried about you heading in there alone."

"Don't let a few wrinkles fool you, Captain Kaeg," Leia said. "We can take care of ourselves."

Kaeg shook his head almost desperately. "You wouldn't say that if you had ever been inside the Rift," he said. "It isn't the kind of place you should go without a guide on your first visit. The plasma in there kills S-thread transmissions, so HoloNet transceivers are worthless—and even emergency transmitters aren't much good."

"What about the RiftMesh?" Han asked. "All that communications hardware, and you're telling me it doesn't work?"

"The 'Mesh works, but it's slow. It can take an hour for a beacon to relay a signal." Kaeg tapped the holopad controls again, and a multitude of tiny white points appeared in the holochart. "And it's not unusual for a message to pass through a thousand beacons before being picked up. Trust me, there's no lonelier place in the galaxy to be stranded."

"It's a wonder any rock grabbers go in there at all," Han replied. "I can't imagine a worse place to be dragging around half a billion tons of ore."

"It's worth it." Ignoring Han's sarcasm—or possibly missing it altogether—Kaeg flashed a square-toothed grin. "The tumblers in the Rift are fantastic, my friend. There are more than anyone can count, and most are heavy and pretty."

By *tumblers*, Kaeg meant asteroids, Han knew. *Heavy and pretty* was slang for a high content of precious metals. According to Lando, the Chiloon Rift contained the largest and most bountiful asteroid field anywhere, with more capture-worthy tumblers than any other place in the galaxy. Unfortunately, its roiling clouds of plasma and a sudden infestation of pirates meant it was probably also the most dangerous.

"Which is why the pirates are hitting asteroid tugs instead of ingot convoys," Leia surmised. "The convoys have combat escorts, but the tugs are hauling all that valuable ore around alone, with no one to call for help."

Kaeg nodded eagerly. "It's terribly dangerous. You can send a message and go gray waiting for an answer." He winced almost immediately, then said, "No offense, of course."

"None taken," Leia said, a bit stiffly. "But with all of those asteroid tugs running around, I can't imagine the pirates coming after a small vessel like the *Falcon.*"

Not seeming to notice how he was being tested, Kaeg shrugged and leaned forward. "Who knows?" he asked. "Even if the pirates aren't interested in the *Falcon*, there are many other dangers."

"And let me guess," Han said. "You're willing to make sure we have a safe trip—for the right price?"

"I could be persuaded to serve as your guide, yes," Kaeg said. "As I said, any friend of Lando Calrissian's is a friend of mine."

"How very kind of you." Leia flashed a tight smile, and again Han knew what she was thinking. No trick was too low for a pirate gang, and one of their favorites was to slip a saboteur aboard the target vessel. "But you *still* haven't explained why Lando didn't meet us here himself."

"Your guess is as good as mine," Kaeg said. "As I mentioned, he didn't give a reason."

Han leaned toward Kaeg and pointed a finger at him. "You see, now, that's where your story falls apart. Lando isn't the kind of guy who fails to show with no explanation. He would've said why he couldn't make it."

Kaeg showed his palms in mock surrender. "Look, I've told you all I know." He focused his attention on Leia. "Lando kept the message short. I'm assuming that's because he didn't want everyone in the Rift to know his business."

"And why would *that* happen?" Leia asked. "Do you have a habit of breaking confidences?"

Kaeg scowled and shook his head. "Of course not," he said. "But I told you—Lando sent that message over the RiftMesh."

"And?" Han asked.

Kaeg sighed in exasperation. "You *really* don't understand how things work here," he said. "The RiftMesh is an open network—*open,* as in one single channel. Everybody listens, with nothing encrypted. If a message *is* encrypted, the beacons won't even relay it. That makes it tough to keep a secret, but it also makes life hard on the pirates. They can't coordinate a swarm attack if everybody is listening to their chatter over the RiftMesh."

"And that works?" Han asked.

Kaeg waggled a hand. "It's not perfect. The pirates find other ways to coordinate," he said. "But the 'Mesh is better than nothing. And it helps the rest of us track one another, so our tugs don't pile up when a good hyperspace lane opens."

Han turned to Leia. "That actually makes sense."

"As far as it goes." Leia did not take her eyes off Kaeg. "But he's been working pretty hard to get us to take him on, and that just doesn't make sense."

"Yeah, I know." Han glanced back at their confused-looking table companion. "Since when do tug captains have time to take on extra work as tour guides?"

The confusion vanished from Kaeg's face. "Is *that* all that's troubling you?" he asked. "My tug has been in for repairs for a month. That's how Lando knew I would be here to give you his message. And, quite honestly, I could use something to do."

Han considered this, then nodded and holstered his blaster. "Maybe we're being too hard on the kid," he said. "After all, he *did* know about Lando's stock of Corellian Reserve."

Leia continued to study Kaeg for a moment, no doubt scrutinizing him through the Force, then said, "Fair enough. But he's worried about something."

"Yes," Kaeg said. "I'm worried that you aren't going to let me guide you to Sarnus." He glanced toward the door again. "But if you don't want my help, you know how to use a holochart."

He started to rise.

"Not so fast, kid." Han grabbed Kaeg's arm. "You've been watching the door since you got here. You expecting someone?"

"Not anymore," Kaeg said, still watching the front of the cantina. "If you don't mind, I have things to do."

Han pulled the asteroid miner back down, then followed his gaze and saw a huge, scaly green figure entering the cantina. The reptiloid was so tall he had to duck as he stepped through the entrance, and his thick arms hung from shoulders so broad that they rubbed both sides of the doorframe. His spiny skull crest almost scraped the ceiling, and a thick tail swept the floor behind him. The creature stopped just inside the room, vertical pupils dilating to diamonds as his pale eyes adjusted to the dim light.

"Who's *that*?" Han asked, keeping one eye on the newcomer.

"No one you'd ever want to meet." Kaeg slid into the back of the booth and slumped down in the shadows. "One of the Nargons."

"Who are the Nargons?" Leia asked. "I'm not familiar with that species."

"Lucky you," Kaeg said, sinking even deeper into his seat. "You should try to keep it that way."

"Care to explain why?" Han asked. "And while you're at it, maybe why you're hiding from that one?"

As Han spoke, two more Nargons ducked through the door, their big hands hanging close to the blasters in their knee holsters. They stepped forward to flank the first one and began to scan the cantina interior.

Kaeg was careful to avoid looking in their direction. "Who says I'm hiding?"

"Kid, I was ducking bounty hunters before your grandfather met your grandmother." As Han spoke, the first Nargon's gaze reached their table and stopped. "I know the signs, so answer the question—or you're on your own."

Kaeg's brow shot up. "You would back me?"

"Assuming you're really a friend of Lando's," Leia said cautiously, "and *if* you start being honest with us. Then, yes, we have your back."

The first Nargon said something to his companions. They eased away in different directions, one going to the far end of the bar, the other drawing angry glares as he jostled his way into the opposite corner.

Kaeg swallowed hard. "Deal."

"Good," Han said. "Tell us what you know about Nargons." He reached over and tapped the holopad controls, and the chart dissolved in a rain of sparkles. "Like, where do they come from?"

"Kark if I know," Kaeg said. "I never saw them before the new outfit brought them in, when the pirates grew so bad."

"New outfit?" Han asked. He was no expert on the Chiloon Rift, but he knew the miners there were mostly independent operators whose families had been in the business for generations. "*What* new outfit?"

Kaeg's lip curled in distaste. "Galactic Exploitation Technologies," he said. "GET. You know them?"

Han had never heard of GET, but he didn't bother to ask for details. His attention was fixed on the entrance, where two more figures were just stepping through the doorway. Unlike the Nargons, this pair was not an exotic species. Standing less than two meters tall, with shoulders no broader than Han's, they were almost certainly human. But they were also wearing full suits of colored armor and blocky helmets with opaque visors, and that could mean only one thing.

"Mandalorians!" Leia whispered.

"Yeah." Han hated Mandalorians. Like their leader, Boba Fett, they had a bad habit of selling their fighting skills to the highest bidder—and the highest bidder was almost always on the side opposite Han. He turned to Kaeg. "What are Mandos doing here?"

"They work security for GET. They're handlers for the Nargons." As Kaeg spoke, the first Nargon leaned down to say something to the taller Mandalorian. "Is this going to be a problem? Because if you can't deal with Mandalorians, then you really can't deal—"

"Relax, kid," Han said. "We can deal with Mandos. We can deal with *anything* in this room."

Kaeg looked doubtful. "Tell me that after you figure out what a Nargon is."

The first Nargon raised a long arm and pointed toward their booth, then fell in behind the two Mandalorians as they crossed the room. The muffled rhythms of the smazzo music continued to reverberate through the tranquillity screen, but the cantina fell otherwise uneasy and still. Judging by all the worried brows and averted eyes, Han half expected the other patrons to clear out. Instead, most remained in their seats, and the miners in the crowd turned to glare openly as the trio passed.

"Not real popular, are they?" Han remarked.

"Nobody likes rock jumpers," Kaeg said. "Galactic Exploitation came in fast and hard with a whole fleet of those giant asteroid crushers. Trouble is, vessels that big aren't nimble enough to run the Rift—and even if they were, GET crews have no nose."

"No nose?" Leia asked.

Kaeg scowled. "You need a sixth sense to operate here," he said. "Outsiders can't smell good rock, and they can't see a lane getting ready to open. They have no feel for how the Rift moves."

"So they trail independent operators instead," Han said. "And then push in on your finds."

Kaeg nodded. "*Push in* is one way to say it. *Steal* is another."

"And when did that start?" Leia asked.

"About a standard year ago. GET showed up a little before the pirate problem erupted in such a big way." Kaeg's face clouded with anger. "And we're pretty sure GET is buying from pirates, too."

Leia shot Han a look that suggested she found the timing as suspicious as he did, and he asked, "What makes you say that?"

"Where else can you take a stolen asteroid?" Kaeg asked. "GET bought up all the small refineries. Now their only real competition in the Rift is Lando's operation on Sarnus, and *he* would never buy from pirates."

Before Han could agree, the Mandalorians arrived with the lead Nargon. Too huge to fit completely inside the tranquillity partition, the reptiloid stopped halfway through and, untroubled by the gold static dancing over his scales, loomed over Leia. The short Mandalorian—a squat fellow in yellow armor—came to Han's side and stood with one hand resting on his holstered blaster.

The taller Mandalorian placed a chair at the table across from Kaeg, then removed his helmet and sat. He had dark curly hair and a burn-scarred face that appeared half melted along the left side. Barely glancing at the Solos, he placed the helmet in front of him, then folded his hands on top and leaned toward Kaeg.

"Skipping out on your marker, Kaeg?" he asked. "I took you for smarter than that."

"I'm not skipping out on anything, Scarn." Kaeg's voice was a little too hard to be natural. "I'm just catching a ride so I can get what I owe you."

A muffled snort sounded inside the helmet of the shorter Mandalorian, and Scarn sneered. "Why do I doubt that?"

"Look, you know what those pirates did to my tug," Kaeg said. "There's no way she's leaving the repair docks for another two weeks, minimum."

Scarn shrugged. "So?"

"So I'll be back for her," Kaeg said. "But it's going to take more credits than I had *before* our game to pay for repairs. I'm heading to Sarnus to make arrangements. I'll get what I owe you at the same time."

"Arrangements with Calrissian?" Scarn rubbed his chin just long enough to pretend he was thinking about it, then shook his head. "I don't think so. We don't like Calrissian, and he doesn't like us. We'll do this another way."

"That's the only way we're going to do it," Kaeg said. "I'm not giving you the *Roamer*—that ship has been in my family for two hundred years."

Kaeg overtly dropped his hand below the table, and Han tried not to wince. Hinting at violence was usually a bad idea when you were outnumbered and outflanked. But at least he was feeling better about the kid's story. Gambling debts he could understand. He'd had a few himself, and the debt explained why Kaeg was so eager to get off Brink Station.

Han rested a hand on his own holstered blaster and tried to look bored, as though firefights against armored Mandalorians backed by overgrown lizards were a common occurrence for him . . . and, really, that wasn't much of an exaggeration.

The Nargon hissed and started to pull the blaster from his knee holster, but Scarn called the reptiloid off with a two-fingered wave.

"There's no need for anyone to get hurt today." The undamaged half of his face smiled at Kaeg. "The last thing I want is that crate of corrosion you call an asteroid tug."

It was hard to say whether Kaeg's frown was one of confusion or outrage. "The *Roamer* may not look like much, but she's all pull," he said. "She's dragged moons out of orbit."

Scarn looked unimpressed. "If you say so. But I have another idea." He extended a hand toward his Mandalorian subordinate. "Jakal?"

Jakal withdrew a pair of folded flimsies from a pouch on his equipment belt and handed them to Scarn.

Scarn unfolded the sheets and pushed them toward Kaeg. "Considering the size of your marker, that's more than fair."

Kaeg eyed the flimsies skeptically, then reluctantly picked them up and began to read. Scarn waited with a bored expression, as though the kid's consent was irrelevant to what was about to happen. Han kept his hand on his blaster grip and watched the Nargon watch him. Jakal's helmet pivoted from side to side as he kept an eye on the rest of the miners in the cantina, who were all carefully observing the situation at Kaeg's table. The other two Nargons continued to stand guard in opposite corners of the room, their tails bumping the walls as they, too, scanned the crowd. But no one was watching

Leia, who was probably the most dangerous person in the Red Ronto.

Maybe the situation wasn't as bad as it looked.

Kaeg was still on the first page when he stopped reading and looked across the table. "Galactic Exploitation wants my family's share of the miners' cooperative?"

Scarn nodded. "That's right," he said. "You sign your share over to GET, then GET pays me, and your debt is settled. Simple."

Kaeg looked more confused than alarmed. "Why?"

Scarn shrugged. "All I know is, the bosses want to join your little co-op," he said. "Maybe they're worried one of their yachts will need to be rescued or repaired or something."

"Then they can pay for an associate membership." Kaeg tossed the flimsies in the middle of the table. "I'm not giving you a founder's share. I'd be run out of the Rift."

Scarn's expression grew cold. "Either you put your thumb in the verification box, or Qizak here rips your arm off and does it for you. Your choice."

A nervous sheen came to Kaeg's lip, but he looked into the Nargon's eyes and managed to fake being calm. "Just so you know, Qizak, you touch me and you die. Clear?"

Qizak bared a fang, then looked to Scarn. "*Now,* boss?"

Leia raised a hand. "Hold that thought, Qizak." Her voice was calm and soothing, the way it always was when she made a Force suggestion. "There's no rush here."

The Nargon studied her, as though considering whether to rip her limb from limb or to simply bite off her head.

Leia ignored the glare and focused on Scarn. "How much does Omad owe, *Ver'alor?*"

The eye on the good side of Scarn's face flashed at her use of the Mandalorian word for *lieutenant.* But the eye on the scarred side merely pivoted in her direction, its cybernetic cornea fogging as it adjusted focus.

Scarn studied Leia in silence. His sneer of contempt suggested that he had no idea she was Princess Leia Organa Solo, sister to Jedi Grand Master Luke Skywalker, and a famous Jedi Knight herself. And if Scarn hadn't recognized Leia, it was a pretty good bet he didn't realize that her companion was Han Solo, one of the finest gamblers in the galaxy—and someone who would know how a cybernetic eye might be used to cheat a kid in a high-stakes sabacc game.

Finally, Scarn asked, "What do you care? You his mother or something?"

Leia's eyes grew hard. "Or something," she said. "All you need to know is that I'm a friend who might be willing to cover his debt . . . once you tell me how much it is."

She pointed at the transfer document and used the Force to summon both pieces of flimsi into her hand.

Scarn's jaw dropped, then his gaze snapped back to Kaeg. "If you think hiring some old Jedi castoff will get you out of your marker—"

"She's not exactly a castoff," Kaeg interrupted. "But you'll get your money, Scarn. Omad Kaeg is no shirker."

"Yeah, but he *is* kind of a rube," Han said. He looked Scarn square in his artificial eye, but when he spoke, it was to Kaeg. "Omad, the next time you play sabacc, make sure it's not with someone who has a cybernetic eye. Those things can be programmed to cheat in about a hundred ways."

Kaeg's voice turned angry. "You have a cybernetic eye, Scarn?"

"He didn't mention that?" Han shook his head and continued to watch Scarn. "You see, now that's just bad form."

Scarn's face grew stormy. "You calling me a cheater?"

His voice sounded exactly like the voices of all the other cheaters Han had spotted over the years—well-rehearsed outrage with no real astonishment or confusion. "Because you weren't even there."

"No, but Omad was." Being careful not to look away from Scarn, Han nodded toward Kaeg. "What do you think, kid? Fair game or not?"

It was Leia who answered. "*Not*, I think." Her eyes remained on the flimsi. "Omad, a million credits on a *marker*? Really?"

"I needed to pay for repairs," Kaeg explained. "And I'm usually very good at sabacc."

"Oh, I can see that," Han said. He was starting to wonder about the convenient timing of the pirate attack on Kaeg's ship—and he was starting to get angry. "And I'll bet after the pirates had you limping back into the station, someone at the bar was buying drinks and talking about the Mando sucker in the back room."

"As a matter of fact, yes." Kaeg sounded embarrassed. "How did you know?"

"It's an old trick, Omad." Leia's voice was kind. "Han has fallen for it himself a few times."

"You have?" Kaeg asked. "Han Solo?"

"No need to talk about that now," Han said. *A few times* was exaggerating, but he knew Leia was just trying to keep Kaeg from starting a fight she didn't think they would win. Deciding she was probably right, he shifted his gaze back to Scarn. "So now that we know your marker is no good, why don't you sign it paid—"

"I didn't cheat," Scarn said, sounding a little *too* insistent. He raised a thumb to the damaged side of his face, then popped out his cybernetic eye and slapped the device on the table. "Check it yourself."

Han barely glanced at the thing. "I'd rather check the eye you used during the game."

"That *is* the one I used."

Scarn's tone remained aggressive and hostile, but the mere fact that he had switched from intimidation to arguing his innocence told Han the balance of power had shifted. Scarn recognized the Solo name, and he was no more eager to start a fight with Han and Leia than *they* were to start one with him and his Nargons.

"Maybe that's the cybernetic eye you were using," Han said, "and maybe it's not. But you didn't tell the kid you had one, and you gotta admit that looks bad." When Scarn didn't argue, Han extended a hand. "So give me the kid's marker, and we'll put all this behind us."

Scarn remained silent and looked around the table, no doubt weighing his chances of actually leaving with Kaeg's thumbprint against the likelihood of surviving a fight. Han risked a quick peek in Leia's direction and was rewarded with a subtle nod. She could feel in the Force that Scarn was worried, and *worried* meant they were going to avoid a battle.

Then Kaeg asked, "What about the rest?"

"The rest of what?" Han asked, confused.

"I lost ten thousand credits *before* I signed that marker," Kaeg said. "It was all the money I had."

Han frowned. "You took your last ten thousand credits to a sabacc table?"

"I didn't see another choice," Kaeg said. "And don't tell me *you* haven't done the same thing."

"That was different," Han said.

He glanced over at Scarn and caught him glaring at Kaeg in fiery disbelief. There was no way the Mandalorian was going to return the ten thousand credits, probably because most of it had already been spent. Han shifted his gaze back to Kaeg.

"Look, kid, ten thousand credits may seem like a lot right now, but it's not worth starting a firefight over. Why don't you think of it as tuition?"

"No," Kaeg said, glaring at Scarn. "Nobody cheats Omad Kaeg."

"Omad," Leia said gently, "*we're* going to pay you for serving as our guide. It will be more than you lost, I promise."

Kaeg shook his head. "It's not about the credits. These Out-Rifters come pushing in here, thinking they can just take what's ours." In a move so fast it was barely visible, he laid his blaster on the table, his finger on the trigger and the emitter nozzle pointed in Scarn's direction. "It's time they learned different."

Han groaned but slipped his own blaster out of its holster and placed it on the table with a finger on the trigger. Scarn did the same, while Jakal pulled his weapon and held it nozzle-down, ready to swing into action against Han or Kaeg. Leia simply laid the transfer document in front of her and dropped one hand onto her lap, where it would be close to her lightsaber. The Nargon watched them all and snarled.

When no one actually opened fire, Han let out his breath and shifted his gaze back and forth between Kaeg and Scarn. "Look, guys, things can go two ways from here," he said. "Either everyone in our little circle dies, or you two come to an understanding and we all walk away. Which will it be?"

Kaeg stared into Scarn's remaining eye. "I'm good with dying."

"Then why are you talking instead of blasting?" Scarn asked. Without awaiting a reply, he turned to Han. "Jakal is going to put his blaster away and hand over that marker. Then we're done here. Clear?"

"What about the kid's ten thousand?" Han didn't really expect to get it back, but he wanted Kaeg to understand that some mistakes couldn't be fixed, that sometimes the only smart move was to cut your losses and move on. "Jakal going to hand that over, too?"

Scarn shook his head. "The ten thousand is gone," he said. "You think I'd be out here on the edge of nothing, wrangling a bunch of overgrown lizards, if I didn't have problems of my own?"

The question made Qizak's skull crest stand erect, and the Nargon studied Scarn with an expression that seemed half appetite and half anger. Han contemplated the display for a moment, wondering just how much obedience the Mandalorian could truly expect from his overgrown lizards, then turned to Kaeg.

Kaeg sighed and took the finger off his blaster's trigger. "Fine." He held a hand out toward Jakal. "Give me the marker."

Jakal holstered his weapon, then pulled another flimsi from his belt pouch and tossed it in the middle of the table.

And that was when Qizak said, "*Coward.*"

Scarn craned his neck to glare up at the Nargon. "Did you say something?" he demanded. "Did I *tell* you to say something?"

Qizak ignored the question and pointed to the unsigned transfer document, still lying in front of Leia. "The bosses need Kaeg's share," he said. "That is the plan they have."

Kaeg's eyes flashed in outrage. "*Plan?*"

Shaking his head in frustration, Han said, "Yeah, kid, *plan.* I'll explain later." Hoping to keep the situation from erupting into a firefight, he turned back to Scarn. "Like you said, we're done here. Go."

Qizak pointed a scaly talon at the transfer document. "When Kaeg gives his share to the bosses."

"No, *now,*" Scarn said, rising. "I give the orders. You—"

A green blur flashed past Han's face, ending the rebuke with a wet crackle that sent Scarn sailing back with a caved-in face. The blur hung motionless long enough to identify it as a scaly green elbow, then shot forward again as Qizak grabbed Kaeg's wrist.

Jakal cursed in Mando'a and reached for his blaster again—then went down in a crash of metal and snapping bone as the Nargon's huge tail smashed his knees. Han stared. *How do we stop this thing?*

By then Qizak was dragging Kaeg's hand toward the transfer document. Han checked the other Nargons and found them both in their corners, still watching the crowd rather than the trouble at the booth. Good. If they were worried about the other patrons getting involved, it would take them longer to react. That gave the Solos ten or twelve seconds to even the odds—maybe longer, if the miners really did jump into the fight.

Han pointed his blaster at Qizak's head. "Hey, Finhead. Let—"

A green streak came sweeping toward Han's arm. He pulled the trigger, and a single bolt ricocheted off Qizak's temple. Then a scaly wrist cracked into Han's elbow; his entire arm fell numb, and the blaster went flying.

From the other side of the booth came the *snap-hiss* of an igniting lightsaber. The acrid stench of burning scales filled the air. Qizak roared and whirled toward a spray of blue embers that made no sense, and then an amputated forearm dropped onto the table, trailing smoke and sparks.

Sparks?

Too desperate to wonder, Han launched himself at Qizak, burying his shoulder in the Nargon's flank and pumping his legs, driving through like a smashball player making a perfect tackle.

Qizak barely teetered.

But the huge alien *did* look toward Han, and that gave Leia the half second she needed to jump onto the booth seat. Her lightsaber whined and crackled, and Qizak's remaining arm dropped next to the first. Two arms, maybe three seconds. Not fast enough. Han drove harder, trying to push the Nargon off balance . . . or at least distract him.

Leia buried her lightsaber in Qizak's side. The Nargon roared and pivoted away, but not to retreat. Remembering how the lizard had smashed Jakal's knees, Han threw himself down on the huge tail, slowing it just enough to give Leia time to roll onto the table. The lightsaber fell silent for an instant, then sizzled back to life.

Qizak let out an anguished bellow, then his tail whipped in the opposite direction. Han went tumbling and came to a rest against a flailing heap of armor—Jakal, writhing with two broken legs. Han spun and reached for the Mandalorian's blaster—then discovered that his numb hand lacked the strength to wrench the weapon from Jakal's grasp.

Jakal pulled it free and started to swing the nozzle toward Han.

"Are you crazy?" Han jerked his thumb toward Qizak. "He's the one who smashed Scarn's face!"

Jakal paused, and Han used his good hand to snatch the blaster away. So far, the fight had lasted six, maybe seven seconds. The other Nargons would join in soon. A tremendous banging sounded from the booth, and suddenly Leia was trapped against the wall as the armless Qizak tried to kick the table aside to get at her. Kaeg stood next to her, pouring blaster fire into the lizard's chest, but the bolts bounced away with little effect.

"What *are* those things?" Han gasped.

Jakal might have groaned something like *scaled death,* but Han was already attacking Qizak from behind, firing with his off-hand. The storm of ricochets was so thick, he did not realize he was caught in a crossfire until he stood and nearly lost his head to bolts screeching in from two different directions.

Han dived and began to kick himself across the floor behind Qizak. The bolts had to be coming from the other Nargons, blasting on the run as they tried to push through the panicked crowd to help their companion. But who would do that—fire into a brawl when their buddy was right in the middle of it?

He continued to squeeze his own trigger, pushing himself toward Qizak's flank and firing toward the smoking hole Leia had opened in the Nargon's ribs. Finally, he saw a bolt disappear into the dark circle.

And *that* drew a reaction. Qizak spun as though hit by a blaster cannon, pupils diamond-shaped and wide open. Gray smoke began to billow from his chest, followed by blue spurting blood and something that looked like beads of molten metal. The Nargon lurched toward Han, his legs starting to shudder and spasm as he prepared to stomp his attacker into a greasy smear.

Leia came leaping over the tabletop, her lightsaber flashing and sizzling as she batted blaster bolts back toward the other Nargons. She pivoted in midair, bringing her bright blade around in a horizontal arc. Qizak's head came off and went bouncing across the durasteel floor.

Han saw the body falling and tried to roll away, but he was too slow. The huge corpse crashed down atop him, and the air left his lungs.

In the next instant, the weight vanished. He saw Leia crouching at his feet, one arm outstretched as she used the Force to send Qizak's body flying into a charging Nargon.

"You okay, flyboy?" she asked.

"I'm—" Han had to stop. His chest hurt something fierce, and the breath had definitely been knocked out of him. Still, he managed to get his feet under him. "Fine. I think."

Kaeg scrambled from beneath the table. A flurry of

blaster bolts nearly took his head off. He cried out in surprise, then waved an arm toward a dark corner.

"Emergency exit!"

He scrambled away, staying low and not looking back.

Han did not follow immediately. Recalling the strange sparks that had sprayed from Qizak's arm as Leia amputated it, he grabbed one of the limbs off the table—and was so surprised by its weight that he nearly dropped it. He flipped the stump around and saw that, instead of bone, the Nargon's flesh was attached to a thick metallic pipe with just room enough for a bundle of fiber-optic filaments.

"*Han!*"

Leia used the Force to send the last Nargon stumbling back toward the bar, then grabbed Han by the arm and raced down a short passage, past the refreshers and out through an open iris hatch. It wasn't until Kaeg sealed the hatch behind them and blasted the controls that she finally released Han's arm and took a good look at what he was carrying.

"Really, Han?" She rolled her eyes in disbelief. "*Souvenirs?*"

Two

The objective was simple: don't break the egg. But like every test at the Jedi Academy on Shedu Maad, success was easier defined than achieved. The obstacle course was littered with fallen *kolg* trees and flattened *maboo* cane, and the academy's best sniper–instructor was laying fire while two apprentices gave chase.

The subject, a young Togorian male with copper-colored fur and a feline's grace, was springing from log to log, holding the thin-shelled sharn egg in one hand and his lightsaber in the other. The Togorian's defense was precise and fluid, with no wasted movement or strength-sapping tension. His counterattacks came in whirling bursts of blade and boot, with enough power and misdirection to impress even the Grand Master of the Jedi Order, Luke Skywalker.

Always, the egg remained safe. As Luke watched, one of the pursuers, a sixteen-year-old human female, dropped into a tangle of *maboo* cane. Her hand rose to deliver a Force shove, but the Togorian was already pirouetting past her slender Bith partner, delivering a powerful hip check that knocked the fellow into the path of her attack. The Bith flew off the log backward, his thin limbs flailing wildly as his oversize cranium led the way toward the rocky ground.

The young woman's eyes brightened in panic, and

when she reached out in the Force to cushion her partner's fall, a sly grin crossed the Togorian's boxy snout. He waited half a heartbeat for her to bring the Bith under control, then tossed the egg into the air so he could switch to a two-handed lightsaber grip and deflect two of the sniper's stun bolts into her flank.

The young woman collapsed in a heap, leaving her partner to hit the ground at a safe speed. By then the Togorian had caught his egg and was holding his lightsaber with a single-handed grip. He leapt off the *kolg* trunk and began to advance on the sniper sideways, deflecting fire toward his last, still-prone pursuer. It took only a couple of steps before a stun bolt struck, sending the Bith's entire body into a paroxysm of clenched muscles.

The Togorian continued toward the sniper at a leisurely stroll, not even bothering to dodge as he deflected a steady torrent of stun bolts. The display sent a cold shiver through the Force, but neither Luke nor the other Masters allowed their expressions to betray their feelings.

"His combat skills are impressive," said Jaina Solo. Han and Leia's last surviving child, Jaina was approaching thirty-six. She looked a lot like her mother at the same age, but she wore her dark hair longer, and she had more steel in her eyes than fire. "There's no doubt of that."

"There certainly isn't," agreed Corran Horn. A short, fit man in his sixties, Corran had wise green eyes, a weathered face, and a gray-streaked goatee. "In fact, I'd say that Bhixen is as good as *you* were at that age, Master Solo."

"He is," Luke agreed. "And he knows it."

As Luke spoke, the Force behind him stirred with the familiar presence of Seha Dorvald, the Jedi apprentice who was currently serving as his aide. Her aura felt nervous and a bit reluctant, as though she was unsure whether her errand warranted an interruption. Luke motioned her forward without turning around.

"Excellent timing, Jedi Dorvald." He drew his blaster and extended the butt toward her. "Take my sidearm and shoot the egg out of Candidate Bhixen's hand."

Seha hesitated. "Uh, Master Skywalker, I have an urgent message—"

"*Now,* Jedi Dorvald," Luke said. Bhixen was only a Force leap away from the fallen tree that Jagged Fel was using as a sniper's nest, and Luke was not ready for the test to end. "And make sure the candidate sees you."

"Very well." Seha took the blaster from Luke's hand. "But, Master Skywalker, this weapon's power selector is set to—"

"*Now,* Seha," Luke ordered. "Open fire—and make it convincing."

Seha stepped two paces away from Luke and the other Masters, then began to spray full-power bolts toward Bhixen's flank. At a range of more than twenty meters, the blaster pistol was not very accurate, and it was difficult to tell whether she was firing at the Togorian or the egg. Bhixen instantly launched himself into an evasive Force tumble, his blade flashing and crackling as he deflected her attacks. For a moment, he seemed too surprised and overwhelmed by the live fire to react emotionally, and Luke dared to hope the Togorian's arrogance was no more than a minor character flaw.

Then Bhixen landed, ducking behind a massive *kolg* trunk that protected him from the sniper's nest. He spun to face Seha's pistol fire, and when he saw who was attacking him, the Force boiled with his outrage. Dropping the sharn egg into the soft bed of *maboo,* he switched to a two-handed grip—and began to bat Seha's attacks back at her so quickly that Luke barely had time to Force-tug his aide to safety. Even then, the Togorian sent the last bolt flying directly into the gathering of Masters, and Luke had to raise a Force-shielded palm to deflect it.

Bhixen froze in mid-whirl. He stopped with his body sideways to Luke, keeping his lightsaber at high-guard and one leg cocked, ready to spin into another Force leap. His presence was quivering with shock and shame, but his outrage remained, as though the attack from an unexpected quarter had been an undeserved indignity.

"Stand down!" Luke called, using the Force to project his voice over the entire testing arena. He summoned the sharn egg from the spot where Bhixen had dropped it. "The exercise is over."

The director of the academy, a tall, dignified Jedi Master named Kam Solusar, signaled Bhixen to remain where he was, then took the egg from Luke.

"Bhixen's pride has always been his greatest weakness," Kam said. "I fear his skill only contributes to it."

"There is a darkness inside him," Luke said. "And the days are gone when the Jedi can afford to train their own enemies."

As Luke said this, he was remembering the long line of Knights who had gone to the dark side under the constant stress of combat and subterfuge that was the everyday life of a Jedi. The most recent had been his oldest nephew, Jacen Solo, who had become the Sith Lord Darth Caedus. To end Darth Caedus's reign of terror, Luke had been forced to assign Jacen's twin sister, Jaina, to hunt down and kill her brother. It had been one of the most difficult decisions of his life—one that had left him heartbroken and doubting his own ability to prepare young Jedi Knights for the spiritual tests in their futures.

Kam continued to study Bhixen in thoughtful silence, and his wife, Jedi Master Tionne Solusar, stepped forward to ask the question on everyone's mind.

"So, dismissal?"

Corran was quick to shake his head. "I think that

would be premature," he said. "The Sith are still out there, and someday they will show themselves again."

"And when they do, we're going to need superb fighters like Candidate Bhixen," Jaina said. "Plenty of them."

"So we lower our standards?" Kam asked. He cast an uneasy glance at Tionne's prosthetic leg—just one of the artificial limbs she needed after a torture session with a henchman of Darth Caedus. "We don't dare—not when we might be creating the next Sith Lord."

"Kam, that's not fair to Bhixen," Corran said. "He's still a youngling. Mistakes are to be expected."

"Mistakes, yes," Luke said. "But faults in character? No."

"It's hard to know the difference at Bhixen's age," Jaina said. "Character isn't merely genetic. It's built through experience."

"And through instruction," Corran added. "If a candidate isn't ready, we mustn't advance him. But does that mean our only alternative is dismissal? Because if it does, *we* are the ones who have failed."

Luke fell silent for a moment, then finally said, "You're right, Master Horn." He motioned Bhixen to approach. "After bringing him this far, we should not give up easily."

The Togorian marched forward, chin held high and ears erect, trying to conceal the anxiety he was pouring into the Force. It was clear that he regretted batting a blaster bolt back toward the Masters, but there was also indignation in his aura, as though he refused to accept that the mistake had been his.

When Bhixen came within a couple of steps, Luke motioned him to stop. The Togorian was already close to two meters tall, with red-brown fur and a powerful build that would have made him an imposing figure even without a Jedi lightsaber hanging from his belt. After the combat test today, there could be no doubting that he would one day be a formidable warrior. But whether that would be in the service of the Jedi or someone else remained to be seen.

"Candidate Bhixen, that was an impressive performance," Luke said. "Do you think you're ready to become Master Solo's apprentice?"

Bhixen's ears pricked forward, and then he spoke in a gravelly Togorian voice that was already deep and confident. "I don't *think* so, Master Skywalker. I *know* so." He switched his gaze to Jaina. "I'll make you proud, Master Solo."

"Not so fast," Jaina replied. "Grand Master Skywalker asked if *you* thought you were ready to become my apprentice. He didn't say *he* thought so. And I haven't said *I* think so, either."

Bhixen looked from Jaina to the sharn egg, then back to Luke. "So my test was not successful?"

"To the contrary, Bhixen," Luke said. "It was very successful. We learned a great deal about your weaknesses."

Bhixen's ears went flat against his head. "My weaknesses?"

"You lost your temper," Luke said.

"But Jedi Dorvald wasn't part of the exercise," Bhixen objected. "You *cheated*!"

"And your enemies won't?" Luke asked mildly. "The greatest danger a Jedi faces is not injury or death, or even failure. It's what he feels inside—his pride, his fear, his anger. His emotions are what feed the dark side."

Jaina nodded in agreement. "You have great potential, Bhixen," she said. "Too much. We can't train you only to have you turn to the dark side and become our greatest enemy."

Bhixen's jaw fell, and he looked from Jaina to the rest of the Masters. Finding only stern, unreadable faces, his fur bristled, and he turned to Luke with disbelief in his eyes.

"Then you're dismissing me?"

Luke continued to watch the Togorian in silence, waiting to see how the stunned candidate would react—whether he would burst into an angry diatribe or beg for another chance, or simply spin on his heel and storm off.

When Bhixen awaited an answer without doing any of these, Luke said, "We're not ready to advance you, but whether you leave or start again depends on you."

"Start again?" Bhixen asked.

"As though you had just arrived at the academy," Luke confirmed. "Whatever you did not learn before, you must learn now. We won't give you a third chance."

Bhixen dropped his gaze. "Of course," he said, not even hesitating. "If that is what you wish."

"No, Bhixen," Jaina said. "If that is what *you* wish. Do you truly want to do this? To start over from the beginning? Think hard."

Bhixen furrowed his bushy brows and stared at Jaina for a long time, and Luke had the impression that the Togorian was looking for the trick in her question, as though his entire future hung on his ability to avoid a verbal trap. But, finally, a gleam of understanding came to his eyes, and his expression began to soften.

He let out a long breath, then said, "I understand. I have too much pride."

"That's right," Luke said. "And your pride is the great weakness in your defenses."

"I agree." Bhixen flipped his lightsaber around and offered the hilt to Luke. "And I want to start over."

"Good." Luke took the lightsaber. "This will be returned when you are ready. Now take the sharn's egg back to its nest, then report to the quartermaster droid for reassignment to a berth in the novice barracks."

Bhixen accepted the egg from Kam, then took his leave with a formal bow. But before he started back into the forest, he made a detour to check on the two apprentices he had put out of action.

Luke began to feel more confident about the Togorian's chances.

Just then, the sniper–instructor who had been firing stun bolts at Bhixen arrived: Jagged Fel. A tall, fit man with a white streak in otherwise dark hair, Jag was a former Imperial head of state, a superb pilot, a lifelong military man—and Jaina Solo's husband. Although not a Jedi himself, he had developed compensating strategies that had turned him into the Jedi Order's finest commando leader.

He stopped at the edge of the group, with his long-blaster slung over his shoulder. "Nice shooting, Jedi Dorvald," he said, grinning at Luke's aide. "I haven't seen many marksmen who could've fired that many pistol bolts at an evading target and still avoided the egg."

Seha's face flushed with embarrassment. "Thank you, Commander." She shot a glance in Luke's direction, then admitted, "But my orders were to *hit* the egg."

"You came close enough, Jedi Dorvald," Luke said, smiling. He motioned at the datapad tucked into the belt of her robe. "Didn't you say you have a message for us?"

"I did." Seha pulled the datapad from her belt. "The Solos have run into some trouble at their rendezvous."

"The Solos?" Corran asked. "Weren't they going to the Chiloon Rift?"

"That's right," Jaina said. "Lando asked them to investigate a pirate ring that's been causing problems there lately. Why do you ask?"

"Because Jedi Soroc is in the Chiloon Rift, and she hasn't checked in for a month," Corran explained. Ohali Soroc was one of ten Quest Knights whom Luke had dispatched a year earlier to search for Mortis, a legendary world that had once been home to a trio of mythic

Force entities known only as the Ones. Jedi lore suggested that the Ones had been associated with keeping the Force in balance for tens of thousands of years, and it was Luke's hope that finding Mortis would help the Jedi Order prepare for the challenges rising in its own future. "We've already diverted Ben and Tahiri to investigate, but it wouldn't hurt to ask your parents to keep an eye out for her."

"Sure, if we can reach them," Jaina said. "From what Lando says, communications in the Rift are tricky."

"Well, since Han and Leia managed to get a message to us, let's see what they have to say."

With that, Luke turned to Seha and nodded. She clicked a few keys, then handed the datapad to Luke. Jag, Jaina, and the others quickly gathered around as the grainy, bouncy image of the *Millennium Falcon* appeared in the display, standing on its struts in a cavernous space-station hangar. The screen instantly started to strobe in green and blue as blaster bolts whistled through the picture.

Han's voice began to issue from the speaker. "Solo here," he said. "Sorry for talking on the run, but we're about to head into the Rift, and I want to send this while our communications are still secure. Lando missed our rendezvous at the Red Ronto and sent a miner pal named Omad Kaeg to fill in. Turns out he's in trouble with some Mandalorians working security for a company named Galactic Exploitation Technologies."

Despite the blaster bolts flashing past and the obvious fact that he was under pursuit, Han sounded calm and unconcerned.

"This GET outfit has been moving into the Rift in a big way, taking over small refineries and muscling in on independent operators. We think they're running the pirates, too."

The image—no doubt recorded on a portable datapad—whirled past a dark-skinned, wide-eyed human male running in one direction and firing in the other, then passed a flashing lightsaber that could only be Leia's, deflecting blaster bolts.

"So we need someone to do some serious digging and get a report to us at Lando's refinery," Han said. "And—sorry about this part—but, like I said, communications in the Rift are not secure. So we need someone to hand-deliver it."

As Han spoke, the image continued to swing around the hangar, until it finally settled on a spray of blaster bolts erupting from the far end. Rather than the Mandalorians that Han had mentioned, the attackers were a pair of scaly green bipeds who—judging by the hatchway behind them—looked to be the size of Wookiees. The image zoomed, and the pursuers grew large enough for Luke to see that each had a spiny skull crest atop its head and a long, spike-tipped tail whipping around behind it. Both carried short-barreled blaster rifles, firing on the run as they raced after their quarry.

"Meet the Nargons," Han said. "They're muscle for GET—and they're big trouble."

The image spun back toward the *Falcon*, which rapidly swelled into nothing but a blur as Han raced toward it and boarded. A thump sounded, and the image shifted to a huge green-scaled arm lying on the deck of the *Falcon*'s main cabin. The limb appeared to have been cleanly amputated above the elbow—by Leia's lightsaber, Luke assumed.

Han's voice sounded from the datapad speaker again. "And there's one more thing."

His hand appeared in the image, rolling the dismembered arm around to display the blackened circle of its cauterized stump. Instead of the usual disc of charred bone, there was a hollow silvery oval of freshly cut metal.

"These Nargon things aren't natural," Han continued. "Someone has to be building them—or maybe growing them. Either way, they're no joke. They just about took us out."

The image shifted to Han's face, and a cocky half grin flashed across his face. "Time to fly," he said. "Solo out."

The message ended with a terminal bleep, and the display went dark. Luke reversed the vid until it showed the Nargons entering the hangar, then enlarged the image until only one filled the display. The magnification revealed vertical pupils and a mouthful of needle-sharp teeth, but not much more.

"Anyone seen one of these guys before?" Luke asked.

"No, but they can certainly shoot," Corran said. "That hangar must be three hundred meters across, and they were putting bolts in a tight cone."

"And with close-assault weapons," Jag added. "I think those are Merr-Sonn Verqs. Powerful, but their effective range isn't anywhere near three hundred meters."

"Are you suggesting that they're using the *Force*, Commander Fel?" Kam asked.

Jag considered his answer for a moment, then shrugged. "I wouldn't have any way to judge that. What I *can* tell you is that those Nargons are as good as I am. I could lay a cluster that tight with that weapon—but just barely."

"Good point," Luke said. "You don't have to be Force-sensitive to excel at something. You're proof enough of that." He paused. When no one else commented, he passed the datapad back to Seha. "Ask Master Cilghal to give me her thoughts on these Nargons, and have a research team start an analysis on Galactic Exploitation Technologies. Then have the *Jade Shadow* prepped for travel."

"The *Shadow*?" Jaina's tone was disapproving. "Are you planning to take this assignment yourself?"

"You don't think I can handle a courier mission?" Luke asked, putting a little indignation in his voice. "Or a few pirates?"

Jaina rolled her eyes. "You know better than that."

Her gaze dropped to Luke's chest, where his robe covered a mysterious, slow-to-heal wound. He had received it the year before from an ancient being named Abeloth, who seemed to be a chaos-bringing agent of the Force itself. Luke had ultimately triumphed, but the fight had cost him a rib and part of a lung.

"I'm fine. You know the wound only bothers me when I have a Force vision." Luke had to work to keep a civil tone, for the Masters' concern over his health had grown tiresome over the last few months. He was the Grand Master, after all, and they insisted on coddling him. "I doubt that will be required."

"Which raises the question of why *you* need to go," Corran said. "Courier runs are the kind of mission we assign to a new Knight, not the Grand Master of the Order."

"Usually, yes," Luke allowed. "But, with the passage of the Neutrality Act, I doubt that Senator Wuul will agree to meet just *any* Jedi."

"You're going to ask Luewet Wuul for a briefing?" Kam asked.

"Of course," Luke said. "He chairs the minerals committee. If anyone can tell us what *isn't* public knowledge about Galactic Exploitation Technologies, it's Luewet."

"But will he?" Jaina asked. "He could be accused of treason for just talking to a Jedi."

Jaina was exaggerating. The Galactic Alliance Neutrality Act was simply a formal declaration of the Alliance's intention to stay out of the war between the Jedi and the Sith. But when it came to a government official sharing information with either side, there were a lot of gray areas where a crafty old senator like Luewet Wuul would not tread boldly.

"That's why I plan to speak with Wuul personally," Luke said. "Wuul is the only friend we have who might be able to tell us what's going on behind the scenes with this GET, and he'll need to know we're not asking for this favor lightly."

"Fair enough," Corran said. "That explains why you might take the first assignment. But I still don't see why a Grand Master needs to carry the report to the Chiloon Rift personally."

"*Need* is a strong word, Corran," Luke said, quietly chafing at his old friend's not-so-subtle effort to keep him from exerting himself. "But I think it should be me, yes."

Jaina studied him for a moment, then finally asked, "Because your son is going to be in the Chiloon Rift, too, and you haven't seen him in six months?"

"It would be nice to see Ben, that's true," Luke said. "But there's another, more important reason."

The Masters all frowned, trying to puzzle out the answer, but a crooked grin tugged at the corner of Jag's mouth.

"Because," Jag said, "you've been stuck recuperating on Shedu Maad for an entire year, and you need to get out of here before we drive you crazy."

Luke smiled. "Exactly," he said. "Sometimes, Commander Fel, I swear you *do* have the Force."

Three

From the purple heavens fell an endless rain of fiery stream-ers, chunks of asteroid plunging into the atmosphere as the breaker crews pushed them out of orbit. "The Drop" was just one of a hundred inefficient steps in an ore-smelting process as backward as the Rift itself, and watching it from the unadorned offices of the Sarnus Refinery administra-tive building, Marvid Qreph could scarcely believe that such an antiquated operation could be the source of so much trouble for him and his brother.

Marvid allowed himself to glare out the viewport for a moment longer, then set his puny jaw and turned his ornate powerbody toward the office interior. In the cen-ter of the room, his brother, Craitheus, hovered at the conference table in his own powerbody, floating a bit high in an effort to intimidate their hosts. Like all mem-bers of the Columi species, Craitheus was largely head, with huge eyes, no nose, and a web of blue veins throb-bing over his giant cranium. Beneath his tiny chin, a ropy neck descended to an atrophied body barely large enough to carry the organs required to keep blood puls-ing through his enormous brain. His limbs were tiny and vestigial, ending in hands and feet curled into use-less lumps of bone and flesh.

". . . Chiloon holdings are nothing but a headache

to you," Craitheus was saying to the refinery's owner, Lando Calrissian. "And the pirate situation is only going to deteriorate. Our offer won't be as good next week."

"And I wouldn't accept it if it were," Calrissian replied.

Despite his age, Calrissian was handsome, fit, and suave—a combination that Marvid always found irksome. A gambler who had parlayed his winnings into an industrial empire, Calrissian was intelligent and cunning by human standards, but he was too smooth for his own good. Not a black-dyed hair was out of place, and he was always quick to flash his annoying white smile.

"I may be relatively new to the Rift myself," Calrissian continued. "But the Sarnus Refinery has been processing asteroids for centuries. It has survived bigger problems than a few pirates."

"Perhaps so," Craitheus said. "But how much are you willing to gamble on that resilience? The smart play is to attend to your holdings outside the Rift—before problems erupt *there*, as well."

The smirk on Calrissian's face did not change. "Should I take that as a threat?"

"Perhaps you should take it as good advice," Marvid said from his spot near the viewport. He was risking his brother's wrath by softening the statement, but Craitheus's fondness for intimidation did not always serve their purposes. "We're all businessmen here, and it's rather early in the negotiations for threats."

"I'm glad you think so," said Dena Yus.

A statuesque, auburn-haired woman who appeared to be in her forties, Yus was seated next to Calrissian and opposite Craitheus. She was the refinery's operations chief and Calrissian's point woman in the Rift, even though she had been running the refinery for only six months. Marvid knew all about her, because he was the one who had forged the employment records and recommendations that convinced Calrissian to hire her.

"Because if you're making threats," Yus continued, "one might wonder if *you're* behind the problems here in the Rift. Are you?"

"Blaming *us* won't deflect attention from your incompetence, Chief Yus," Marvid said, playing along.

Like any good industrial spy, Yus was taking pains to establish herself as a loyal employee in the eyes of her target. But she was also warning the Qrephs to go easy, letting them know that intimidation would not work against Lando Calrissian. It was rather impertinent of her, but, in this case, Marvid concurred with her opinion.

Marvid glanced toward the far end of the table, and his powerbody—responding to a thought that had barely risen to the level of consciousness—drifted into position directly opposite Calrissian.

"Selling is in your best interests," Marvid said. "The Sarnus Refinery has been draining Tendrando finances for months now, and it's only going to get worse."

"And so of course you just *have* to buy it," Yus retorted. "The pirates are a temporary problem, and you certainly know that—probably better than anyone."

"Chief Yus, that's the second time you have made a thinly veiled accusation against us," Craitheus said. Overacting as usual, he spoke in a wispy, menacing voice. "I would advise against a third."

The humor left Calrissian's eyes, and Marvid knew his brother had gone too far with the intimidation tactics. Hoping to undo the damage, he dropped his powerbody until his feet were almost on the floor, bringing him eye-to-eye with the famous industrialist and gambler.

"Chairman Calrissian, you're an astute businessman," Marvid said, his tone reasonable and almost apologetic.

"So I'm sure you understand why we're making such a generous offer."

"Because those asteroid crushers of yours are too big and clumsy to compete in an environment like the Rift," Calrissian said. "And you want to shut down my refinery, so the asteroid tugs will have no other place to sell and you can drive down the price of raw ore."

"Close enough," Marvid said, allowing himself a tiny smile.

Despite his legendary acumen as a gambler, Calrissian saw only one level of the brothers' plan. This was to be expected. Calrissian was only human, after all, with a tiny human brain in a tiny human head. The Qrephs were super-geniuses, bigheads even among the giant-headed Columi.

"Our process *is* immeasurably more efficient," Marvid continued patiently. "The haulage savings in the first year alone will be worth more than this entire planet."

"And put a million independent asteroid miners out of work," Lando replied.

"Economics is a cruel science," Marvid said. His power-body wobbled as its mechanical shoulders reacted to a mental shrug. "There's nothing we can do about *that*."

"You need to think about yourself, Calrissian," Craitheus added. "Chief Yus hasn't been able to turn the refinery's situation around, and you won't, either. These are no ordinary pirates. If they were, our Mandalorian security force would have hunted them down by now."

"Assuming your Mando thugs have actually been *trying*," Dena said. "We have only your word for that."

"And how many pirate bases has *your* security contractor eliminated?" Marvid asked.

Dena dropped her gaze. "We're concentrating our resources on delivery protection."

"*Of course* you are," Craitheus sneered. His power-body pivoted to face Calrissian. "You simply don't have the resources to mount a search-and-destroy operation *and* continue operating the refinery at a loss."

"And even if we *were* behind the pirates, as Chief Yus insinuates, it would change nothing," Marvid added. "Your problems in Chiloon would *still* be drawing money away from your more valuable enterprises."

"And robbing time from your family," Craitheus added. "Think of them, Chairman Calrissian. Wouldn't you rather be spending your evenings with Tendra and Lando Junior in one of your homes closer to the Core?"

Something flashed in Calrissian's eyes. It might have been pain or agreement, but it was gone too quickly for even Marvid to catch. Instead, the human displayed his white teeth in a smile so wide and well rehearsed that it seemed quite condescending.

"*Chance,*" he said.

The wrinkles above Craitheus's brow dropped into a wedge of confusion, and even Marvid did not understand the reference. Hoping for some insight, he accessed the last few seconds of his video archive, which was being constantly recorded by the vidcam in his powerbody's breastplate. Calrissian's face appeared in his mind, transmitted directly from his powerbody. Marvid replayed the vid slowly, trying to identify the emotion that he had seen flashing across the industrialist's face.

He soon found what he was looking for: a microexpression that came and went in a millisecond—the tip of a tongue darting between the lips, the eyes growing round and wide.

Fear.

For just an instant, Calrissian had taken Craitheus's remark about spending time with Tendra and Lando Junior as a threat to their safety—and *that* had worried him.

When neither Marvid nor his brother spoke, Calrissian filled the silence. "*Chance* is what we actually call Lando Junior," he said. "If your researchers were any good, that would have been in their report."

"Our apologies," Craitheus said, his voice growing ominous. "We'll do better next time."

"Assuming there *needs* to be a next time," Marvid said. Deciding to press the target on the one weakness Calrissian had exhibited so far—his concern for his family—Marvid had his powerbody transmit a string of numbers to the datapad resting in front of Calrissian. "You need to be with your family, Calrissian. Believe me, it would be better for everyone if you accepted our offer and let us take over your Chiloon holdings."

Marvid pointed at the datapad. A flash of defiance lit Calrissian's brown eyes, but his gaze dropped to the screen anyway. His brow rose in shock.

"That's a bit more than I expected," he admitted.

"It's for *all* of your Chiloon holdings," Craitheus said. "All you need do is accept, and the credits will transfer to an account of your choice."

Calrissian's gaze remained on the datapad. "I didn't realize you were in a position to offer that much," he said, "especially in an immediate transfer."

"There are a great many things you don't know about us, Chairman," Craitheus said. "That is how we prefer it."

Calrissian nodded, silently acknowledging that their unannounced arrival and request for an urgent meeting had left him little time to investigate *them*—not that he would have discovered much. The Qrephs had learned how to manage information as mere younglings, from a mother who had earned her livelihood brokering information on the black market. Now her sons could work behind the scenes better than anyone in the galaxy—with the possible exception of the Sith, of course. Even Marvid and Craitheus had failed to anticipate the brief

Sith takeover of the Galactic Alliance government the year before. The mistake had cost them close to three trillion credits in lost opportunities.

Lesson learned, Marvid thought.

Finally, Calrissian pushed the datapad in front of Yus. She studied it for a moment, then said, "That's a nice offer, Lando." There was just enough reluctance in her voice to make her disappointment sound sincere. "No one would blame you for taking it."

"No?"

Calrissian's eyes went back to the datapad. His fixed gaze and tilted head suggested that he was seriously contemplating the offer, as well he should have. Marvid and his brother had selected the figure very carefully. It was high enough to suggest the Sarnus Refinery was hurting them more than they wanted to admit, yet not so high that Calrissian would wonder what else the Qrephs had in mind for the Rift.

But there was no hint in Calrissian's face of whether he was inclined to accept or refuse. Marvid initiated an immediate playback of the video archive, slowing the feed to search for micro-expressions that might suggest whether now was the time to remain patient or to make another threat and play on Calrissian's fear for his family.

Still nothing.

Calrissian was inscrutable, one of the few humans who seemed truly capable of hiding his emotions. Marvid might even have admired the man, had he not posed a threat to the Qrephs' own plans in the Rift.

Realizing that any additional pressure would only backfire, Marvid elected to let Lando ponder the figures on his own. The Qrephs were offering as much as the refinery would net in three years—even without the pirate troubles. Any rational being would jump at such an offer.

Apparently Craitheus had come to the same conclusion. He allowed his powerbody to settle to the floor and fold into a lounging-chair configuration, and that was when the door slid open and Yus's obsolete CZ-19 secretary droid rattled into the conference room.

"I apologize for the intrusion, Chief Yus," it said. "But Chairman Calrissian requested notification as soon as his guests arrived."

"It's about time," Calrissian said. He turned to Dena. "Have someone show them up right away."

"That won't be necessary, Chairman," the droid said. "Your guests are waiting in the anteroom now. Captain Kaeg escorted them up from the hangar."

Marvid had to force himself not to look in his brother's direction. By now Omad Kaeg was supposed to be rotting in a Brink Station trash compactor. The fact that he *wasn't* undoubtedly meant that Craitheus's thug—a Mandalorian lieutenant named Scarn—had failed to secure Kaeg's seat on the support cooperative. That was *not* good news.

As Marvid contemplated Kaeg's survival, Calrissian's mustache lifted in a grin of relief. "What are you waiting for?" he asked the secretary droid. "Show them in!"

"You're entertaining guests?" Craitheus demanded. "In the middle of *our* meeting?"

Calrissian squared his shoulders. "Our meeting is over for now," he said. "You've made your offer, and I need time to consider it."

Craitheus's eyes grew angry. "You *have* no time, Calrissian. The situation is deteriorating. So will our offer."

"I'll take that chance," Calrissian said, rising. "I have a feeling things in the Rift are about to change."

He stepped around the table and started for the door, where a pair of humans was just entering from the adjacent anteroom. The male looked roughly the same age as Calrissian, with lighter skin, untidy graying hair, and a lopsided grin. The female appeared to be about ten years younger, with long hair shot with gray and a high-cheeked face. Her big brown eyes were shining with wit and vigilance, and Marvid found her quite attractive. Behind the pair followed a young olive-skinned human with a scarred chin and crooked nose—no doubt the target of Scarn's failed assignment, Omad Kaeg.

Calrissian spread his arms wide. "Han, Leia—thanks for coming," he said. "Your timing is perfect."

This time, Marvid did not even try to avoid exchanging glances with Craitheus. Both Qrephs knew of Calrissian's famous friends, Han and Leia Solo. But they hadn't expected Calrissian to turn to the Solos for help. That development added a whole new dimension to their business in the Rift—one as personal as it was troubling. Marvid and Craitheus continued to look at each other for a moment, silently acknowledging that they had some new contingencies to plan for, then finally turned toward the jabbering humans.

"You'd *better* thank us," Han Solo was saying. "This place is a nightmare to reach. I blew the *Falcon*'s entire sensor package in a plasma pocket, and we just about bumped noses with an asteroid the size of the Death Star."

The corners of Craitheus's mouth dipped in disappointment, and Marvid knew he and his brother were thinking the same thing: *how unfortunate you avoided that.*

Calrissian's brows shot up, and he glanced past Han's shoulder toward Kaeg. "Omad, you let *Han* take the yoke? His first time in the Rift?"

Kaeg shrugged, his twitching eye betraying the casual smirk he affected. "He threatened to have the princess mindwipe me—whatever that is," he said. "But Captain Solo did pretty well for a Rift virgin. The asteroid bump was the only time we almost died."

Calrissian cocked a brow. "That you *know* of."

He released Han and turned to embrace Leia. She was dressed in a white, form-fitting flight suit that made Marvid wonder if Jedi women aged at the same rate as normal humans.

"Leia, I appreciate this," Calrissian said, flashing his broad smile. "I know the Order is stretched thin right now. I'm sure you had a real job convincing the Jedi Council to let you come."

"It was no problem at all," Leia said, returning the embrace. "The Council is always happy for an excuse to send Han offbase."

Calrissian laughed. He seemed so at ease that Marvid was starting to think their investigators had missed a lot more than Lando Junior's nickname. Where the Jedi were concerned, *stretched thin* was an understatement. A Hutt–Yaka spice war was threatening to erupt into full-blown interstellar combat, while a Falleen charlatan was using her pheromones to build an interstellar church devoted to nonregulated, free-market anarchy. And there were dozens of similar crises building across the galaxy, all ready to erupt without Jedi intervention. The Order wasn't *stretched thin*—it was at the breaking point.

Yet the Jedi Council had answered Calrissian's request by sending not only the Solos to the Chiloon Rift, but also a Duros Knight named Ohali Soroc—who had actually reached Base Prime before being captured by the Qrephs' security force. And Luke Skywalker's son, Ben, had been snooping around the planet Ramook, an agricultural world located just beyond the far end of the Rift. Ostensibly, Ben and his companion had been searching for a mysterious Sith vessel named *Ship*—but Marvid knew a cover story when he heard one. The Jedi were responding in force to Calrissian's call.

And Marvid had a good idea why. The balance sheet of Tendrando Arms, the Calrissian family's most successful concern, showed three billion credits in payments to unspecified vendors. Both Marvid and his brother had assumed the payments were to the top-secret suppliers any weapons manufacturer required. But there was another possibility: perhaps Tendrando's secret payments were being sent to the Jedi Order. *That* would certainly provide some incentive to help Calrissian solve his problems in the Rift.

Clearly, the Qrephs had underestimated Calrissian's reach. Marvid turned to suggest they depart, and he found Craitheus glaring at Han with such obvious hatred that even Calrissian had noticed.

Obviously, a diversion was in order.

Marvid spun his powerbody toward Calrissian. "You have *Jedi* on call? Very impressive."

"I asked my friends to appraise the pirate situation," he said. "I trust you and Craitheus have no problem with that?"

"Only if their presence delays your decision to sell," Marvid said.

Kaeg's eyes widened in alarm, and he turned to Calrissian. "You're selling?"

"Marvid and Craitheus made an offer." As Calrissian spoke, his gaze remained fixed on Craitheus. "I haven't said yes. I doubt I will."

Craitheus's eyes flattened to horizontal ovals. "Then you'll wish you *had,* Calrissian," he said. "Bringing Jedi into this was a mistake. They can't save you."

Both Solos tightened their lips almost simultaneously, and Marvid realized Craitheus had just committed a serious blunder. *Very* serious.

"What my brother means to say," Marvid said, attempting to cover, "is that it's too late for a few Jedi to drive out the pirates. The problem has already grown too large."

Craitheus shot Marvid an angry glare, and Marvid

realized he didn't have the faintest idea what his brother was thinking. True, forty years ago Han Solo had been the last person to consult their mother before someone put a blaster bolt through two of her cerebrums. But emotional outbursts were *not* how Columi operated. Columi followed a plan.

Seeing that all three humans were now staring at *him*, Marvid realized that he had no choice except to follow his brother's example. Fixing his gaze on Calrissian, he tipped his powerbody forward in intimidation.

"Your only hope is to accept our offer and count yourself lucky." As Marvid spoke, his powerbody reported a surge of high-frequency radio waves—a signal of approval from Craitheus. "If you don't, you'll leave the Rift with nothing."

"If you leave at all," Craitheus said. He spun his powerbody away and started toward the exit. "Don't underestimate us, Calrissian."

"It wouldn't be smart," Marvid added.

Following his brother's lead, Marvid turned toward the door—and found Leia Solo standing in front of him with folded arms. He armed his powerbody's weapon systems with a thought—and her hand dropped to her hip and came up holding her still-inactivated lightsaber.

"You know what wouldn't be *smart,* Marvid?" she asked. "Underestimating Han and me. That's what your thugs at Brink Station did, and they paid with their lives. All of them."

"Yeah, it was a real mess," Han added. "Scales and bits of Mandalorian armor everywhere. I'll bet they're still scrubbing that blue stuff off the walls."

"Then we'll have to send *more* next time," Marvid said, moving his powerbody higher. "Fortunately, our security force is more than ample."

With that, he crossed over the top of the table and shot through the door after his brother—then ran straight into the Solos' golden protocol droid, who was two steps inside the anteroom, still reeling from his encounter with Craitheus.

Marvid lashed out with a vanalloy arm and sent the 3PO unit stumbling.

As the 3PO sputtered behind him, Marvid followed his brother down the corridor toward the turbolifts. Though he kept his weapon systems armed, Marvid wasn't expecting trouble. The refinery was bustling with sentient staff, and Calrissian was too soft to jeopardize innocent lives by deploying his dreaded YVH security droids. Both brothers reached the turbolift bank without incident.

Before he slipped into a tube behind Craitheus, Marvid activated his powerbody comlink and opened a channel to their confidential assistant, Savara Raine. "We're returning to the *Aurel Moon* now," he said. "Be there when we arrive, or you may be left behind."

"I'm already aboard and waiting." As always, Savara's voice was silken and alluring, with a hint of accent so exotic that Marvid often found himself accessing his archive just to hear it. "Trouble?"

"Coming soon, I think," Marvid said. "Prepare for launch."

"As we speak," Savara replied. "Anything else?"

"Were you able to complete your assignment?"

Savara's voice grew indignant. "I *said* I was aboard and waiting."

"Of course." Marvid took no exception to her peevish tone; in fact, he relished it. There were very few beings who had the confidence to speak to him in such a manner—and even fewer dangerous enough to survive it. "Were you observed?"

"Now you're just being rude," she retorted. "They won't even find the bodies."

"Excellent," Marvid said. "Be sure to award yourself a bonus. A substantial one."

"Oh, *thrilled,*" she said, sounding just the opposite. "Look, Craitheus is crossing the hangar . . ."

"Of course," Marvid replied. "Go ahead—"

The channel popped shut, leaving Marvid oddly warm within. He wondered whether the girl understood the effect she had on him. It wasn't her disdain he found so appealing, but the intimacy it created between them— as though Savara understood exactly what he was and accepted it, because monsters didn't frighten her . . . because *nothing* frightened Savara Raine.

Marvid slipped into the lift tube and dropped a hundred meters into a cavernous subterranean hangar. A dozen spacecraft of varied sizes and shapes sat berthed in an area that could have held three times that number. He recognized a handful of ships—the elegant crescent of the Qrephs' own Marcadian luxury cruiser, the *Aurel Moon;* the plump wafers of half a dozen ScragHull commando boats, workhorses of the Sarnus security force; and the fork-nosed disk of the Solos' YT-1300, the famous *Millennium Falcon.*

The hangar's maintenance crew was swarming over the *Falcon,* repairing the damage from what appeared to have been a *very* rough first journey into the Rift. It was impossible to tell whether any extra Jedi were aboard the vessel, but even if there were, it would be a few days before they moved against him or his brother. Calrissian and the Solos might have their *suspicions* about who was behind the pirate attacks, but the Jedi Order would never sanction violence on suspicion alone. So, while the Solos wasted time searching for evidence, the Qrephs would be executing their plan to drive Calrissian and the miners from the Rift.

Seeing no immediate threats, Marvid hurried across the hangar to the *Aurel Moon* and ascended the boarding ramp into its vestibule. There, he was surprised to find Craitheus and Savara Raine waiting with the commander of the Mandalorian security force, Mirta Gev. A compact human woman in orange and gray armor, Gev had light-brown eyes and dark-brown hair, which she wore short and neat so it could be tucked beneath her helmet. She had a pensive gaze that made Marvid suspicious of her loyalty, as though there were some things she would not do even for money.

Savara was a much younger woman, with light-brown hair that fell to her shoulders and dark-brown eyes that often shaded to black. She was only a few years out of childhood, but her gaze seemed infinitely older than Gev's, as cold and deep as that of an Anzati assassin. She sometimes carried a crimson lightsaber—a souvenir, she had said, from her time with the Jedi—but she could kill easily and efficiently with any weapon at hand . . . or even none at all. The only sign that she had ever fought someone who had challenged her skills was a small hooked scar at the corner of an otherwise perfect mouth.

Surmising that his brother and the two women were meeting him here to discuss something in private, Marvid extended his powerbody's struts and let it rest on the deck.

"You wish to adjust our plan?" he asked Craitheus.

The veins in Craitheus's temple throbbed in eagerness. "We didn't anticipate the arrival of the Solos," he said. "That was shortsighted. But it gives us an opportunity to eliminate them."

Marvid considered the suggestion for a moment. Could they actually kill the legendary Han and Leia Solo that easily? He looked from Craitheus's enthusiastic gaze to the reluctance in Gev's and finally to the neutral confidence in Savara's.

"You can arrange it?" he asked Savara. "For the Solos to be there?"

"I don't have to arrange anything," she replied. "Lando is *going* to show them around. All I need to do is wait."

"But then you'll take out Calrissian, too," Gev said. She turned to Marvid. "Won't that complicate your plan?"

"It's a small thing," Craitheus said, dismissing her objection with a wave of a vanalloy arm. "Eliminating Calrissian has *always* been a possibility."

"True enough," Marvid agreed. He and Craitheus had debated Tendra Calrissian's reaction to her husband's death many times. They had never been able to decide whether she would give up the Sarnus Refinery—or grow more determined to keep it open. "But an event of this magnitude will draw scrutiny, and we already have too many Jedi inside the Rift."

"It won't draw scrutiny if it looks like an accident," Savara said. "And it will. Tractor beams fall out of alignment all the time."

"They do," Gev said. "But you'll need three sets of safety overrides to fail. That's asking the accident investigators to overlook a lot."

"We can handle the investigators," Marvid said. "That's routine."

"And the Jedi are *already* here," Savara said. "You need to deal with them sooner or later—and they'll be much easier to kill in a confused situation."

"Very astute," Craitheus said. He turned to Marvid. "And, of course, there is the added bonus."

Marvid thought for a moment, then said, "Agreed. Killing Solo and his wife would be a nice bonus, indeed."

Craitheus actually smiled. "Then it's decided."

Gev shook her head. "This isn't what my people signed on for," she said. "Chasing a bunch of asteroid miners out of the Rift is one thing, but this—"

"*Your* people won't be doing this," Savara said. She

locked gazes with the older woman, and even Marvid felt the chill that passed between them. "*I* will."

Gev returned Savara's glare without flinching. Marvid began to fear it might actually come to a fight, and as entertaining as that might be, it would also be unfortunate timing. The Mandalorians would probably lose their leader, which meant the Qrephs would likely lose their Mandalorians. And without Mandalorians to oversee them, the Nargons were too slow and brutish to function as an effective security force.

Deciding he had no choice but to intervene, Marvid said, "Commander Gev, the terms of our contract are clear. Are you suggesting you intend to break that contract? The granddaughter of Boba Fett, renege on her word?"

Gev's eyes flashed, but she immediately looked away from Savara. "No, of course not," she said. "I was just letting you know how my people are going to feel about this kind of attack."

"Then I suggest you don't *tell* them it was an attack," Craitheus said. "Unless, of course, you don't expect us to help you and your grandfather with *your* problem."

Gev's face grew stony, and she spoke to Craitheus through clenched teeth. "I *said* I'd honor the contract. You make sure you do the same."

Craitheus's eyes twinkled. "Oh, we will," he replied. "Have no fear of that."

Savara made a point of catching Gev's eye, then curled her lip into a victorious sneer. "It looks like I have work to do." She turned toward the boarding ramp, then said to Marvid, "I won't be carrying a comlink, so you two had better be sure you want this done."

"We're quite certain." Craitheus made a shooing motion with his powerbody's hands. "Just be sure we're offplanet when it happens."

Savara rolled her eyes, reminding Marvid of the teen-age human she still was, at least physically. "I think you'll be safe, Craitheus."

"Of course we will," Marvid said. "But what about *you*, my jewel? The Solos should not be underestimated. If something were to raise their suspicions, I doubt you would survive."

"And then you wouldn't complete your assignment," Craitheus added. "Are you sure you can do this alone? We could spare a squad of our bodyguards to provide support."

"The Mandalorians wouldn't need to know what you're doing," Marvid added. "Only that it's *their* job to protect you."

He left unsaid the next part, the part he knew Savara would not need explained—that once her assignment was over, the bodyguards would have to be eliminated. No one but Savara and Gev could be allowed to know the Qrephs' role in the upcoming *accident*.

Savara thought for a moment, then met Marvid's gaze and asked, "You're only talking about Han and Leia, right? Jaina isn't with them?"

"That's correct," Craitheus said. "Does that make a difference?"

"Of course it does," Savara said. "*Leia* Solo I can handle myself. But Jaina . . . well, a squad of Mandalorians wouldn't be enough."

"So you intend to go alone?" Craitheus confirmed.

Savara nodded. "I'm less likely to be spotted that way. And even if someone does notice me, I'll have an easier time talking my way out of trouble without a squad of armored guards clunking around behind me."

"No doubt." Marvid hesitated for a moment, then asked, "You *do* have a plan to escape unharmed, cor-rect?"

The question actually brought a smile to Savara's face, and she reached up to pat his cheek. "Why, Marvid—I do believe you're worried about me." Marvid did not usually like being touched, but it was not so bad when Savara did it. "That's so *sweet*."

Four

At the far end of the service hangar sat a SoroSuub Ur-menung 300, its unique three-pods-on-a-disk silhouette so distinctive that Luke could identify its model at a glance. Heavily armed and armored, the "Urmi" was the yacht of choice for anyone who valued security as well as luxury, so it wasn't unusual to see one at an up-scale resupply depot like Crossing Lanes Station. At the same time, the yachts were too expensive to be common, so it seemed likely that this one belonged to the person he had come to meet.

And the fact that Luewet Wuul had yet to show him-self suggested just how much the senator wanted to avoid being seen with Luke. Not that Luke could blame him. At the moment, the Jedi were almost pariahs in the Galactic Alliance—especially on the capital world. Most of Coruscant's citizens still held the Jedi responsible for the devastation their planet had suffered during the bat-tle to dislodge Abeloth and her Sith minions.

Nonetheless, Wuul had agreed to the meeting, because he understood that the public wrath was misplaced. Without the Jedi, there would be little to prevent the Sith from returning in strength and trying again to sub-vert the Galactic Alliance.

From the stern of the *Jade Shadow* came the muffled thump of a supply nozzle pushing into a load socket.

R2-D2 tweedled from the droid station at the rear of the flight deck, then a message appeared on the pilot's display, requesting permission to accept a thousand liters of hyperdrive coolant. Luke confirmed that the routing valves were set properly, then opened the tank.

"Go ahead, Artoo," he said. "But tell them to take it slow. I don't want any blowback corroding our hull."

R2-D2 gave an affirmative whistle, and Luke watched the tank's status gauge start to rise. It was during quiet moments like these, sitting alone at the helm, that he still felt Mara's presence at his side. The *Jade Shadow* had been his wife's ship and—all too often—their temporary home as one crisis or another turned the Skywalkers into interstellar nomads. At the time, Luke would not have guessed that those periods of close living would be among his most cherished memories, but they were—the uninterrupted hours with his wife and son, the week-long stretches when the only faces he saw belonged to Mara and Ben.

Now Mara was dead. And Ben was a Jedi Knight, only a bit younger than Luke had been when he began his training with Yoda.

R2-D2 chirped again, and another message scrolled across the pilot's display. THE CLEANING SERVICE REQUESTS PERMISSION TO BOARD.

Luke hadn't ordered any services that required access to the interior of the vessel, but he *was* expecting a visitor. "Can you put up a vid of the cleaners?"

The display switched to the image of a squat little Sullustan in a cap and blue overalls. He carried a bag of cleaning supplies slung over his shoulder. Beside him sat the multi-armed cylinder of a SoroSuub JTR cleaning droid.

Luke smiled. The Sullustan's face was hidden beneath the bill of his cap, but the cleaning droid was a dead giveaway. A Sullust-based manufacturing conglomerate,

SoroSuub was known for everything from its battle cruisers to its comlinks. But its cleaning droids had been an abysmal failure. Only Sullust's senator, who would never risk being seen with an item made by any of Soro-Suub's competitors, would have a JTR.

"Permission granted," Luke said, rising. "Lower the boarding ramp, Artoo."

By the time he went aft to meet his guests, the ramp was down and the cap-wearing Sullustan was leading the cleaning droid across the threshold. With heavily wrinkled dewflaps, rounded ears sagging forward, and deep circles ringing his huge dark eyes, he was clearly an elder of his species—and he was clearly Senator Luewet Wuul. He quickly caught Luke's gaze, then shot a glance toward the wall control.

"We normally leave the boarding ramp down while we clean," Wuul said, his voice bright and cheerful. "But of course it's your choice, Captain."

"Thank you. I'd prefer to keep the vessel closed," Luke said, flipping the toggle button.

As the ramp rose into position, Wuul moved his cleaning droid into the main cabin, then knelt down and pressed a switch hidden between its treads. The entire front casing swung open, revealing a hollow interior filled with equipment essential to any clandestine meeting. The wily senator removed the silver half ball of a full-spectrum eavesdropping jammer, then activated it and placed it on the galley prep counter. Next, he withdrew a bottle of Maldovean burtalle and a pair of cut-crystal tumblers, which he promptly filled. He passed one to Luke and took the other himself, then raised his glass and clinked rims.

"To old friends and honest deals."

"Wealth and health for everyone," Luke replied, completing the traditional Sullustan toast. "And may the Force be with us all."

The addition caused Wuul's eyes to cloud with concern, but he tipped his glass and drained the burtalle in one gulp. Luke sipped his, relishing its smoky flavor as Wuul refilled his own glass. This second glass, Luke knew from his sister's notes on the senator, was only for show and would go mostly untouched until their business was done.

Once Wuul's glass was full again, he took a seat at the table. "Sorry for all the subterfuge," he said. "But we can't be too careful. They have eyes everywhere."

"Who—the Senate?" Luke asked. "The Sith? BAMR News?"

Wuul scowled. "Sith? BAMR? No." He hopped out of his seat and fetched a flimsiplast file from the droid's secret compartment. "Who are we here to talk about? *GET!*"

"Right—Galactic Exploitation Technologies," Luke said. He sensed a growing fear in the senator's Force aura. "I take it you've heard of them?"

"More than I'd like." Wuul returned to his seat, but instead of placing the file on the table, he kept it close to his chest. "Let's start with the Jedi's interest in them. How are you involved with GET?"

"*Involved* probably isn't the right word," Luke said, taking a seat across from Wuul. "GET's name came up in association with a piracy problem we're investigating."

"A problem in the Chiloon Rift?" Wuul asked.

"That's right," Luke replied. "But the Rift is well outside Galactic Alliance territory, so I didn't expect you to be familiar with our situation there."

"Of course I'm familiar with it," Wuul retorted. "It involves minerals and metals, doesn't it?"

"Indirectly, I imagine," Luke replied. Even without the Force, Wuul's suspicion was as evident as it was surprising. "Han and Leia were handling the initial investigation alone, so I'm not really sure."

"Initial? Then you're sending more Jedi into the Rift?"

Luke paused, trying to decide how much he should reveal before he knew the reason for Wuul's wariness. "As a matter of fact, I'm going there myself."

"You?" Wuul asked. "Why?"

Luke pointed at the file. "Your turn," he said. "So far, I'm the only one who's been sharing."

"Fair enough," Wuul said, keeping the file close to his chest. "Chiloon may be outside Alliance space, but that doesn't mean we have no interests there. The Rift supplies a tenth of our beryllius, a quarter of our quadranium, and most of our duralium. And the list of other minerals is as long as my arm. *Of course* I want to know why the Jedi are there."

Luke merely smiled. "And?"

"*And* we're not the only ones who regard the Chiloon Rift as vital to our economy," Wuul continued. "You might have noticed that it's located midway between the Corporate Sector and the Imperial Remnant—and it's a lot closer to them than to us."

"So you're worried about annexation?"

"I'm *always* worried about someone annexing the Rift," Wuul said. "The only reason nobody has tried it yet is that the asteroid chasers out there are crazy and fiercely independent. All they'd really have to do to wipe out a war fleet is retreat into the Rift and wait for the enemy to come after them."

"That sounds like an old problem."

"You asked for background," Wuul replied, still evading.

"On GET."

A spike of fear shot through Wuul's Force aura, and he surprised Luke by draining half the burtalle in his glass.

"Okay. You understand that we impose a mineral tax on everything imported from the Rift into the Alliance," Wuul said. "It's the only way to give a fair break to the miners working our own asteroid fields."

"I still don't see the connection," Luke said. "What does that have to do with GET?"

"They don't like paying taxes," Wuul replied. "And when the Qreph brothers don't like something, it's a problem."

"The Qreph brothers?" Luke asked.

Wuul tapped the file. "They own Galactic Syndicated," he said. "Which, in turn, owns Galactic Exploitation Technologies. It's all in this file. It's an interesting read, I promise."

When Wuul did not pass the file over, Luke asked, "So how do I get a look at it?"

"First you tell me what the Jedi are doing in the Rift," Wuul said. "Then we'll see."

Luke paused to examine Wuul's Force aura again, searching for the oily touch of deception or the tang of a bluff. When he found only the electric bite of fear, he realized that the senator was not trying to dupe him— only to be sure that Luke did not hold back any secrets himself.

"We have nothing to hide," Luke said. "GET might be involved in the piracy problem I mentioned earlier. The attacks are really cutting the supply to Lando Calrissian's asteroid refinery on Sarnus. We sent Han and Leia to investigate as a favor to an old friend, and their last message hinted that it might not be your usual pirate problem."

Wuul's eyes gleamed with sudden comprehension. "GET is bringing more product into the Alliance now than ever," he said. "I thought they were just taking a bite out of Lando's market share, but I'm beginning to think it's something else—something more typical for them."

"*More* typical?" Luke asked.

Wuul nodded and placed the flimsi on the table between them. "Piracy isn't GET's only sideline," he said. "Just because GET is bringing metal into the Alliance doesn't mean we're collecting taxes on it."

"So—they're into smuggling, as well," Luke said, taking the file.

"Just read." Wuul drained his glass, then eyed the bottle as though fighting the temptation to pour another. "Piracy and smuggling are only the beginning."

Luke opened the file. As Wuul had explained, GET was owned by Galactic Syndicated, an interstellar conglomerate with interests in livestock gene development, advanced cyborg technology, interstellar transportation, and a dozen other fields. Over the last thirty years, their companies had been associated with crimes ranging from gene rustling to slave making. During the war against the Yuuzhan Vong, there had even been a Syndicated starliner service that specialized in selling whole shipfuls of refugees to Yuuzhan Vong priests for rites of mass sacrifice.

Luke looked up. "Why aren't these guys living in a detention center somewhere?"

"Because Marvid and Craitheus Qreph are masters of working behind the scenes," Wuul replied. "Their mother was an information broker and statistical prognosticator on Ord Mantell, until someone put a blaster bolt through her head."

"They were orphans?"

Wuul shook his head. "That might have been easier on them," he said. "The bolt didn't kill her. It just left her unable to form new memories."

"Which meant she couldn't earn a living anymore," Luke surmised.

"Right. The Qrephs grew up poor—so poor they had to share a powerbody." Wuul pointed at the file again. "Keep reading. It's all in there."

Luke returned to the file. Growing up in poverty had been a deeply motivating factor for the Qrephs. On their eleventh emergence anniversary, the brothers had embezzled a million credits from a local crime lord. They had used the money to buy a small product-evaluation laboratory, then began a lucrative program of testing Kuati cosmetics on stolen pets and orphaned younglings.

After that, the Qrephs had virtually disappeared from the official record until shortly before the war against the Yuuzhan Vong. At that point, security and police services all over the galaxy began to trace an astonishing array of crimes, corruption, and deceitful business practices back to the parent company, Galactic Syndicated. Even then, it wasn't until recently, just after the Second Civil War, that Marvid and Craitheus Qreph had been identified as the sole owners of Galactic Syndicated.

Luke set the file aside. The Jedi Order's own researchers had discovered some of the same information. But the Galactic Alliance's investigation had clearly been going on for a much longer time, and their file was far more complete. He looked across the table at Wuul.

"You're right, it's an interesting read," he said. "Now tell me what's *not* in the file."

"Those are the facts as we know them, Master Skywalker," Wuul said. "Anything else I might say is merely observation and speculation."

"Understood," Luke replied. "That's what I came to you for."

Wuul's dewflaps rose in the Sullustan version of a smile. "Well, since you ask . . ." He took the file and opened it to a long list of Galactic Syndicated's recent acquisitions. "What strikes me is the sudden growth. In the last six months alone, GS has bought two dozen companies, most for a fraction of their true value—and many of those concerns are behemoths in their own right."

Luke studied the list. "And a lot of them are duplicates in strategic industries," he noted. "I see three Tibanna-gas suppliers, two starfighter manufacturers, *four* ship builders, five freight companies . . ."

"Exactly," Wuul said. "At the SoroSuub Business Academy, they teach that a sudden acceleration in corporate acquisitions usually means someone is attempting to corner a market. But the acquisitions tend to be clustered around a single industry."

"And these *aren't*," Luke said. "They're all over the place."

"Precisely, Master Skywalker," Wuul said. "It's a bit premature to say this, but if the pattern continues to accelerate as it has, I would have to conclude that the Qrephs aren't attempting to corner *one* major market. They want them *all*."

"*All?*" Luke repeated. "That's pretty ambitious, isn't it?"

"It is." Wuul glanced away, and once again Luke felt a bolt of fear shoot through his Force aura. "But so was disbanding the Senate and turning the Galactic Republic into the Empire."

"Point taken," Luke said. "Is that what the Qrephs are after? Total control of the economy?"

Wuul spread his hands. "You're the Jedi, Master Skywalker. You tell me."

"Better to avoid assumptions," Luke said, nodding. "You said the Qrephs have been buying companies at a fraction of their true value. How are they doing that?"

"The same way they avoid paying import taxes, I imagine," Wuul said. "Spies, bribery, extortion, intimidation, murder—whatever they need to do."

"And what is it that *you're* frightened of, Luew?"

Wuul's ears dipped ever so slightly. "I thought you

might notice that," he said. "But I assure you, I'm not allowing my own concerns to influence my decisions— any more than I would consider taking a bribe."

"*What* concerns, exactly?"

"The threats, of course." Wuul met Luke's gaze again. "Have you been *listening,* Mâster Skywalker?"

"Yes," Luke replied. "But I'm having trouble believing it. The Qrephs are actually threatening a Galactic Alliance *senator?*"

Wuul's dewflaps tightened. "Heavens no, Master Skywalker," Wuul said. "Even *they* aren't that brazen. But I've had to ask my warren-clan to go into hiding."

"Threatening a senator's family is still a crime," Luke observed.

"And I'm sure they would be prosecuted for it," Wuul said. "*If* we could bring the Qrephs to justice inside Galactic Alliance space—and *if* I had the kind of evidence that could be used to embarrass Wandara Dekort into pursuing the case."

Luke raised his brow. "The minister of justice is on their payroll?"

"Bribed, blackmailed, threatened—or perhaps just overly cautious." Wuul spread his hands. "Who is to know?"

"Has Minister Dekort at least opened . . ." Luke paused when he sensed a jittery presence underneath the *Shadow,* up near the bow, then continued, ". . . an investigation of the threats against your family?"

"Not that I know of," he said.

Luke rose and turned halfway toward the presence. Wuul tipped his head but quickly resumed the conversation when Luke twirled a finger to keep it going.

"Dekort claims that mere innuendo is no grounds for an investigation," the Sullustan said. "But she *has* assured me that if anyone in my warren-clan vanishes or comes to harm, she'll be happy to open a file."

"What about Senate Security Services?" Luke asked. "Isn't it the Senate's duty to protect you *and* your family?"

"Duty and deed are very different things, Master Skywalker," Wuul said. "If the Qrephs can subvert senators and high-court judges—and they *have*—they can certainly subvert a bodyguard or two."

The presence was underneath the *Shadow*'s main cabin now, creeping closer to the galley table where Wuul was sitting. Luke felt more apprehension than sinister intent in its Force aura, which suggested that the intruder was probably a spy rather than an assassin—or perhaps merely an unscrupulous member of the service crew looking for something worth stealing.

Motioning Wuul toward the boarding ramp, Luke said, "We might be able to send a Jedi to help your family."

"Do you want me tossed out of the Senate, Master Skywalker?" Wuul asked. He rose and started aft. "A lot of my colleagues actually believe that nonsense about the Jedi drawing us into war after war—and the rest are happy to blame *you* instead of their own bad judgment."

"It wouldn't have to be obvious," Luke said, waiting until Wuul reached the boarding ramp. "We *do* have Sullustan Knights, you know."

Wuul thought for a moment, then shook his head. "The Alliance has to handle this problem on its own." He reached the boarding ramp, then placed a thumb over the control pad and raised his brow in silent inquiry. "With the Jedi gone, it's the only way we'll ever build the kind of robust institutions we need to fight corruption like this."

Luke pointed at the control pad and nodded, signaling Wuul to lower the ramp. At the same time, he reached for the spy in the Force, grabbing him in its invisible hand and slamming him into the hard durasteel of the *Shadow*'s belly.

A muffled thunk echoed through the hull, and a voice cried out in pain and astonishment. Whoever was beneath the *Shadow*, Luke realized, was not a professional spy. Luke allowed the eavesdropper to fall back to the hangar deck, then hurried aft.

By then Wuul was already kneeling near the top of the ramp, peering forward under the *Shadow*'s belly. *"Suuas?"* he called, clearly astonished. "Didn't I tell you to wait aboard the ship?"

A reedy voice replied, "I, uh . . . I'm sorry, Uupa." *Uupa* was the Sullustan word for one of the clan-matriarch's mates. "I thought something might be wrong."

"Is that why you're carrying an eavesdropping saucer?" Wuul retorted. "Even I know that's not pilot kit."

Luke had to descend the ramp about halfway before he saw a young male Sullustan lying on the deck beneath the *Shadow*'s belly, a purple lump forming on the crown of his head. Resting on the deck beside him was a device that resembled a stethoscope with a giant suction cup on the end.

"You're *spying* on me?" Wuul hissed, struggling to keep his voice down. "My own warren-spawn?"

Suuas shook his head urgently. "No, Uupa!" He picked up the eavesdropping saucer and stared at it as though it were a fang eel. "This was already here. That's what I was coming to tell you!"

He was, of course, lying. Luke could sense the deception and panic in the young Sullustan's Force aura.

"That's not what you said two moments ago." Wuul's voice was calm and cold. "You said you thought something might be wrong."

"Because I saw *this* hanging beneath the vessel's belly," he said, shaking the listening device at Wuul.

"Then you'd better come aboard," Luke said. He

didn't have to look to know they were attracting the attention of the crew who were still servicing the *Shadow*. "Let's have a look at it."

"Yes, bring it to us," Wuul said, catching Luke's concern almost immediately. He glanced around beneath the vessel, as though searching for someone hiding behind one of the struts. "Did you see who put it there?"

A warm wave of relief rolled through the Force as Suuas fell for his uupa's trick and believed he might actually get away with his misdeed. The young Sullustan rose and came toward the boarding ramp.

"Just some service crew," he said. "It might have been one of them."

"That would make sense," Wuul said, his tone so convincing that, had Luke not sensed the suspicion in his Force aura, he would have believed the senator accepted Suuas's lie. "We'll sort this out inside."

Wuul took one last look around, then quickly withdrew into the ship. Luke waited on the ramp, watching to make certain the bump on Suuas's head hadn't given him a concussion. When the young Sullustan started to ascend the ramp without lurching or stumbling, Luke extended a hand for the device.

"Let me have a look at that."

Suuas shook his head. "I work for the senator," he said. "I should give it to him."

"As you like," Luke said, lowering his hand. "And I'm sorry about banging you into the hull. I assumed from the apprehension I sensed in your Force aura, and the care with which you were creeping forward, that you were trying to avoid notice."

Suuas looked away without speaking, then climbed the rest of the way into the *Jade Shadow*. Luke took a moment to glance toward the stern of the vessel and found a pair of Duros service technicians making a point of *not* looking in his direction. He knew better than to hope they had failed to recognize him, but Crossing Lanes Station was the kind of place where clients demanded discretion—and were willing to pay for it.

Luke took a pair of hundred-credit chips from his belt pouch and went back to the hoverlift the Duros were using to reach the *Shadow*'s service socket.

"In case I don't see you before I depart." He reached up to place the chips on the hoverlift deck. "I appreciate your professionalism."

Both Duros glanced down, their gazes lingering on the chips long enough to show their appreciation, then nodded curtly.

"Our pleasure, Captain," said the older one. "You have a safe journey, now."

"I will," Luke said, smiling at the use of *captain*. "Thank you."

He climbed back aboard the *Shadow* and raised the ramp again. In the main cabin, Wuul had already taken possession of the eavesdropping cup and was waving it in Suuas's face.

". . . not even SoroSuub!" the senator roared. "This is Loronar! How could you, Suuas? *Loronar?*"

The younger Sullustan looked at his boots and said, "Uupa, I keep trying to tell—"

"That it belongs to someone else," Wuul finished. "I know—and that's a load of drutash castings." He flung an arm toward Luke. "He's a Jedi, you idiot. And a Jedi always knows when you're lying."

That was close enough to accurate for Luke to nod. "I've been sensing your feelings since you drew near," he said. "You weren't coming to tell us about anything. You were having trouble eavesdropping, so you decided to try the saucers."

Suuas's eyes flattened to angry ovals. "Cheap Loronar trash," he said. "I *told* them I wanted SoroSuub."

"Who?" Luke asked.

"Who do you *think*, Jedi?" Suuas snarled. He turned to Wuul. "And it's not like you left me a choice, Uupa. When you wouldn't work with them, *someone* had to put our warren first."

Wuul's shoulders fell. "What did you do, Suuas?"

"Galactic Syndicated has eyes everywhere," Suuas replied. "You told me that yourself. It's impossible to hide a whole warren from them—even for you."

"So you struck a deal," Wuul surmised. "The warren's safety in exchange for spying on me?"

"And I'd do it again," Suuas confirmed. "Throw me in a detention center, hire another pilot and put a bad reference out on me, even have the Jedi dump me down a black hole. I make no apologies."

Before Luke could object to the idea that Jedi disposed of bodies, Wuul stepped close to his warren-spawn and began to speak in a low, gravelly voice.

"Oh, no, Suuas—you're not going to be that lucky," he said. "We're going to handle this through the warren-clan. The Dame will decide your fate."

Five

The Sarnus Refinery stood scattered across the barren plain below, spanning a hundred square kilometers of dust and stone. Hundreds of fleck-sized landspeeders were whizzing back and forth, running between the dark polygons of distant structures. Studying the far horizon, Leia could just make out a line of fiery orange crash pits—a series of jagged notches still aglow with the heat of recent impacts. In the middle of the plain, she saw the enormous spinning domes of more than twenty grinding mills, surrounded by a web of the transport tubes that fed and emptied them.

"A lot of those repulsi-veyer lines are over fifty kilometers long," Lando was explaining over the comm channel.

Dressed in a yellow standard-issue pressure suit, he stood at the edge of a narrow pullout, pointing to the facilities they would soon be visiting. Lando wanted the Solos to understand the refining process so they would be able to recognize any illicit refineries they happened to come across. But clearly he enjoyed having the chance to show the place off.

"Our crash pits are located well away from the work areas," Lando continued. "When those astroliths come down, they can scatter debris for dozens of kilometers."

"Of course, we try to contain the scatter with deflector shields," added Lando's operations chief, Dena Yus. She was standing by the landspeeder, watching for approaching traffic, because they had parked in the only pullout on the switchbacking route down into the production basin. "But we still lose three percent of our ore to spray-out."

Leia chinned the microphone toggle inside her helmet, then asked, "How much of the astrolith do you lose to other causes?" *Astrolith*, Dena had explained earlier, was the term mining engineers used for the asteroid fragments prepared by the breaker crews. "I'd think a lot of ore would vaporize on impact—or simply sink into the crash-pit walls."

"That's why we have beam generators and particle shields," Lando said. "As the astrolith drops into the atmosphere, we slow it down with repulsor beams and guide it in with tractor beams. And crash pits are lined with particle shields to keep the ore inside the pit where we want it."

"The process is quite controlled," said Dena. "The astroliths arrive with just enough momentum to smash one another into chunks. When those chunks are small enough to transport, they fall down a collection funnel into the repulsi-veyer line and are transported to a grinding mill."

"You must have a lot of safeguards, right?" Han asked. He was standing at the opposite end of the pullout, studying the nearest crash pit—Crash Pit One— through a pair of electrobinoculars. "I mean, there's no chance a 'lith could get away from you, right?"

"Of course not," Dena said. "Sarnus has a thin atmosphere and weak gravity, but those astroliths run ten million tonnes. An uncontrolled drop would cause a huge burn-off, and we'd have massive impact disintegration. We'd lose most of what we dropped."

"And probably half the refinery, too." Lando's tone

grew wary. "But I'm sure you know all that, Han. Why are you asking?"

"It's probably nothing," Han said, raising the shoulders of his bright-yellow pressure suit. "I'm just wondering if those beam nozzles should be pointing at the smelter houses."

"What?" Lando crossed the pullout in three quick strides, then took the electrobinoculars from Han and turned them on the nearest crash pit. "Dena, do you have any maintenance scheduled for Crash Pit One?"

"Not until next week."

"Then something's wrong," Lando said. "I see three— no, make that *four* tractor beams out of alignment. And Han's right. It looks like they're turned toward the smelting center."

"That can't be," Dena said. "The turret mounts have safety chocks on them. The beam nozzles can only turn a few degrees—just enough to help with the lock-on."

Lando laid a finger over the control pad on top of the electrobinoculars, then said, "Well, they've turned around *somehow*. You'd better get on the comm to plant control and find out what's happening—*now*."

"Of course," Dena said.

A soft click sounded in the helmet speaker as Dena switched her transmitter to plant control's channel. Leia crossed to Lando's side and took a turn with the electrobinoculars. At this distance, the beam generators looked like seven black drops surrounding a gaping red maw. But instead of the narrow ends pointing into the sky above the pit, four seemed to be turned toward the near side of the basin, where the cone-shaped towers of the smelting houses stood belching smoke into the thin Sarnusian atmosphere.

Leia felt a cold prickle of danger sense creeping down her spine. "Lando," she asked, "what happens if a breaker crew drops an asteroid chunk while the tractor beams are pointed at the smelting center?"

"They can't," Lando assured her. "The breaker crews can't start their drop until all four tractor-beam operators have a firm lock-on. There's a fail-safe shutdown."

As he spoke, the crimson thread of a friction fire appeared high in the sky, fluttering and brightening as it chased the flaming trails of three previous drops toward the surface.

"I see . . ." Leia continued to look through the electrobinoculars. "Just like the safety chocks that *should* be keeping those beams from turning more than a few degrees?"

Lando fell silent for a moment, then asked in a low voice, "You're thinking sabotage?"

Leia lowered the electrobinoculars. "Lando, there are *four* tractor-beam nozzles pointed toward your smelting center," she said. "Does that sound like an accident to you?"

"Not to me," Han said. "And Lando just made some nasty competition pretty angry."

Lando nodded inside his helmet. "The Qrephs. *Of course,*" he said. "I shouldn't be surprised, but I am. I didn't expect them to be this bold—or to move so fast."

"That's the trouble with Columi," Han said. "They're always three steps ahead."

"*Now* you tell me." Lando started back toward the landspeeder. "Dena, what does plant control say about those tractor beams?"

A small pop sounded over Leia's helmet speaker as Dena switched her transmitter back to the group channel. "Nothing yet. I haven't been able to raise them."

Lando hissed a curse, then asked, "What about security?"

"I can't raise *anyone,*" Dena replied. "The only comm

I have is suit-to-suit. There must be a problem with the satellite relay."

"Yeah, because somebody vaped it," Han commented, following Lando toward the landspeeder. "How many workers are down there right now?"

Lando looked to Dena. "Chief?"

She checked her chronometer. "We're just starting the shift change," she said. "That means we'll have thirty thousand workers on site, give or take a few hundred."

A cold lump formed in Leia's stomach. With millions of tonnes of mass, an astrolith impact would cause an unimaginable explosion. Even at a reduced velocity, it could easily level the entire Sarnus Refinery and kill most of the on-site employees.

"How quickly can you evacuate?" she asked.

"Fifteen minutes, once the order is issued," Dena said. "But with the comm net down—"

"You can't issue the order," Han finished. "These are some bad Columi. *Really* bad."

They all fell silent for a moment, contemplating Han's words.

Then Dena asked, "Are you saying the saboteurs are trying to take out our entire workforce, too?" Despite her calm exterior, her presence was bleeding rage and hatred into the Force, so raw and powerful that it felt almost inhuman to Leia. "That would cripple us for years!"

"Dena, this isn't about capital assets and labor pools anymore." There was just a note of irritation in Lando's voice. "It's about saving our people. Let's see if we can raise someone down there without the satellite relay."

He reached inside the landspeeder and flipped a switch on the dashboard. The steady beep of an emergency beacon sounded inside Leia's helmet, and a yellow strobe began to flash atop the landspeeder roof.

She glanced back toward the crash pits and watched

the sky for a moment, studying the four ribbons of flame as they continued to stretch and grow longer. The two lowest streamers seemed to be headed for the middle and far horizon, where Crash Pits Three and Six were located. But it was impossible to say where the two highest streamers were going, and Leia knew there would be many more astroliths even higher, too far above the atmosphere to betray their presence with a friction trail. Clearly, any attempt to estimate time-to-impact would be nothing but a wild guess.

Leia turned back toward the landspeeder. Lando and Dena stood at the front bumper, facing in opposite directions, their lips moving in sporadic bursts as they attempted to establish a line-of-sight comlink connection with the production basin. Han was in the pilot's seat, stabbing at the dashboard buttons as he attempted to raise someone—*anyone*—on the vehicle's more-powerful communications array. Judging by the ferocity of his jabbing, he was having no more success than Lando or Dena.

Leia opened a channel to the *Falcon* and tried to raise C-3PO or Omad Kaeg, whom Lando had hired—with Han's reluctant blessing—to oversee the repair of the *Falcon*'s damaged sensor suite. If the ship's military-grade rectenna happened to be turned their way, it might pick up even a semi-deflected transmission.

When the only reply was an empty hiss, Leia began to despair. A typical drop took seventeen minutes from lock-on to impact, Dena had told them earlier. And it took almost that long to evacuate. Leia switched her transmitter back to the group channel, then waved to get her companions' attention.

"We don't have time for this," she said. "If an emergency evacuation takes fifteen minutes, we're out of time already. Even if we connect with someone—"

"Hold on," Han said. He turned to Dena. "*Emergency* evacuation? What triggers that?"

"Plant control sounds an alarm, of course," Dena said. "But I don't see how—"

"I mean what triggers it *automatically*?" Han interrupted. "Say something big explodes. Would that do it?"

"Of course, if it was big enough to be seen," Dena said. "But I don't see how—"

"Get in," Han said. "I've got an idea."

Leia went for the front passenger seat. Lando took the seat behind her. Dena, who until then had been the group's driver, went to the pilot's seat.

"Sorry, sister." Han jerked his thumb toward the seat behind him. "Get in. I'll take it from here."

Dena's jaw dropped behind her faceplate, and she made no move toward the rear door. "Captain Solo, this is *my*—"

"Han's driving," Lando interrupted. "Take the backseat. *Now.*"

Leia felt a wave of outrage roll through the Force, but Dena obeyed. Han hit the throttles before the doors had even dropped shut, and the vehicle shot down the narrow road, weaving and bouncing as it descended toward the production basin.

"We need something that will go up with a big flash," Han said. "Maybe a processing core or something."

"The closest processing core is down in the slag well," Dena said. "About ten kilometers from here."

"Too far," Leia said. Given the long series of switchback curves, it would take at least five minutes to travel that far—even with Han behind the controls. "We need something closer."

"What about those storage tanks at the bottom of the scarp?" Lando asked Dena. "Didn't you put them out here to protect the plant if there was an accident?"

Dena did not reply immediately. A green light activated in the ceiling panel, indicating that the landspeeder interior was now fully pressurized. She covered her pause by making a show of deactivating her suit's air supply and raising her faceplate.

Leia chinned a release tab inside her own helmet. She didn't quite trust Dena. The woman had a habit of thinking too long before answering a question, and Leia didn't like the way Dena had offered to secure the closures on Han's pressure suit. That was just too familiar—*oddly* familiar, given that he was her boss's married best friend.

Leia flipped her own faceplate up, then turned to ask, "Is that a difficult question, Chief Yus?"

"It isn't," Dena replied, a little too quickly. "I'm just trying to recall what we have in each tank at the moment—and wondering whether we can breach them. They're triple-walled durasteel, sandwiched around two ten-centimeter layers of duracrete. Crashing a landspeeder into one wouldn't even crack it."

"Crashing a landspeeder . . ." Han let his sentence trail off, then asked, "Are you crazy? We've got a Jedi with us."

He started to elaborate but stopped to fight for control as they rounded a blind corner and discovered a hairpin curve coming up fast. Han decelerated hard and spun the yoke. The landspeeder's stern swung around, tipping the vehicle onto its left side, and Leia felt the repulsorlifts starting to flip them.

Then Han hit the throttles again, and the speeder shot forward. Dena let out an audible sigh of relief as the vehicle dropped onto its repulsorpads and sped down the next straightaway. Leia's gaze returned to the sky. The first two astroliths were almost on the horizon, their streamers so long and bright that Leia could see the jagged notches of the crash pits beneath them.

But the third streamer remained high up, its tail so

short that it was visible only as a fan of orange. Before Leia's eyes, the head blossomed into a red fireball the size of her fist, and by the time she comprehended what she was seeing, it had grown as large as her head.

"We're not going to make it," she said.

In the time it took her to speak the words, the fireball had swelled to the size of a starfighter, and the entire sky was orange.

"Han, stop!" Leia cried. "We're too late!"

Han was already decelerating, braking so hard that Leia had to brace against the dashboard.

The fireball continued to swell, blotting out the sky, burning so bright it hurt Leia's eyes, continuing to expand until . . . it touched ground.

A white flash filled the dust basin. Leia saw the smoking cones of the smelters tumbling sideways before they were engulfed by a curtain of flame and dust. The curtain rolled out toward the edges of the silver plain, hurling the white flecks of landspeeders and the dark polygons of buildings high into the air. It swallowed everything in its path, growing ever higher and brighter as it drew near.

Han slammed the landspeeder into reverse, then started up the switchbacks backward, struggling to put some distance between them and the rolling curtain of fire. A pillar of yellow-white flame rose from the impact site, climbing thousands of meters into the sky before the atmosphere finally grew thin enough for it to boil across the heavens.

A wall of billowing dust began to climb toward them, and Leia knew the legendary Solo luck had finally run out. No way, she thought . . . no way could they outrun a shock wave. She laid her hand over Han's, then reached out in the Force and *pushed*. The wave hit. The landspeeder bucked, *hard,* and the world shattered.

Six

All that remained of the smelting center was a ten-kilometer impact basin ringed by a rim of sheer cliffs and broken stone. A day after the strike, the crater floor continued to glow and smoke, and Luke saw no activity there. But the surrounding plain shimmered with tiny flecks of color—the running lights and flood lamps of emergency crews digging through rubble sprays that had once been milling domes and flotation tanks. Though the effort was still being called a *rescue operation,* it had been twenty hours since anyone had been found alive.

"I'm going to kill them," Lando said. He was standing next to Luke in the infirmary, watching the rescue operations through a waiting-room viewport. Despite three broken ribs and a badly gashed face, he had spent the last twenty-four hours personally directing the rescue effort from this makeshift headquarters. "Craitheus and Marvid both. I'm going to hunt them down and put a pair of disruptor beams through their heads. Maybe three or four."

"You have a disruptor?" Luke asked. Disruptor weapons disintegrated their targets at the molecular level—causing so much pain in the process that they were banned in nearly every civilized society in the galaxy.

Lando shot him a glower. "I can afford to buy one, you know."

"I'm sure you can," Luke said. The rage in Lando's Force aura made it impossible to read his true intentions, so it seemed possible that he was serious. "But you might want to hold off on that."

"And why would that be, Master Skywalker?" asked Dena Yus, who was also standing next to Luke, opposite Lando. Though she still had a few bruises on one side of her elegant face, she had avoided any serious injuries by ducking behind a seat as the shock wave hit. "Perhaps you intend to make the kill yourself?"

"There isn't going to *be* a kill," Luke said, a little taken aback by her suggestion. "At least not until we have proof of the Qrephs' guilt—and even then, only if there's no other way to bring them to justice."

Dena's lips tightened in mock disappointment. "That's very noble, Master Skywalker. But we have all the proof we require. The Qrephs' threats were quite explicit." She shot him an odd smile, then continued, "I'll happily swear to it, if that will soothe your Jedi conscience."

"That won't be necessary," Luke said. He couldn't quite decide whether she was trying to flirt with him or sic him on the beings she held responsible for the destruction of the refinery. "It's not my Jedi conscience that concerns me—it's our emotions. Anger clouds judgment. So does fear."

"And that way lies the dark side—I know." Lando's voice grew bitter. "I've got news for you, old buddy. The dark side is already here. It just killed twenty-eight thousand of my people and put Han and Leia *both* into a coma."

"And rushing to judgment won't change that," Luke said. *Anger* did not begin to describe how he felt about what had happened to the Solos. The shock wave had caught them head-on, blowing the shattered viewscreen into their faces and leaving them both so badly injured that their recovery remained doubtful even now. A part of Luke wanted to join in Lando's rage and pursue the vengeance Dena advocated, but he did not dare act on those emotions—not while they remained so powerful and raw. "We need to confirm our suspicions before we act."

"That's easy to say," Dena replied, "but hard to accomplish. All we really know about the attack is that someone used a laser torch to cut away the safety chocks on all four tractor-beam generators at Crash Pit One."

Luke raised his brow. "Are you sure it was a laser torch?" he asked. "There are other ways to cut—"

"I know what you're thinking," Lando interrupted. "But forget about Sith—it wasn't a lightsaber. We found pieces of a torch rig near one of the generator turrets."

"What we *can't* figure out is how they took control of the beam targeting," Dena said. "To do it from inside the control facility, they would have had to override the fail-safe lockouts."

"And that should have triggered safety alarms at *both* ends of the drop," Lando added.

"Maybe the control code was compromised," Luke suggested. "That would have been child's play for most Columi."

Dena gave him an approving smile. "Excellent thought, Master Skywalker. We already have a team of slicers analyzing our control systems. So far, they swear the programming is secure."

"Which is all the more proof that the Qrephs were behind this," Lando said. "Had it been anyone else, we would have known by now how they did it."

"Perhaps," Luke allowed. Beyond the observation wall, an amber beacon began to brighten and swell as a distant craft rose into the air and turned toward the infirmary. "But I think it's more important to figure out *why* they did it—and what they intend to do next."

Dena's Force presence suddenly grew cool and wary. "Don't you think their goal is fairly obvious, Master Skywalker?" she asked. "They need to eliminate their competition in the Rift. It's the only way to make their investment here profitable."

Luke shook his head. "This is going to bring a lot of unwanted attention to their operations in the Rift—attention that will make it harder, not easier, to make a profit. Whatever is going on here, it's about more than mining and money."

"That's hard to believe," Lando said. "Money is a powerful motivator, and the Chiloon Rift has the largest concentration of high-value asteroids in the galaxy."

"And it's still small change to the Qrephs," Luke said. "No offense, but Calrissian Holdings is nothing compared to Galactic Syndicated."

Lando fell into a shocked silence, then finally asked, "*The* Galactic Syndicated?"

"Good. You know the company," Luke said. "I'd barely heard the name until recently."

"I didn't say I knew them," Lando corrected. "Nobody *knows* Galactic Syndicated. They're a ghost corporation."

"Ghost corporation?"

"An invisible mover," Lando explained. "You can't actually see them, but you know they exist because of a clear pattern of events."

"And in Galactic Syndicated's case, this clear pattern of events is . . ." Luke asked.

Lando rubbed his chin. "Well, the most noticeable is all these surprise takeovers lately," he said. "The big players keep whispering the name Galactic Syndicated. But the buyouts are always through cutout corporations, so it's impossible to be sure who's responsible. A lot of people don't even believe that Galactic Syndicated exists."

"It definitely exists," Luke said, recalling his conversation with Luewet Wuul. "In fact, I have it on good authority that the Qrephs are the sole stockholders of Galactic Syndicated. And asteroid mining is just a tiny piece of their empire. They started in livestock genetics, then moved into droid manufacturing and cyborg technologies. Now they hold companies that specialize in chemicals, privatized detention services, high-risk finance, reinsurance, waste disposal, nutritional synthesis, interstellar mass transportation—the list goes on."

Without revealing the source, Luke went on to recount what Wuul had told him about the Qrephs' most recent acquisitions, as well as the senator's suspicions that they might be trying to take control of the galactic economy.

"And they're not being subtle," Luke said. "They're using blackmail, extortion, bribery, even murder to make their purchases at a good price."

Lando turned from the viewport toward Luke. "You say this buying spree started six months ago?"

Luke nodded. "About the same time your piracy problem really heated up," he said. "And my contact says GET has been smuggling more product than ever into the Galactic Alliance."

"And you think the Qrephs are using *piracy* to finance their acquisitions binge?" Dena was beginning to seep cool fear into the Force. She turned to Luke and laid her hand on his arm. "Luke, even if that were feasible, I don't see why the Qrephs would base themselves in the Chiloon Rift. It can't be easy to run an industrial empire from way out here, and they *aren't* leading pirate raids personally."

"No, but remember that the Chiloon Rift is beyond the reach of any galactic justice." Luke was as puzzled by the fear he felt from Dena as he was by her sudden attempt to establish a level of intimacy with him. "Craitheus and

Marvid are breaking laws all over the galaxy. Their base of operations needs to be somewhere law-enforcement agencies can't touch them."

"So the Jedi are here to bring them to justice?" Dena asked.

"That's more of a byproduct," Luke said. "Our primary mission is to stop the piracy, but the Qrephs have certainly made themselves a high priority of mine."

Dena considered this for a moment, then shook her head. "There's something you're not saying," she said. "Stopping the pirates was the Solos' mission, and you *aren't* here because of what happened to them. You were already in transit when the Qrephs sabotaged the drop."

Luke gave her an appreciative smile, then tried to dodge the question by turning to Lando. "I see why you place so much trust in your operations chief," he said. "She doesn't miss much."

Lando grinned. "She's also right," he said. "Hunting pirates *does* seem way below the Grand Master's pay grade, and there's no way you made the trip to Sarnus in a day. So, what's really going on?"

Luke remained silent, trying to decide why Dena was pushing so hard to learn his "real" reason for coming to the Chiloon Rift. Lando obviously trusted her, but there was a troubling note of desperation in her Force aura. And her clumsy attempt to manipulate him had certainly aroused his suspicions.

"Very well," he said. He allowed his gaze to slide toward Dena's reflection in the viewport. "But I don't think you'll believe me."

"Try us," Lando said. When there was no immediate reply, he took the hint and turned toward Dena. "Why don't you let us talk in private?"

Dena looked through the viewport, where a string of running lights was growing brighter as an airspeeder approached the infirmary, then turned and nodded.

"Of course. They're bringing in another load of bodies." The sorrow in her voice was genuine. "I should go down to the morgue and see who they've found."

"I'd appreciate that," Lando said. "I'll fill you in if Luke and I discuss anything that affects recovery operations."

"Thank you." Dena turned to Luke and squeezed his elbow. "Master Skywalker, if I can be of any assistance to you—at all—please don't hesitate to ask."

"I won't," Luke assured her. "You're kind to offer."

As the door hissed shut behind Dena, Lando asked, "Is there something I should know about her, Luke?"

Luke studied the door for a moment, reaching out in the Force to see if Dena would linger on the other side to eavesdrop. When he felt no sign of her presence, he finally shrugged.

"I can't say for sure," he said. "But didn't she seem to be coming on a bit strong?"

"You shouldn't hold *that* against her, old buddy." Lando's grin was more than a little sad. "You *are* a pretty eligible widower—even if you don't think about it yourself."

Luke felt a familiar pang of sorrow, then said, "So they tell me. But with Han and Leia's recovery still so uncertain, it feels like Dena is trying to manipulate me—and very clumsily."

Lando smiled in amusement. "Clumsy, yes," he said. "But manipulative? I wouldn't go that far. Dena fast-tracked through the ranks as a mining engineer."

Luke frowned. "So?"

"So don't let her good looks fool you. She grew up studying fracture patterns and stress loads." Lando waved his hand toward the scene beyond the viewport. "And for most of her adult life, she's been working on rocks like Sarnus. I doubt she's up on the latest dating etiquette."

"That's possible, I suppose," Luke said. "But *you* can't

feel her in the Force. She's a little too curious about what I'm doing here."

Lando sighed. "Dena isn't the only one, Luke. I'm curious, too. And she's right—it's not like you *knew* what was going to happen to Han and Leia before you left Shedu . . ." He let his thought trail off, then cocked his head and studied Luke from the corner of his eye. "You *didn't*, did you?"

Luke shook his head. "No, Lando. Even Jedi Grand Masters can't see the future."

Lando continued to eye him sidelong. "You sure about that?" he asked. "Your timing was pretty impressive."

"Coincidence," Luke said. "I was coming here anyway."

"Because?"

Luke gave him a melancholy smile. "For several reasons, none of which are all that mysterious," he said. "Mostly I wanted to have some fun."

"Fun?" Lando echoed. "In the Chiloon Rift?"

Luke shrugged. "I hadn't left Shedu Maad in a year, and I was tired of everyone fussing over my recovery," he said. "And Han and Leia were out here with you. It seemed like a nice low-key mission."

"Sure. Chasing pirates through an asteroid maze filled with banks of hot plasma is just low-key fun for you Jedi." Lando's brows came together in disbelief and annoyance. "What do you take me for, Luke? Some nerf herder sitting in on his first sabacc game?"

"Okay, maybe I wanted to test myself a little," Luke said, showing his palms in surrender, *"and* have some fun with you and the Solos while I let the Masters get used to the idea that they can run things without me. Is there something wrong with that?"

Lando's expression began to soften. "You're not here hunting for the Sith homeworld or something?" he asked. "You just came out here to see if you're all healed up?"

"Well, and maybe to set up a rendezvous with Ben," Luke said. "I haven't seen him for six months."

"*Ben's* here? In the Rift?" The suspicion returned to Lando's face. "Luke, old buddy—"

"It's *not* a mystery," Luke interrupted. "Ben and Tahiri were on Ramook to investigate a *Ship* sighting—"

"A *Ship* sighting?" Lando's eyes grew wide. "As in Vestara Khai's *Ship*? The Sith meditation sphere *Ship*?"

"It was only a *sighting*," Luke insisted. *Ship* was a sentient vessel created thousands of years in the past to train Sith adepts in the ways of war. Its most recent pilot was a young woman named Vestara Khai. A defector from the Lost Tribe of Sith, she had spent over a year earning Luke's trust—and winning his son's heart—only to betray them both during the Sith occupation of Coruscant. "And we don't know that *Ship* was actually there. They never picked up its trail."

Lando appeared unconvinced. "Then why are Ben and Tahiri still in the Rift?"

"They're trying to track down Ohali Soroc," Luke said. "She hasn't checked in for a month."

"Okay," Lando said, now seeming as confused as he was suspicious. "Who's Ohali Soroc?"

"One of my ten Quest Knights," Luke said.

"A *Quest Knight*?" Lando's jaw dropped, and he turned toward the viewport. "*Now* I get it. You think you've found—"

"No, we don't," Luke said. As someone who made his considerable resources across the galaxy available for Jedi use, Lando had been informed of the hunt for Mortis shortly after the ten Knights departed on their mission. "The Quest Knights are searching *everywhere*. We're only looking for Jedi Soroc because she's missed so many check-ins—and I'm sure *that* has more to do with the communication difficulties here in the Rift than with Mortis."

Lando fell silent, obviously thinking.

Luke waited a few moments for him to calm down, then said, "On my honor, Lando. I'm telling you everything."

Lando exhaled slowly, then finally turned around. "Okay, maybe you are," he said. "But doesn't it all seem a little strange to you?"

"All what?" Luke asked. "The coincidences?"

"Exactly." Lando raised his hand and began to tick points off by lifting his fingers. "First, there's a *Ship* sighting at Ramook. Then one of your Quest Knights goes quiet inside the Rift. Next, Han and Leia show up to help me deal with some pirate problems. And then *you* decide to play courier so you can see your son and decide if you're healed yet."

Lando folded his four fingers back down and lowered his arm. "I'm no Jedi, but that's either the Force at work or—"

"Or the Qrephs," Luke finished. "I see your point, but I don't feel the Force behind this. It's too . . . soulless."

Lando scowled. "Actually, I was going to say *Sith*," he replied. "Could they be the ones behind my pirate problems? Or could they be working *with* the Qrephs?"

Luke considered the question, then spread his hands. "You tell me," he said. "You've met the Qrephs, and I haven't. *Could* they be working with the Lost Tribe?"

Lando frowned for a time, then finally shook his head. "I can't see it," he said. "That would be like two sarlaccs in the same pit. It wouldn't be long before they started to eat each other."

Luke nodded. Lando was undoubtedly right about how quickly the Qrephs would turn on any possible Sith allies. But sarlacc digestion was notoriously slow. It could take a thousand years for a sarlacc to fully digest its victim—and that made Luke wonder if they shouldn't be more concerned about how long an alliance between the Qrephs and the Sith might last before one finally destroyed the other.

Luke was still wondering when the door whispered open behind him. He glanced at the reflection in the view-port, half expecting to see Dena Yus. Instead, he was sur-prised to find C-3PO's golden shape rushing into the room.

"Please excuse the interruption," the droid said. "But Captain Solo has asked me to fetch you at once."

As quickly as Luke turned, Lando was even quicker, and Luke found himself following his friend toward the door.

"Han's *awake*?" Lando asked, charging out of the room—and nearly bowling C-3PO over. "Are you kid-ding?"

The droid threw his arms up to steady himself. "Cap-tain Solo is *quite* awake," he said, turning after Lando. "He said to tell you he has a plan."

Seven

Dena found Tharston Kharl's body on the fourth shelf of a ten-level storage litter, in a quiet corner of the makeshift morgue—a cold underground hangar bustling with outdated medical droids and numb-eyed attendants. Emergency services had run out of body bags within the first few hours, so he had been left in his shredded pressure suit. Dena could still read the employee number—CC6683—stenciled on his chest tab. Given what the flames and the flesh-scouring wind had done to his rugged face, it was the only way to identify him, and she found herself hoping someone else had been wearing Tharston's uniform that day. Maybe he had needed to borrow a crew member's heavy-duty hazard suit and had forgotten to switch chest tabs when they traded suits. Or something.

Anything.

Because while Tharston Kharl may have been an obnoxious jerk at the sabacc table and a cheating husband to his wife back on Telos, he had also been Dena's first and only lover, cheerful, supportive, and surprisingly gentle when the occasion called for it. And for that she owed him more than a coffin and a trip home in the cold hold of a death ship. She owed him justice and remembrance and something she did not quite understand, something that she felt gnawing at the cold, aching void inside her.

Dena had never experienced such feelings before, and she did not know how to interpret them. The more she thought of Tharston, the more powerful the feelings grew. And yet she could not stop. She felt as though some insidious parasite had taken control of her emotions, as though it were driving her toward some mad act that would ultimately destroy her.

Behind Dena, a young woman said, "So, you were in love with him." The voice was smooth and thin, almost a girl's. "Foolish woman."

Dena dropped her arm and cupped her hand, letting her holdout blaster slip down from beneath her sleeve. Only when she had the weapon securely in her grasp did she turn to face the newcomer. Slender and strong, in a form-fitting flight suit, the woman was no more than nineteen, with fair skin, light-brown hair, and dark smoldering eyes. She glanced at the weapon in Dena's hand, then looked up and cocked her brow.

"*Really,* Chief Yus?" Savara Raine placed one hand on her hip. "You might want to rethink that."

Dena raised the blaster higher. "Maybe I did love Tharston," she admitted. "And you killed him."

"So?" Savara rolled her eyes. "You helped."

"Me?" Horrified, Dena shook her head. "No. It was only you. You alone."

"Then I suppose someone *else* copied the control code for us? Someone else gave us the production schedule?" Slowly, Savara reached into her breast pocket and removed a datachip bearing the golden-asteroid logo of the Sarnus Refinery. "Because I'm pretty sure this has *your* access number embedded in it."

"You were supposed to strike during the maintenance break!" Dena objected. "There would have been no more than a thousand beings at work. And they would have had time to evacuate."

Savara shrugged. "Not my fault," she said, slipping the datachip back into her pocket. "Your makers changed the schedule."

There was no arguing with that, Dena knew. The Qrephs took no counsel but their own, and they regarded any concern for *collateral damage* to be the folly of a weak mind.

Still, Dena was confused. The attack had been a hundred times deadlier than needed to put the refinery out of business—and overkill was not the Qrephs' style. They prided themselves on efficiency, believing that excessive force was a waste of resources likely to lead to unintended consequences.

After a moment, she said, "I doubt they told you to sabotage our entire communications system."

"They *told* me to succeed," Savara retorted. "I did what was necessary—no more, no less."

"Really? To me, it looks like you murdered twenty-eight thousand beings in cold blood. And *that* will bring a lot of unwanted attention to the Rift." Dena met Savara's hard gaze, then continued, "Had I been able to sound the alarm, this disaster *might* have looked like a simple industrial accident. Instead, you turned it into the largest mass murder the galaxy has seen since the Yuuzhan Vong were driven off."

A glimmer of doubt flashed through Savara's eyes, but her voice remained confident. "So what? Twenty-eight thousand died instead of the few hundred you expected. If you think that makes you innocent, go ahead and blast me. Then have fun explaining yourself to Lando Calrissian and his Jedi pets. I'm sure you'll find them in a forgiving mood."

For a moment, Dena seriously considered the suggestion. She pulled the blaster trigger back to the arming click, then felt a guilty thrill as the blood drained from Savara's face. But Dena did not dare fire—not yet— because she did not know how to spin the story for Lando and his Jedi friend Luke Skywalker. Certainly, they would be happy to hear that Dena had killed the saboteur. But they would also have questions—many questions—and Dena doubted she would be able to fool Luke Skywalker for long.

So the question was exactly as Savara had framed it. If Dena came forward and explained that she had expected only a few deaths, or a few hundred at most, would Lando and his Jedi friend forgive her? Would they help her?

Dena simply did not have the background to know. Her makers had loaded her memory with a plausible family history, and they had given her more knowledge than a mining executive of her station would ever need. They had even imprinted her with a personality specifically engineered to make her a key employee at the Sarnus Refinery.

But there was no substitute for *experience*. Despite all of her neuroprogramming and the accelerated learning and synaptic stimulation, Dena had been living among humans for less than a year. She simply had not accumulated enough behavioral data to project their likely response to an emotionally charged situation like this. Would Lando and his friend be so grateful for her help that they would overlook her own small role in the atrocity? Or would they take vengeance on *her,* too?

The only real data available to Dena was the irony in her tormentor's voice, and it was easy enough to interpret *that*. Savara Raine would not have suggested putting a blaster bolt into her own head if she had believed that to be a wise course of action. Quite the opposite. The challenge had been issued to drive home the point that Dena *had* no other allies. No matter how much she hated her makers and their teenage pet—no matter how desperately she might want the help of Lando and his Jedi friend—she *needed* the Qrephs.

They had designed her that way.

The thought had barely crossed Dena's mind before Savara pushed the holdout blaster aside. With her other hand, she grabbed Dena by the throat and shoved her against the storage litter, so hard that it almost toppled.

"If you ever point a weapon at me again, you die," Savara said. "Are we clear on that?"

Dena considered trying to bring the blaster to bear again, not because she believed she was strong enough to kill the girl, but because, at the moment, dying did not seem so terrible—not with Tharston's scorched corpse on a shelf behind her and a future ahead of her that promised only more of the same despair.

But the Qrephs had designed her to resist such temptation. As hopeless as she felt, her survival instinct remained primary. Her hand opened of its own accord, and the blaster clattered to the floor.

The hand on her throat tightened. "I asked if we were clear."

Dena managed only a nod and a garbled croak, but Savara seemed to understand.

"Good." The hand relaxed, and the teenage terror retreated two steps, then held out her hand expectantly. "I believe you have something for me?"

Dena nodded. "I do."

It hurt her throat to talk, but she tried not to show her pain. She reached into her pocket and withdrew a pair of clear steriplas bags. Each contained a bandage soaked with still-damp blood. Dena checked the labels, then passed them over, one at a time.

"The first is from Captain Solo, and the second is from Princess Leia," she said. "I collected them right after the shock wave hit, while I was tending their wounds."

Savara inspected the bags, then nodded her approval. "Well done." She tucked both into an empty thigh pocket. "But your makers would have been happier if you had let the Solos die."

"Then someone should have told me that," Dena replied, more surprised by the suggestion than she should have been. "Besides, it wasn't an option. Lando was conscious and trying to help, too. It was all I could do to collect the blood samples before he closed their face-plates."

Savara's eyes remained cold. "And you couldn't have taken him out, too? He's practically an old man."

A cold lump of anger began to form inside Dena's stomach. "Again, I had no orders to—"

"It's fine. It's hardly your fault if your makers went too light on your sense of initiative." Savara's eyes were twinkling with amusement, and Dena realized the girl had been toying with her. "But perhaps it's not too late. How likely are our patients to survive?"

"How would I know?" Dena asked icily. "I wasn't loaded with medical expertise, either."

"No, but the infirmary director does report to you," Savara said. "Surely, Chief Calrissian has asked you to inquire about the Solos' condition?"

Dena reluctantly nodded. "He has. They've been unconscious since they arrived, so the medicos are having a hard time evaluating how much brain damage the concussions may have caused. Captain Solo was in a coma—"

"*Was?*" Savara asked. "Does that mean he's awake?"

"By now, probably. There have been clear signs that he's coming around," Dena said. "He was still unconscious when I left Lando's command center to come down here, but he was removed from the bacta tank a few hours ago."

"And Princess Leia?"

"She's still in her tank," Dena said. "She won't wake up, but she's not in a coma. The medical droid doesn't understand why she remains unconscious."

Savara's face grew unhappy. "Jedi healing trance," she said. "Any other injuries?"

"She suffered a fractured skull and had one arm broken in several places, but those have already mended. The surgical droids have no explanation—"

"Healing trance," Savara repeated, her tone darker than ever. "What else?"

"Their eyes have been repaired and should function well," Dena said. "But one of Captain Solo's eyes is from a donor. We lost the original at the crash site."

"A *donor*?" Savara scowled in distaste. "A prosthetic wouldn't work?"

"We're running short on prosthetics right now," Dena said, biting back her anger. "Perhaps they'll replace it when he returns to the Hapes Consortium."

"I don't think returning to the Consortium is going to be in his future," Savara said. "At least, it better *not* be. Do I make myself clear?"

Dena felt her eyes widen. "You want *me* to kill the Solos?" she gasped. "Both of them?"

Savara studied her, then finally shook her head. "I suppose not. You'd only get caught, and your makers don't want your biology exposed. Not yet."

Dena exhaled in relief. "That's probably wise," she said. "I doubt I would be able to withstand a Jedi interrogation."

Savara's eyes narrowed. "Is that a threat?"

Dena paused, taking time to evaluate what the girl had just revealed about the Qrephs' fear of her exposure. Perhaps she had more leverage than she realized.

After a moment, Dena said, "No, it's a fact. But you can take it however you like."

That actually drew a smile from the girl. "I see I've made a mistake, letting you know how important you are." She reached into one of her thigh pockets and withdrew a black pouch about the size of her palm. "Perhaps I should just give you what you need and leave before I do any more damage."

"That might be for the best."

Dena knew she should mention the arrival of Luke Skywalker, but he and Lando had been going to great lengths to keep Skywalker's presence here a secret—and the fact that Savara hadn't asked about the Grand Master suggested they were succeeding. Reasoning that it might be best to keep at least *one* of her bargaining chips hidden, Dena extended a hand to accept the pouch.

Instead of passing it over, Savara suddenly frowned and drew it back. She opened the top, then withdrew three vials about half the length of her little finger and held them up to the light, pretending to study the clear oil within.

"What are you doing?" Dena gasped.

"Checking the contents, of course," Savara said, watching as the oil grew cloudy and gray. "I wouldn't dare short you—not now, when you realize how valuable you are to us."

"Please, don't!" Dena lunged for the vials, but Savara anticipated her and quickly retreated out of range. "They mustn't be exposed to light."

"Is that so?" Savara continued to study the vials, watching them turn from gray to silver. "And I suppose they're no good to you after that?"

"They'll be poison!" Dena lunged again. "They'll kill me faster than no enzyme at all!"

Savara waited until Dena's hand was almost on hers, then jerked her arm aside—and let one of the vials go flying. It broke with a distant tinkle, and Dena could not help letting out a cry of despair. There were still two more in Savara's grasp, and there would be seven more inside the pouch. But each vial contained only a single day's dose, and deliveries were always ten days apart.

"Please—don't." She motioned at the two vials remaining in Savara's grasp. "Put them back before the color comes. I need it all to make it until next time."

"Come now, we both know that's not quite true," Savara said. "You might look a little wan and lose some hair, but if you stretch the interval, you'll survive."

She let another vial slip from her grasp. Dena tried to catch it, only to have Savara block the attempt with a well-placed foot-tap. The second vial shattered, and Dena watched in horror as the enzyme—the enzyme she needed to metabolize her food, the enzyme that the Qrephs had engineered her to need—spread across the duracrete floor in a darkening stain.

Dena looked up. "Why are you doing this to me?"

"Because I don't like being lied to."

"But I'm not lying!" Dena objected. "I've told you the truth."

"As far as it goes."

Savara let the third vial drop and did not try to stop Dena from catching it, but the oil was quickly turning pink. Injecting it now would be painful and deadly. Dena looked back to her tormentor, who was already reaching back into the pouch.

Savara smiled, then said, "Is there something you neglected to tell me?"

Dena closed her eyes, then reluctantly nodded. "Luke Skywalker."

She did not understand why the revelation made her feel like such a traitor, but it did. Perhaps it was because if anyone in the galaxy was capable of freeing her from the control of the Qrephs, it would be the Grand Master of the Jedi Order.

And Dena desperately wanted to be free.

"Luke *Skywalker*?" Savara's voice sounded brittle and alarmed. "What about him?"

When Dena opened her eyes again, Savara had withdrawn her hand from the pouch, empty. The girl's face was pale and her eyes were large and round. She *almost* looked afraid.

"Upstairs with Lando," Dena said. Suddenly she felt so powerful she had to fight not to smile. "Luke Skywalker is here."

Savara allowed her fear to show only in the way her nostrils flared, but it was enough to confirm what Dena had already guessed—that the Skywalker name was the one thing capable of rocking the girl onto her heels. Dena extended her hand, reaching out to take the enzyme pouch . . . only to have Savara snatch the bag away again.

"You weren't going to tell me," she said. "You think Skywalker can help you."

"Nobody can help me," Dena said. "I know that."

"But you have dreams," Savara insisted. "You have hopes."

"What do dreams and hopes matter? Skywalker can't formulate my enzymes." Dena paused, then gave a resigned shrug. "Besides, he wouldn't help me even if he could. He doesn't trust me."

"Why not?"

"I tried to establish an emotional connection with him," Dena said. "I don't understand why it failed. I used the voice you taught me, I teased, and I touched. Your system didn't work."

Instead of anger, the accusation elicited a laugh—a cruel one, but genuine.

"You tried to seduce *Luke Skywalker*—with his sister

and brother-in-law lying half dead in the infirmary?" Savara shook her head, laughing harder than ever. "You biots are such vac-heads."

"If you failed to teach me properly, whose fault is that?" Dena asked. "But the damage is done, and I don't see how it can be undone."

Savara finally stopped chuckling. "That's because you have no imagination." She thought for a moment, then asked, "You said in a status report that Tharston had a weakness for sabacc, correct?"

"Yes," Dena said. "He went to the casinos on Valnoos every month, whenever he had a recreation break."

"Good." Savara thrust the enzyme pouch into Dena's hand, then withdrew the datachip from her pocket and passed that over, too. "Take the datachip to Calrissian."

Dena stared at the datachip in confusion. "But this has my access number *and* a copy of the control code. Lando will know in an hour that it was used to sabotage the beam generators at Pit One."

"Exactly," Savara said. "You'll say you found the chip in Tharston's locker."

"*Tharston's?* Why?"

A sly grin came to Savara's lips. "Because you're going to confess to Calrissian and Skywalker," she said. "You're going to tell them all about Tharston being your lover and how he often visited your quarters."

Dena began to feel queasy inside. "You want me to blame *Tharston?*"

Savara rolled her eyes. "No, I want you to answer their questions," she said. "Let *them* blame Tharston."

Eight

Leia's dream began as it ended, with a gauze pad dragging across her torn face. The distant shriek of decompression sang in her ears, and the biting cold of thin air chewed at her nose and cheeks. Her head was spinning, her lungs aching, and she felt herself dropping into hypoxic oblivion. But she could not reach up to close her faceplate. Someone was kneeling on her arms, holding her motionless while the gauze drank up her blood.

Not yet, Jedi Solo, a woman's voice was saying. *I need more. Just a little more.*

Then Leia awoke as she always did, floating in the blue liquid warmth of a bacta tank, with her pulse pounding in her ears and angry knots slithering in her stomach. An outdated FX-4 medical droid stood at the monitoring station next to the tank, but there was no one else in the room. Not even Han.

The droid rotated its mushroom-shaped dome in her direction. There was a momentary delay as a central monitoring computer translated the FX's query from droidspeak into Basic, then a stilted gender-neutral voice rippled through the auditory buds sealed into Leia's ears.

"Good afternoon, Jedi Solo. Do you know where you are?"

Before answering, Leia took a second to calm herself,

trying to sort out how much of the dream had been memory and how much had been misinterpretation—or even pure fabrication. Clearly, her subconscious mind was trying to warn her about *something*, to make her understand that she had been betrayed. But dreams should seldom be taken literally—and, really, what would anyone want with her blood? The warning had to be about something else, something that could be symbolized by blood.

"Jedi Solo, can you answer me?" the droid asked. "Do you know where you are?"

Leia sighed at the droid's insistence, then swirled her hand through the green fluid in which she was floating. "I'm in a bacta tank." She spoke directly into her breath mask, which had an integrated microphone that would relay her words to a speaker on the tank exterior. "In a hospital somewhere."

"An infirmary," the droid corrected. "Sarnus has no true hospitals."

Sarnus. Of course. The planet was deep in the Chiloon Rift, the location of Lando's refinery. She remembered that much.

"You are in the Recovery and Close-monitoring Unit," the droid continued. "Room Ten, Floor Five."

"What happened to me?"

"You arrived with facial trauma, multiple fractures in your left arm, and a concussion," the droid informed her. "But your recovery is well under way. Your arm has mended incredibly fast. Both of your eyes have been repaired and are completely functional. Your nose has been reconstructed according to visual references obtained from the infirmary's historical library. Your facial lacerations have been closed—"

"—and are expected to heal without visible scarring," Leia finished. "I have a feeling I've heard this before."

"Excellent," the droid replied. "The symptoms of your

concussion seem to be receding. What else do you recall?"

Leia thought for a moment, fighting to retrieve any memory associated with Sarnus. "I recall being in an office with Lando and . . . *Han.*"

As she spoke her husband's name, Leia's heart climbed into her throat, and she found herself close to panic. Could that be what her dream was about? Could *Han* be the blood that was taken from her? She had no memory of what had happened to him after the astrolith impact—but that was no comfort, as she could not recall what had happened to *her,* either.

"What else do you remember about the meeting?" the droid asked. "Who else was there?"

Leia did not even try to recall. "Stop trying to diagnose me," she ordered. "Just tell me where my husband is."

"Captain Solo is on his way—"

"Then he's okay?" Leia asked. "He's not hurt?"

"He no longer requires bacta immersion to continue healing," the droid said carefully. "And since there is a shortage of tanks, he has been in the staff lounge, waiting for you to awaken. Chairman Calrissian and two other gentlemen are with him. Your protocol droid asked to be alerted as soon as you were available. Are you not available?"

"They're here?" Leia was more relieved than disquieted, of course, but she *was* disquieted. Bacta-tank wraps were not exactly modest. "In the hospital?"

"Yes, coming down the corridor," the droid confirmed. "Though we are an infirmary, not a hospital. I am concerned that you have forgotten that so soon. Do you recall what we were talking about a moment ago?"

"That Han is on his way with three other men. Please raise the privacy shield." Leia reached out in the Force and felt not only Han's familiar presence but that of the young miner who had accompanied them from Brink Station and—much to her surprise—that of her brother, Luke. "This tank *does* have a privacy shield, doesn't it?"

"Of course," the droid responded. "Our equipment here is seldom more than twenty years out of date."

A band around the middle of the tank turned opaque, concealing Leia from mid-thigh to just below her armpits. An instant later the door to the room slid open, and Han stepped into view. He was not quite hobbling, but he was moving slowly and using a cane. He paused briefly, his eyes betraying his concern as he turned toward the bacta tank. His face was a red mesh of half-healed laceration scars, both eyes were black, and his nose was covered by a protective guard. He gave her a lopsided grin, then stepped over and pressed his palm to the wall of the tank.

"Hi there, Princess." Han's voice sounded a bit tired and hollow over the bacta tank's comm system. "You're looking good."

Leia chuckled into her breath mask. "Not if I look anything like you." Pressing her own hand to the tank interior, she paused to see if Han's presence triggered the same kind of fear she had experienced in her dream. The only thing she felt was relief at seeing him alive. Whatever the dream was about, it wasn't him. "Han . . . how bad is it?"

Han's expression turned grim. "Leia, we need to get these guys." He finally removed his hand from the wall of the bacta tank. "They murdered almost thirty thousand beings."

Leia was stunned. She recalled sensing a certain malevolence in the Qrephs, but she had not realized that they were capable of this magnitude of evil. How could she have missed that? She could not help feeling partly responsible—because she *had* missed it, and she hadn't stopped them.

"Count me in," she said. "But I can't believe the Qrephs expect Lando—or *us*—to roll over. Do they really think controlling production in the Rift is worth the trouble they're bringing down on themselves?"

"Good question. We were just about to discuss that ourselves," Han said. He turned and motioned toward the door. "Come on in, fellas."

Lando entered first, looking far less battered than Han, but still moving stiffly and holding a protective arm over his ribs. Omad Kaeg followed behind him, grim but uninjured. Luke followed, looking calm and determined in his gray flight suit, then C-3PO and R2-D2.

"Oh, dear," C-3PO lamented. "You look absolutely terrible, Princess Leia. I do hope these outdated first-aid droids haven't been interfering with your recovery."

The FX droid spun around and shot a burst of static at C-3PO.

"Well, I fail to see why you should be offended," C-3PO replied. "You *are* outdated."

Leia ignored the droids and turned to Luke. "I hope you didn't come all this way just to send me home to recover," she said. "Because that's not going to happen."

Luke smiled. "The thought never crossed my mind," he said. "Actually, I came to deliver that background report you and Han wanted on GET. But I think I'm going to stick around and try to figure out what the Qrephs are *really* doing in the Rift."

"How so?" Leia asked.

"The Rift is valuable," Luke replied. "But it's hardly worth making an enemy of the Jedi."

"Maybe the Qrephs miscalculated," Kaeg suggested. "Maybe they thought they wouldn't be blamed for the sabotage. Or maybe they didn't realize how the Jedi would react to mass murder."

"I'm sorry, Captain Kaeg, but that is extremely unlikely," C-3PO said. "In any intellectual contest, the odds of a Columi miscalculating the opponent's response are—"

"Thank you, Threepio," Luke interrupted, "but the odds don't matter." He tripped the FX-4's circuit breaker to prevent it from making a record of their conversation, then assigned R2-D2 to prevent any eavesdropping by the central monitoring computer. "This is about more than trying to corner the Galactic metal markets, I'm very sure. It's bigger than that."

"And you're sure of that *why*?" Leia asked.

"I'll fill you in more completely later," Luke said. "But Lando and I were talking, and I don't think we can ignore the possibility of Sith involvement. The *Ship* sighting on Ramook may be nothing more than a coincidence, or it may hint at what's really going on in the Rift. The only thing we know for sure is that the Qrephs are up to something out here we don't understand—and we'd better figure it out quick, before it becomes any more of a problem for the rest of the galaxy."

"More of a problem?" Han asked. "You mean the Rift isn't the only place they're blighting?"

"Far from it," Luke said. "Their holdings in the Galactic Alliance have more than *tripled* since they relocated to the Chiloon Rift—despite this being a very strange base from which to run a financial empire. The question is, why are they here?"

"You're suggesting there's something in the Rift that makes it all possible," Leia surmised. "And you think it might be Sith."

"*Sith*." Han snorted in disgust. "Well, that might explain why the Qrephs aren't too worried about Jedi. If they've got a bunch of Sith on their side, they might feel pretty confident about dealing with Leia and me."

Leia frowned. "But it doesn't explain the Mandalorians and the Nargons," she said. "First, Mandalorians don't like Sith any more than they like us. Second, if the Qrephs have an army of Sith at their disposal, why would they pay for mercenaries?"

"My thoughts exactly," said Lando, who had been standing on the far side of the room listening quietly. "I've been running some figures since Luke and I talked. By the time the Qrephs pay for those big asteroid crushers of theirs and an army of Mandalorians to push everyone else around, they're *losing* money on their Chiloon operation—and that's assuming they aren't paying for the pirates, too."

"They're protecting a secret," Luke said. "That *has* to be it. If they don't want anyone to know there are Sith here, they can't have a security force armed with light-sabers running around, or a bunch of Force-sensitive pirates trying to drive miners out. They need someone *else* to do that—so they hire the Mandalorians."

Han's jaw dropped. "Wait a minute. Are you saying *Kesh* is in the Rift? Is *that* their secret?"

"The thought had crossed my mind, but, no," Luke said. "If Kesh were here, there wouldn't be any Manda-lorians *or* miners running around the Rift. The Sith would never take that chance."

"If you say so," Kaeg said, sounding a little doubtful. "So, what *is* this Kesh?"

"It's the homeworld of the Lost Tribe of Sith," Han explained. "But its location is a big secret, mainly be-cause it's so far outside the hyperspace lanes that the Lost Tribe was marooned there for five thousand years."

"I see," Kaeg said. "Then how unfortunate it is that Kesh cannot be here."

"Why?" Leia asked.

"Because then we would know why the Qrephs wanted my share of the miners' support cooperative," Kaeg explained. "It would give them a seat on the RiftMesh Committee."

Han frowned. "And that's important *why*?"

"Because the RiftMesh isn't static," Lando said. "It's constantly being expanded and repaired—and it's the 'Mesh Committee that decides when and where."

"So, if the Qrephs had a seat on the committee, they could influence which beacons to repair—and where to place new ones," Kaeg said. "And even if they failed to win the vote, they would know the committee's plans."

Leia frowned. "I'm still not following," she said. "How does knowing the committee's plans keep people away from Kesh—or *whatever* the Qrephs are trying to protect?"

"Because it's dangerous to operate beyond the Rift-Mesh," Kaeg explained. "*Too* dangerous. Without a beacon signal, it is easy to lose your way—and it is impossible to summon help."

"There aren't many miners who like to operate out of touch in the Rift," Lando added. "If the Qrephs know where the cooperative is putting new beacons, they can destroy the ones that are too close for comfort. That way, there isn't much chance a tug captain could stumble across their secret."

"And if one did, he and his crew would just disappear," Kaeg said. "It may not be this Kesh that the Qrephs are hiding, but it must be something like it. Something big and immobile. We only need to figure out what."

"Agreed." Han nodded, then looked from the bacta tank to Luke and Lando. "I say we do it."

Leia felt a lump form in her chest. There was a certain glee in Han's voice that she never liked to hear, a mad enthusiasm that came only when he had decided to attempt something wild and dangerous that he would not be talked out of.

"Do *what*, exactly?" Leia asked.

Han continued to look at Luke and Lando, awaiting their replies.

"Han," Leia said, trying not to sound worried. "Do what?"

Han continued to watch Luke and Lando.

At last, Luke shrugged, and Lando nodded.

"I guess I don't have any better ideas," Lando said.

"Better than *what*?" Leia demanded.

Han grinned, then finally looked back to her. "It's okay," he said. "I have a plan."

Nine

With polished larmalstone floors and gold bioluminescent chandeliers hovering in midair, the Blue Star casino was more Lando's style than Han's. It was the kind of place where the staff frowned on whooping in delight when you won a fat pot and where they would escort you straight out the door if you cursed a string of bad luck too loudly. But formal attire was required and weapons were restricted, which made it a hard place to flood with hired thugs, and it had top-notch security with state-of-the-art weapon detectors at every door. All in all, Han thought it was a pretty good spot to draw out the enemy—especially since he was still a little too banged up to want another firefight.

A few days of bacta therapy and some close attention from the medical droids had taken care of his superficial wounds and stopped the ringing in his ears, and he could see even better out of his new eye than he could with the one that had gone missing when the astrolith hit. But his bruised chest and ribs were another matter. They had to heal on their own, and, unlike Leia, he couldn't enter a Jedi healing trance to speed things along. He just had to be patient and try to avoid laughing too hard, or breathing too hard, or lifting too much—or doing any of a dozen things that might drop him to his knees, gasping in pain.

A slender hand touched Han's shoulder as Dena Yus returned from a break and slipped into the adjacent seat. "This isn't working," she said, leaning in close and whispering. "Tharston always went to the Durelium Palace. I think that must be where he met his contact."

"Yeah, but we're not supposed to know that, remember?" Han replied. Dena had been making the same argument since confiding that it might have been her dead lover who helped the Qrephs destroy Lando's refinery. Her tune was starting to get old. "Relax. Tharston's handler will find us."

"I don't see how," Dena said. "This isn't the kind of place where hired thugs hang out—and Valnoos has dozens of other casinos that *are*."

"But there's only *one* Lando Calrissian and *one* Han Solo. In case you hadn't noticed, we're kind of famous around the tables." Han nodded toward the crowd of local high rollers gathered behind the observation rail, all hoping for a chance to play their local sabacc variant, Riftwalker, against a pair of galactic legends. "Trust me, Tharston's handler has already heard that we're here. Sooner or later, he'll want to know why."

A card went spinning toward the dealer's station, and Lando announced, "Discard." He slid a stack of thousand-credit wagering tokens into the hand pot and another equal stack into the game pot, then leaned back and smiled broadly. "The bet is ten thousand . . . to each pot."

Han sighed and glanced over at his friend, who now had only three chip-cards—all locked—on the table before him. There were only two reasons Lando would play with just three cards: either he was bluffing or he had a sure win with the idiot's array. Like nearly every scheme Lando employed—in business or gambling—it was an effective long-term strategy, designed to present his rivals with an agonizing choice time after time.

Han knew of only one way to prevent that strategy

from working. He looked at his chronometer. Seeing that the second counter was on an even number, he locked his own chip-cards and pushed *twenty* thousand credits into each of the pots.

"I'll raise," he said.

The declaration drew an approving murmur from the spectators but groans from two of the other players still in the hand. They discarded their chip-cards without matching Han's bet, which meant they were no longer eligible to collect either pot.

The third player, Omad Kaeg, smiled broadly.

"I was *hoping* you would say that, Captain Solo." He pushed all of his betting tokens into the center of the table, exceeding Han's bet by two thousand credits. "In fact, I have been waiting for it."

Instead of replying, Han turned to Lando, who now had to decide whether to match both raises. If Lando called or re-raised, Han would know he was beat and discard his own chip-cards. But if Lando retired from the hand, Han would call Kaeg's extra two thousand credits. There was a good chance the kid had his own idiot's array and Han was beat, of course. But Kaeg was young and cocky, and that meant he was likely to mistake good hands for great hands, and great hands for unbeatable hands. Considering the size of the pots—well over a hundred thousand credits—it was worth a couple thousand credits to see what the young asteroid miner was holding.

When Lando took too long thinking, Han knew his friend had been bluffing. "Go ahead and bet everything," he said, smiling. "I *might* fold."

Lando scowled in disgust and threw his chip-cards toward the dealer's station. "How do you *do* that?"

Han just smiled and glanced at his wrist. The truth was, his decision had been random chance. Had the second counter on his chronometer been showing an odd number the first time he looked, he would have folded to Lando's bluff instead of raising it.

"Lucky, I guess." Han matched Omad's extra two thousand credits, then turned his four cards faceup, revealing the master of coins, the master of flasks, a star, and the commander of staves. "That's twenty-three. How about you, Cap'n Kaeg?"

Omad's face fell. "You have *positive* sabacc?" He shook his head in disbelief, then tossed his chip-cards toward the dealer's station and rose. "I'm out."

"Tough break, kid." Han's sympathy was genuine. It might have been Lando's money that Omad was playing with, but losing big always tore at the guts of a young sabacc player; it was too easy to keep replaying bad decisions and bad breaks. "You'll do better the next time."

"Until then, *I'll* take the seat."

The female voice came from the middle of the line, but it was so hard and authoritative that those ahead of her made no objection. Han glanced over to see a pale, compact woman with short brown hair ducking beneath the observation rail. She was dressed simply but formally, with a long black dress that showed flashes of muscular thigh through a high slit and a top that revealed shoulders so strong that Han found himself thinking of one-armed push-ups.

Han turned away and collected his winnings, being sure to leave a nice tip for the dealer, then glanced over at the adjacent table, where Luke and Leia sat disguised as a high-rolling Devaronian tug captain and his Twi'lek companion. Both seemed completely absorbed by their own game, Luke joking as he splashed betting tokens into a sizable pot, Leia laughing and using the Force to animate the fake head-tails hanging down her back. He let his gaze dart toward the approaching woman and saw Leia flutter her eyes in acknowledgment. She was keeping a close eye on Han and Lando and would not hesitate to intervene if something went wrong.

As the newcomer took her seat across from him, Han was surprised to realize he recognized her small oval face.

"Mirta Gev," Han said, smiling to hide his surprise. Granddaughter to the infamous bounty hunter Boba Fett, Gev had a complicated history with the Solo family. She had once considered Jaina a friend, but that relationship had gone south after Darth Caedus had tortured her. "I thought you had better taste."

Gev returned Han's smile with a cold glare. "You have a problem with halter-necks, Solo?"

"The dress is nice," Han said. "It's your bosses I don't like. The Qrephs—*really?*"

Gev shrugged. "I should care what a Solo thinks?" She took Omad's seat, next to Lando. She was careful to avoid looking at Dena Yus, which told Han she knew exactly who Dena was. "Now, what are we doing here?"

"Playing sabacc, I trust," said the dealer. A tall noseless Duros with red watchful eyes and a droll curl to his lipless mouth, he did not seem to care in the slightest that he was in the presence of two sabacc legends. "The minimum buy-in is twenty thousand credits."

Gev ignored him and continued to study Han. "You're already trying my patience, making me come to a place where I have to wear something like this." She plucked at her clingy dress, then said, "And I'm not fond of Rift-walker, either. You ask me, it's not even real sabacc."

"But *we* like it," Lando said, giving her a big grin. "If you're a little bit short of the buy-in, I'd be happy to front you."

Gev sighed. "That won't be necessary." She drew a voucher chip from her clutch and passed it to the dealer. "Give me half."

The Duros glanced at the voucher chip, then gave an

approving nod. He placed the chip facedown on the table, on an interface pad in front of his supply of wagering tokens.

"Purchasing one hundred thousand." He counted it out in a variety of denominations, then displayed the stacks for the overhead vidcam to record. "Subtract one hundred thousand from the Mirta Gev voucher."

A confirmation beep arose from the interface pad. The Duros pushed the wagering tokens across the table to Gev, and that was when Han realized there might be a problem. Mirta Gev wasn't the kind of mercenary who'd walk around carrying two hundred thousand credits in ready gambling funds—especially if she didn't like playing Riftwalker—and that could mean just one thing. Not only had Gev expected them to come to Valnoos to hunt for Tharston's contact, she had known they would try to level the odds by choosing the most security-conscious casino on the planet.

The Qrephs had anticipated them again.

Or maybe they had help from a spy inside Lando's inner circle.

Han moved his two antes for the next game into the appropriate pots, then glanced over at Dena and found her studying Gev with a furrowed brow. Gev might know who Dena was, but he didn't think the reverse was true. Besides, Dena hadn't even been *told* they would be going to the Blue Star instead of the Durelium Palace. The only thing she knew about Han's plan was that they were on Valnoos to find Tharston's contact.

He leaned close to Dena's ear, then asked, "What do you think? Ever see her talking to Tharston at the Palace?"

"No," she said. "But I only came to Valnoos with him once."

Han frowned. "Then how do you know he always went to the Durelium Palace?"

Dena rolled her eyes at him. "How do you think, Captain? Sometimes we actually talked." She paused, then, almost as an afterthought, added, "And he brought home souvenirs marked with the Palace's three ingots—hats, drink tumblers, even a sabacc deck. Trust me, Tharston went there a lot."

The explanation seemed reasonable enough that Han began to think he was being overly suspicious. Luke and Leia were convinced that Dena was hiding something. But even Han could see she felt bad about what her lover had done, and that alone might have been enough to explain the guilt the two Jedi were sensing in her Force presence.

Then a big man dressed in the pale-blue tabard of a Blue Star security guard stepped up. In his hands, he held a large white handbag that matched Dena's white gown.

"Excuse me, Chief Yus," he said. "But I was asked to return your bag. Another guest found it in the females' lounge."

Dena's eyes widened in surprise, but only for an instant, then she smiled and said, "Thank you. I didn't even realize I'd left it." She took the purse and placed it in her lap. "I'll have to keep a closer watch on it."

Had Dena been the kind of woman who carried a big handbag, Han might not have found the exchange so suspicious. But she had not been carrying this bag when they arrived. He was sure of it. She had been carrying a tiny satchel, which was now nowhere to be seen. Maybe she *had* left a purse in the refresher, but it wasn't this one.

By the time the guard left the table, Han's first two chip-cards had arrived. He tipped them up and saw a nine of sabers and a ten of flasks, then looked back toward the observation rail.

The mix of the crowd had subtly changed. There were

more guards at the rail now, and while they wore the standard uniforms of the casino staff, they were all large human males with rugged faces and calloused knuckles. Even more telling, their blue security coats were often too small—sometimes so small they looked more like tunics than tabards.

No wonder the high rollers hadn't protested when Gev cut ahead of the line. She was backed by Mandalorians. Han looked around the room and saw that extra guards had been posted at the doors, and there were more quietly slipping into the room. When he glanced at Leia, it was clear she hadn't missed the new development, either.

"The bet is to you, Captain Solo," the Duros said. "It stands at five thousand credits to each pot."

Han turned back to find Mirta Gev's gaze fixed on him, her lip curled into a faint sneer. The only player with two wagers stacked in front of her, she was clearly the person who had opened the betting.

"Something wrong, Captain Solo?" Gev asked. "In over your head, perhaps?"

"Not likely, sister." Before responding to the bet, however, Han turned to the Duros dealer and asked, "Say, when did this place change hands?"

"I'm sorry, but management has recently asked us not to discuss ownership." The faintest hint of a smile flashed across the dealer's noseless face, then he continued, "I hope you understand, Captain."

"Sure, no problem," Han said, understanding exactly why the Duros had used the word *recently*. In essence, he'd answered Han's question. It was one of the benefits of being a good tipper: dealers liked to keep him happy—short of cheating, of course. "Thanks anyway."

"Sorry I couldn't be more helpful," the Duros replied. "Will you be calling the lady's bet?"

Han studied Gev's cool expression, wondering how

much of his plan the Qrephs had anticipated—and how much Dena Yus had told them. Yus hadn't known which casino Han would pick, but she *had* known they were heading to Valnoos. In fact, she had maneuvered them into it by fingering Tharston as the guy who'd leaked the tractor-beam control codes.

Han felt like a fool, but what mattered was how much the Qrephs had figured out. Did they realize that Han and his companions weren't actually trying to capture Tharston's handler—if such a person even existed? Han's real objective was to drive a wedge between the two brothers. Had the Qrephs figured *that* out, too?

Probably, he decided. They were Columi, after all.

Fortunately, at the moment, it wasn't the Qrephs that Han and his companions had to fool—only Mirta Gev. He smiled, then counted out two stacks of wagering tokens.

"Actually, I'll be raising . . . to ten thousand each pot," Han said. He placed the two stacks on the table in front of him, then looked up at Gev. "What do you say we drive out the weak hands?"

Gev smiled. "Fine by me."

Dena quickly withdrew from the hand, as did the Arconan tug captain seated next to her.

Gev called Han's raise, then turned to Lando. "What about you?" she asked. "Are you here to play, Calrissian—or just watch?"

Lando smiled. "I was about to ask you the same question."

He doubled Han's bet to both pots, drawing a chorus of murmurs from the spectators and forcing the next three players to withdraw. Normally, Han would never call a bet like that with such terrible chip-cards, but winning was hardly the point. He called Lando's bet, then watched Gev do the same.

Once the dealer had placed the tokens into the appropriate pots, Gev turned to Lando and said, "Correct me if I'm wrong, but you haven't looked at your hand yet."

"You're not wrong," Lando said. "Where's the fun in looking?"

He nodded to the dealer, who announced, "Lock any chip-cards you want locked."

Gev glanced at her cards again, then slid one of them into the stasis field. Both Lando and Han left their cards where they lay.

Gev gave them an approving smile. "You two like to live dangerously, I see."

"Not so dangerous," Lando said.

"We're just playing a different game," Han added.

A glimmer of uncertainty flashed through Gev's eyes. "And what game are you playing?"

"Odd man out," Lando said.

He leaned close to Gev and began to whisper. Though Han could not hear the words, he knew that Lando was asking her to carry an offer to Craitheus Qreph. In return for Craitheus cutting Marvid out of the deal, Lando would agree to a partnership that gave them equal control over the entire Chiloon Rift. The offer came with a threat, too: If Craitheus refused, Lando would call in his markers and go to war against the Qrephs.

When Lando finished, Gev drew her head away and studied him in open suspicion. "You're not serious," she said. "You can't be."

"Actually, I'm desperate," Lando said. "And desperate men do desperate things. Maybe I'll even convince my good friend Luewet Wuul that the situation in the Rift is so dire that the Galactic Alliance needs to intervene."

The threat sent a disapproving murmur through the crowd—which, after all, consisted mostly of independent tug captains and asteroid hunters who had struck it rich in the Rift. Lando, who always knew when to press a bluff, merely narrowed his eyes and doubled down.

"Of course, when the Galactic Alliance comes in, the Empire and the Corporate Sector Authority will feel compelled to protect *their* interests, too." He leaned toward Gev, then added, "Tell your boss to take the deal, or things will get very messy, very fast."

Gev leaned forward, mirroring Lando's aggressive posture. "Obviously you haven't heard," she said. "Luewet Wuul is dead. And so is most of his staff."

Lando frowned in disbelief. "What are you talking about?"

"It's very unfortunate. There were explosions on his yacht." Gev smiled and locked gazes with Lando. "Alliance Security thinks it was probably the work of a disgruntled employee. But he was about to introduce a bill authorizing military action to stop mineral smuggling from the Chiloon Rift, so of course there's talk of an assassination. Like any politician, Wuul had enemies."

Lando was so stunned he actually let his jaw drop. "You *killed* Luew?" he gasped. "Are you crazy? He—"

"*Maybe* Luew is dead," Han said. It wasn't like Lando to let anything shake him during a negotiation, and the fact that he was allowing his shock to show made Han worry about what else his friend might let slip. "Or maybe Gev here is just trying to see if you really have pull with the senator."

Gev smirked in his direction. "A fine idea, Captain Solo, but I'm afraid the news is true. We heard it this morning." She turned to the dealer, then added, "I'm sure we weren't the only ones."

"I did hear some gossip," the Duros said warily, clearly seeing Gev in a dangerous new light. "But you know how unreliable these kinds of rumors can be in the Rift."

"Not *this* one," Gev said, turning back to Lando.

"But whoever killed Senator Wuul, it wasn't a Mandalorian. We're mercenaries, not assassins."

"I wasn't aware there's a difference," Lando replied. His eyes grew hard again. "But Luew's death doesn't change my offer."

Gev shrugged. "Maybe not. But you're a fool if you think Craitheus will even consider it."

"And you're a fool if you think he wouldn't want to hear it," Lando replied.

Gev remained silent for a moment, then her gaze slid toward the two huge pots sitting on the sabacc table. "If I deliver the message, what's in it for me?"

Han snorted. "Sorry. There's business, and then there's sabacc." He sneaked a look at his chip-cards and was happy to see that the nine of sabers had changed into a three of staves, giving him a bit more breathing room. "If you want those pots, you'll have to win them."

Gev sighed, then flipped her chip-cards over, revealing an ace of sabers and a mistress of flasks. She had exceeded a score of twenty-three and bombed out.

"It wasn't my money anyway." She pushed her remaining tokens toward the dealer, then said, "Put those back on the voucher, please. I'm done here."

The Duros scowled, no doubt unhappy that his game was proceeding in such a disorderly fashion, but reluctantly accepted the tokens and began to count.

Lando leaned back in his chair and said, "Tell Craitheus he has two days to say yes."

Gev rose and studied Lando until the dealer returned her deposit voucher, then said, "Actually, I won't be the one telling him."

Han frowned. "What's that supposed to mean?"

Gev gave him a cold smile. "It means you can tell him yourself, Captain Solo." She looked toward the observation rail and nodded. "You're coming with us."

Han glanced over and saw six security guards approaching, all with blaster pistols in hand. "What are you, nuts? You think you're taking me hostage?"

Gev shook her head. "No, I'm collecting a *bounty*. The Qrephs put a million credits on you." She smirked. "I bet it feels like old times for you—but, lucky for me, the Qrephs pay better than Jabba the Hutt."

"Come on, you're kidding, right?" Han glanced at Dena, but she looked as confused as he was. "A million credits? I don't believe it."

"Does it look like I'm kidding?"

Han eyed the cadre of guards. "Maybe not," he said. "But a *million* credits? What for?"

Gev shrugged. "The Qrephs don't like you much—or maybe they're commissioning a carbonite wall hanging." She motioned for him to stand. "Now, please don't make me have you blasted. The bounty is only half if I kill you."

"Be serious," Lando said, rising. "You won't walk out of here alive if you try this. Do you really think we came without backup?"

"You two have done crazier things," Gev said. Despite her words, she took the precaution of glancing around. Her gaze passed over the Devaronian and Twi'lek at the nearby table without even pausing. She turned back to Lando with a little smile. "I've seen the history vids."

Lando's face grew stormy. "Like I said, try this and you'll regret it."

"I doubt that," Gev said. "In fact, maybe I should bring *you* along, too. The Qrephs might give me a bonus."

"Not for starting a war, they won't," Lando said. "Han's brother-in-law is the Grand Master of the Jedi Order. And my wife and I own the biggest war-droid manufacturer in the Galactic Alliance."

"Tell me something I *don't* know," Gev said. "Because, so far, I'm not that scared."

"You should be," Lando said evenly. "What do you

think happens if we *both* don't leave here as free men? It won't be just the Jedi coming after you and the Qrephs. It will be every YVH war droid my wife can put on a transport and every bounty hunter she can hire. And it will *never* end."

As Lando threatened, Han was looking around, trying to count guards and figure odds. Between the guards with Gev at the table and the others standing at the rail, he counted maybe a dozen guys that looked tough enough to be out-of-armor Mandos—and all of them carried blaster pistols in plain sight. And then there was Dena. Han couldn't be sure what she had in that big purse of hers, but he knew it couldn't be good.

On their side, Han and Lando had Omad Kaeg, who was trying to blend into the now-worried crowd, and Luke and Leia, whose lightsabers were hidden inside scan-shielded pockets in Leia's fake head-tails. Given two Jedi and the element of surprise, Han felt sure his side could take out Gev and her unarmored thugs— eventually. But at what cost? He and Lando were in a bad spot. They would probably take a dozen blaster bolts apiece, and the odds of surviving *that* were a little long, even for Han Solo.

More important, if Luke and Leia revealed themselves too early, Han's plan would be ruined. The smart play would be to go along now and let the two Jedi rescue him later, inside the hangar. With any luck, they would be able to plant their tracking beacon during the heat of battle and nobody would notice.

The decision wasn't even close.

Han rose and turned to Lando. "It's okay, buddy. I'll go with Mirta. The Qrephs are businessmen, after all. We can work something out."

Lando scowled. "No, Han. You're not going any-where."

"Yeah, I am," Han said, wishing he could put the

Force behind his words. "Look around. We're outnumbered six to one."

Lando dropped his gaze, then reluctantly glanced around the tension-filled gaming floor. The fact that he was careful to avoid Luke and Leia told Han that his message had gotten through—that it would be smarter to get the drop on Gev and her thugs later.

When Lando spoke this time, there was less certainty in his voice. "Han, I can't let you do this," he said. "Who knows what they really want with you?"

"I'll be okay, Lando. They just want a little leverage against you. And I'm it. They know if they hurt me, they lose the leverage." Han wasn't entirely convinced, but he wanted to put Lando at ease. He stepped away from the table, placing himself between two of the big security guards, then looked back over his shoulder. "Tell Leia I'll see her real soon, okay?"

Lando bit his lip and dropped his eyes again. "I'll do that, buddy. No worries."

Han swung his gaze toward the adjacent table, where a still-disguised Luke and Leia continued to sit among the other players. He ran a hand over his hair, giving Leia the signal not to intervene. She flicked a fake headtail in acknowledgment, her expression just shocked and disinterested enough to let Han know she understood what he wanted her to do.

That was the thing about working with a familiar crew. When the plan went a little astray, a good team improvised.

Han looked away, then shrugged at the crowd and shot them a quick *what can you do* smirk. He let the guards take his arms and turn him toward the side exit.

And that was when Omad Kaeg appeared at the observation rail. The kid pushed forward between two glittery-eyed Arconans dressed in brand-new tabards, then glanced toward the exit. Han gave him a quick headshake and a half grin to show he appreciated the offer.

Omad furrowed his brow, then glanced toward the exit again. Whether he was confused or simply disagreed, Han could not tell. He scowled and shook his head again, harder.

Omad nodded and withdrew into the crowd.

"Smart move," Gev said, having noticed the exchange. "We wouldn't want any innocents caught in—"

Her sentence was cut off by the crash of an expensive roo-wood chair shattering across a pair of shoulders. Han spun toward the sound and was shocked to see Omad Kaeg leaping over the observation rail, one foot planted between the shoulders of a stunned security guard who was already halfway to his knees. Omad drove him the rest of the way to the floor and dropped atop him, then pulled the Mandalorian's blaster from its holster, rolled, and came up firing.

A string of blaster bolts screamed past, so close that Han smelled his own singed hair. The hands holding his arms went limp, and both guards crumpled with smoking holes in their heads. In the half second of stunned silence that followed, Han turned to find Omad smirking in his direction, clearly proud of his marksmanship.

Before Han could ask the kid what part of a headshake he didn't understand, the rest of the Mandalorians were pouring bolts back at Omad. The kid raised his weapon again, and Han turned to dive for cover.

Han wasn't fast enough. Gev already had him by the collar and was spinning him around, putting him between her and Omad. She started to yell an order in Mando'a, but by then Han was driving backward into the sabacc table, pushing Gev onto its black velvet surface and sending thousand-credit tokens in every direction.

They both landed on their backs, Han atop Gev, and

he found himself looking into the eyes of a much-stunned Dena Yus. She still sat in her chair, clutching her mysterious white purse to her chest.

From beneath Han, Gev's angry voice called, "Chief Yus! What are you doing? Open your purse!"

Yus glanced down at the bag but seemed too shocked to obey. She shook her head and clutched the purse more tightly.

"Chief Yus, open the—"

Han slammed the back of his head into Gev's face, and the order ended in a loud crackle. Gev's small hand shot under Han's arm and came up behind his neck, then her other hand snaked across his throat and grabbed his collar. Her arm began to pull, cutting off the blood supply to Han's head, and his vision narrowed.

Han tried to slam his head into Gev's face again, but the hand behind his neck held it motionless. He tried to drive his elbows back into her ribs and only banged them against the table instead. The darkness began to creep in from the edges of his vision. He kicked his legs against the edge of the table, hoping to draw the attention of Lando or Omad or *someone* . . . and knew he had succeeded when he felt the Force lifting both him and his attacker into the air.

Gev was so astonished that she relaxed her choke hold. They continued to rise, twenty centimeters, fifty, maybe a full meter above the table. Han's vision returned, and he saw Lando come up holding a blaster. He was positioned behind Dena and firing at the guards, who continued to pour bolts at Omad. There were maybe seven or eight of them left, all staggering around as if they had spent too much time in the bar before coming on duty.

Luke or Leia, of course, using the Force to shove them off balance.

Han suddenly dropped, landing hard atop Gev. The

breath left her in a sharp groan, and her arm fell away from his throat. He immediately slammed his head back into her nose again, and as it crackled, he felt her other hand slip from behind his neck.

Han launched himself away. As his feet met the floor, he caught a glimpse of Dena, still clutching the purse and crawling beneath the table to hide. Luke and Leia remained at their own table, crouching on the floor with the other patrons, maintaining their cover as they surreptitiously used the Force against Gev's team. Han smiled. That was the thing about experience. Even when a plan went *totally* astray, veterans knew how to get it back on track.

Han dropped and rolled, taking cover behind an overturned chair. Dena was now fully under the table, continuing to clutch the mysterious handbag. Half a dozen Mandalorians lay dead or wounded on the floor, and the rest were caught in a vicious crossfire between Lando and Omad. All Han needed was a little extra firepower, and then he could send Gev scurrying back to the Qrephs.

Seeing no blasters within safe reach, Han turned to snatch the handbag from Dena's grasp.

She jerked it away. "What are you doing?"

"Cut the innocent act, sister." Han could not be sure what Dena had inside that handbag, but since she'd received it *after* she passed through the weapon detectors, he was betting it was something useful. A blaster, maybe, or even a grenade. "Whatever they brought you in that purse, I want it."

Dena shook her head. "No, Captain Solo." She continued to pull it away. "Trust me, you—"

Han stretched and caught the purse, then yanked it out of her grasp. Something clinked inside. It didn't sound like a grenade or a blaster, but when Dena lunged and got hold of the bottom, he knew it had to be *something* important.

Han ripped the purse flap open, then thrust his hand inside and felt what seemed to be two or three tubes about as large as his hand. He grabbed a couple, and that was when Dena planted a spiked heel on his still-tender sternum.

"No!"

She wrenched the bag away, and the tubes went flying.

Dena's gaze dropped to a tube that had ricocheted off the table bottom and landed about a meter away from Han. Her eyes grew wide, and she dropped her hands to the floor and began to crab-walk backward into the fire-fight. Han turned toward the tube and saw something white and bristly inside. It seemed to be pushing the ventilated stopper out of the end.

What the blazes?

Han reached for the tube, but the stopper was already popping free. The bristly white thing scrambled out, unfurling itself as it moved, and Han was astonished to see a white, fist-sized arachnid stepping onto his wrist.

He whipped his hand and sent the thing flying. It landed beneath the adjacent table, where it paused and began to wave its long antennae in the air. After a moment, it spun around and raced toward Luke and Leia's end of the table.

The arachnid made it almost halfway before it passed in front of a crouching three-eyed Gran, who screeched and slammed an empty cocktail glass on it.

The Gran vanished in a blast of white flame, and the table was hurled onto its side. Han didn't see what happened to Luke and Leia, but suddenly the cries of the panicked and injured were drowning out the scream of blaster fire.

Han's plan was history.

When he glanced around, he found two more tubes lying on the floor. Both were open and empty. He spotted one of the bristly white things scampering toward the toppled table where he had last seen Luke and Leia.

The other one was headed toward Lando.

Han lurched toward Lando and grabbed him by the shoulder. "White spiders!" he yelled. "Big white spiders! Blast them!"

Lando spun around and saw the spider heading for him. He pointed his blaster and pulled the trigger, and a ball of white flame erupted beneath the table. Han felt himself tumbling across the floor, chest aching and face stinging, until he finally slammed into a dead security guard.

A second blast sounded from farther away. By then Han's ears were ringing and his vision was blurry. But he still knew where he was—and that the fight wasn't over. He spun around and began to search for the dead guard's blaster.

His fingers were just closing around the handle when a black high-heeled pump with a peep toe came down on his wrist. He looked up to find Mirta Gev staring down at him, dripping blood from a broken nose, pointing the emitter nozzle of a blaster at his head.

"Oh, no, Captain Solo," she said, motioning for him to rise. "Like I said, you're coming with me."

Ten

One thing casinos usually had in abundance was surveillance, and Marvid loved surveillance. He could measure the intelligence of his subjects by how long it took them to start acting as though the vidcams were not recording. He could predict how reliable they were by comparing their behavior when they *knew* they were being watched to their behavior otherwise. He could even tell whether someone was a good liar by monitoring the number of times he or she placed a finger somewhere impolite.

What Marvid could not do, however, was change plainly visible facts.

He and Craitheus were meeting on the owners' deck of their mobile headquarters in the Rift, the asteroid crusher *Ormni*. Their powerbodies were resting side by side in the conference cabin, with Mirta Gev standing left of Craitheus and Savara Raine to Marvid's right. A pair of Nargon bodyguards flanked each of the two doorways, their raised skull crests reflecting the tension in the room. A surveillance vid from the Qrephs' most recent acquisition, the Blue Star casino on Valnoos, was playing on the wall screen.

And, despite Savara's claim that *she* deserved the million-credit bounty for capturing Han Solo, the vid suggested otherwise. So far, it showed a bloody-nosed, formally dressed Mirta Gev dragging a wildly kicking Solo across the floor of a casino hangar. Behind her followed a squad of ten Mandalorians in full armor and a handful of firefight survivors, wounded and still dressed in Blue Star security tabards. One of the wounded men had his arm around a blaster-burned Dena Yus, half dragging and half carrying her as he limped after the others.

An inset in the bottom corner of the screen showed the Mandalorians' destination, a boxy, Mandalorian Tra'kad space-transport with the boarding ramp extended. A second inset showed a current-time image of Han Solo, lying battered and unconscious on a bare durasteel bunk in the *Ormni*'s brig. Marvid liked that image the best.

He looked toward Savara. "I see nothing to support your contention."

"Not yet," Savara replied. "Keep watching."

Craitheus sent a powerbody transmission: THIS IS A WASTE OF OUR TIME. YOUR PET IS JUST ANGRY THAT WE PUT GEV IN CHARGE OF THE BLUE STAR OPERATION.

THE AMBUSH *WAS* SAVARA'S IDEA, Marvid said. I SUGGEST WE GIVE HER *TWO* MILLION CREDITS FOR ELIMINATING WUUL. WE HAVE NO ONE ELSE WHO COULD HAVE DEFEATED THE SECURITY OF A GALACTIC ALLIANCE SENATOR, AND THE BONUS SHOULD MAKE HER FEEL BETTER ABOUT MISSING THE ATTACK ON THE JEDI.

WHAT DO I CARE HOW SHE *FEELS*? Craitheus demanded. SHE FEARS THE JEDI AS MUCH AS SHE HATES THEM. IF SHE IS UNHAPPY WITH HER ASSIGNMENTS, IT WILL BE A SMALL MATTER TO ARRANGE A SURPRISE MEETING.

PERHAPS, BUT AN UNHAPPY OPERATIVE IS A SUSPICIOUS ONE. SHE WOULD NO DOUBT BE WATCHING FOR SUCH A BETRAYAL.

ALL THE BETTER, Craitheus replied, AS LONG AS SHE ALSO *FEARS* IT. IF WE KNOW WHAT SHE FEARS, WE KNOW HOW TO

CONTROL HER. As they conversed, two points of light appeared in the vid, about head height on the hangar door behind Gev and the Mandalorians. At first, Marvid did not recognize what he was seeing. Then the two points separated and began to glide in opposite directions, creating the glowing orange outline of a doorway.

A pair of lightsaber tips, cutting their way into the hangar.

In the vid, Gev waved her armored Mandalorians back toward the glowing outline, then Solo suddenly let his legs go limp and dropped, dragging her down with him. By then the two lightsabers were nearly at the floor, cutting through the thin interior door as though it were plastoid instead of durasteel.

The door blew off its hinges, and a pair of Jedi—one Devaronian, one Twi'lek—came whirling into the hangar, their lightsabers weaving baskets of color as they deflected blaster bolts back toward their attackers. A trio of Mandalorians dropped in an instant, and Savara's claim to the bounty suddenly began to look more plausible.

Deciding that now might be a good time to undermine his brother's excessive faith in Mandalorian solutions, Marvid stopped the vid and turned to Mirta Gev.

"You were in charge of the ambush, Commander," he said. "Tell me, how did *two* Jedi manage to smuggle lightsabers into the Blue Star?"

"They were in disguise," Gev said. "The lightsabers were hidden inside the Twi'lek's lekku."

"Ah, that explains it." Marvid smiled. Gev was blundering straight into his trap, of course. "And didn't they go through the weapon detectors at the main entrance?"

Before Gev could do more damage to her cause, Craitheus said, "The point is noted and conceded, Marvid. Savara would have seen through the Jedi disguises *before* taking Solo prisoner. But we still have Solo."

"Which is hardly the issue," Savara said. "If I had been in command, Dena would have released the arachnokillers *first*. The ambush would have *started* with the deaths of Calrissian and the Jedi, and taking Solo captive wouldn't have left you paying the death benefits on a dozen contracts."

"Assuming your plan worked," Craitheus countered. "But there was never any guarantee. As you are so fond of reminding us, Jedi are difficult to kill."

"And now Mirta has made it impossible." Savara pointed at the vid. The frozen image showed the Devaronian Jedi in midair, hurling himself into a somersault with three blaster bolts simultaneously ricocheting off his blade. "That's Luke Skywalker you're looking at. You only get one chance at him—*if* you're lucky."

Savara glared across the table at Gev, then continued, "And Mirta just wasted that *one* chance capturing an old man who can't even use the Force. The only thing *she's* done is bring the Qreph empire one step closer to ruin—and bring both of you *five* steps closer to death."

Marvid's powerbody registered a blast of transmission static that could only be his brother's rage. But when Craitheus spoke, it was in a carefully measured tone.

"Nevertheless, Commander Gev *has* delivered Han Solo to us alive, which is all that is required to collect the bounty." Craitheus turned to Marvid. "We're done here."

"Not yet, you aren't," Savara said. She looked to Marvid. "Keep playing. You'll be glad you did."

Marvid restarted the vid, then watched in grudging admiration as Jedi Skywalker downed two more armored Mandalorians. The phony Twi'lek—Leia Solo, no doubt—sent a third flying across the hangar. The last three men began to fall back. They were clearly overmatched and destined to fail.

That changed when Savara Raine appeared in the doorway behind the two Jedi and sent a separate grenade flying at each one. Skywalker and his sister sensed the danger and sprang away in opposite directions, then the vid flared orange and stayed that way for nearly three seconds. When it cleared, it had resolved into a split screen, one half showing the Mandalorian vessel shuddering on its struts, the other half showing a trio of Nargons charging into the hangar, firing their blaster rifles toward an unseen enemy.

Savara was not visible on either half of the screen, but Gev was on the first screen, dragging a badly beaten and now-unconscious Solo up the Tra'kad's boarding ramp. They were almost inside when they suddenly stopped and seemed to teeter on the verge of tumbling back to the hangar floor—caught, Marvid assumed, in an invisible Force grasp.

Then more Nargons appeared and began to pour fire at the unseen Jedi, and Gev disappeared into the transport with Solo. The vessel started to rise off its struts even before the boarding ramp had retracted, and Craitheus stopped the vid.

"Savara has made her case," he said, turning to Marvid. "She deserves a share of the bounty."

"Agreed," Marvid said. "I suggest a fifty percent split."

"*Fifty* percent?" So strident was Gev's voice that the Qrephs' Nargon bodyguards stepped forward, ready to protect Marvid and his brother. She merely glared at them, then continued, "I lost a dozen good men in that operation. If you think we'll settle for a single credit less than the full million—"

"You don't deserve a million," Savara interrupted. "You don't deserve a single credit." She turned to Marvid. "Didn't I tell you to keep playing?"

Marvid knew he shouldn't smile—it would betray his bias to Craitheus—but he couldn't help himself. She was so arrogant.

"If you insist," he said. "But I really don't see you receiving more than half the bounty."

"That's not the point." Savara waved at the wall screen. "Just play."

Marvid restarted the vid and watched in growing concern as Skywalker went after the Nargons, while his sister began to Force-hurl armored Mandalorians into the hangar walls. By the time the transport was departing through the barrier field, the Nargons had been reduced to piles of scale-covered flesh and metal. Gev's Mandos lay strewn across the hangar floor, missing limbs and armor. Most were clearly dead, but several appeared to be merely wounded or unconscious. A moment later, Lando Calrissian and Omad Kaeg entered the hangar and began to interrogate the survivors.

Marvid and Craitheus had the same thought simultaneously.

"Were any *pilots* captured?" Craitheus asked, spinning his powerbody toward Gev. "Did you risk anyone who knows how to find Base Prime?"

Gev's eyes grew resentful. "Of course not," she said. "We *do* know how to follow a directive."

Marvid ran a replay of her facial expressions and determined that she was not entirely confident. After a quick, silent consultation with his brother, he spun his powerbody toward Savara.

"You'll go to Sarnus immediately," he said. "Commander Gev will want her personnel rescued—if possible. If not, the Jedi are not to have time for a lengthy interrogation."

Gev's eyes flared in anger. "Those are my—"

"A rescue won't be necessary," Savara interrupted. "The Jedi didn't take any prisoners."

Gev whirled on her. "What did you do?" she demanded. "If you harmed my people—"

"If I did, it was *your* mess I was cleaning up," Savara replied, just as hotly. "Besides, loose tongues are the least of the problems you caused. Do you *really* think Calrissian was on Valnoos to strike a dirty deal?"

The word *deal* hit Marvid like a gamma blast to a cerebellum. He hadn't heard anything about a deal—or any other offer from Calrissian—and that could mean only one thing. He directed his powerbody to arm its weapon systems, then designated Craitheus and Gev as first and second targets.

"Deal?" Though the question was directed at Savara, his attention was locked on his brother. "What deal?"

Savara's eyes went wide with shock, and her attention remained fixed on Gev. "You didn't tell them together?"

"How did *you*—" Gev stopped herself, glaring at Savara. "The message was to *Craitheus*, and I'm not paid to involve myself in their business."

"You fool." Savara shook her head. "The message was nothing but a ploy—and now you have it working on two levels."

"What message?" Marvid demanded. To encourage an answer, he aimed a blaster cannon at Gev's face and uncovered the emitter nozzle. "*What* levels?"

"There's no need to arm your systems," Craitheus said. "The only reason you haven't heard about it is that it wasn't worth mentioning."

Marvid kept his weapon systems live. "It might be worth mentioning *now*."

"Calrissian is trying to drive a wedge between us." Craitheus switched to their private comm channel. I DIDN'T WANT TO LET THAT HAPPEN.

SO HE OFFERED TO STRIKE A DEAL WITH YOU AND SUP- PLANT ME, Marvid replied. He continued to keep his weapon systems live. This was a new experience for him. His brother had never kept a secret from him be- fore, and it had his thoughts reeling. PREDICTABLE.

AND FUTILE.

Craitheus had not armed his own weapon systems yet, no doubt because the attempt would force Marvid to make a preemptive strike.

"Calrissian certainly knew that I would never cut you out."

Craitheus spoke aloud, no doubt because he hoped to elicit support from Gev. Perhaps he could sense Marvid's confusion and thought a smallhead opinion might actually influence him.

"It was only an attempt to create strife between us," Craitheus continued. "We've used the same divide-and-conquer strategy a hundred times. I was determined not to let it affect us."

YET IT HAS, Marvid transmitted, BUT ONLY BECAUSE YOU KEPT IT FROM ME. WHAT AM I TO THINK, EXCEPT THAT YOU WERE CONSIDERING IT?

SO WHAT IF I WAS *CONSIDERING*? Craitheus countered. CONSIDERING IS NOT DOING.

There lay the truth, Marvid realized. Craitheus *had* been tempted. The one being Marvid had always trusted— the one being *he* would never betray—had been thinking about turning against his own brother.

For what? Certainly not for money. Craitheus was already wealthier than most interstellar empires. No, Craitheus wanted power. He wanted to be the sole holder of Galactic Syndicated—and all it controlled.

Marvid considered his options. Given the limited confines of the conference room, he decided the blaster cannon would be best—then felt his head rocked by an invisible Force slap.

"Marvid, *stop* that," Savara ordered. "So your brother was tempted to sell you out. Disarm your weapons and deal with it. We need to talk about the real reason Calrissian made the offer, and we're running out of time."

Marvid did not disarm his weapons. "We *know* the reason," he said. "Calrissian was trying to drive a wedge between us. It worked."

"Better than he ever imagined, I'm sure," Savara said. "But that's not our problem at the moment."

"Then what is?" Craitheus asked, eager to change the subject.

"Reverse the vid, and I'll show you," Savara said.

She waited until the image showed the transport resting on its struts again, with Gev and her companions disappearing inside. She ordered him to stop, then to magnify the image and restart the vid in slow motion.

"Watch carefully." She pointed at the wall screen, then said, "Right . . . *here.*"

A tiny gray disk appeared on the screen and began to accelerate toward the transport. By the time the vessel was gliding out through the hangar exit, the disk had caught up and attached itself to the hull.

"You're looking at a Jedi tracking beacon," she said. "And *that* is our problem."

Eleven

The asteroid crusher *Ormni* hung in the distance ahead, a gray wedge silhouetted by the fiery glow of its own smelter vents. Beneath its belly billowed a dust cloud three times its size—all that could be seen of the asteroid it was slowly devouring. Both ship and cloud were surrounded by a swirling mesh of blue slivers—the efflux tails of the *Ormni*'s tender craft going about their business.

Sitting in a little ScragHull spyboat on loan from Lando, Leia was still too far away to see the tender craft with her naked eye. But on her dimly lit tactical display, she saw the transponder codes for dozens of blasting yawls and ram galleys—the slaveships that broke the asteroid apart and pushed the pieces into the *Ormni*'s processing maw. She also counted four huge cargo transports clustered around the *Ormni*'s stern, five Bes'uliik starfighters on patrol, and three assault transports departing on a mission.

By now Han could be aboard any one of those vessels, being moved from the *Ormni* to a new location before she had a chance to rescue him.

Leia longed to reach out in the Force and search for him. But during the last moments of the firefight at the Blue Star, both she and Luke had felt a dark presence working against them, and now it seemed entirely possible that the Qrephs might be working with Sith. If so, using the Force would alert the enemy to their approach just as surely as firing the ScragHull's engines. Leia had no choice but to watch and worry as they drifted toward the *Ormni*, unpowered, all the while terrified that Han would be gone—or already dead—by the time they arrived.

Leia was no stranger to worry, of course. During the Rebellion, she and Han had risked their lives almost daily. As a diplomat of the New Republic, she had seen her children kidnapped and used as political hostages. Later, she had watched those same children become Jedi Knights and leave on dangerous missions of their own. Twice she had suffered the anguish of losing a son to war. And now, with her daughter known as the "Sword of the Jedi," a month seldom passed when Leia did not find herself wondering whether her last surviving child would return from a mission alive.

So Leia knew all about worry, and she knew how to handle her fears—even how to use them.

But this time felt different. Han called on luck the way Jedi called on the Force—and luck *wasn't* the Force. The Force was all-encompassing, eternal, and infinite. Luck was fickle. It came and went, favored some and spurned others. Luck was mathematics, the rules of probability. Mathematics said you simply could not win every long shot.

And yet Han had been taking long shots his whole life. If this turned out to be the time his luck finally ran out, the Qrephs and Mirta Gev would pay dearly for taking him. Leia would see to that—even if she had to spend the rest of her life hunting them down.

"Careful," Luke said. He was seated next to her in the cockpit's dim blue light, monitoring the tracking beacon they had attached to Gev's transport as she fled with Han. The vessel was still aboard the *Ormni*—that much they could be sure of. But who knew where Han was? "Hatred leads to the dark side. So does vengeance—even plotting it."

"Who says I'm plotting?" Leia asked.

Luke only looked at her through the dim light—patiently.

"Sorry," Leia said, realizing she must have been allowing her rage to seep into the Force. "I wouldn't call it *plotting* . . . but it's hard not to dwell."

"I understand," Luke said. "But you know there's no sense in it. Han has been in worse situations, many times over."

"This feels different. The Qrephs are always two steps ahead of us. And that scares me."

"Me, too," Luke admitted. "And I keep asking myself, *Why Han?* What makes *him* worth a million-credit bounty, when they were trying to kill Lando and us?"

Leia considered the question for a time, trying to recall anything in her husband's past that might explain the Qrephs' interest in him, then finally shook her head.

"All I can think of is a hostage situation," she said. "They probably know that Ben and Tahiri are in the Rift looking for Ohali. Maybe they were hoping to have some leverage after they killed you and me."

Luke shook his head. "They're too smart to believe that would work," he said. "And that spider-bomb operation was a mess. I still don't know why Dena Yus was trying to hold on to those things."

"You don't?" Leia asked. The Blue Star surveillance vids had gone "missing" by the time R2-D2 could access the casino's security computer. But she and Luke had managed to piece together a decent picture of Dena's actions during the firefight from their own memories and Lando's account. "It's pretty obvious—she froze."

Luke considered this, then nodded. "I guess, but why? She's been working with the Qrephs from the beginning, that much is clear. And she's the one who set us up for the ambush. So why hesitate to finish us, when she just helped the Qrephs kill thousands of refinery workers?"

"Maybe she was supposed to hit us somewhere else, or maybe the firefight vacced her brain, or maybe the purse latch was stuck." The speculation was beginning to frustrate Leia, for it only served to remind her how little they actually knew about the Qrephs and their organization. "She didn't stick around to take questions, so all we can say for sure is that Dena Yus works for the Columi. And whatever *they* have planned, by the time we figure it out, it could be too late for Han."

"It won't."

Luke's hand settled on Leia's arm and squeezed, and she began to feel a little less helpless—if not entirely confident.

"Han is going to be fine," Luke said. "I promise."

"Thanks. I appreciate the reassurance." Leia patted Luke's hand, then removed it and said, "But I don't want you making promises that may get you into trouble. These guys are too dangerous for that."

"You seem to be forgetting who I am, Jedi Solo," Luke said sternly. "We are *going* to get Han back. And we are going to stop the Qrephs." He paused for a moment, then let out an exaggerated sigh. "Once we figure out what they're doing here, of course."

Leia had to smile. "Well, at least you have a plan—sort of," she said. "I feel like Han is back already."

An alert chime sounded over the cockpit speaker, then a standard distress message scrolled across the pilot's display. INCOM RECONNAISSANCE CRAFT X396 REQUESTS EMERGENCY ASSISTANCE. ALL SPEED.

Leia's brow went up. "Three ninety-six," she repeated. "Isn't that—"

"Ohali Soroc," Luke finished. Over nonsecure comm networks, Jedi StealthXs were currently identified only as Incom Reconnaissance Craft. "Artoo, give us the co-ordinates."

R2-D2 replied with a negative chirp, then loaded a routing report onto the pilot's display. It showed that the message had passed through only one repeater beacon.

"Wherever that came from, it's definitely close," Leia said, already starting to feel torn. She wasn't about to leave without Han, but the first law of space travel was *Respond to a distress signal.* And this was a *Jedi* in distress. "She has to be less than a light-year away."

R2-D2 gave a confirming tweet. A schematic appeared on the display, showing the repeater beacon within a quarter light-year of the ScragHull, somewhere within a 140-degree arc to the stern.

"Why behind us?" Leia asked.

Another chart appeared on the display, this one showing the location of every repeater beacon nearby. The *Ormni* was hanging at the absolute edge of the 'Mesh, with nothing beyond it but a huge bubble of uncharted Rift. Since the message had come over a RiftMesh repeater beacon, it *had* to have come from behind them.

Leia began to feel even more worried and lonely. She could not count the number of times that she had stood on the edge of the abyss, staring down into its black heart. But it had never felt quite so literal before—perhaps because Han had usually been there, staring down into the darkness along with her.

Leia's contemplation was interrupted when Luke asked, "Artoo, is there any indication that Jedi Soroc is still with her craft? Or whether she's still alive?"

The droid responded with a negative chirp.

"So, maybe a trap," Luke said. "Gev could have found our tracking beacon."

"*Probably* a trap," Leia corrected, her heart climbing into her throat. If the Qrephs knew about the tracking beacon, they would be expecting Luke and her to make a rescue attempt on Han. "It seems very unlikely that Ohali Soroc just happened to run into trouble nearby while you and I are trying to sneak aboard the *Ormni*."

"Right. And if something had *just* happened to her this close, we would have felt it in the Force." Luke paused to think, his face growing more sad and worried as he worked through Ohali's possible fates. "This is no coincidence. They've captured Ohali's StealthX, and they're trying to use it to draw us out."

"And if the Qrephs have *Ohali's* StealthX . . ." Leia let the sentence trail off as she sorted through the implications of the distress signal, then finally asked, "Luke, what about Ben and Tahiri? If they've been looking for Ohali, they might have run into the Qrephs themselves."

Luke shook his head. "They're fine," he said. "At least, Ben *felt* fine when I tried to summon him."

"When did you do that?" Leia asked. She did not need to inquire *how* Luke had tried to summon his son. Force-sensitive relatives could usually sense each other across vast distances. "After they took Han?"

Luke nodded. "Before we left the Blue Star," he said. "I thought we could use some backup."

Luke did not need to add that it was impossible to know whether Ben had actually understood what he wanted. For all its power and mystery, the Force could provide only a vague impression of a loved one's condition—it wasn't a comm network.

"Backup couldn't hurt," Leia said. "But even if Ben and Tahiri haven't tangled with the Qrephs yet, I'm worried about that distress signal. We need to warn them off."

"Maybe," Luke said. "Let me think."

He fell silent, no doubt contemplating the same dilemma as Leia. Trying to warn Ben now—even by reaching out in the Force—would probably alert the enemy to their own presence. That would compromise their attempt to rescue Han and probably put him in even greater danger. Leia did not think she could bear turning back, but neither could she risk her teenage nephew's life to save her husband's.

"Luke," Leia said. "There's nothing to think about. Ben will respond to that beacon—"

"Ben is a Jedi Knight," Luke interrupted. "So is Tahiri. If I didn't trust them to handle situations like this, I wouldn't send them out."

"Luke, we *know* this is a trap. Han wouldn't want us to risk Ben—"

"And Ben wouldn't want us to sacrifice Han," Luke said, cutting her off again. "But it's not *their* decision, or even *yours*. It's mine—and I have faith in Ben and Tahiri."

Leia fell into silence, unsure of whether to thank Luke or defy him. No matter what they did, they were putting someone in grave danger—which was probably exactly what the Qrephs intended.

As Leia struggled to adjust her thinking, Luke turned to R2-D2 and asked, "How long will it take that distress signal to reach the *Falcon*?"

Even before he had finished the question, Leia's stomach sank. Lando and Omad were waiting aboard the *Falcon*, just two light-years away—and they didn't have the Force to warn them off. When Ohali's distress signal reached the *Falcon*, they would no doubt respond—and fly straight into the Qrephs' trap.

R2-D2 spent a few moments calculating, then tweedled in uncertainty. A brief message scrolled across the pilot's display. MINIMUM TWENTY MINUTES. MAXIMUM UNKNOWN.

They pondered the droid's answer for a moment, then Luke said, "I think we proceed as planned. Even if the distress signal reaches the *Falcon* in *just* twenty minutes, it will take time for Lando and Omad to pinpoint the source and plot a course. And then they'll still need to make the trip. So we have at least forty minutes—and, more likely, four or five hours."

Instead of answering immediately, Leia paused to think. Beyond the forward viewport, the *Ormni* had already stretched to the length of her forearm—large enough that she could see tiny specks of astrolith tumbling down the intake maw in its bow. But there was nothing to suggest that she and Luke had been spotted yet—which was not surprising, given the nature of their borrowed vessel.

Lando's little ScragHull spyboat used some of the same sensor-defeating technology as a Jedi StealthX— and it was better armored. Its biggest drawback was the lack of low-visibility sublight engines, but that deficiency could be overcome by simply drifting to the target—as Leia and her brother were successfully doing at that moment.

Leia glanced back at R2-D2. "Artoo, if we get jumped, the first thing you do is warn Lando and Omad off that distress signal. I don't like gambling with their lives."

R2-D2 emitted an acknowledging bleep.

"Good," Luke said. "And may the Force be with us—*all* of us."

But it seemed the Force *wasn't* with them. A few moments later, a spray of blue darts exploded from a hangar mouth on the near side of the *Ormni*. Leia recognized the sight as a launching starfighter squadron, and her assessment was confirmed when the designator symbols for ten Mandalorian Bes'uliiks appeared on the tactical display. She reached for the engine igniter switch—but instead of fanning out to attack, the Bes'uliiks arranged themselves into a delta formation and circled back over the *Ormni*.

"They're forming up for escort duty," Leia said. "Someone is getting ready to leave."

As she spoke, the silvery crescent of a personal transport rose from a docking berth atop the *Ormni*. The tactical display identified the vessel as the Marcadian luxury cruiser *Aurel Moon*, but its transponder code quickly grew unreadable as its escorts swarmed around it. Leia looked up again to find the entire formation turning away, heading deeper into the Rift—beyond the RiftMesh.

"The Qrephs must be more frightened of us than we thought," Leia said. "That's uncharted Rift they're heading into."

Luke remained silent and stared out the viewport, his face clouding with worry. Leia needed only a second to realize what was bothering him. The Qrephs had paid handsomely to take Han captive—and Leia didn't see them leaving their investment behind.

"They're taking Han with them," she said.

Luke nodded but said, "Assuming that's actually them in the *Aurel Moon*." His gaze remained fixed out the window. "But these are Columi. If we try to outthink them, we'll lose."

"So we need to locate Han," Leia said, coming to the same conclusion. "Which means using the Force."

"We don't have a choice anymore," Luke said. "The only way our drift approach makes sense now is if we *assume* Han is still aboard the *Ormni*—and how likely does that seem?"

"Not very."

"Not at *all*," Luke said. "You'll have a better feel for where Han is, so you take the yoke. I'll ready our weapons."

Luke armed their entire magazine of proton torpedoes and began to designate targets. Leia watched just long enough to see that he was preparing a close-range shock attack, then closed her eyes and extended her awareness toward the *Aurel Moon*.

She sensed dozens of Force auras around and aboard the yacht. There was the cold focus of the Mandalorian escort pilots, the embittered anxiety of the *Moon*'s crew and domestic staff, the arrogant self-satisfaction of the Qrephs themselves . . . and a groggy, slumbering, cranky presence that had slept next to Leia for decades.

Han.

"Found him," Leia reported. "He's on the *Moon*."

This was one of those rare times Leia wished Han were Force-sensitive, so he would feel her presence nearby and know she was coming for him.

"How does he seem?"

"Drugged," she said. "And pissed off."

Luke smiled. "Good. Pissed off is when Han is at his best."

He started to reach for the torpedo launchers—then Leia felt something dark and oily brush her in the Force.

"Wait!"

She pulled Luke's hand away from the launchers, then tried to follow the dark tendril of Force energy back to its source. But the presence retreated as swiftly as it had appeared, and she was left with nothing but the chill it had sent down her spine.

"We have Sith," Leia confirmed. "And they know we're here."

As she spoke, the *Aurel Moon*'s escort squadron was already going into stealth mode, deactivating their transponders and bringing their sensor negators online. They even deployed the efflux baffles that made their Bes'uliiks slower and less maneuverable—but far more difficult for conventional weapons to target.

Fortunately for Leia and her brother, Jedi were not conventional weapons. She simply called up the Scrag-Hull's systems and began to disable the proton-torpedo guidance and propellant modules. Beside her, Luke closed his eyes and began to breathe in a steady rhythm, no doubt reaching out in the Force to search for their deadliest enemies—the unseen Sith.

"Where are they?" Luke asked.

"I couldn't tell," Leia said. "I only felt one touch, and it was faint. If we're lucky, it's only one or two."

Luke opened his eyes. "Let's hope," he said. "I can't feel any Force-users now, so they're probably waiting until we make our move."

Leia nodded. Now that they had been detected, the safe move would be to withdraw and find another way to rescue Han.

But the safe move wasn't always the right move.

Leia looked over.

Luke nodded. "Han wouldn't turn back now." He opened the launch tubes. "We won't, either."

Leia felt the soft thump of ejector charges pushing proton torpedoes out of their carrying racks. Four slender white cylinders slid into view, gliding ahead of the ScragHull. Normally, the thrust engines would ignite once the torpedoes were a safe distance from the cockpit, but with their guidance and propellant systems disabled, the cylinders merely continued to glide.

By then the *Ormni* was a looming wedge of durasteel, its gray hull blotted by the radiant squares of open hangar mouths. The steady stream of blasting yawls and ram galleys entering and leaving suggested that no battle alarms had yet been sounded.

Leia glanced over and found her brother staring into the darkness above the *Ormni,* his gaze fixed on a cluster of tiny delta-shaped shadows that kept appearing and disappearing against the glow of passing tender craft.

Without looking away, Luke said, "I'll take starboard. You're port."

"Good."

As Leia spoke, she opened herself to the Force and felt the cold, focused presences of perhaps ten pilot-and-gunner teams swirling above the *Ormni*. She used the Force to grab two of the proton torpedoes they had set adrift earlier, then accelerated them toward the left edge of the formation above them.

The *Ormni* continued to swell as the ScragHull closed, growing so large that it stretched across the entire viewport. After a few moments of Force-use, she felt the oily brush of the dark side again, and this time it did not withdraw. No matter. Soon enough, the Sith would not be the only enemy who knew where to find Leia and her brother.

The salvo passed above the *Ormni*. Leia guided her first torpedo into the nearest Bes'uliik and was rewarded with the symmetrical white blossom of scattering protons. The viewport dimmed as the ScragHull's blast-tinting activated, and she felt the hot sharp surprise of two lives being torn from the Force—then felt it again as Luke's first torpedo found its target.

Leia put the deaths out of her mind and reached for a pair of alarmed presences near the back of the Mandalorian formation. A heartbeat later, the viewport darkened again, then darkened even more as Luke's second torpedo also detonated, and four more Mandalorian auras dissolved into fiery anguish.

A flashing tangle of energy erupted ahead: the remaining Bes'uliiks opening fire. With the ScragHull's engines still inactive and no Force to help find their targets, the Mandalorian attacks were as ineffectual as they were desperate. Leia did not even bother to bring the spyboat's nose up to reduce the likelihood of a cockpit strike.

But with the *Aurel Moon* carrying Han away and at least one Sith out there who *could* target the ScragHull, continuing to glide was no option. Leia hit the engine igniters. As Luke brought up the shields, enemy cannon bolts began to converge on the little spyboat.

Leia went into an evasive roll, then gave the control yoke over to instinct, jinking and juking without conscious thought, simply trusting to her training and the Force to keep the spyboat out of trouble. A steady patter of cannon bolts blossomed against their forward shields, but many more glanced off harmlessly or missed altogether.

In the blink of an eye, the distance between the Scrag-Hull and its attackers had closed to mere kilometers. Leia opened the launch tubes again and felt the soft thump of torpedoes being expelled. She grabbed two in the Force and accelerated them toward the enemy. At this distance, the exhaust baffles did little to conceal the Bes'uliiks' efflux, and she could see the Mandalorian starfighters as they approached head-on, a half dozen faint blue halos growing steadily larger and brighter as they weaved and bobbed closer.

But where were the Sith? Leia could find no sign of them on her tactical display. She turned her attention back to the Mandalorians, reaching out in the Force and guiding a torpedo toward the largest halo. The Bes'uliik vanished in a white bloom of light and anguish. By then Leia had found another pair of targets near the back of the formation. The mercenaries felt as terrified as they were angry, confounded by Jedi weapons and sorry they had sold their lives so cheaply.

Leia gave them no chance to surrender. These were Mandalorians, and Mandalorians expected no mercy because they gave none. She merely held on to their fear until it vanished in a flash of pain and heat.

By that point Luke had destroyed two more Bessies himself, and the last pair was flashing past in a blazing storm of color and damage alerts. R2-D2 reported an

overloaded forward shield generator and a breach in the
ScragHull's upper cannon turret.

But where were the Sith? Leia had no time to search
for them. The *Aurel Moon* was accelerating away, and
weapon ports were opening along the *Ormni*'s hull. The
last two escorts were wheeling around to attack the
ScragHull from behind, and the tactical display showed
five distant patrol teams rushing back to join the fight.

Clearly, the shock-and-awe phase of the attack was
over.

The *Ormni* loomed ahead, a massive durasteel wall
mottled by the bright ovals of external operating lights.
Its tender craft were scattering, their ion tails lacing
space with long threads of blue light.

Leia eased back on the yoke, bringing up the Scrag-
Hull's nose, and the *Ormni*'s turbolasers opened up, filling the void with billowing blossoms of fire. Leia let the
Force guide her hands, barely aware of the yoke slamming to and fro as the little spyboat dodged through the
stabbing forest of flame. R2-D2 reported that the forward shield generator was operating at 50 percent and
the upper laser cannons remained operable, though the
turret was stuck at 190 degrees.

"Set all cannons to automatic fire," Luke ordered,
"and open a hailing channel to the *Aurel Moon*."

Leia raised her brow. "You're going to *negotiate*?"

"I'm going to threaten," Luke said calmly. "Artoo,
lock a torpedo on the *Aurel Moon* as soon as you can
resolve a target."

R2-D2 let out a three-note whistle of disbelief.

"Of course I know Han is aboard," Luke said. "Just
do it."

Leia was also surprised by the order, but she had no
time to question it. The ScragHull lurched as one of the
Bes'uliiks slipped a cannon bolt through the rear shields
and gouged a divot in its hull armor. Leia rolled the craft

upside down, using the still-functional belly turret to discourage their pursuers. The spyboat shuddered as the dual laser cannons began to fire.

R2-D2 gave a READY chirp for the hailing channel, and Luke spoke into his throat mic. "Jedi pursuit boat hailing the *Aurel Moon*," he said. "Acknowledge."

The cockpit speaker remained silent. The *Ormni*, which now appeared to be floating upside down ahead, drifted high enough to provide a clear view of space beyond. The *Aurel Moon*'s crescent-shaped hull was shrinking fast as the yacht's big ion drives pushed her into a starless abyss between two plasma clouds.

R2-D2 reported a target-lock with a single chirp, and Luke launched the torpedo.

Leia watched with dropped jaw as the torpedo shot away in a flash of white heat.

"Luke!" she gasped. "What are you—"

Luke raised a hand. "Wait. I need to . . ."

He closed his eyes, and the blinding white sphere of a detonating proton torpedo appeared between the *Moon*'s twin ion drives.

"Jedi pursuit boat hailing the *Aurel Moon*," Luke repeated into his throat mic. "*Acknowledge.*"

An instant later, the image of Craitheus Qreph's pear-shaped head appeared above the cockpit holopad.

"*S-S-Sk-Skywalker!*" the Columi spat. "Are you mad? That explosion cracked the viewport on our flight deck."

"And the next one will take out the entire deck," Luke said calmly. "Artoo, lock two more torpedoes on the *Aurel Moon*."

Leia pictured Han imprisoned somewhere aboard the yacht and found her heart climbing into her throat.

Craitheus sneered in derision. "You'll never launch those torpedoes, Skywalker," he said. "Then it would be you killing Han Solo, not us."

"Han dies either way," Luke said. "The only question is whether we all die with him."

Craitheus's eyes narrowed. "You're offering a trade?" he said. "Our lives for Solo's?"

"And *ours,* of course," Luke said. "You call off your Mandalorians and put Han in a rescue pod for us to pick up. Otherwise . . ."

Craitheus's tongue flicked into view between his thin lips. "You drive a hard bargain, Jedi." The Columi's head turned as he looked at something beyond camera range, and he said, "I'll have to consult with my brother."

Luke started to nod, but by then the little ScragHull was passing the leading edge of the *Ormni,* and Leia's spine had gone icy with danger sense. The last two escorts had dropped so far back that they were no longer landing effective shots, and no one else seemed to be hurrying to rush in.

"Luke, he's stalling!" she said. *Where were the Sith?* "Tell him it's now or never."

As Leia spoke, she felt herself pulling the yoke and toeing the thruster-control pedals. They rolled left—just in time to see a hatch the size of the *Falcon* open in the *Ormni*'s top hull. Leia was expecting a flight of Bes'uliiks or a concussion missile to come streaking out of the opening. Instead, she saw a flock of silver birds spraying into the void on tails of rocket fire.

The birds spread into a fan-shaped cloud and swung to block the ScragHull's route. Leia pulled the yoke back farther, spinning and diving away from the strange flock. She had no idea what the things were—they looked like mynocks with jetpack tails—but it was clear that she didn't want to fly into them.

The flock swirled around to follow, but they were too slow to catch the ScragHull. Leia pulled out of her dive and started after the *Aurel Moon* again. The blue circles of the yachts' big drive engines were still visible—perhaps the size of her thumbnails—but dwindling fast.

Leia accelerated after them, crossing the immense breadth of the *Ormni*'s top hull in the span of a few heartbeats.

Luke spoke into his throat mic again. "Last chance, Craitheus."

"Oh, I quite agree, Master Skywalker." A sneer came to the tiny mouth on the Columi's image. "Just not *ours*."

Luke scowled and reached for the torpedo launchers. Leia started to object, but as the ScragHull reached the far side of the *Ormni,* a bloated amber orb that Leia instantly recognized as a Sith meditation sphere rose into view. Covered in a web of pulsing red veins, it had four hideous wings connected to its body by a network of ugly brown struts. In the center of the sphere, an organic hatch was gaping wide, spitting balls of white-hot plasma in their direction.

"Ship!" Luke hissed.

He launched a torpedo, but it was too late. The white cylinder had barely cleared its launching tube before the first ball of white-hot plasma engulfed it. Leia jerked the yoke hard, spinning the ScragHull away from the detonation, then felt the spyboat leap sideways as the blast wave sent them tumbling.

Leia hit the thrusters, trying to power her way back into control as they spiraled toward the *Ormni.* Somewhere behind her, R2-D2 shrieked in alarm as he crashed into a bulkhead, and the cockpit erupted in a frenzy of alarms and lights and sparks.

The *Ormni*'s gray hull approached fast. Leia gave up on regaining control and reversed the thrusters, but the collision was inescapable. She turned to warn Luke to brace and saw him reaching for the torpedo launchers, then felt the thump of the ejector charges and . . . *white*.

Twelve

Ben Skywalker sat stunned and shaken, trying to figure out what he had just felt. It had come to him through the Force, a blast of alarm and determination and hope so powerful it had stolen his breath, and then . . . *nothing*. No wave of searing pain, no tearing in the Force, no reaching out in farewell, just a cold emptiness in the place in his heart where he usually carried his father.

"Ben?" Tahiri Veila's voice came from close beside him, urgent and confused. *"Ben!"*

A hand punched his shoulder, then pointed into the blue miasma beyond the cockpit. A pear-shaped ball of rock and ice came spinning into view, as large as a mountain and so close that Ben could have leapt onto it from the nose of their little Miy'tari Scout. It was the third asteroid to emerge from the plasma in as many minutes, and a barely perceptible gravity field suggested the cloud concealed hundreds more. Ben used the craft's maneuvering thrusters to ease the Miy'tari backward, navigating as much by Force and feel as by sight and sensor, his gaze dancing from the luminescent murk beyond the canopy to the infrared display to the StealthX distress beacon blinking on the navigation screen.

"What was *that*?" huffed Tahiri. She was in her early thirties and had wavy blond hair, piercing green eyes, and a trio of faint scars on her brow—relics of being tortured by the Yuuzhan Vong when she was only fourteen years old. "This is no time to be daydreaming."

"Sorry," Ben said. "I just felt . . . I don't know what. But it was bad."

"Bad?" Tahiri asked. "Be specific, Skywalker."

"It was my father," Ben said. "Something happened to him. I felt it."

"Something as in . . . dead?"

"How would I know?" Ben asked. He wanted to shout, but that was his fear working on him, trying to rob him of his ability to think and act. "I felt a wave of alarm and . . . I guess, *hope.* Then I didn't feel anything. He just isn't there."

Tahiri's face went neutral—a bad sign. She was trying to hide her feelings.

"That could mean a lot of things," she said. "And right now we don't have time to worry about *any* of them."

She turned her eyes forward again, and he followed her gaze out into the blue fog beyond the canopy.

"That's going to be hard," he said.

"I know it is," Tahiri said. "But we have our own mission, Ben, and our own problems. Whatever has happened to your father, you *know* what he expects of you."

Ben took a deep breath, centering himself. A Jedi couldn't lose focus, not when that would endanger him, his mission partner, and everyone counting on them.

Finally he nodded and checked his sensor display. Nothing.

"Our sensors are as blind as I am," Ben said. "This would be a lot easier if we could go active."

Tahiri's voice turned mocking. "You think?" she asked. "Fighting a close-quarters pirate assault would be easier than dodging a few asteroids?"

"Well, it would be faster," Ben said, shrugging. "And more satisfying."

A shadow appeared to starboard, a nugget of darkness that rapidly began to swell as it tumbled through the foggy luminescence. Ben eased off the thrusters and watched as the nugget became a boulder and the boulder a monolith. He would have felt a lot more confident of being able to avoid trouble had he been using the Miy'tari's ion drives rather than its maneuvering thrusters. But even through the plasma cloud, the drives would light up the sensor arrays of anyone lurking in ambush.

Finally, their R9 astromech droid—Ninette—tweedled an alert and displayed the asteroid's projected course on the navigation screen. Ben came to a dead stop, then watched in awe as a three-kilometer mass of pure, dark nickel–iron tumbled across their travel vector.

Almost immediately, the hair on his arms stood on end. He double-checked the asteroid's projected course on the navigation screen. Seeing no indication that Ninette had misjudged either its size or course, he scanned the plasma cloud for more shadows. He saw none, but the hair on his arms started to prickle. He glanced over at Tahiri and found her staring out the forward canopy, her expression blank and distant.

"You feel that?" he asked.

Her gaze dropped toward the deck, and she nodded. "Coming up under us."

Ben fired the thrusters again and rolled the Miy'tari ninety degrees up on its side—then cringed when he saw a ball of speeder-sized durelium crystals whirling up beneath them. He slid the power glides forward and pulled the yoke back, and the scoutboat slid forward, the nickel–iron asteroid now seeming to drop away beneath its belly.

They had barely cleared the asteroid before an irregular circle of shadow appeared ahead and began to swell in their forward canopy. Ninette chirped a navigation alert, and Ben looked down to discover that they were now traveling directly toward Ohali Soroc's distress signal. It was impossible to tell whether the source of the signal was floating free or coming from the surface of an asteroid, but the signal was growing rapidly stronger.

Ben brought the Miy'tari to a dead stop, then said, "I think we've found the crash site."

"What makes you think Jedi Soroc *crashed*, Ben?"

"Sorry," Ben said, realizing he was speaking as though they were responding to a mere accident. "It appears we've found the source of the distress signal."

Tahiri nodded. "That much I agree with," she said. "Let's see if anyone else is here."

Ben checked the sensor display just long enough to identify the drifting masses of half a dozen nearby asteroids, then carefully began to extend his Force awareness to the surrounding area. He kept expecting to feel a sudden prickle of danger sense racing down his spine. He and Tahiri had been searching for Ohali Soroc for weeks without finding any hint of her or her StealthX, so it seemed very suspicious to have the signal activate just after they had sent a message to the Jedi Council reporting their decision to break off the search and go to Sarnus.

Ben was far from surprised to feel the dim, hungry presences of a dozen hunters waiting patiently for their prey to arrive—and apparently unaware that their prey was now stalking them. He reached out more strongly in the Force, taking careful note of the position and mood of each of the presences that he felt.

After a minute, Ben said, "I have three groups of four beings, arranged at seventy-five, a hundred eighty, and two hundred ninety degrees, surrounding the distress beacon."

"Same here," Tahiri said. "It feels like they're in two-seat fighters, two craft at each spot, just waiting for someone to respond to Ohali's distress signal."

Ben thought for a moment, then nodded. "And none of them feel like Force-users," he added. They had found no reason so far to suspect Sith involvement in Ohali's disappearance. But because their initial mission in the area had been to investigate a *Ship* sighting on the planet Ramook, they were being careful to avoid excluding the possibility. "Those pirates—or whatever they are—don't even know we're here."

"Then we'd better keep it that way," Tahiri said. "So far, the plasma is masking us fairly well, but this thing is hardly a stealth fighter. Let's shut down everything we can, then try to look like a hunk of nickel–iron asteroid."

Ben frowned. "And do what?"

"The same thing as the pirates," Tahiri said. "Wait. It's the only way to figure out what they're after."

Ben was quick to shake his head. "That could take days," he said. "It's better to hunt them down, then follow the signal to Ohali's StealthX and learn what we can from its memory chips."

"What makes you think the whole StealthX is down there?" Tahiri asked. "I don't see why they would bother towing the whole starfighter in here when all they need is the astromech, the pilot's seat, and the rectenna array."

Ben frowned. "You don't?" he asked. "Haven't you been reading the technical updates?"

Tahiri's ears reddened. "I may have skipped a few," she admitted. "What am I missing?"

"The distress signal has a dead-man switch now," Ben explained. "Anytime the seat comes out of the cockpit or the astromech is ejected from its socket, the astromech activates both beacons automatically. That way, if you take a big hit and your StealthX comes apart, the rescue teams still have a chance of finding you—or at least your astromech. It's been that way for a year."

"Okay, so the distress signal would have gone off earlier if the StealthX had been disassembled outside this cluster," Tahiri said. "That still doesn't make going after our would-be ambushers the smart play. They have *six* craft, and this Miy'tari is hardly a top-notch starfighter."

"They're *pirates,* Tahiri," Ben said. "We can handle them."

"We *think* they're pirates," she said. "Ben, the last status report we received was days ago. For all we know, those are Chiss out there."

Ben could hardly argue. Their last contact with the civilized galaxy had come when the Jedi Council sent a message telling them that Ben's father would be joining the Solos and would like to arrange a rendezvous. So far, scheduling a rendezvous in the Rift had proved problematic, mostly because events had been escalating so fast.

When Ben remained silent, Tahiri continued, "And whoever they are, they managed to capture a Jedi StealthX. It would be foolish to underestimate these guys, Ben."

Ben exhaled in frustration. "And *we're* not in StealthXs, I know," he said. "But the longer we sit here, the better the chance of them stumbling across us by accident."

Tahiri cocked her brow. "Really, Ben? You don't think we'd sense them coming?" She reached over and squeezed his arm. "I know you're worried about your father. But if he needed help—if there was anything he thought you could *do* to help—you would feel it in the Force."

Ben looked away. He wasn't so sure—and that was the problem. He simply didn't know what had become of his father. Did the cold hole in his heart mean that Luke Skywalker was lying unconscious somewhere, his life seeping out of him in breaths and warm red drops? Or had his father simply drawn in on himself, hiding his Force presence from some dark being powerful enough to come hunting for him?

After a moment, Ben turned back to his mission partner. "What about Ohali?" he asked. "She could be alive and hurt down there."

"Did you feel her Force aura when you reached out to find our ambushers? Because I sure didn't." Tahiri removed her hand. "Ben, you're letting your emotions influence your judgment, and you *know* better. We need to let things play out here." She paused and flashed him a smile. "*Then* we'll see if the Grand Master of the Jedi Order really needs *us* to rescue him."

Ben sighed in frustration, but nodded. "Okay, deal."

Three hours later, he glanced at the sensor display and was dismayed to see a pair of dark blobs converging on their Miy'tari. He activated the reverse thrusters and began to back out of their path, only to have his neck tingle with danger sense as a third asteroid appeared on the display, rising up to block their retreat.

Ben deactivated the reverse thrusters and fired the forward thrusters, but he had his doubts about whether the tiny air jets could move them away quickly enough to escape damage.

"Ninette, give me a collision analysis on those three asteroids," he ordered. "How much distance do we need to be safe?"

Ninette answered immediately with an alert tweedle, followed by a message on the display. IF YOU WISHED TO BE SAFE, YOU SHOULD NOT HAVE FLOWN US INTO A PLASMA CLOUD FILLED WITH ASTEROIDS.

A red bogey dot appeared on top of the tactical display.

AND IT WOULD BE PRUDENT TO CHANGE COURSE. WE CURRENTLY HAVE A 53 PERCENT CHANCE OF COLLIDING WITH THE UNKNOWN TRANSPORT.

The red dot vanished as quickly as it had appeared.

"Unknown transport?" Tahiri demanded. "What transport?"

Preliminary mass and size estimates suggest the craft is CEC YT-1300 transport, heavily modified for speed.

"The *Falcon*?" Tahiri gasped.

Identity impossible to confirm at present time. The bogey dot reappeared, weaving its way down the display at breakneck speed. Contact appears to be concealing its approach behind asteroids.

"It's the *Falcon*," Ben said, keeping one eye on the sensor display. "Has to be. Only Han Solo would be crazy enough to come in *here* that fast."

The bogey dot vanished again.

Then six more dots flared to life, two at each of the locations where Ben and Tahiri had sensed lurking ambushers. All six craft began to converge on the *Falcon*'s vector, with one pair swinging around to cut off the transport's retreat and the other two positioning themselves for a crossfire attack from opposite flanks.

"I'm beginning to think it wasn't *us* they were trying to bait," Tahiri said, reaching for the drive ignition. "Maybe your aunt and uncle have been giving the pirates a harder time than we realized."

"I wouldn't be surprised." Ben clasped her arm to stop her from igniting the drives, then glanced down at the sensor display, watching the three asteroids behind them drift ever closer to a collision with one another. "I'll handle the drives. You take weapons."

Tahiri saw where he was looking, then smiled. "Smart boy." She started to bring the Miy'tari's weapon systems online. "If you time this right, those pirates will never know what hit them."

"Let's hope they're the only ones."

Ben watched his sensor display as the asteroids drifted closer, then ignited the sublight drives as the last sliver of darkness vanished between the closest two. The Miy'tari chugged and hesitated as the engines shuddered to life, and Ben could not help cringing as the dark globs on the screen merged into one huge clump.

The white glow of an impact detonation lit the miasma beyond the Miy'tari canopy, and the sensor display filled with static. Ben slammed the throttles the rest of the way forward and felt the Miy'tari buck as the extra fuel collected in the still-cool ignition chamber. He pulled the throttles back, giving the igniters a chance to clear.

By then the miasma outside was fading to blue, and he could hear asteroid gravel pinging off the hull.

"If you're trying to impress me, please don't," Tahiri said. "If that energy bloom gets any closer, it's going to incinerate us, not hide our approach."

"No worries," Ben said, easing the throttles forward. Nothing happened. "Okay, *now* you can worry."

A loud clang reverberated through the hull, and a damage alarm began to chime. Ben ignored it and pumped the throttles again, then pushed them to their overload stops. This time the Miy'tari shot forward like a missile. The pinging of the asteroid gravel grew less frequent, but streamers of white heat began to streak past the canopy as rubble continued to overtake them.

Another loud clang reverberated from the stern of the ship.

Ben forced the throttles past their overload stops, clear to the end of the lever channel, then sank back into the pilot's chair. The nacelle temperatures climbed into the danger zone, and Ninette began to tweedle warnings about everything from hull friction to fuel volatility.

"Better." Tahiri's gaze remained on the tactical display. "And don't ease off. We have no time to waste."

Ben glanced at the tactical display and saw that Ninette had designated the *Falcon* a friendly YT-1300. The six newcomers had been changed from unknown bogeys to enemy bandits, but the astromech was still working to identify the type of craft. Judging by how quickly they were closing with the *Falcon,* it seemed clear they were starfighters.

Ben reached out in the Force, searching for his aunt or father—any Jedi at all—and felt two male presences. One was confident and calm and familiar enough that Ben recognized it as Lando Calrissian. The other presence was reckless and excited and so cocky it *had* to be Han Solo—except that it felt a few decades too young.

Tahiri glanced over. "Ben, your uncle doesn't happen to have any long-lost sons . . ."

Ben laughed, despite the situation. "I doubt it. They would have to be *before Leia.*"

Tahiri winced. "Right." She shook her head, then added, "But it's not impossible, I guess."

"What's not impossible?"

"That there could be *two* men in the galaxy brash enough to fly a beat-up old YT-1300 like it was a starfighter." Tahiri sighed. "I just hope he lives long enough to meet me."

"Uh, okay . . . I'll see if we can arrange that," Ben said, not quite sure what to make of Tahiri's comment. "Right now let's take the starboard bogeys with missiles, then hit the tail-chewers with our laser—"

Ben stopped when all six bogey symbols vanished from the tactical display.

"What the *kark*?" Tahiri demanded. "*Stealth* fighters?"

"Have to be Bes'uliiks," Ben said, making the logical assumption. "Ninette had trouble making an ID so we know they can beat our sensors. And they didn't disappear until they had closed to attack range, so they were deploying exhaust baffles."

Tahiri's expression grew hard. "Mandalorians." She practically spat the word. "They get one chance, Ben. If they don't surrender—"

"We take them out," he finished. "Mandalorians always fight dirty."

Ninette whistled an alarm, and Ben looked down to discover that one of their vector plates was starting to melt. He backed off the throttles to let their control surfaces cool before initiating combat, then looked over to find Tahiri arming their small complement of concussion missiles. With just four missiles and a pair of blaster cannons mounted beneath its belly, the Miy'tari was no match for six heavily armed Bes'uliiks—which simply meant they would need to make every attack count.

Ben checked his sensor display and was more than a little surprised to see the *Falcon* continuing toward the distress signal. Lando and his companion would have had to be flying sensor-blind to miss the Bes'uliiks when they powered up, so they certainly realized they were flying into an ambush. And yet here they were, proceeding as though this was a standard rescue operation.

What did they know that Ben and Tahiri did not?

Ninette chirped a comm notification, then a stern female voice began to speak over the cockpit speaker. "This is Galactic Exploitation Technologies security team five-niner hailing the *Millennium Falcon*. Acknowledge or prepare to accept incoming fire."

The challenge was answered immediately by Lando Calrissian's smooth voice. "No need to worry about us, sweetheart," he said. "We're prepared for whatever you bring."

"I'm nobody's sweetheart, Calrissian, least of all yours," the woman replied. "Power down and prepare for boarding."

"I'm afraid we're unable to comply," Lando said. "We happen to be responding to a distress signal. Maybe you heard it?"

"Of course we heard it," the woman shot back. "We're the ones who activated it."

"You *faked* a distress call?" Lando asked, feigning outrage. "Don't you know that's a violation of the Galactic Navigation Accords?"

"So report me," the woman replied. "Last chance, Calrissian. Power down."

Ben and Tahiri were so close now that the *Falcon* was visible to the naked eye, a tiny fork-nosed disk riding a fan of ion efflux past the dusty gray face of a crater-pocked asteroid. The transport's challengers were not yet visible, though Ben could see several long trails of swirling plasma that seemed to be converging on the same asteroid. He pointed the Miy'tari's nose at a pair of trails to the *Falcon*'s starboard and pushed the throttles forward again.

"Sorry, sweetheart," Lando replied. "But I think you should hear what I have to say before you open fire."

"I'm done talking, Calrissian," the woman said. "And I'm *not* your sweetheart."

"Only because we haven't met yet," Lando retorted. "And before you make that a permanent impossibility, you might want to consider something."

As Lando spoke, Ninette reported that the Miy'tari had become the subject of an active sensor probe.

"I doubt it," the woman said.

"Don't be so sure," Lando said. "You *do* know that your boss kidnapped Han Solo, right? That's bound to make a *whole* bunch of Jedi really—"

"Calrissian's stalling!" a Mandalorian voice interrupted. "It's a trap!"

A flurry of cannon bolts erupted ahead and came streaming back toward the Miy'tari. Ben put them into an evasive roll and continued to close with the targets, but the Mandalorian gunners were good, and cannon strikes began to blossom against the forward shields in rapid succession. Ninette tweedled, and Ben glanced down to see a message scrolling across the display.

Forward shield generators *already* 20 percent over specified capacity. Miy'taris are not designed to take heavy fire.

"Tell me something I *don't* know," Ben muttered.

Now that the Bes'uliiks had opened fire, Ninette had designated them Bes1 and Bes2 on the tactical display. The information wasn't much help. Their stealth qualities still made it impossible to achieve target-lock on them, and the constant stream of bolts coming from their cannons was a pretty good indication of their location.

Ben opened himself to the Force, and the Miy'tari whirled into an erratic, unpredictable spiral as his hands swung the yoke to and fro. The cannon bolts continued to stream toward them, but the number that flowered against their shields quickly dwindled by half.

Forward generators 40 percent over specified capacity, Ninette reported.

Ben felt the bump of a missile being ejected from a launch tube. An instant later, its engine ignited, and the missile became a disk of white-hot exhaust.

"Follow that bird," Tahiri said.

Her gaze remained distant and unfocused as she concentrated on their targets. Realizing that Tahiri was using the Force to guide the missile, Ben swung in behind its rapidly shrinking disk—then quickly lost sight of it in the storm of energy bolts coming their way.

A tiny pair of dark wedges appeared ahead, their bellies flashing with cannon fire as they tore through the plasma cloud. At least they weren't attacking the *Falcon,* Ben thought. He activated the Miy'tari's laser cannons and started to return the attacks.

Golden forks of dissipation static began to crackle across the Miy'tari's shields, and the tiny wedges ahead swelled into hand-sized silhouettes with cockpit bubbles in the center. The lead Bes'uliik diverted its fire to the missile, apparently realizing that its stealth capabilities were no match for a Force-guided weapon. The hint of a smile crept across Tahiri's face, and the lead Bes'uliik went into an evasive roll.

Ben reached out and found the Force presence of the second Bes'uliik pilot. He launched another missile and grasped it in the Force, gently guiding it toward its target. By then the enemy starfighters were the size of Wookiee heads, ringed by the flickering haloes of their baffled exhaust. The second Bes'uliik detected the missile coming its way and peeled away.

Too late.

A blinding white flash appeared ahead of the Miy'tari as Tahiri's missile reached its target and detonated. An eyeblink later, the black delta of a half-crumpled Bes'uliik emerged from the other side of the explosion, wobbling and pouring the anguish of its badly injured crew into the Force.

In the next instant, Ben's missile found its target. Instead of taking the detonation on his Bes'uliik's sturdy beskar hull armor, the second pilot had made the mistake of turning his engines to the missile as he tried to evade. The blast tore through his exhaust nozzles into the engine nacelle, and the starfighter's entire stern vanished in a ball of flame and flotsam.

By then the Miy'tari was past the point of initial engagement and was advancing on the surviving Bes'uliiks. Ben could feel their crews perhaps twenty kilometers directly ahead, a knot of nervous Force presences clustered in the tight diamond of a defensive formation. The *Falcon* was fifty kilometers to port, gliding past their flank, unmolested, silent, and blasting the area with target-locking sensor scans.

"We need to let them know who we are," Ben said. "Without the Force, we're the *only* craft they can find."

"I've got it. You keep an eye on those Bessies." Tahiri

opened a hailing channel, then said, "This is Jedi Strike
Force Beta ordering all four Mandalorian Bes'uliiks to
leave the area immediately. Failure to comply *will* result
in your swift destruction."

Tahiri had carefully chosen her words to reveal the
size and nature of the enemy forces in the area, but that
message seemed lost on whoever was flying the *Falcon*.
The old transport immediately began to decelerate and
turn toward the distress signal, as though the pilot actually *believed* that a Jedi strike force had miraculously
arrived just in time to save him from a Mandalorian
ambush.

Or maybe that was Lando playing out their bluff.

During the tense silence that followed, Ben took a
moment to study the asteroid from which the beacon
seemed to be coming. As far as he could tell from their
sensors and his eyes, it was an unremarkable hunk of
nickel–iron covered in a dusty silver-white regolith and
pocked by impact craters. If there was any reason that a
Quest Knight should have been interested in it, that reason was certainly not apparent—and that tended to confirm the idea that Ohali's StealthX had been deliberately
brought here to bait a trap.

But for *whom*?

Finally, Ben felt the Mandalorian presences beginning
to move—toward the *Falcon*.

"Blast," he said to Tahiri. "They're not buying it."

Tahiri dropped her chin and studied him from the top
of her eyes. "Ben, we're flying a Hapan *Miy'tari*," she
said. "Do we look like a Jedi strike force to *you*?"

Ben shrugged. "A guy can hope."

He studied the tactical display for a moment, wondering how far the *Falcon* would push the bluff before deciding to cut their losses and abandon the wrecked
StealthX. Then Ben remembered: Lando was aboard the
Falcon.

Lando Calrissian wasn't the kind of gambler who cut his losses and ran. He was the kind who turned an opponent's trap against him, then raked in the pot and left the other player sitting there wondering how he had lost everything he owned.

Ben pushed the Miy'tari's throttles forward, then swung onto a vector that would place them between the approaching Bes'uliiks and the *Falcon*. Tahiri's eyes instantly grew round.

"Uh, Ben, what did I say about trying to impress me?" She began to bring up damage and ordnance reports. "We can't take fire to save the *Falcon*. Our shield generators are still cooling down, and we've fired half our missiles. And you know those laser cannons we're carrying couldn't even *scratch* a beskar hull."

"Scratching is not what I have in mind." Confident that the Mandalorian pilots would be eavesdropping on any communications to the *Falcon*, Ben opened a channel and said, "*Millennium Falcon*, this is Jedi Knight Ben Skywalker suggesting that you run for it. And that's an order."

Tahiri looked at him as if he had lost his mind. "*Suggesting* an order?"

"Well, you know Lando," Ben said, grinning. "You have to be careful how you talk to him."

A moment later, Lando's voice came over the cockpit speaker. "You want us to run for it, Ben?"

"That's right," Ben said. "And that's an order."

Lando chuckled. "Sure, kid, whatever you say."

A fan of blue efflux flashed from the *Falcon*'s stern, and she shot across the face of the asteroid toward the far side. Ben slammed their own throttles past the overload stops again, shooting away in the opposite direction and drawing an immediate whistle of protest from Ninette.

THAT VECTOR PLATE IS ALREADY WARPED, AND THE EN-
GINE NACELLES ARE READY TO MELT.

"Good," Ben said. "I want those Bessies to have trouble keeping up."

As he spoke, a steady stream of cannon bolts began to
flash past from the Miy'tari's port side. He rolled into an
evasive helix, then glanced down at the tactical display.
A pair of Bes'uliik symbols had appeared on the screen,
closing in from one flank. Passing beneath the other flank
was the surface of the asteroid. The last pair of Bes'uliiks
had also appeared on the display, turning to pursue the
Falcon in the opposite direction.

"Ninette, are those positions based on estimates or
sensor readings?" he asked.

SENSOR READINGS. THE MANDALORIANS HAVE RETRACTED
THEIR EFFLUX BAFFLES IN ORDER TO PURSUE.

Ben smiled. "Better and better." He glanced over at
Tahiri. "You should take the turret. They're going to be
behind us any second."

"And do what, exactly?" Despite her question, Tahiri
immediately swung her chair around and opened a deck
hatch at the back of the cockpit. She slipped out of her
seat and dropped into the little nose turret. "Try to daz-
zle them with armor deflections?"

"Wouldn't hurt," Ben said.

By then the Miy'tari had passed beyond the edge of
the asteroid. The two Bes'uliiks dropped in behind them
and began to hammer the rear shields with their blaster
cannons. Tahiri opened up with their own weapons,
pouring a constant stream of fire back past the Miy'tari's
stern—which, of course, did nothing at all to back off
the Mandalorians.

Ninette started to whistle and chirp, scrolling a constant stream of warnings and reports across the main
display, informing Ben of all manner of damage that he

could feel just by the way the scoutboat was shuddering and jumping. The port vector plate was dripping away in molten beads of metal, and the overheated engine nacelles were beginning to burn their own linings. The shields were flickering in and out, resulting in a sporadic serenade of clangs and bangs as Mandalorian cannon bolts gnawed through the Miy'tari's thinly armored hull.

Through it all, Ben kept one eye on the tactical display, watching with no small amount of envy as the *Falcon*'s heavier shields and more-powerful quad cannons forced her pursuers to maintain a healthier distance. Still, her pilot was no Jedi, and it was not long before she began to react a bit sluggishly.

Then the *Falcon* cleared the far edge of the asteroid and went into a tight circle, swinging around toward the back side. Ben mirrored the maneuver, dropping as close to its crater-pocked surface as he dared to prevent the Bes'uliiks from trying to cut across the curve and come up beneath the Miy'tari's belly.

"Pull up—you're raising a dust cloud down here!" Tahiri yelled from the nose turret. "And I've lost my firing angle!"

"One . . . second."

Ben felt himself grinding his teeth, trying not to panic as a steep ridgeline appeared ahead. He had maybe three seconds before he hit it, but he had no way to know what was on the other side, and if he happened to come up in the wrong place . . .

The *Falcon* flashed past overhead, so close that Ben swore he glimpsed Lando Calrissian sitting in the belly turret, grinning wildly as he poured fire back toward his pursuers. The ridgeline became a towering wall of stone and dust, and still Ben held the yoke steady, for one more breath, until the *Falcon*'s two pursuers passed overhead in a river of flying cannon bolts and rippling efflux.

Ben pulled the yoke back, hard, putting the Miy'tari into a steep climb—and drawing a shocked scream as Tahiri suddenly found herself staring at a stone cliff streaking past just meters from her turret.

"Switch targets!" Ben rolled the Miy'tari around so the nose turret was facing the stern of the *Falcon* and her two pursuers. "Switch, switch—"

He did not need to give the command a fourth time. The Miy'tari's little laser cannons began to chug again, and a Bes'uliik erupted in blue flame as the bolts burned through its drive engines. Another fireball erupted below as one of their pursuers slammed into the ridgeline. Tahiri whooped for joy, then fired again, this time for much longer. Finally she let out a second whoop as her bolts found their way into another Bes'uliik drive engine.

Ben dropped the Miy'tari's nose and was dismayed to see the last Bes'uliik still chewing on their tail. Tahiri began to pour fire at its cockpit, gouging divots into its tough beskar hull and doing little else.

Then, suddenly, the Bes'uliik pulled up. Ben thought the pilot had decided to break off and head for home—until the long bright lines of two of the *Falcon*'s concussion missiles appeared on the tactical display. They merged with the target a heartbeat later, and the last Mandalorian starfighter vanished in a spray of static and light.

Ben yelled in triumph—then realized that his own cockpit was filled with shrieking damage alarms and the control yoke was shaking so hard he could barely hold on. He eased back on the throttles and glanced down to find his entire control board blinking and flashing with emergency alerts. He activated the hailing channel.

"Uh, *Millennium Falcon*, this is Jedi Knight Ben Skywalker requesting assistance," he said. "I think we're going to need a ride."

"On our way," Lando said. "And thanks, Ben. I haven't seen flying like that since . . . well, I don't think I've *ever* seen flying like that."

Thirteen

All in all, Han found the room a pretty convincing stand-in for a sabacc parlor. Mirta Gev sat in the dealer's seat, looking resentful and uncomfortable in a tight black vest over a long white tunic. A pair of Nargon thugs stood by the door, taking the place of the security team that usually watched over play in high-stakes sabacc salons. A crooked-nosed Mandalorian named Thorsteg had been assigned to serve as the table butler, fetching drinks, snacks, and anything else one of the players might need. Even the scene beyond the viewport reminded Han of something that might be found at one of the galaxy's finest gaming houses, with clouds of blue plasma rolling across a dark stone plain that dropped away to the void about seven hundred meters out.

Only the chairs were wrong. The Qrephs sat in their powerbodies at opposite ends of the long table, tucked in low and close so they could look at their hands without lifting the chip-cards too high. Han was seated in a modified examination chair across from Gev, with electrodes and probe needles stuck all over his bruised and half-naked body. It was how he had awakened, just a short time earlier, with a headache that would drop a rancor and no idea where he was—or how long he had been there.

Gev flicked her wrist and sent a chip-card spinning across the table to land atop the pair that already lay in front of each player. Before peeking at his hand, Han looked from one Columi to the other and found both of their gazes fixed on him—no doubt searching for micro-expressions that would betray whether he was happy with his hand.

Instead of reaching for his chip-cards, Han asked, "So, what game are we playing here?"

Craitheus's eyes shone with spite. "The game is standard sabacc, Captain Solo. We have made that very clear."

"You know what I'm asking." Han glanced around the room, which had originally been some sort of reading parlor, then waved at himself and his chair. "What's all *this*? You didn't have Mirta and her canheads snatch me just so we could play a game of strip sabacc on some rock in the middle of the Rift. This *is* the Rift, right?"

"Is that your wager, Captain Solo?" Marvid asked.

Han scowled. "It's a question, not a bet."

"A question that *will* be answered—if you win the hand," Craitheus replied.

"And if I don't win?"

"Then you answer *our* question," Marvid replied.

"That should be obvious even to you, Captain Solo," said Craitheus. "If you wish to bet, ask a question. The winner of each hand earns the answer to his question."

"If we ask a question you are unwilling to answer, you can always fold," Marvid said. His voice grew wispy and menacing. "But there will be no lying and no withholding. When you answer, we will be monitoring your biometrics. If you accept the bet and lose, you must be entirely truthful—or die."

Han looked from one huge pulsing head to the other, desperately searching for some hint about the angle they were working. A couple of geniuses like Marvid and

Craitheus had to know what it meant to have Luke and Leia coming after them. Yet here they sat, more interested in challenging Han to a game of *truth-or-die* than in preparing for the imminent arrival of two Jedi legends.

And that puzzled Han big-time. Either they believed the Rift could hide them even from Jedi hunters, or they were more confident than they should have been in their defenses.

Columi—especially *two* of them—were smarter than that.

But there were no clues to be found in the withered faces of the Qreph brothers, only the enigmatic patience of two alien predators waiting for the opportune moment to pounce. Han turned away from them and looked across the table to Gev. A clear plastoid splint protected the nose he had smashed, and her eyes were purple and swollen.

"You have any idea what this is all about?"

Gev shrugged. "They want to play sabacc with Han Solo," she said. "I suggest you make them happy."

"You would do well to listen to her," Marvid said. "Otherwise, we have no reason to keep you alive."

"And what about *after* the game?" Han asked. "You going to have a reason then? Because I might need a little incentive here."

Marvid blinked twice, then looked down the length of the table to his brother. He said nothing audible, but Han knew that Columi could converse with each other via comm waves. That was going to make it more difficult for him to win—and not only at sabacc. Whether the Qrephs chose to believe it or not, Luke and Leia *would* be coming, and when they arrived, the success of their attack would depend on surprise and confusion. So, the way Han saw it, his job was to put Craitheus and Marvid on tilt, to get them so upset and angry that when the assault came, the brothers would be in too much of a rage to think clearly.

After a few moments of silent communication with Marvid, Craitheus finally curled his lip into a thin sneer and turned to Han.

"We accept your terms," he said. "The one who earns the most answers wins. If that is you, you will be free to leave."

"But if *either* of us wins, you will remain here to assist us," Marvid added.

"Assist you in what, exactly?" Han asked.

"I'm sorry, Captain," Craitheus said. "But haven't you already asked a question in this betting round?"

"I guess you could say that," Han replied, still not looking at his chip-cards. "You calling?"

Craitheus extended a pincer arm and tipped his cards up to study his hand. Knowing how impossible it would be to read anything in a Columi's enigmatic face, Han looked out the viewport and tried to appear bored as he used a silent count to measure how long it took Craitheus to make his decision.

He was at three when Craitheus finally said, "Yes, I call. And if I win, my question will be this: how did you feel when Chewbacca died?"

The question took Han by surprise. It had been nearly twenty years since the Wookiee had sacrificed himself to save the Solos' youngest child, Anakin, during the war against the Yuuzhan Vong. The loss of his best friend was one of the most painful things Han had ever endured, and it still gnawed at him inside.

"Is that a fold, Solo?" Gev asked.

She started to reach for his chip-cards, but Han covered them before she could take them away.

"The bet's not on me yet." Han turned to Marvid. "What about you, Marv? You still in?"

A tiny smile came to Marvid's small mouth. "I intend

to make that decision after you look at *your* hand, Captain Solo."

"Show me a rule that says I have to," Han replied. There was no question of outplaying a pair of Columi, either observationally or on the mathematics of the game. If he was going to beat them, it would have to be with attitude and luck. "You in or out?"

Marvid's furrowed brow grew even more wrinkled, and he quickly fluttered one of his powerbody's pincer arms in Gev's direction.

"I'll withdraw."

Han glanced across the table and locked gazes with Gev, then rolled his eyes. "That figures."

"It was the only prudent play on my part, Captain Solo," Marvid said. "*You* may be playing blind, but I assure you Craitheus is not. If my brother is still in the hand, it's because he has a substantial advantage over me."

"Sure." Han continued to hold Gev's eyes, trying to give the impression that they shared a secret. "I guess you're used to that."

Marvid's voice sizzled with anger. "I fail to understand your implication, Captain Solo."

"Then you're not as smart as you think," Han replied.

He smiled at Gev and motioned for his next chip-card. She looked to Craitheus, who responded with a terse nod, then dealt another chip-card to both Han and Craitheus.

Again without looking at his cards, Han turned to Craitheus and said, "So, how does the second round work? Do I ask another question? Or do we just check it down and see how the cards come?"

"Perhaps we ask questions ancillary to the first," Craitheus suggested. "That would allow sufficient opportunity to raise the stakes and require some careful betting strategy."

"Then that's the way we'll do it," Han said. "After all, you're the boss around here, right?"

"Actually," Marvid interjected, "Craitheus and I are equal partners in all of our ventures. We make our decisions jointly."

"If you say so." Again, Han glanced across the table at Gev and rolled his eyes, then looked back to Craitheus and said, "My next question is this: where are we, exactly?"

"That can be rather difficult to answer," Craitheus said.

"That mean you're folding?" Han asked.

Craitheus glared at Han's still unexamined hand, then finally used his pincer arm to lift his own chip-cards for a peek. Again, Han counted to three before the Columi finally laid the trio down.

"I'll accept the bet," Craitheus said. "I just want to be sure you're aware the payment may not be in the form you expect. As you know, coordinates tend to be imprecise within the Rift."

"How convenient," Han said.

"My answer will be truthful and complete," Craitheus replied. "As will yours, I hope. My second question is this: why didn't you mourn your son Anakin's death as deeply as you mourned that of your Wookiee friend?"

If the first question had been painful, this one felt like a vibrodagger sliding into Han's gut. Anakin had died just a couple of years after Chewbacca, one of several young Jedi Knights who perished on a mission to neutralize a Yuuzhan Vong weapon. Not a day went by when Han's heart did not ache with the loss, when he did not regret every harsh word he had ever said to his youngest son. And yet Craitheus's question wouldn't be easy to answer. After Chewbacca's death, Han had sunk into despair and fled his home for a time. When Anakin died, he had not had that luxury. The loss had nearly destroyed Leia, and Han had needed to stay strong—or he would have lost Leia, too.

Gev finally asked, "Well, Solo?"

Han nodded. "Sure, I'll call the bet." He waited until Gev put her thumb on top of the deck to deal another chip-card, then said, "But no card for me. Let's see what Craitheus does."

Craitheus tipped his powerbody forward in a gesture of intimidation, then said, "If you have no wish to actually play the game, Captain Solo, I am quite sure Marvid and I can learn what we wish to know through more . . . *efficient* means."

Han shrugged. "I'm playing by the rules," he said. "I just have my own style. If that's a problem for you, fold."

Craitheus peeked at his hand again, checking to make sure that none of the card values had shifted while they were talking, then said, "I think not. The advantage remains mine."

He flicked his pincer arm, and Gev dealt him a fifth chip-card.

Han locked his chip-cards at their current values by pushing them into the stasis field in front of him, then turned to watch Craitheus. The Columi glowered at Han's cards for perhaps a dozen heartbeats, then gathered his five cards into a fan and lifted them to study.

Craitheus's motions were exactly the same as before, and if there was a change of expression, Han could not recognize it on a Columi face. But this time the count reached six before Craitheus laid his chip-cards flat, and Han felt sure the value of Craitheus's hand had just shifted.

"So, my bet." Han plucked at one of the lead wires attached to his chest. "Why all these electrodes and probe needles?"

When Craitheus looked up, his eyes gleamed with

comprehension. "Very clever, Captain Solo," he said. "You have been playing *me* instead of your own hand."

"Is that your next question?" Han asked.

"Of course not," Craitheus replied. "That was an observation, not an inquiry. My question is this: why did you love your son Jacen less than you loved Anakin?"

Now Craitheus was twisting the vibrodagger, trying to tear Han apart emotionally. After Jacen's capture and torture during the war against the Yuuzhan Vong, Jacen had begun a long, slow fall to the dark side, which eventually ended with his sister, Jaina, having to hunt down and kill her own brother. The decision to give their blessing to that mission had been the most anguishing of the Solos' lives, and even the memory of it filled Han with an acrid, churning ache that made him want to spit bile in Craitheus's face. But Han couldn't let the Qrephs rattle him now—not when so much depended on rattling *them*. Leia and Luke would be arriving soon.

After a moment, Han nodded. "Okay, I'll take the bet."

Craitheus smiled. "Excellent."

The Columi gestured for his next chip-card.

And Han knew that he *probably* had Craitheus beat. Because Han was playing blind, the Columi would need to assume that Han's four chip-cards gave him a mediocre hand. And since Craitheus was still trying to improve his own hand with a *sixth* card, it was safe to assume that the Columi had been unable to beat even a mediocre hand with five chip-cards—which almost certainly meant that Craitheus *had* suffered a value shift earlier and that it had been disastrous.

As soon Craitheus's sixth card hit the table, Han said, "I call the hand."

Immediately, the backs of all six of Craitheus's chip-cards turned red, indicating that Han had caught the

Columi when the value of his hand exceeded twenty-three—the maximum allowable score in sabacc.

"Look at that," Han said, smirking. "A bomb-out."

Craitheus glared at his chip-cards, then gathered them up and tossed them to Gev without revealing what he had held. Han returned his own cards without even looking, then turned to Craitheus.

"You owe me some answers," Han said. He continued to smirk.

"And you shall have them," Craitheus said. "Here is the simple answer to your second question: you are in a lounge in our laboratory on Base Prime. And, yes, you are still in the Rift."

"I asked for our *exact* location," Han said. "*Base Prime* is pretty vague."

"As Craitheus warned you it would be," Marvid replied. "The more complete answer is rather complicated. I doubt you will be able to comprehend it."

"I don't care what *you* doubt," Han said, being careful to keep his gaze on Craitheus. "My bet was with your brother, and if he thinks he's going to back out of it now—"

"Reneging on our agreement is the last thing I intend to do," Craitheus said. "If I did, how could I expect you to answer my questions?"

Han was pretty sure that Craitheus already knew the answer to his questions and was just asking them for the pleasure of being cruel, but he gave a quick nod.

"Glad we understand each other," Han said. "Now, how about that answer?"

"The truth is, I can't give you exact coordinates," Craitheus replied. "Nobody can."

Han scowled, but before he could open his mouth to object, Gev said, "Don't blow a brain vein, Solo. Craitheus is telling it to you straight. Base Prime is . . . well, it sort of sits in a big bubble in space."

"To be more precise," Craitheus said, "Base Prime is located on a space station of unknown origin, which expands space–time around itself in a way that makes it impossible to speak of a location in terms of physical coordinates. The most that can be said is that it occupies the heart of the Chiloon Rift. Or, perhaps, it would be more accurate to say that the way to reach it is *through* the heart of the Chiloon Rift."

"Are you trying to tell me we're sitting on some sort of black hole?" Han scoffed. "How gullible do you think I am?"

"We didn't say that Base Prime is located on the surface of a black hole," Marvid said. "Quite the opposite. We said that it bends space–time outward, not inward. You are the one who suggested the false analogy."

"And I consider the bet paid," Craitheus added. "If you are unhappy with my answer, Captain Solo, we can forgo the sabacc game and switch to more conventional methods of interrogation."

"You mean torture," Han said.

"Call it what you will, Captain Solo." Craitheus spread his powerbody's arms. "But I assure you, any chance you have of winning your freedom lies in our little sabacc game—not in any ill-advised attempts to escape on your own."

"Assuming you intend to honor your word," Han replied. "And that remains to be seen. You still owe me two answers."

"One, actually," Craitheus replied. "The answers to your first and third questions are the same. The *game* we are playing is data collection, which is why you have a network of sensors attached to your body and inserted into your brain."

Han's throat went dry. *"Inserted?"*

He started to reach for his head—and felt a sudden jolt of electricity shooting down his spine. His arms went numb and dropped, limp and useless, to the sides of his examination chair.

"Forgive the neuro-restraint," Marvid said. "But you really shouldn't attempt to remove the probes by yourself. Some of them run all the way down into your corpus callosum."

"*What?*" Han yelled. "You've stuck my brain full of needles?"

"Exactly," Craitheus replied. "As I was about to explain, we're using stress reactions to map your mind's functionality and to stimulate memory retrieval. In our other subjects, it has proven to be a highly effective method of modeling."

"You're making a map of my mind?" Han repeated, growing more horrified by the moment. "Why in the blazes would you do that?"

Marvid smiled. "Is that your opening bet for the next hand?"

Fourteen

A tiny electric jolt stabbed through the singeing fog and bit into Luke's shoulder. Not flinching, he lifted himself from the healing sea of the Force and came instantly awake. There were no surprises. He still lay on the floor of a stale, smoky locker room, with his sister lying in her own healing trance beside him. On his other side, R2-D2 was still standing watch. Once again, the little droid extended its charging arm and hit Luke with a tiny—but painful—jolt of current.

"Enough, Artoo. I'm awake."

Luke reached up and used the adjacent bench to pull himself into a seated position. The agony of his broken ribs had faded to a dull ache and his belly wound had closed, but he had not been able to mend all of the damage he had suffered during the ScragHull's crash. His burns felt worse than ever—hot and throbbing—and he knew he had an infection starting.

R2-D2 softly chirped an inquiry. Luke glanced over to check his sister's condition and cringed. So far, she had managed to close the mesh of lacerations that had torn her face before she lowered her faceplate. But her brow and cheeks remained red and covered in weeping blisters. And she had lost all her eyelashes and eyebrows, as well as a lot of the hair on the right side of her head. Even her fireproof vac suit had been half melted down its right arm and body panel, and he felt sure the flesh beneath was in much the same condition as her seared face.

After a moment's inspection, Luke whispered, "No, Artoo. Let her stay in her healing trance." He kept his voice low—not to avoid disturbing her but to keep their hiding place secret. "For now."

Luke checked his chronometer. Nearly five hours had passed since they had blasted their way into the *Ormni*. When he and Leia had crawled into the half-wrecked locker room and sealed themselves in, he had not expected to have nearly that long before R2-D2 woke them. He unhooked his lightsaber from his equipment harness, then carefully rose to his feet. He winced. His burns still rubbed against his half-melted vac suit, and it felt like a vibro-sander was peeling away layers of skin. But he could stand and walk.

Or at least hobble. He had torn some ankle ligaments during the crash, and they did not feel quite healed.

"Okay, Artoo," Luke said softly. "What is it?"

R2-D2 spun on his treads and headed for the exit hatch, which the droid had evidently reopened. Beyond the threshold lay a small control room in complete disarray. Flimsies and datapads were strewn across the floor amid hard hats, breath masks, and other safety equipment. A bank of control cabinets sat across from a half-transparisteel observation wall. The viewing wall had once overlooked the vast production vault into which Luke and Leia had crashed their spyboat. Now the entire wall was a buckled wreck, so smoke-stained that it was transparent only where the explosion had ruptured it.

And coming through the rupture was a muffled male voice.

". . . that grinder bank will be out of production for days as it is," someone was complaining loudly. "I have three freighters still waiting to be loaded, and more on the way. This is going to cost us hundreds of millions."

"The production schedule is not my concern." The second voice—also muffled—was young, female, and vaguely familiar. "My concern—and *yours*—is confirming the deaths of the ScragHull crew. It should never have taken this long to give me access to the crash site."

"Their fusion core blew," the male replied. "So we *know* they're dead. We had to send in droids to decontaminate the entire vault before it was even safe to enter."

"And yet . . . no body parts," the female said. "No proof."

As the voices continued, Luke crawled into the control room, then raised his head to peer through the ruptured viewing wall. Immediately after the crash, the production vault beyond had been choked with billowing dust and flying debris. Now it was a scorched crater packed with shapeless metal and fused stone.

In the middle of the wreckage, about thirty meters away from Luke's hiding place and fifteen meters below, stood the two beings who were talking. The male was a Duros dressed in half-open blue coveralls over a white captain's tunic, his noseless face drawn into an angry grimace. The female was a young human, no more than twenty, with light-brown hair and large dark-brown eyes.

Luke's stomach knotted in cold fury. The woman was Vestara Khai, the Sith defector who had betrayed Ben and him during the Sith occupation of Coruscant. A part of Luke still longed to make her pay for her treachery, but now was not the time. It was more important to find out how the Sith were involved in the Qrephs' plans and to learn what had become of Han. And to do that, he and Leia had to escape alive.

Vestara seemed to contemplate the Duros's excuse for

a moment, then finally said, "You should have sent in more droids. If those ScragHull pilots survived, they could be anywhere by now."

"No one could have survived this, Mistress Raine." The Duros gestured toward the deck, where twisted shards of metal surrounded a meter-wide melt hole. "As I told you, their fusion core blew. We're lucky we didn't lose the entire *Ormni*."

Vestara laughed darkly.

"I'm sure *luck* had nothing to do with it," she said. "Hasn't it occurred to you to wonder how a little two-person spyboat—moving at a relatively low velocity—managed to penetrate the hull of an asteroid crusher? They used a *torpedo* to clear their way. For all we know, they didn't even crash. They could have touched down nice and soft, then blown their own fusion core to cover their escape."

The suggestion wasn't far from the truth, but the Duros remained unconvinced. "That's pretty far-fetched, mistress. And even if it *were* true, they would have had to survive an explosive decompression. Trust me, the ScragHull's pilots are stardust. I see no reason to delay repairs, and since I am the captain of the *Ormni*—"

"*Don't* make me relieve you." Vestara used the Force to grab the Duros by the throat and lift him off his feet. "Trust *me*, Captain Palis, you wouldn't like that. Are we clear?"

Palis's mouth began to work without making any sound. Unable to say yes, he simply nodded.

"Excellent," Vestara said.

She let him drop, then began to circle the twisted wreck of the ScragHull. After a moment, she pointed at a sagging rectangular frame a half meter taller than she was.

"Tell me, Captain Palis, what does this look like?"

"I believe that's a hatch, Mistress Raine," he said, rubbing his throat. "It's in the right place."

"Yes, Captain, it's a ScragHull hatch," Vestara said. "An *open* hatch."

Palis's red eyes grew wide. "That isn't possible," he said. "It just can't be."

"I assure you it can, Captain Palis. These are Jedi we're dealing with, not . . ." Vestara let her sentence trail off, her head cocking as she slowly turned to scan the rest of the vault. "Wouldn't there be an emergency air lock for crews in this area?"

"Of course." Palis raised his gaze to the ceiling, where ten square meters of durasteel patch had been welded over the hole opened by the ScragHull's torpedo. "But with a hull breach that size, there would have been no time to use it. We can only hope all of those poor beings died quickly."

"I care nothing about them," Vestara said. "I want to know where that air lock is."

She started to turn and scan the walls, and Luke knew she would be reaching out in the Force, searching for him and his sister. With Leia deep in a healing trance and Luke's own Force presence drawn in tight, Vestara would have a hard time detecting either of them. Their hiding place was a different matter, however. Once she passed through the emergency air lock, it wouldn't take long to find the locker room.

Luke ducked out of sight, then turned to R2-D2 and whispered, "Can you jam the emergency air lock we used after the crash?"

The droid gave a quiet chirp, then extended his interface arm and turned toward the nearest control cabinet.

"Wait until they're inside the compartment," Luke whispered. "Then secure the hatches and fry the circuits."

R2-D2 replied with a barely audible tweedle and

stopped in front of an interface socket. Luke gathered some of the safety equipment strewn across the floor, then returned to the locker room.

Leia remained in her healing trance, her face a mask of tranquillity as she used the Force to repair her injuries cell by cell. Luke knelt at her side and placed the safety gear he had collected on the bench beside her, then gently shook her shoulder.

"Time to move, sis," he said.

Leia's eyes snapped open, then flashed in pain as she became fully aware of her body. "Why did I think I would feel better than this when I woke up?"

"Wishful thinking," Luke whispered. "Keep your voice down—we have company. How's your shoulder?"

Leia braced her hands on the floor and, wincing, pushed herself upright. "I can manage," she said. "How about your ankle?"

"I won't win any races, but I can hobble along." Luke grabbed two suitably sized pairs of blue GET coveralls from nearby lockers and added them to the pile of safety equipment, then began to strip out of his vac suit. "We need to get moving. Vestara Khai is here, and she knows we survived. Artoo won't be able to stall her for long."

"You were close enough to identify her, and she's still walking?" Leia began to undo her own suit's closures. "You must be hurt worse than I thought."

Luke shrugged. "I'll deal with Vestara later. First we need to know how she's involved in all this," he said. "And we need to find Han."

"Absolutely," Leia said. "I'll need to know how he is before I decide how I'm going to kill that—"

"Leia—"

"Little Sith," Leia finished. She turned one eye on him. "What, like *you* don't intend to kill her?"

Luke decided not to remind his sister that vengeance

led to the dark side. Right now they could *both* use the extra motivation, just to keep themselves going.

After he had removed his vac suit, he passed the smaller set of coveralls to Leia, and soon they were both disguised as refinery workers, complete with hard hats, safety glasses, and respirators dangling from their necks. Luke would have preferred to conceal their faces by actually wearing the respirators, but no legitimate workers would wear the uncomfortable masks outside the dusty production areas where they were actually required.

They had finished donning their disguises and had just begun to stuff their vac suits down a disposal chute when R2-D2 returned, softly tweedling an alarm.

"It's okay, Artoo," Luke said. "We're ready to go."

The droid chirped in relief, then immediately spun around and left the locker room. They followed him across the control room to a rear access hatch, which opened onto a durasteel walkway suspended high above a bank of massive transfer tubes. Both the handrails and floor grating were shiny from frequent use, but the walkway was completely deserted at the moment. Luke guessed that the entire production area had been sealed off to serve as a buffer zone around the crash site.

As they followed R2-D2 toward the far end of the walkway, the smell of molten metal began to waft through the stale air, and a steady drone sounded from below. Luke glanced over the railing. Ten meters beneath them, the tip of a crimson lightsaber was slicing through the hatch of an emergency air lock.

"Vestara won't think that hatch jammed by coincidence," Leia said. "Let's move it along, before the place is crawling with Mandos and Nargons."

R2-D2 whistled, then sped away at nearly double his original pace. Luke found himself struggling to keep up, limping on his half-healed ankle and trying to ignore the anguish of his burn-blistered skin rubbing against his coveralls. He could see by the grim determination in Leia's face that she was also suffering.

They reached a much larger walkway, which seemed to run along the asteroid crusher's length instead of across its beam. R2-D2 turned toward the *Ormni*'s stern. The cavernous space remained empty and illuminated by silver-blue glow panels. The walkway was flanked on both sides by long runs of massive transfer tubes and the durasteel shells of sealed production vaults, all eerily silent now that operations had been stopped because of the ScragHull crash.

"Our first priority is going after Han," Luke said. "But, as much as I hate to say it—"

"We're in no condition to succeed," Leia finished. "If we don't get some bandages and bacta salve on these burns soon, we won't be rescuing *anyone*."

"Exactly," Luke agreed.

A muffled clang sounded in the distance behind them—Vestara freeing herself from the air lock, no doubt. Luke forced himself not to look back. If they were going to escape, they had to stay focused on what they were going to do, not what was happening behind them.

"And it won't do any good to steal a Bessie and take off in pursuit of the *Aurel Moon*," Luke continued. "We need to figure out where the Qrephs were headed."

Leia frowned. "How are we going to do that?"

"I don't know yet," Luke admitted. "It may come down to capturing Vestara. She seems to be in charge around here. I'm not sure anyone else would know where the Qrephs went."

R2-D2 emitted a confident chirp, then they came to a sealed bulkhead, its emergency door still lowered against the possibility of a ship-wide decompression. Luke pressed his ear to the metal and heard murmuring voices and whirring machinery on the far side.

He would have liked to reach out in the Force to see if he could sense any particular danger on the other side of the bulkhead. But he did not dare. He could not be certain that Vestara was the only Sith aboard the *Ormni*, and he did not want to take the chance of drawing attention by expanding his Force presence.

Instead, he tried the slap-pad on the adjacent wall.

When nothing happened, Leia said, "Vestara's doing, I'll bet. She would have wanted to keep the entire area sealed until she could take a look around the crash site and see whether we survived."

"Probably," Luke agreed. "Artoo, can you override these locks without tripping an alarm?"

The droid replied with an indignant buzz, then inserted his interface arm into the socket beneath the control panel. A moment later, the status light changed from amber to blue, and a huge bulkhead door started to slowly slide aside.

Knowing they would draw less attention by simply stepping into traffic than by standing there trying to get their bearings, Luke started across the threshold—only to find himself staring at the helmet and armored back plate of a Mandalorian guard looking in the opposite direction. The Mando was flanked on each side by scaly green walls that Luke eventually recognized as Nargons.

Standing beyond the Mandalorian and his assistants were hundreds of beings. They all wore the same blue coveralls that Luke and Leia wore, and most were heavily burdened with tools and repair supplies. Several were seated at the controls of heavy equipment. As soon as the huge bulkhead door was completely retracted, a big horn-headed Devaronian grumbled, "About time," and started his hoversled, and the entire mass lurched forward as one body.

Luke and Leia barely had time to clear the way by pressing themselves against the walkway railing, and even the door guards had little choice except to move aside. The Mandalorian, of course, chose to join the Nargon standing on Luke and Leia's side of the walk-way.

"What happened to you two?" he demanded, staring at Leia's burned face. "Let me see your identification badges."

Clearly, Vestara had not yet alerted the security teams to watch for them. Whether that was because she did not realize how close behind she was or simply wanted to avoid tipping her hand, Luke could not say. He knew only that their best chance of escape lay in getting away from the crash site as quickly as possible. He reached into his pocket as though to extract his identity badge but brought his hand out empty and waved it in front of the Mandalorian.

"There is no need to see our identification," he said. "We lost it when we were injured. We're on our way to the infirmary."

The Mandalorian's visor remained fixed on Luke's face, and Luke began to wonder if his Force suggestion was going to work. But, finally, the guard nodded.

"There is no need to see your identification." He turned toward the crowd, then extended a hand down the rail and ordered, "Make way! These people were injured in the explosion. They're on their way to the infirmary."

The crowd quickly began to move away from the rail. But the Nargon stepped into Luke's path, then cocked his crested head and studied his Mandalorian officer out of a huge, slit-pupiled eye.

"No badges?" he asked.

"There's no need to see their identification," the Mandalorian repeated. Still under the influence of Luke's Force suggestion, he motioned the Nargon away from the safety rail. "Stand aside. They're on their way to the infirmary."

The Nargon hissed but obeyed, then watched with a suspicious sneer as R2-D2 rolled into the lead and started down the walkway. Although Luke was careful to avert his gaze, he kept one hand tucked into the front seam of his coveralls so he could reach his lightsaber quickly if the green hulk made a sudden move.

But the Nargon seemed content to do as he was told, and Luke and Leia were soon following R2-D2 past the tail of the repair column. They quickly returned to the middle of the walkway, trying to put as many bodies between themselves and the guards as possible, and continued toward the *Ormni*'s stern. They passed through another bulkhead—this time unsealed—and began to see the huge transfer tubes curving off to enter the durasteel spheres and ovoids of different varieties of flocculation tanks.

After fifty meters, R2-D2 turned down an intersecting walkway that led past a series of assaying labs and production offices to a bank of turbolifts. Most of the lift-tube control panels had blue status lights, indicating they were ready for use. Their destination plates named decks such as CREW QUARTERS, MAINTENANCE, and INFIRMARY.

But two turbolifts at the end of the bank had amber status lights, denoting restricted access. The destination plate of one of these lifts listed half a dozen decks dedicated to the security hangars, training facilities, and guard quarters.

R2-D2 went to the other restricted turbolift, where the destination plate contained a single line: ADMINISTRATIVE DECKS. The droid extended his interface arm and plugged it into the droid socket beneath the control panel.

Almost instantly, a low, rasping voice boomed behind them. "Where do you go?"

Luke turned to see two Nargons striding toward them from the far end of the walkway. It was difficult to tell whether they were the same pair who had been with the Mandalorian at the sealed bulkhead, but both had empty holsters on their knees and E-18 blaster rifles cradled in their long arms.

"There's no need to bother with us." Luke spread his hands in a placating gesture, using the motion to hold the attention of the Nargons while he used a Force suggestion to deflect their suspicion. "We're injured and on our way to the infirmary."

The Nargons continued to approach. "The executive infirmary is not for crew," said the second. "Real crew members know this."

"Who are you?" demanded the other one. "Are you the crash survivors?"

He pointed his blaster rifle in their direction.

"Whoa! There's no need for threats." Luke glanced over at Leia, then said, "I think we'd better show them our identification."

"I don't think we have a choice," Leia replied.

"You lost your identity badges," the first Nargon objected. "You *said*."

"Yes, we lost our *badges*," Luke said. "But we have other identification."

This only seemed to make the Nargon more suspicious. "*Other* identification?"

"Credit chits, operator certifications, storeroom keycards," Luke said, naming a string of possibilities that he hoped would sound plausible. "Stuff like that."

"Things only crew members would have," Leia added. She turned to Luke and said, "Just make sure you show it clearly. These guys don't have very good eyesight."

Luke nodded, recalling what the Solos had told him about the fight in the Red Ronto cantina. Nargons didn't go down easy.

A soft chime sounded from the turbolift, and Luke glanced over to see that the status light had changed to ready-blue.

Now the second Nargon also pointed his blaster rifle at them. "Move away."

The Nargons were about three quarters of the way down the walkway, still six meters or so from Luke and Leia. It was certainly possible to take them out at that distance, but the fight wasn't going to be a quiet one. Trying to stall, Luke turned to R2-D2.

"I think he means you, too," Luke said. "You'd better uncouple and display your serial number."

R2-D2 swiveled his dome back and forth, giving a negative chirp. By then the Nargons were only four meters away.

Luke shrugged. "It's your scrap party."

R2-D2 emitted a falling whistle, then withdrew his interface arm and turned his holoprojector toward the approaching Nargons. A string of holographic numerals and letters appeared in the air in front of them.

The Nargons walked through the holograph, then stopped two meters away.

Two meters would do.

The first Nargon flicked the safety off his blaster rifle. "No one cares about the droid." He pointed the emitter nozzle at Luke's chest. "Identification *now*."

"Sure." Luke opened the chest closures on his coveralls and, moving very slowly to avoid alarming the Nargon, reached inside. "Here it is."

"Mine, too," Leia said, doing the same thing. "How many pieces do you want?"

"All pieces," the first Nargon replied.

"Sure."

Luke used the Force to shove the Nargon's blaster nozzle toward the ceiling, then pulled his lightsaber from inside his coveralls and leapt. The Nargon's finger closed on the trigger anyway and sent a string of blaster bolts pinging into the ceiling. Luke hit the ignition switch beneath his thumb, and his lightsaber snapped to life, filling the air with the acrid stench of scorched scales.

A huge claw tore into the ribs beneath Luke's upraised arm, and a blast of fiery pain spread through his entire torso. He ignored the wound and used the Force to press his own strike home, driving his lightsaber blade up through the Nargon's clavicle into his throat.

Then Luke felt the Nargon's hand sweeping him aside and found himself flying sideways into Leia. He bounced off, then slammed into a durasteel wall and slid to the deck, bleeding and gasping for air.

By that point Leia was leaning over her fallen Nargon, stirring her blade through his chest as he raked a set of claws down her back. Luke used the Force to hurl himself to his feet, lashing out with his lightsaber to remove the Nargon's arm at the elbow, then spun back toward his own attacker—and discovered him lying on his back, arms and feet hammering at the deck as his body awaited signals from the head now only half attached to its shoulders.

Luke's entire chest ached, but he had no trouble drawing a deep breath when he tried, so it seemed unlikely that he had suffered any internal damage—at least any *serious* internal damage. He turned to find Leia staggering away from her Nargon, her back a bloody tangle of shredded cloth and skin.

Luke deactivated his lightsaber, then asked, "How bad?"

"Not . . . bad," Leia said, obviously understating the case. She turned, her gaze dropping to the red gashes down Luke's torso. "You're worse."

Alarmed voices began to sound from the far end of the walkway, and Luke looked up to see a handful of workers in blue GET coveralls pointing toward them. He waved a hand over the fallen Nargons and whipped it forward, using the Force to send both huge corpses flying through the air toward the astonished spectators. Murmurs of alarm became cries of surprise, and the crowd dispersed in panic.

Leia deactivated her own lightsaber and stowed it in a thigh pocket, then slipped a supporting hand through Luke's arm.

"Let's get out of here."

She dragged him into the turbolift tube R2-D2 had prepped, then wrapped her arms around him so they would not be separated. R2-D2 tweedled once, and Luke had to fight to keep from retching as the repulsorlift shot them upward.

As they ascended, Luke slid his lightsaber up inside his sleeve, where it would be both out of sight and handy if he needed it. His head cleared enough to realize just how desperate their situation had grown. Vestara was hunting them, and by now she had a pretty good idea where they were. Even with the mess below, it would not take her long to find them. Clearly, they were in for a fight—and probably sooner rather than later.

The turbolift stopped after a few seconds, then swished open to reveal an elegant, round maleristone foyer filled with lacy green frond plants. Corridors fanned out in all directions, and from several came the sound of murmuring voices and chiming office machinery. Directly across from the turbolift, an RC-7 receptionist droid stood behind a curved lindakwood counter, her triangular head tilted expectantly as she waited for Luke and Leia to approach.

Standing behind the RC-7 were two Mandalorians in polished beskar'gam armor. As soon as they saw Luke and Leia's blood-soaked coveralls, they drew their blaster pistols and stepped forward to intercept them.

"Quick!" Leia called, pointing back toward the turbolift. "Jedi!"

The Mandalorians looked in the direction she had indicated. Luke did not even glance toward Leia. He used
the Force to push aside the closest one's blaster hand, let
the lightsaber drop out of his sleeve into his hand, and
jammed the end into the unarmored area beneath the
Mandalorian's arm.

"Don't make me."

The Mandalorian's helmet pivoted toward his companion, who was in a similar position with Leia. For a moment, Luke thought his guard would be foolish enough to
resist, but the Mando quickly opened his hand and let his
blaster clatter to the floor.

When his partner did the same, Leia nodded and said,
"Now take off your helmets—and I'd better not hear
anyone asking you to confirm a report about intruders."

As the two Mandalorians obeyed, Luke turned toward
the RC-7 droid and used the Force to push her away
from the desk. "You—stay. And no messages, or you're
scrap."

The droid raised her arms immediately. "Please, you
have no need to threaten me," she said. "Security is *their*
assignment."

As the droid spoke, the turbolift door opened with a
soft chime, and R2-D2 rolled out of the tube. Luke motioned him toward the reception counter.

"Isolate this deck," Luke ordered. "And see if anyone
knows where we are yet."

"You're kidding, right?" said a Mandalorian.

Luke turned back to find that the now-helmetless
guards appeared to be brother and sister, with the same
blue eyes, golden-blond hair, and broad flat faces.

"Vestara has already put out an alert?" he asked.

The woman, who looked no more than twenty-two,
frowned in confusion. "Vestara?"

"The Sith girl giving orders around here," Leia said. "The one who flies that round spacecraft with the pulsing veins and hawk-bat wings."

"They mean Lady Raine," the young man said to his sister. He turned to Luke. "And, yeah, she just ordered us to hold you. The entire security force is on its way up."

As the Mandalorian spoke, a bitter note came to his Force aura, and Luke knew the claim was a lie.

He leaned close. "That had better be the last time you try to bluff me . . ." Luke paused, waiting for a name to rise to the top of the Mandalorian's mind, then finally said, *"Joram."*

Joram's eyes widened in alarm, but he said, "It hardly matters, Jedi." He glanced at the floor. "With the trail you two are leaving, the Nargons will be on you in about three minutes flat."

Luke looked down to find a pool of red spreading around his feet and a similar one around Leia's.

"The kid has a point," Leia said. "We need to do something about these wounds—and soon."

R2-D2 gave a whistle, then rolled out from behind the reception counter and stopped in the mouth of an adjacent corridor. Before following, Luke stepped behind the counter and tripped the RC-7's circuit breaker, then used his lightsaber to disable the computer interface sockets.

R2-D2 tweedled impatiently.

"What's down there?" Leia asked the female Mando.

"The executive infirmary," she replied.

"Then what are we waiting for?" Luke asked, motioning the Mandalorians after R2-D2. "We'll *all* go. Pick up your helmets and fall in."

Joram glanced at his sister, then shrugged and did as he was told. Luke and Leia retrieved the pair's blaster pistols and followed, using Force flashes to momentarily blind the surveillance cams they passed every ten meters or so. Soon, the maleristone floors and walls gave way to polished durasteel, and they came to a pair of transparent doors that automatically drew aside as they approached.

Inside, an FX-2 nursing droid stood behind a circular counter packed with medical monitors. Most of the equipment was inactive, but three sets of displays did seem to be tracking a patient's vital signs. As Luke and the others drew nearer to its workstation, the FX-2 turned and began to run its photoreceptors over first Leia, then Luke. It raised an arm and pointed to a pair of rooms directly adjacent to the station.

"Female to examination room one, male to examination room two. The Two-One-Bee will be in to evaluate you shortly." It picked up a datapad and started out from behind its counter. "Please have your identification badge ready for verification of executive status."

R2-D2 whistled something loud and rolled past the counter.

"You can't go back there," the nursing droid responded. "Access to that area is restricted."

R2-D2 buzzed a rude reply and continued down the corridor.

"Stop!" The FX-2 turned to whir after him. "Don't force me to summon the security contractors! Stop at once, or—"

The protest came to an abrupt end as Leia put a blaster bolt through the back of the FX-2's brain housing. The droid continued down the corridor in silence, veering left until it finally struck a wall and crashed to the floor. Leia quickly followed, then knelt down behind the wreck and tripped the FX-2's primary circuit breaker to be sure the droid would not be sending any messages via an internal comm unit.

As Leia started to rise, Joram looked over at his sister and cocked a conspiratorial brow.

Luke grabbed them both in the Force and slammed them into the wall. "Don't make me regret letting you live," he said. "It's not too late to change my mind."

The woman's eyes flashed in alarm, and she raised her hands in placation. "Why would we try anything? You're never getting off this ship alive anyway."

"I remember when I was your age," Leia said, peeling an identity badge off the FX-2 droid's torso. "I was wrong about a lot of things, too."

She stepped over to the storeroom and pressed the badge to the control panel. The door slid aside and an interior light activated, revealing a cool, compact chamber lined by drawers filled with medical supplies. Leia entered and began to load a steel medical tray with supplies—wound glue, bacta salve, antibiotics, hypos.

Luke saw her studying the anesthesia section and realized what she intended. He glanced back to their prisoners. The brother was probably a size smaller than Luke was, and the sister a couple of sizes larger than Leia— but close enough.

"Okay, helmets on the floor," Luke said. He waved his blaster at their torsos. "The rest of your armor, too."

The woman's eyes flashed in anger. "You can't take our beskar'gam," she said. "Do you know what that means to a Mandalorian?"

"It means you need better training." Luke pointed a blaster at her head. "But we can do it the hard way, if you'd rather."

Joram began to open his torso armor. "Just take it off, Jhan," he said. "Gev will cancel our contracts either way."

Jhan glared daggers at Luke but began to open her own armor, as well. "I hope you cook in it."

"Thanks for that," Leia said. She stepped out of the storeroom with a pair of hypos. "That makes this easier."

She jabbed the hypo into Jhan's neck and activated the injector.

"Hey!" Jhan turned to look at her. "What was . . ."

Her eyes rolled up, and she collapsed.

Joram caught his sister, then checked her pulse and turned to Leia. "Knockout drug?"

"You'd rather I used something stronger?" Leia asked.

"Of course not," Joram replied. "But why don't you settle for just locking us in the storeroom? No need to put me out, too. I won't try to escape."

"Sure you won't," Leia said. She waited until he had removed the last of his armor, then motioned for him to do the same with his sister's. "But I'll have Artoo raise the temperature so you don't freeze."

Joram's voice turned sarcastic. "Thanks. You're a real sweet smooka." He did as instructed, leaving two piles of armor on the floor, then rose and dragged his sister into the storeroom. "You *do* know we'll be coming after you. No Mandalorian can let someone steal his beskar'gam. It's an honor thing."

"Funny," Leia replied. "I didn't know hired killers *had* honor."

That actually drew a smile from Joram. "Now that you mention it, maybe it's more of a pride thing," he said. "But we *will* be coming."

"How polite—a warning." Leia jabbed the second hypo into his neck and activated the injector. "I can hardly believe you're Mandalorian."

She waited until he had collapsed next to his sister, then grabbed her tray of supplies and returned to the corridor. Luke was surprised to see that her lips were taut and her eyes brimming with unshed tears.

"You can't possibly be worried about that kid's threat," Luke said. "If he and his sister were anything to be nervous about, he would have known better than to give us a warning."

"Joram doesn't worry me." Leia looked around, obviously searching for a good place to tend their wounds. "But we're not winning this thing, and I'm starting to wonder if I'm going to see Han again."

"You will," Luke said. "We just need to patch ourselves up and find someplace to hide while we figure out where they took him."

"It's that last part that troubles me," Leia said. "The Qrephs are *always* two steps ahead of us, and we keep trying to beat them at their own game. We need to change the dynamic."

"We will," Luke promised. "The Qrephs may not realize it yet, but they've already made one very bad mistake."

Leia cocked her brow. "They took Han?"

"That's right," Luke said, smiling. "Nobody is harder to figure out than Han Solo. I know it's hard to hear, but if they wanted him dead, he would have been dead before they left the *Ormni.* So, whatever those two want with him, he's going to make them crazy trying to get it."

Leia studied Luke for a moment, then finally nodded. "Maybe so," she said. "He's certainly driven *me* crazy enough times."

R2-D2 appeared a few meters down the corridor and whistled impatiently, then disappeared into the adjacent room—where he continued to whistle.

Luke gave Leia's shoulder a squeeze. "Either Artoo found us a medical droid or we have company on the way," he said. "You check on that, and I'll jam the doors."

Leia nodded and disappeared down the corridor with her tray of supplies. Luke used his lightsaber to cut the legs off a durasteel bench, then returned to the infirmary entrance and slipped them into the tracks of the sliding door. When he finished, he still saw no sign of anyone coming down the corridor beyond, but he took the precaution of disabling the control panel, as well. His precautions probably wouldn't delay Vestara and her Mandalorians for long, but at least they would have to make a lot of noise trying to get through.

The floor, of course, was spattered with blood from his wound. Deciding that cleaning up wouldn't delay their hunters much anyway, Luke simply left it and returned to the room R2-D2 had sought out.

Instead of the surgical droid he had expected, Luke found Leia with a female patient with auburn hair and a bandaged torso. Her face was so pale, and her eyes so sunken, that it took him a moment to recognize her as Lando's treacherous operations manager, Dena Yus.

When Yus heard him enter the room, she looked up and smiled. "Luke Skywalker." She raised her free arm, motioning for him to take her other side. "Hurry. We don't have much time if you want to save Captain Solo."

Fifteen

The object in the holograph was unlike anything Ben had ever seen, natural or artificial. Shaped like two pyramids stuck base-to-base, it had black granular facets that occasionally flashed white. There was nothing else in the image for comparison, so its size was impossible to determine. As it spun on its long axis, it threw off wisps of blue haze, and Ben could just make out three silver specks drifting across its midline.

"What *is* that thing?" he asked, leaning closer to the image. "Could it be a chromite crystal?"

He was in the *Falcon*'s main hold, kneeling among the scattered remnants of the R9 astromech droid he had salvaged from Ohali Soroc's wrecked StealthX. Lando and Omad Kaeg were with him, while Tahiri was at the helm, headed for his father and Aunt Leia's last known position. Ben had not been able to find either his father or aunt in the Force since the last blast of emotion he had felt, but that probably only meant that they were hiding their presences for some reason. At least, that's what he kept telling himself.

"It could also be magnetite," Omad Kaeg suggested. "It does look like a mineral crystal of *some* sort."

Ben turned to C-3PO, who was standing behind the astromech's half-melted casing. "See if you can get him to enlarge the image."

"I can try," C-3PO said. "But, as you can see, Nine-ball is no more than an operating system now. With all of his memory cards and datachips removed, it's remarkable that he recalls his own identifier."

"Just ask," Ben said.

Before using Nineball to bait their trap, the Mandalorians had stripped the droid to his barest components. Fortunately, Jedi R9s were designed to protect mission data at all costs. While trying to retrace Ohali's journey through the Rift, Ben had come across several holovid fragments buried in a string of corrupted operating code.

C-3PO shot a blurp of static toward Nineball's new comm receiver, which they had borrowed from Ben and Tahiri's own astromech.

Nineball squawked a reply that was more death rattle than chirp, but the holograph's perspective slowly began to draw tighter. After a moment, the crystal became a pair of immense black facets sloping away from each other at a ninety-degree angle, and the silver flecks became two starfighters and a medium transport.

"That's *some* crystal," Ben said, awed by what he was seeing. "Do they grow that big in the Rift?"

"I've seen a few durelium and cardovyte crystals the size of an asteroid tug," Omad replied. "But that thing must be as big as a Star Destroyer."

"Or a moon," Lando said. He scowled down at the wrecked R9 unit, which Ben had reduced to a warped motherboard surrounded by cables and borrowed parts—then asked, "Are you sure you don't have some data-merging issues?"

Ben looked up with an expression that suggested Lando's circuits were as scrambled as the droid's. "You're kidding, right?" he asked. "We probably have a hundred issues—none of which we have time to address right now. His processor could go at any second."

"Forget I asked," Lando said. "But if that's an asteroid, why hasn't someone hauled it in? The prospector's cut alone would be enough to buy a world."

"Because that's not an asteroid." Ben's thoughts were beginning to race. Though he was reluctant to say so before he had evidence to support his suspicions, he was starting to believe they might be looking at something very special—something that he had secretly feared might not even exist. "Whatever that thing is, Nineball thought it was important to protect an image of it when things went bad—and Ohali wasn't hunting asteroids."

Lando's brow shot up. "Are you saying that's—"

"I'm not saying anything yet," Ben said. "I don't want to leap to *any* conclusions, especially not before we've learned everything we can from Nineball."

Ben looked to C-3PO, who shot another burst of static at the borrowed comm receiver.

The R9 gave a barely audible rasp, then the holograph flickered and switched to a tactical display. The asteroid was designated UNKNOWN SPACE STATION, and the orbiting vessels were identified as two Mandalorian Bes'uliiks and the Marcadian luxury cruiser *Aurel Moon.*

Omad's jaw dropped. "That's the Qrephs' yacht!"

"Which probably means that, uh, *thing* is their secret base." Lando's voice dropped. "I think we know who's behind Ohali's disappearance."

"Maybe," Ben said. "Or maybe not. Think about it— Ohali was in a long-range StealthX, so she had a lot of fuel and no real firepower. After recording this, her first move should have been to bug out and send a report to the Jedi Council."

"Maybe she tried," Lando said. He turned to C-3PO. "Ask him how Jedi Soroc came to find this *Unknown Space Station.*"

When C-3PO relayed the question, the tactical display flickered out and the R9 fell silent. It remained that way for almost a full minute, and Ben began to fear the astromech had finally suffered a catastrophic failure. He stuck a finger inside the warped chassis and began to push cables and wires aside, looking for broken solder or an overheated relay—anything that he might be able to repair.

Finally the droid began to creak and sputter, so softly that it was nearly imperceptible. Then his motherboard cooling fans began to whir, a sign that he was engaged in some heavy-duty processing. Ben froze, afraid that if he withdrew his finger again, he would disrupt the circuit.

"Oh, dear," C-3PO said. "All this effort is straining his processing unit. Perhaps we should withdraw and let his circuits cool."

Ben shook his head. "Whatever just happened, there's no guarantee I can make it happen again," he said. "And I can still hear him drawing power. Let's give him a chance to work it out."

"It's our best shot," Lando agreed.

They fell silent, listening to the hum of the cooling fans—and trying not to wince at every little pop and hiss.

After a moment, Lando said, "Ben, we both know that Ohali Soroc was looking for the Mortis Monolith, and that certainly qualifies as a monolith."

Ben nodded. "So you're wondering if the Qrephs could have found the Mortis Monolith? I've been wondering the same thing." He paused, then—a bit reluctantly—asked, "But if Ohali thought she had found *the* Mortis Monolith, why does Nineball call it a space station?"

"I see your point," Lando said. "*Ohali* must have thought she was looking at a space station."

"Exactly," Ben said. "Until we know better, we have to assume that's what she found."

"Could the Qrephs have built such a thing themselves?" Omad asked.

"Absolutely," Lando said. "They're on the cutting edge of all kinds of technology, and they have more money than most galactic empires."

"Then maybe we're focusing on the wrong problem," Omad suggested. "Instead of asking ourselves *what* this thing is, maybe we should be asking *why* they have brought their work to the Chiloon Rift."

"Because they *really* want to keep it a secret, of course," Ben said. A frightening thought occurred to him, and he turned to Lando. "They couldn't be building some sort of Death Star, could they?"

Lando's eyes grew wide, but he shook his head. "They're certainly capable, but even something like the Death Star is not much good without a sizable navy to support it. And if they had a navy that large, they wouldn't be hiring Mandalorians to do their dirty work out here."

Nineball emitted a rasp, and their attention returned instantly to him.

"Threepio, what's he saying?" Lando asked.

"It may not be reliable," C-3PO said. "But he *claims* that when Jedi Soroc found the space station, she was following a Sith meditation sphere."

"A meditation sphere?" Ben repeated. His stomach began to churn, for the only meditation sphere he knew of was the one flown by Vestara Khai, and *betrayed* did not begin to describe what she had done to him. She had played him for a fool, claiming his heart and stomping it into a bruised mass, and there was no Sith in the galaxy whom he wanted to hunt down more. *"Ship?"*

Nineball gave a long, half-audible hiss.

"Nineball cannot confirm the identity of the meditation sphere," C-3PO said, "merely that Jedi Soroc followed it to the . . ."

C-3PO paused and shot a burst of static at Nineball. The R9 responded with a sharp crackle.

C-3PO turned back to Ben. "I'm afraid he's merging data again. Now he seems to think that *Ship* led Jedi Soroc into a Mandalorian trap."

The R9 emitted a soft, angry rumble. The holograph of the strange space station reappeared, then suddenly vanished into a boiling orange flash. When the image returned, it was shaky and filled with static. A trio of bright halos seemed to materialize out of nothingness and rapidly swelled into three Mandalorian Bes'uliiks. Bright bolts of energy began to flash back and forth between the StealthX and the oncoming starfighters. The holo spun and shook as Ohali went into evasive maneuvers, then stretched into a flashing blur as the StealthX jumped into hyperspace.

Nineball—or, rather, Nineball's remnants—emitted a series of blurts.

"There is no need to be rude," C-3PO replied. "I was only suggesting that we be careful, considering your condition."

"Ask him what happened after the jump," Ben said.

C-3PO relayed the question. The astromech hissed something soft, then fell silent.

"He doesn't know," C-3PO translated. "Jedi Soroc ordered him to plot a route back to the RiftMesh and issue a distress call, but Nineball was hit by a cannon bolt as they entered hyperspace. He did not have time."

Nineball added another short hiss.

"The next time he returned to awareness," C-3PO translated, "Jedi Skywalker was working to repair him."

"What about navigation coordinates?" Omad asked. "Where is this space station?"

Nineball responded with a string of coordinates that drew instant frowns from everyone present.

"That can't be right," Lando said. "It's halfway to the Core. How about a dead-reckoning history?"

"Don't bother," Omad said. Ben noticed that a glimmer of recognition had come into Omad's Force aura. "It won't help."

"You know where this is?" Ben asked.

"No, but I know where to look for it," Omad said. "I think it's in an area called the Bubble of the Lost."

"That doesn't sound good," Lando said. "What is this Bubble?"

"A zone of ghost ships," Omad replied. "Many tug captains claim it is half myth, but it *does* exist. No one really understands what it is—only that going there is very dangerous."

"As in normal dangerous?" Lando asked. "Or dangerous by Rift standards?"

"Dangerous as in no sane miner would try to work it," Omad said. "The support cooperative gave up trying to extend the RiftMesh into the Bubble more than a hundred years ago. The beacons kept drifting out of range of each other, no matter how many the repair crews placed."

"And where did the beacons go?" Ben asked.

"That's just it," Omad said. "They weren't really going anywhere. The repair crews often found them in their original positions relative to *one another*—but the distance between them was much greater than it should have been."

"And they were still functional?" Ben asked.

Omad nodded. "Exactly. It seemed as though space kept growing between them, until they were out of range of one another."

"Like space–time being stretched," Lando said. "Could there be a black hole in there?"

"Maybe, but only if it's a hole that nothing ever falls into," Omad said. "Ships that disappear into the Bubble don't vanish forever. They just seem to lose their way. They always show up again . . . eventually."

"Define eventually," Ben said. He was beginning to have a bad feeling about his chances of seeing his father again. "And how is the crew when the ships return?"

"Sometimes a vessel is lost for only a few weeks. The crew is usually shaken but fine," Omad said. "Other times, the ship is gone for centuries. When that happens, the crew is nothing but bones and dust."

"So there's no event horizon," Lando said. "The Bubble is simply a big sphere of expanding space–time, with that weird space station at the center."

"Exactly," Omad said. "Except that I don't really know whether the station is at the center of the Bubble or in some other part. I've never even heard of it, so I can't be sure that it's inside at all."

"It's inside," Lando said. "It has to be. The pieces don't fit together like this unless they all come from the same puzzle. My only question is, how do we actually find the station?"

"If the Qrephs and their Mandalorians can find it, *we* can find it," Ben said. For probably the tenth time that day, he began to expand his Force awareness ahead of the *Falcon*. He was searching for his father's presence, of course—but this time he intended to reach well beyond the *Ormni*, all the way into the Bubble. "We might not be as smart as a couple of Columi, but *we* have the Force."

Sixteen

The voices coming over the helmet's integrated comlink were urgent and brusque, the way soldiers sounded when they were closing in on an enemy. Leia didn't speak Mando'a, so she didn't know exactly what they were saying—but she had a good idea. It probably concerned the two dead Nargons she and Luke had left outside the turbolift on the production level. And if that was true, she and her brother had about three minutes before their pursuers traced them to the infirmary. Next, someone would find two guards lying unconscious in their underclothes, and then the *Ormni*'s entire security staff would be looking for two Jedi disguised in white Mandalorian armor.

Leia glanced down at R2-D2. At the moment, his interface arm was jacked into the droid socket next to a sealed utility hatch. The little droid was softly chirping to himself, his single photoreceptor turned toward a captured 2-1B surgical droid, who stood on the opposite wall supporting Dena Yus. Luke had disabled the medical droid's internal comlink, but R2-D2 remained wary and made a point of watching the 2-1B.

"Let *me* worry about security, will you?" Leia asked. "Just get us out of here."

R2-D2 replied with one last irritated tweet, then turned his photoreceptor toward the hatch. As the droid

worked, Leia felt a familiar touch in the Force. Thinking
it was her brother, she glanced up the service corridor
toward the intersection, where Luke stood pretending to
be a Mandalorian guard. But instead of looking back
toward Leia, his helmet was cocked slightly to the side,
as though he were feeling the same Force touch she was.

Not Luke's touch, she realized, but his son's.

With Vestara Khai still pursuing them, there had been
no chance for Luke to reach out to Ben. The young
Knight would probably be worried—especially if he and
Tahiri had responded to the StealthX distress signal.

Leia held the contact long enough to let Ben know she
was alive and more or less well, then turned her attention back to their escape. If R2-D2 didn't finish soon,
she and Luke might have to start looking for the nearest
trash chute to jump down.

The little droid spun his dome around and gave an
inquisitive chirp.

"About time," Leia said. "Do it."

The raucous blare of an emergency alarm gave three
long bursts, then a synthesized female voice came over
the intraship address system.

"This is a catastrophic-event alert. Proceed in an orderly fashion to your assigned evacuation stations and
launch your escape vessels. I repeat . . ."

R2-D2 emitted a triumphant whistle.

Leia pointed at the hatch. "Forget something?"

The droid bleeped indignantly and opened the hatch,
then withdrew his interface arm. Leia peered into the
corridor beyond and quickly located a wide-angle security cam overhead, then used a silent blast of Force energy to blind its lens.

She glanced back to find Luke coming to join her, not
quite hobbling but in obvious pain. His captured blaster
pistol was holstered on his hip, but his lightsaber—like
Leia's—was hidden safely out of sight in one of the stor-

age compartments R2-D2 normally used for spare utility arms.

The emergency alarm sounded again, and the same synthetic voice repeated the evacuation order. At the far end of the service corridor, GET administrative staff began to rush past the intersection, heading for the executive hangar. Luke gathered Dena Yus in his arms, then glanced toward Leia.

"Ben is here," he said.

"Aboard the *Ormni*?" Leia gasped.

Luke shook his head. "But somewhere close," he said. "He seemed . . . eager."

"You think he found Ohali?"

Luke shrugged. "I guess we'll find out," he said. "Assuming Dena's plan works."

"It will," Yus said. The wounds she had suffered during the casino firefight were already healing, yet her voice remained frail and her body weak from malnourishment. "It *has* to work."

"It better," Leia said. There was no deception in Yus's Force aura, but Leia thought it wise to remain watchful. Yus had obviously been working for the Qrephs all along, and there had been no time to explore the reasons for her recent change of heart. "If this is a trap, you're the first to die."

Yus responded with a patient smile. "If it comes to that, you will be doing me a favor." She directed her gaze through the hatch. "We should try for a SwiftLux pinnace. They're designed for passenger protection, and there will be several departing."

Leia stepped through the hatch, then led the way down a crooked corridor into the silvery vastness of the executive hangar. She quickly blinded two more security cameras overhead, then started across the hangar. There were probably three dozen craft resting on the spotless deck, grouped by model and arrayed in orderly rows.

Near the center of the hangar sat the blue wedges of five SwiftLux pinnaces.

The emergency alarm and the synthetic voice continued to cycle, urging the crew to evacuate. The first crush of administrative staff was already arriving through the main entrance, pushing past a pair of Mandalorian guards and four edgy-looking Nargons. Leia spotted one Nargon staring in their direction and, through her helmet viewplate, held his gaze long enough to suggest she did not regard him as a threat.

The Nargon ruffled his skull crest. Raising an arm to point out Leia's group, he turned toward his Mandalorian superiors.

"Don't look now," Leia said to her companions. "But I think we're in—"

Before Leia could finish, a flurry of Mando'a came over her helmet comlink. Fearing the message could be a warning to watch for two intruders in white armor, she quickly dropped back next to R2-D2, where she would be able to retrieve her lightsaber quickly. But instead of turning to stop them, the security squad stepped into the hangar entrance and began to motion the would-be evacuees to turn back.

With the alarm continuing to sound and a steady flow of personnel arriving behind them, the administrative staff was in no mood to cooperate. A trio of older, dignified-looking beings—probably high-ranking executives—stepped forward to argue with the guards. Everyone else simply circled around them.

By the time the Nargons had finally formed a line across the entrance, it was too late. Dozens of beings had pushed their way inside the hangar and were rushing toward the nearest vessels.

Leia and her companions kept moving, too—and they were almost at the SwiftLuxes. She hit the overhead security cams with another wave of Force energy, then turned to R2-D2.

"How long before the *Ormni*'s bridge cancels the evacuation alarm?"

R2-D2 emitted a negative tweet.

"Any guesses?" Luke asked.

Again, R2-D2 gave a negative tweet, but this time it was more insistent and sharp.

"Your astromech has a rather inflated opinion of himself," said the 2-1B droid. "He claims the alarm cannot be canceled without disabling the entire intraship address system."

R2-D2 gave an affirmative beep, then sped ahead, into the row of gleaming SwiftLuxes. He veered under the middle craft and stopped behind the forward landing strut, then inserted his interface arm into a diagnostics socket. A moment later, the landing lights blinked to life, and a section of blue hull swung down to serve as the boarding ramp.

R2-D2 turned his photoreceptor on the 2-1B and emitted a long, mocking trill.

"You have not succeeded *yet*, little droid," the 2-1B replied. "There is a difference between sneaking aboard a GET starcraft—and actually flying off in it."

"That's enough, Two-One-Bee," Yus said. As Luke carried her up the ramp, she scowled at the medical droid. "Or are you *hoping* the Jedi will give you a memory wipe?"

The 2-1B's head pivoted toward her. "They would never dare," he said. "I am a surgical droid!"

"You're scrap metal unless you move it," Leia said, waving the 2-1B up the ramp. "We only brought you along to look after Dena, and, frankly, I'm not that fond of her."

The droid sputtered in indignation, then hurried up

the ramp, avoiding Leia's gaze. "The sacrifices I make for my patients," he muttered.

The moment the 2-1B had boarded, R2-D2 withdrew his interface arm from the diagnostics socket. The ramp began to rise immediately. Leia leapt on and rushed into the SwiftLux's cramped-but-elegant cabin, then found the interior controls and lowered the ramp again for R2-D2.

By then Luke had already removed his helmet and was strapping the ailing Dena Yus into a nerf-hide chair. Leia waited impatiently for their droid to roll up the ramp, knowing that using the Force to lift him aboard would draw unwanted attention.

With the alarm still sounding and the synthetic voice continuing to repeat the evacuation orders, the situation at the hangar entrance was deteriorating. A hundred angry beings were trying to push their way past the four Nargons, who had begun to bowl interlopers back into the crowd. The three executives were making rude gestures at the Mandalorians, who were stubbornly standing their ground—and resting their hands on the butts of their still-holstered blasters. The beings who had already made it into the hangar were clambering up the boarding ramps of five other vessels, including several SwiftLuxes.

R2-D2 finally rolled aboard. Leia raised the ramp and turned to go forward—then stopped when her helmet comm fell silent. She stepped to a viewport and, with a sinking feeling, peered out.

The Nargons were still doing their best to keep would-be evacuees out of the hangar, though another couple dozen had sneaked inside and were running for the nearest spacecraft. But the Mandalorians had turned away from the executives and were now tapping control pads on their wrists—no doubt switching to a new comm channel.

Leia removed her helmet. "They know we're listening, which means they found our friends in the infirmary." She motioned R2-D2 toward the flight deck. "Artoo, fire this thing up. We need to leave *now*."

"No—we can't be first," Yus said. "The *Ormni* is the heart of GET operations in the Rift, and most of the security force is based here. If we leave first and without authorization, we'll be jumped before we've traveled three kilometers."

"That's better than having the blast doors slammed in our faces," Luke said.

"There *are* no blast doors," Yus said. "The *Ormni* is an asteroid crusher, not a Star Destroyer. The hangar mouths do have some serious deflector shields—but only to prevent exterior attacks. From the inside, the shield generators should be easy to take out."

Luke glanced toward Leia, clearly as conflicted over the advice as Leia was. There was still nothing in Yus's Force aura to suggest she was lying to them. But delaying would only give the operations crew more time to react—and that could easily backfire. Leia looked out the viewport and saw that the security team had left its post to begin a search of the hangar. Behind the team, hundreds of would-be evacuees were about to complicate that task by pouring into the hangar.

"We *might* have half a minute," Leia said. "But no more."

The SwiftLux gave a little pop as R2-D2 brought the fusion core online.

"A minute would be better," Yus said. "We need some cover. We just don't want to be the first to leave the hangar."

"I heard you the first time," Leia said. She stepped onto the flight deck and looked out toward the hangar mouth. The atmospheric barrier field remained a faint translucent gold. But the operations crew was standing in the control room above the hangar mouth, peering out through their own viewport at the pandemonium below, and Leia had no doubt that they were discussing ways to bring the situation under control.

"We don't *have* a minute," Leia said. She turned back and pointed the 2-1B droid into a chair. "Strap yourself in. I won't be giving any launch warnings."

Luke arched a brow. "Looks like I'm taking the cannons."

"Good idea," Leia said, smiling. "Let me know if those hangar guards start heading in our direction."

She moved onto the flight deck and took the pilot's seat, then waited impatiently while nearby vessels began to cold-fire their engines. After ten seconds or so, Luke's voice came over the intercom.

"We have Mando reinforcements entering the hangar." He opened up with the laser cannons—no doubt trying to delay the reinforcements—and filled the hangar with flashing light. "Get us out, now!"

Other vessels were beginning to rise around them. Leia eased the throttles back and lifted off the deck, then fell into line behind another SwiftLux and started toward the exit.

R2-D2 chirped an alert, and Leia glanced down to find the comm system blinking for attention.

"If that's hangar control—"

Before Leia could say, *Ignore it,* a nasal voice came over the cockpit speaker.

"Attention all vessels: the deflector shields are being activated. There is no emer—"

The message dissolved into blast static as cannon bolts from half a dozen vessels converged above the hangar mouth. The shield generators vanished in a blossom of sparks and molten metal, and then someone fired again—and hit the barrier-field generators by mistake.

At least, Leia hoped it was by mistake.

Suddenly the hangar was filled with flying bodies and tumbling equipment, and the Force trembled with the cold terror of hundreds of dying beings.

Leia shoved the throttles forward and, trying to ignore her own shock, followed a boiling circle of ion blast out through the hangar mouth and into clear space. She extended her Force awareness farther out into space . . . and was not entirely surprised to sense Ben Skywalker's familiar presence off to starboard.

Leia pulled up and pushed the throttles past the overload stops, then saw the twinned ion tails of three Bes'uliiks lacing the black void ahead. Ben's presence grew stronger, more urgent. She shoved the yoke hard to starboard, turning toward the wispy bank of Rift plasma where he seemed to be hiding.

A tingle of danger sense ran down her spine—the Mandalorian pilots lining up behind her. The SwiftLux shuddered as Luke opened up with their laser cannons, and an instant later the enemy counterattack overloaded their shields. The cockpit erupted in damage alarms, and the hull screamed with the sound of cannon bolts burning through the pinnace's thin armor.

Then R2-D2 emitted another alert chime, and the familiar voice of Lando Calrissian came over the comm channel.

"Dive, dive, dive!" he ordered. "We have you covered!"

"*Lando?*" Leia exclaimed. "What are you . . ."

Too relieved to finish, Leia simply pushed the yoke forward—then gasped as the *Millennium Falcon* emerged from the plasma barely a hundred meters above, cannons blazing and concussion missiles flying. She pulled up hard, swinging around to cover their savior's stern, but by the time she finished, the Bes'uliiks were already blossoming into fireballs, and the *Falcon* was halfway through its victory roll.

Luke's voice came over the comm speaker. "Lando!" he exclaimed. "You *do* know how to make an entrance."

Seventeen

Even the simple act of pulling chip-cards across a velvet tabletop sent needles of anguish shooting up Han's arm. He told himself the pain was no big deal, that his thumb had not actually been crushed and he still had all of his fingernails. All he was feeling were inflamed nerves, the result of injections and shocks delivered by the Qrephs' sophisticated torture droid, DSD-1. But his body wasn't cooperating. His hands were shaking, his brow was wet with perspiration, his breath had grown quick and shallow—and that was a bigger problem than the pain itself.

Han had developed a tell.

The pain had started to wear on him, and he knew by the reactions of the new players—by Ohali Soroc's averted gaze, and by Barduun's hungry smile—that everyone saw it. They thought he was done, ready to give up. And maybe he should have been. He had been trying to cause trouble between the Qrephs ever since he arrived, and all he had accomplished was to bring out their sadistic side. A more cautious man might have taken the hint and stopped pushing.

Good thing Han had never been a cautious man.

Because Han wasn't playing for himself right now. Leia and Luke would still be out there looking for him. They *had* to be . . . along with Lando and Omad and, by now, maybe even Jaina and a whole bunch of Jedi Masters. He couldn't give up on himself without giving up on *them*. So he had to keep pushing, keep the Qrephs' attention focused on him instead of his would-be rescuers, because that was the only way he had to protect Leia and the others.

Han pinched the cards between a throbbing thumb and two sore fingers, then tipped them up and looked down to find that his new chip-card gave him a score of exactly zero. There was nothing special about zero, except that it was nicknamed "absolute zero" because it was the worst score a sabacc player could have without bombing out. The safe play would have been to fold and let everyone think they were reading him right.

But you didn't beat the Qrephs with safe plays.

Han nodded and said, "I'm in."

The player to his left, Ohali Soroc, used the Force to pull her chip-cards up, then pinched them gingerly between her thumb and two fingers. The other two fingers on that hand remained stiff and extended, a sign of the lingering pain she felt from her earlier losses. Like Han, the Duros Jedi sat unrestrained in a modified examination chair, wearing a loose lab tunic over a mesh of electrodes and probe needles that recorded her brain waves and physiological reactions to the Qrephs' bizarre, pain-wagering game.

The brothers wanted Han to believe she was the Quest Knight who had happened across Base Prime and been captured by their Mandalorians. And maybe she was. After all, she had passed his makeshift identity test with flying colors, correcting Han when he said the last time they had seen each other was at Jaina's wedding on Coruscant. The wedding, she reminded him, had occurred aboard the *Dragon Queen II*—and she had not been present because that was the day she and the other Quest Knights had departed to find Mortis.

Finally, Soroc tossed her chip-cards to Mirta Gev, who was still acting as the dealer. The splint had been removed from Gev's nose, but the bridge was now crooked, and her eyes remained puffy and faintly bruised.

"I'm out," Soroc said.

Gev nodded, almost in sympathy, then turned to the torture droid. "She still owes the ante."

The torture droid—a dark orb adorned with syringes, claws, and electrical prods—quickly floated to her side and extended an innervation needle. Soroc shuddered but turned away and presented her left hand to the droid.

Knowing from previous procedures that the electro-injection would not be allowed to delay the game, Han let his gaze slide past Gev to the *other* Ohali Soroc, who seemed to be some sort of half-wit replica that the Qrephs were experimenting with.

"How about you, Ditto?"

Ditto's bulbous red eyes brightened with irritation. "My name is not Ditto," she said. "I am Ohali Two."

"If you say so." Han glanced at the first Ohali Soroc, who had tipped her head back and was staring at the ceiling as the torture droid used its tools to duplicate the pain of having a fingernail extracted. Then Han rolled his eyes and turned back to Ditto. "You in?"

Ditto flashed a smile that would have been a sneer on a human. On a Duros, it just looked out of place. "What do you think, Captain?"

"Of course you are," he said. "Why do I even ask?"

Ditto was one of those players who didn't seem to understand that sabacc was about more than taking risks. She played too many hands and lost most of them, then trumpeted even minor wins as if she'd won the Core Worlds Open.

Han let his gaze slide past Craitheus Qreph, who had

already folded, to the next player—a heavy-jawed, dark-haired Mandalorian named Barduun.

Dressed in one of the padded bodysuits normally worn under beskar'gam armor, Barduun certainly *looked* ugly enough to be Mandalorian. But he wasn't—at least not any longer. There was something off about him, a fiendish malevolence that seemed entirely too twisted to be human.

That, and he was a Force-user.

At the moment, Barduun was using the Force to hold his chip-cards up where he could see them. He continued to study the cards for a moment, probably for no reason except to make the other players wait. Then, finally, he lowered the cards to the table and caught Han's eye.

"Jhonus Raam raises," Barduun said, calling himself by the brand name stenciled across the chest of his bodysuit. "Jhonus Raam raises to a . . . burned eye."

Han had to force himself not to look away or draw his throbbing hands back toward his lap, and even then the sweat began to roll down his brow more freely. Barduun liked to intimidate and frighten his fellow players by raising the stakes to some new kind of torture that no one had experienced.

Unfortunately, the strategy was proving successful. It had been Barduun who had forced Han to suffer the pain of a crushed thumb on a clever reverse bluff. Then, twice afterward, Han had folded a great score, only to discover that Barduun's bet had been nothing but bluster. But with an absolute zero in his hand, Han had no choice. When the bet came to him, he would need to fold again.

Marvid Qreph, seated between Han and Barduun, said, "I raise."

Han's jaw dropped. Marvid had not been playing

quite as timidly as his brother, but after losing two pain-inflicting bets to Barduun, he had been even less eager than Han to challenge the . . . well, whatever Barduun *was*. If Marvid was raising a bet of a burned eye, he had to have at least a pure sabacc—maybe even an idiot's array.

Marvid turned to Han. "I raise with this question: who blasted Mama?"

Barduun scowled. "A question is not a raise." He turned to Gev, who, as the dealer, was supposed to be the ultimate judge of rules questions. "It is not even a bet. We are playing for pain, not answers."

The challenge made Marvid's eyes narrow to angry ovals. "There are many kinds of pain, Barduun." As he spoke, he kept his eyes fixed on Han. "Some answers cause a great deal of pain."

Gev nodded. "I'll accept that," she said. "The bet stands."

"Fine by me," Han said, thinking maybe the time had come to bluff. He had finally figured out that the Qrephs were the offspring of a Columi information broker he had once consulted on Ord Mantell. Apparently, he had been her last customer before someone put a blaster bolt through her head. Naturally, the Qrephs had grown up blaming Han. "But are you sure you want to make that bet, Marvid? Maybe you ought to ask Craitheus first. I already told you, I didn't blast your mother."

"That's not what I asked," Marvid said. His face had gone tight with resentment, which Han took to mean that his strategy of building animosity between the brothers was still working. "I asked who *did*. Is there some reason you are reluctant to tell me what you know?"

"Yeah," Han said, deciding to offer a little bait. "I can't be sure."

"Come now, Captain Solo. Our rules require only a

good-faith effort." Marvid glanced across the table toward their dealer. "Isn't that correct, Commander Gev?"

Gev nodded. "Those are the rules," she said. "As long as an answer doesn't trigger the lie-detection routine, best guesses count."

Han paused to think. Marvid probably had Barduun beat, but these kinds of stakes were going to scare him—and that meant it wouldn't take much to make the Columi fold. Han shot a conspiratorial smirk across the table toward Craitheus, then looked back to Marvid.

"In that case," Han said. "I re-raise."

A flicker of hesitation came to Marvid's face, and Han knew Marvid had nothing better than a pure sabacc, perhaps even a *negative* sabacc. Either score beat Han's absolute zero, but Han wasn't playing his hand anymore. Now he was playing *Marvid*—and he was pretty sure he was winning. Han peeked at his chip-cards again, then locked the value of his hand at zero by pushing all three cards into the stasis field.

"I want to ask Jedi Soroc—the real one—a question." Han turned to glance out the viewport, which opened onto a dusty black plain so perfectly flat and unblemished by impact craters that it *had* to have been created by an advanced species of sentients. "I want to know if this place is sitting on the Mortis Monolith."

Craitheus's powerbody hissed and tilted forward. "Do we *look* like the Ones to you, Captain Solo?"

"Not really," Han said, looking away to think.

The Qrephs had clearly had plenty of time to interrogate Ohali about her mission as a Quest Knight, so it came as no surprise to hear Craitheus refer to the Ones. What Han *did* find surprising was that the Qrephs didn't seem to care that they might have built Base Prime on the Mortis Monolith. Han was no expert on Force nexuses, but he knew enough to realize that locating a lab on top of such a place of power would be like erecting a house on top of a live volcano to take advantage of the free heat.

Which was not to say that the Qrephs hadn't done exactly that, of course. They were just arrogant enough to think they could exploit something like the Mortis Monolith and manage dangers they could not even perceive. Or maybe Han was misreading the situation entirely. Maybe Craitheus wasn't concerned because he already *knew* this wasn't Mortis.

There was only one way to find out.

Han turned back to Marvid. "But that's *my* raise. If you want to know who blasted Mama, you have to let me ask Ohali if this is Mortis."

Marvid's only response was to turn his gaze to the next player in the betting rotation: Ditto. She used the Force to raise her chip-cards so she could peek at their values, then let her gaze drift to her trembling hands. She closed one eye, as though trying to imagine what she would be able to see if the other became disabled by pain, then checked her cards again. Han could tell that she had, at best, a mediocre hand. But Ditto didn't fold easy—not until the last chip-card had been dealt, when there was no longer any chance of being saved by a last-minute shift.

Finally, Ditto looked up. "I . . . I call the bet."

"Of course you do," Marvid sneered. He directed his attention to Barduun. "I believe the bet is to you."

A veil of dusky anger passed over Barduun's face—the same tell Han had seen half a dozen times before—and Han knew Barduun's hand was not a good one. But that didn't mean he would fold easily. Han put a confident smirk on his face, then looked away as though he were trying to hide his expression.

He had no idea what Barduun actually *was*. So far, the fellow seemed to care less about winning sabacc hands than creating fear in the hearts of other players, as if maybe he was some kind of dark-side fiend who used fear to feed his Force powers. Han could see why the Qrephs might want to create a few Ohali Sorocs—what baron of industry *wouldn't* want an army of Force-using lackeys—but he couldn't see why the two Columi had turned a perfectly good Mandalorian into something like Barduun. Maybe he was a lab accident or something.

After a moment, Barduun hissed in frustration . . . then said, "Jhonus Raam raises."

Good. The stakes would force Marvid to fold. Han glanced over and caught Ohali Soroc watching the two Nargon guards at the door. Clearly, she was thinking the same thing he was—it was about time to make a move.

Barduun remained silent, letting the fear build as his fellow players contemplated what he intended to bet.

The fear was still building when the lounge door slid open and a gravelly Mandalorian voice spoke behind Han.

"Sorry to interrupt, but Lady Raine wants a word with the chiefs."

Marvid cocked his head, half-turning toward the door. "Savara is here already? Excellent."

Craitheus—who could see the door from his seat on the opposite side of the table—nodded to the guard. "Send her in."

"She said to tell you it needs to be in private," the guard said. "And she said it's urgent."

Marvid let out a melodramatic sigh, then used a servogrip to gather his chip-cards. "It appears you will have to continue without me." He tossed the cards to Gev and turned to Han. "As much fun as it would be to see you suffer, Captain Solo, I must withdraw."

His powerbody started to pivot away from the table—until Han clamped a hand on to one of its vanalloy pincer arms.

"Not so fast," Han said. "You owe us a session with the torture droid."

Marvid shot a glance toward his brother, who was just floating around the far end of the table toward the door.

"What are you looking at Craitheus for?" Han demanded. "He can't get you out of this."

Marvid turned back to Han, his temples throbbing. "I am sure you think yourself quite clever, Captain Solo." He tipped his powerbody forward. "You have manipulated me into a position where I must either suffer an unimaginable torment or admit I never intended to honor the bet. Would that be a fair assessment?"

"Look, pal, all I want is what you owe the pot," Han said, growing uneasy. "No one likes a shirker."

"*Likes,* Captain Solo?" A thin smile came to Marvid's puckered mouth. "What do you think this has been? A social event?"

"I think it's a sabacc game," Han said. "And when you play sabacc, you make good on your markers."

Craitheus surprised Han by whirling his powerbody around and stopping next to his brother. "Why?"

Han scowled. "Why *what?*"

"Why should we honor our marker?" Craitheus asked. "So you will tell us who blasted our mother?"

"The thought had crossed my mind, yeah." Han didn't like how the Qrephs seemed to be in sync all of a sudden—as if maybe they had been playing *him* all along. "I thought you wanted to know. Marvid kept asking about it, anyway."

"Only to make certain you understand the reason you are here," Marvid said.

"Sorry," Han said. "I'm still a little unclear on that."

Craitheus glared at him. "Retribution, Captain Solo," he said, "for the poverty we endured after our mother's cerebrums were destroyed and she could no longer earn a living."

"In that case, you have some work to do," Han said. "I already told you *I* wasn't the one who blasted your mother."

"And you expect us to accept that?" Marvid asked. "The word of a smuggler and a rebel, when there is twelve-point-two percent chance that you're lying?"

Han frowned in confusion. "Twelve percent makes the odds better than seven to one that I'm telling the *truth*."

"So it does," Craitheus said. "But we always prefer to minimize our chance of error—and now we have reduced it to zero."

"Zero? How can you . . ." The answer to Han's question came to him before he had finished asking it. "Wait—you've already killed the other possibilities?"

Craitheus tipped his powerbody back and looked at the ceiling. "Is that so difficult to believe, Captain Solo?" he asked. "Yes, we have destroyed the other suspects: Hondo Bador, Cabot Lom, Nevid d'Hon, Berille Ada— anyone Mama might have angered by helping you."

"We even destroyed the bartender," Marvid added. "He had been with Mama for twenty standard years, but she had just refused a salary request, so he *did* have a reason to be resentful."

Han could only shake his head in disbelief. "You two are insane," he said. "Killing, what, *five* innocent beings just to be sure you got the right one?"

"Fifteen innocent beings, actually," Marvid said. "There were quite a few minor suspects."

"And did I say we *killed* them?" Craitheus asked. "I hope we haven't led you to believe we are that merciful, Captain Solo. We *destroyed* them. We took their treasure, their friends, their family—"

"Stop there." Han was growing angrier by the moment. "You two must have a death wish if you think you're going to make threats against my friends and my family."

"Those are not threats, Captain Solo." Again, a tight smile came to Marvid's withered mouth. "After you survived the assassination attempt at Sarnus, we decided to try a more . . . *careful* approach."

"*Assassination* attempt?" Han echoed, reeling from the implications. "You dropped that asteroid on Sarnus . . . to get at *me*?"

A lipless sneer came to Marvid's mouth. "Does that make you feel guilty, Captain Solo?"

"What it makes me is mad," Han said, coming out of his chair. "You kill almost thirty thousand people for a twelve percent shot at *aarrrrggh!*"

Han's outburst came as a blast of electricity tore through his head. When it finally subsided, he dropped back into his chair, quivering and half paralyzed.

Craitheus moved his powerbody so close that the air grew stale with the smell of actuator oil and Columi sweat. "A good plan works on many levels, Captain Solo," he said. "Your arrival merely added a new dimension to our plan to handle Calrissian—one that persuaded us to act sooner rather than later."

Han glared at the Columi. "You're . . . d-d-done," he said, speaking through teeth that were still half clenched. "You know th-that, right?"

"Because Luke Skywalker is coming?" Marvid's tone was mocking. "I doubt that very much. He's already dead, as is your wife. Savara Raine ambushed them both at the *Ormni*."

"And we used *you* to bait the trap," Craitheus added.

"Sure you did." Han's retort was more hope than conviction, since his greatest fear all along had been that

Leia and Luke would get themselves killed trying to rescue him. "That's why you ran out *here* to hole up."

"You are quite mistaken," Marvid said. "Mind mapping requires the proper equipment. That is why we have been here so long."

Han snorted. "Give me a break. You're *hiding* from Luke and Leia, and your problems are only getting worse." He cast a look toward the still-open door, where two Nargons continued to stand guard. "By now half the Jedi Order is on its way here—with a fleet of Hapan Battle Dragons to back them up. If you had any sense, you'd surrender to me. Maybe I can convince them to lock you away someplace nice for the rest of your lives."

Marvid's eyes twinkled with amusement. "A skeptic, I see," he said. "Well, you shall have proof of your wife's death soon enough."

Han waved a dismissive hand. "It's easy to make promises you don't mean to keep." He turned away. "They're kind of like bets that way."

Marvid fell silent to consider his reply, and Han knew he had struck a nerve. He fixed his attention on Barduun, intending to ask how his fellow players felt about shirkers, but was cut short when Marvid finally replied.

"You can be quite persuasive when you wish to be, Captain Solo." Marvid turned to the torture droid. "Our guest is right, I *do* owe the pot the pain of a burned eye. If he fails to win the hand, inflict it on *him*."

"What?" Han demanded, starting to rise again. "You can't bet someone else's *paiagggrrh!*"

Again, Han's objection ended in a debilitating shock as one of the Qrephs sent a jolt of electricity through his head. He dropped back into his chair, shaking and weak.

"Apparently, I can," Marvid said, leading his brother toward the door. "Enjoy your game."

Han heard the door hiss shut behind him, then looked over to find Barduun watching him with a hungry grin.

"A nose," Barduun said. "Jhonus Raam raises to a broken nose."

Han rolled his eyes. "Fine." When Barduun reacted to his call with an involuntary nose twitch, he quickly added, "And I raise *you* to . . . death."

"Death?" Barduun asked. "You cannot bet death."

"But I *can* bet any kind of pain I want to," Han said. "And that's what I'm betting—what it feels like to drown to death." He turned to the torture droid. "You can do that, right?"

"Of course." The droid floated a little higher and hovered over the edge of the sabacc table. "But there is a seventy-six percent probability the subject will fall into a temporary coma. He will certainly become unconscious."

A dusky veil passed over Barduun's face again, and Han knew his opponent wouldn't call. Whatever Barduun *was,* he was feeding on other people's fear—and comatose players didn't fear anything. He held Han's gaze for a moment, then shot him a sneer of grudging respect and turned to the only other player still in the hand: Ditto.

"It seems Captain Solo is going all-in," he said. "Do you call?"

Ditto's eyes grew even rounder than normal, and she turned to the dealer. "He can really do that?"

"Sure I can," Han said, keeping his gaze fixed on Barduun. "I just did."

"Actually, you *can't,*" Gev said. "That was a string bet you made."

"String bet? No way!" Despite Han's objection, Gev was right. After seeing Barduun's reaction to his call—when he said the word *fine*—Han had quickly added a raise. That was a string bet, it was cheating, and, under the circumstances, he didn't care. "You're just sore because I gave you a bent beak."

Gev's eyes narrowed. "*My* nose has nothing to do with it. I'm enforcing the—"

"Then what's the deal?" Han asked, cutting her off. With the Qrephs out of the room, the time had come for the inmates to take over the asylum. "What do the Qrephs have on you, anyway?"

"They pay," Gev said. "They pay very well."

"Yeah . . . right," Han snorted. He pointed at the torture droid. "Not even a Mandalorian would do *that* for money. If those two bigheads didn't have something on you, you wouldn't be here. What is it?"

"Nothing."

Gev made a point of holding Han's gaze across the table, which was how he saw her eyes light when he mentioned the Qrephs. They didn't *frighten* her. There was something about them that she actually *liked*—and Han knew of only one thing that could be.

"Come on, you don't believe they can really clean the nanokillers out of Mandalore's atmosphere, do you?" Han asked. Gev's expression clouded with anger, and he knew he was on the right track. "Not even Columi are that smart."

Barduun's gaze snapped toward Gev so fast his neck popped. "*That* is why you took this contract?"

The fact that Barduun did not ask for details suggested that he knew exactly what Han was talking about. During the Second Civil War, a group of Imperial Moffs had released a genetically targeted nanokiller on Mandalore. It was designed to kill Gev and her famous grandfather, Boba Fett, if they ever again breathed Mandalorian air. The pair had been trying for years to find a way to disable the nanokiller so they could go home, and now it appeared that Gev had turned to the Qreph brothers.

"I *asked,* is that why you brought us here?" Barduun

demanded. "So you and the Mandalore can return home?"

Gev finally turned to meet Barduun's gaze. "What, the money isn't good enough?"

"For *that?*" Han scoffed, gesturing at Barduun. "Even I know Mandalorians well enough to realize your crew didn't sign on to be lab rats for a couple of crossed circuits like the Qrephs."

Barduun's expression flashed from deranged to hurt, prompting Gev to turn back to Han.

"That's enough, Solo," Gev said. Her finger hovered over a control button on the table. "Leave my people out of this."

"Sure, if you say so—but you need to ask yourself how hard the Qrephs are *really* trying to deliver." He glanced over at Barduun and gave him a conspiratorial wink. "After all, we just saw how they feel about honoring their bets."

"I said"—Gev's finger stabbed down on the button, and the probe needles in Han's head unleashed a torrent of white, debilitating pain—*"enough!"*

Eighteen

After several minor surgeries, a skin graft, bacta wraps, and a three-day healing trance, Luke was beginning to feel almost fit. His wounds were closed, his burns had healed into red blotches, and his ankle felt ready for action.

Leia looked much better, too. It would be some time before her hair returned to its normal length. But her burns had faded to inconspicuous scars that would vanish entirely after a few more bacta treatments. And when she turned her body, it was with a natural grace that suggested the gashes on her back no longer troubled her.

In short, Luke and Leia were ready to take the fight to the enemy—just as soon as Omad Kaeg actually *found* the enemy. Assisted by R2-D2 and C-3PO, Omad was on the *Falcon's* flight deck, flying blind from one long-lost repeater beacon to another. Luke felt fairly sure that the young tug captain was completely adrift navigating in the Bubble. Still, he admired the way Omad answered any inquiry about their location with a broad smile and cheery *Almost there!*

It kind of reminded him of Han.

Everyone else was gathered in the crew lounge, developing a plan to rescue Han and neutralize the enemy. Given the group's many disadvantages, Luke was fairly certain that *neutralize* would end up meaning *kill*. But they were trying to keep their options open. Jedi were supposed to be the good guys, after all.

"Five Bessies isn't much of a squadron, but it's more than we have," Lando was saying. "There's no question—we have to hit the hangars with a couple of concussion missiles on the way in."

To emphasize his point, he tapped the square marked HANGAR on the schematic that Dena Yus had drawn of the Qrephs' secret base.

Tahiri thought for a moment, then put her finger on the long rectangle that abutted the hangar.

"I don't know," she said. "That hangar is pretty close to the barracks annex. If that's where they're keeping Han—"

"It won't be," Yus interrupted softly. She was seated in front of the engineering station on the other side of the lounge, slumped in her chair and looking even worse than when they had brought her aboard the *Falcon*. "Captain Solo will be across the courtyard from the hangar, in the laboratory wing."

"The laboratory wing?" Leia demanded, looking up from the schematic. Her expression grew stormy. "Why there?"

"Because the Qrephs don't take prisoners, and they're too arrogant to believe they need hostages." Yus did not flinch as she said this. "If they still have Captain Solo, it's because they are using him for an experiment."

"What *kind* of experiment?" Leia asked.

Yus shook her head. "If I knew, I would . . . tell you." It seemed to take all of her energy just to say that much—which was strange after so many days of medical care. Her blaster burns showed no sign of infection, but she was growing weaker and more jaundiced, almost by the hour. "Trust me."

Leia glared at her for a moment, then looked back to the schematic. "So, on the first pass, we dump a couple of concussion missiles on the hangar and drop two YVHs on the residential annex."

"Battle droids?" Ben asked. He was kneeling on the deck adjacent to the table, tinkering with some cables and circuit boards. He looked up at Lando. "You brought *YVHs*?"

"Of course I brought YVHs," Lando said, frowning. "This is Han we're talking about."

Ben winced. "Sorry, I guess I meant . . . what are they doing in the Rift?"

"They were for a decoy program that Lando hoped to launch against the pirates," Yus said.

"Yeah," Lando said. He shot her a glare. "I guess now we understand why the program never made it past the pilot stage."

Yus dropped her gaze. "I *am* sorry."

A moment of awkward silence followed as the apology went unaccepted.

Then Tahiri said, "Anyway, about these YVHs. How many and what series?"

"Only six," Lando replied. "But they're YVH-Eight, S-series."

Tahiri whistled. "Space assault models." She smiled and turned to Lando. "I could kiss you."

Lando's expression brightened. "Well, under the circumstances, I don't think Tendra would—"

Tahiri laughed. "Later."

"Back to the plan," Leia said, clearly irritated by the diversion. "On the first pass, we drop two YVHs on the residential annex, then take the other four and do a hot-drop into the laboratory wing ourselves."

"What targets do I program into the YVHs?" Lando asked.

"Anything with green scales or beskar'gam armor," Luke said. "But not the Qrephs or their Sith friends. Those, we need to handle ourselves."

"I can do that," Lando said. "But do we really need a hot-drop? That courtyard looks big enough for a landing, and we'll have the *Falcon*'s laser cannons to cover—"

"Sorry, Lando," Leia said. "We need you and Omad flying top cover."

"Top cover?" Lando sounded insulted. "Just because I don't have the Force—"

"And aren't trained in Jedi assault tactics," Ben interrupted.

"Okay, that, too," Lando said. "But let's assume Dena is right about the Qrephs letting only a few Mandalorians know about this place. You're still going to be outnumbered four-to-one by Mandos—and at least twenty-to-one by Nargons."

"Which is why we need *you* to be sure our getaway ship stays in one piece," Leia said. She rose on her toes and kissed him on the cheek. "Lando, I love you for wanting to come, but . . . my husband, my plan."

Lando fell silent, then finally dropped his chin and nodded. "Okay, but you'd better come back." He cast a sidelong glance at Ben, then added, "*All* of you."

Luke clamped a hand on Lando's shoulder and gave it a reassuring squeeze. "We'll do our best, I promise." He turned to Ben. "What do you have for us? Anything yet?"

"Sure—take a look at this."

As Ben spoke, the holograph of a black angular shape—two pyramids stuck base-to-base—appeared in front of R2-D2's projector.

Ben looked across the lounge to Yus. "Does that thing look like what you've been calling Base Prime?"

"Yes, but Base Prime actually sits on its surface," Yus said, looking surprised. "The Qrephs refer to the thing itself as the artifact."

"The artifact?" Luke asked. "What did they mean by that?"

Yus shrugged. "They didn't discuss it with me," she said. "Sometimes I heard the Mandalorians call it 'the station,' but to the Qrephs it was always just 'the artifact.' I'm not sure that any of them actually knows what it is."

"Let's hope not," Lando said.

Yus's brow rose. "Why not?" she asked. "Do you know what—"

"Why don't you let us ask the questions?" Leia interrupted.

Yus studied Leia in silence for a moment, then said, "I thought I might have won a little trust when I helped you and Master Skywalker escape the *Ormni*."

"We'll talk trust when I have Han back," Leia said. "Until then you're still the lying sleemo who helped the Qrephs murder thirty thousand beings. Clear?"

Yus's expression grew even sadder. "I understand why you blame me. But you must also realize by now that I have every reason to help you rescue Captain Solo—that I *must* help you."

"Why would that be?" Leia asked. "And don't expect me to believe you've suddenly grown a conscience."

Yus looked confused. "You really haven't figured it out?"

"Figured out what?" Luke asked.

"That *I* am one of the Qrephs' creations—a *biot*," Yus replied. "My only hope of survival is to help you find Base Prime."

Leia's eyes narrowed. "How convenient."

Luke motioned for Leia to be patient, then asked, "And a biot is *what*, exactly?"

Yus dropped her eyes. "You've already had several fights with the first generation," she said. "The Nargons were designed as soldiers. But they lack the judgment to work on their own, so the Qrephs had to hire Mandalorians to oversee them."

Lando scowled and looked past Luke toward Leia. "Are you buying this?" he asked. "She looks as much like a Nargon as I do."

"Not on the outside," Yus said. "But on the inside I'm basically the same thing as they are: a sentient being, grown on a vanalloy skeleton, with fiber-optic filaments for nerves—and a cybernetic memory chip embedded in my brain."

"You're some sort of cyborg?" Ben asked, incredulous.

"You can't expect us to believe that, either," Luke said. "Your Force presence would feel . . . well, more different than it does."

"Because I'm *not* a cyborg," Yus said. "A cyborg is an organic being enhanced by technology. A biot is a living being *grown* around an inorganic core."

Everyone fell quiet, no doubt trying to imagine—as Luke was—the unconscionable applications of such technology.

Misinterpreting their silence, Yus said, "I'll prove it to you." She motioned to the captured 2-1B droid, then extended her arm. "Show them."

The droid quickly injected her forearm with an analgesic, then produced a scalpel and began to cut. When red blood spilled from the wound, Leia let her hand drop toward the lightsaber hanging on her belt.

"Nargon blood is blue," she said. "That looks just like mine."

"Because *I* am supposed to look human," Yus replied. "I am supposed to blush. I am supposed to bleed and feel pain. I am supposed to *pass*."

The droid used its suction attachment to draw the blood out of the wound, then peeled back a small flap of skin. Yus shakily raised her arm, and Luke saw the silver gleam of vanalloy.

"Is this proof enough?" Yus asked, directing the question at Leia—and looking even more pale than she had a few moments earlier. "Or do I need to show you my fiber-optic nerves?"

"I'll take your word for the nerves," Leia said. "But I still have my doubts about your change of allegiance."

Yus sighed. "You're right. I *haven't* changed allegiance. I could never raise a hand directly against the Qrephs—the chip in my brain would explode." She turned to Luke. "But I *do* want to live. That is the reason I've done . . . well, just about *everything*."

"And helping us find Base Prime helps you stay alive?" Luke asked. "How, exactly?"

"I can't live without a regular injection—an enzyme cocktail the Qrephs create at Base Prime. But they don't consider me useful any longer, so they've stopped supplying me."

Yus paused. Her eyes began to burn with real hatred— at least it felt that way in her Force aura—then she glanced toward the 2-1B droid.

"They didn't even think I was worth killing. They left me in the infirmary to die slowly and alone." She pointed an accusing finger at the droid. "While *he* monitored my decline and recorded the whole process."

Luke cocked a brow at the 2-1B. "Is that true?" he asked. "You didn't try to help her?"

"Her biochemistry is unique," the droid said, sounding almost defensive. "It's impossible to synthesize a replacement without access to the proper formula."

"And it's impossible to reverse-engineer the enzymes," Yus said. "That's how the Qrephs controlled me. It's how they control all their biots. We obey or they stop providing the enzymes."

"*All* their biots?" Leia echoed. "I'm not sure I want to ask this—but how many like you *are* there?"

"I'm guessing dozens," Luke said. He turned to Yus. "Isn't that how the Qrephs have been taking over so many conglomerates? By infiltrating biots like yourself into their management?"

Yus looked away. "It was how they were trying to take Lando's operation." She cast an apologetic look in Lando's direction—and was rewarded with an icy glare. "But I wouldn't know about any other acquisitions."

"You must have *some* idea." Leia crossed the deck to Yus and braced both hands on the arms of her chair. "You've already said you were part of a generation of biots. How many generations are there? And how many in a generation? A hundred? A *thousand*?"

Instead of shrinking away, Yus met Leia's gaze evenly. "Does this mean we have a deal?"

"With *you*?" Lando scoffed. He turned to Luke. "Be careful, old friend. Dena may be desperate for those so-called enzymes, but that doesn't mean helping us is her best shot at getting them. For all we know, she might be hoping to trade us for a lifetime supply."

"Clearly you don't understand the Qrephs," Yus said. "They may *promise* a lifetime supply, but they'll deliver only as long as it suits them. That's why I need you—to help me enter Base Prime and find the formula for my enzymes."

"Then we'll make the same deal with you," Luke said. "We'll do what we can for you—as long as you're useful to *us*."

"I suppose that's fair." Yus turned back to Leia. "To answer your questions, I don't think there could be more than thirty biots in my generation and a few hundred in the Nargons' generation. The lab isn't large, and maturation takes two years—at least it did for me."

"*Two* years? That's impossible," Luke said, starting to

grow angry with her. "The Qrephs have been in the Rift less than a year."

Yus's expression grew more confident. "You need my help even more than I realized, Master Skywalker," she said. "You're not accounting for the time dilation. A year in the Rift is closer to five years at Base Prime."

"*Time dilation?*" Luke echoed. "Are you saying the lab is . . ."

He stopped, trying to understand exactly what Yus was suggesting. Every starship pilot knew that as gravity and velocity increased, time slowed relative to an outside observer. But Yus seemed to be describing the opposite effect—that time moved *faster* in the lab.

"Are you saying the Qrephs have found a way to *accelerate* time?" Tahiri asked, finishing the question for Luke.

"It's not a way so much as a place," Yus replied. "That's why they built Base Prime where they did. Time seems to run faster on the artifact than it does in the rest of the Rift."

"Which sort of makes sense, given what's happening in the Bubble," Ben said. "If space is expanding *around* the artifact, it's not too surprising that time might be dilated *on* it."

"Or that the Qrephs would find a way to exploit the fact," Lando said, sounding almost envious. "If I could expand my production time without affecting my delivery date—that's a heck of an advantage, even for a *legitimate* business."

"But what does that have to do with Han?" Leia asked. "Why would they need him for any of this?"

Yus thought for a moment, then finally shook her head. "I have no idea," she said. "I couldn't begin to guess."

Luke studied her, searching her Force aura for the bitter taste of a lie. All he found was the same cloying despair that he had been sensing all along.

"But you're *sure* that's where they took Han?" Leia asked, pointing at the holograph. "To Base Prime?"

"It's where I *assume* they took Captain Solo," Yus corrected. "But it only makes sense. Base Prime is the ideal place to hide from the Jedi—from *anyone*. Only a handful of beings know how to reach it—and I'm not one of them."

Luke knelt closer to the holograph, his heart starting to pound in excitement as he studied its dark surface. He and the others had already discussed the possibility that Ohali Soroc had actually *found* the Mortis Monolith— as unbelievable as that seemed—and Yus's descriptions of its time-dilation properties only made that more likely. But he didn't want to get his hopes up. Finding a legendary place like Mortis after only a year of searching seemed almost *too* easy, and there was still the question of why Ohali's astromech had referred to it as a space station instead of a monolith.

He turned to Yus. "Who built that thing?" he asked, trying to make the question sound sincere. "Was it the Qrephs?"

Yus shook her head. "I doubt it," she said. "I don't think they understand it very well themselves—at least, they didn't when I was there half a year ago. They were still trying to create a gate so they could go inside."

"They were trying to go *inside*?" Luke asked, more worried than ever. Whatever the Qrephs had found— Mortis or not—it was clearly a place of great power, and the thought of them experimenting with it like some kind of corporate research project chilled him to the bone. "How close were they to succeeding?"

"Close, I think," she said. "But Savara Raine was trying to talk them out of it. I once heard her tell Marvid that only a fool toys with power he can't even perceive."

At the mention of Savara's name, Luke glanced over to check on his son. He had already broken the news about Vestara's new role as the Qrephs' assassin, and now Ben's eyes had gone distant and cold.

After a moment, Ben finally said, "Vestara is playing them. That's just what she does." He paused, then added, "But right now her goals aren't as important to us as whether she's there alone."

"Alone?" Yus looked confused. "Of course she is not alone. There are the Mandalorians—"

"We're not talking about Mandalorians," Tahiri interrupted. "Did there seem to be other people like Savara Raine around? Someone who could use the Force?"

Yus thought about it, then shook her head. "I'm not sure exactly what you are asking," she said. "But the answer is no. There is *no one* like Savara Raine."

Nineteen

Marvid followed Craitheus down a hundred meters of durasteel corridor, all the while fighting the urge to activate an arm cannon and start blasting. Naturally, Marvid had known all along that Han Solo was playing on his emotions—trying to turn him against his own brother. But the human was good. Solo had a way of picking at psychic scabs—even a Columi's psychic scabs—and understanding the man's strategy had done little to stop it from working.

Of course, Marvid recognized that the strategy had worked only because he *already* had suspicions about his brother's loyalty. Calrissian's offer to strike a separate deal had been a crude ploy, which made the delay in bringing it to Marvid's attention even more disturbing. Clearly, Craitheus had wanted time to analyze the offer, and that could only reflect the degree to which he had been tempted.

To Marvid's surprise, the messenger led them completely out of the laboratory wing and into the barracks annex. Craitheus transmitted a complaint about Savara expecting them to come to her. Marvid ignored him. Craitheus felt threatened by the girl's strategy of trying to insert herself between them, and at the moment Marvid wanted his brother to feel threatened. Besides, Savara was a valuable asset to him, one that balanced his brother's control of the Mandalorians, and he was glad to have her safely back at Base Prime.

Finally the Mandalorian opened the airtight hatch of a security-team briefing room and stepped aside. Inside, Savara stood at the front of the room, still dressed in a crimson flight suit as she addressed half a dozen Mandalorian officers. They were all studying the wall-sized vidscreen, which showed a detailed schematic of Base Prime's layout. The heavy-weapons emplacements were highlighted in bright yellow.

As the Qrephs whirred into the room, Savara glanced in their direction, then turned back to the Mandalorians. "That's all for now. I'm sure you'll be receiving orders shortly."

The Mandalorians looked warily at the Qrephs, then nodded brusquely and departed. Marvid started toward the aisle that ran up the center of the room between the metal benches. Craitheus sped up a smaller aisle along the wall and beat him to the front of the room.

"You are growing presumptuous, Savara," Craitheus said. "It is we who issue the orders, not you."

Savara's eyes grew cold and narrow, and she seemed to be debating the wisdom of killing him on the spot. Deciding he wasn't ready to disabuse her of the idea that she might actually be capable of playing the brothers off each other, Marvid raced the rest of the way and stopped at her side.

"Pay Craitheus no attention," Marvid said. "Captain Solo has put us both in a foul temper."

By way of explanation, he looked toward the end of his powerbody's armrest. Savara's eyes quickly followed. But when her gaze fell on his still-inflamed fingertips, her expression betrayed neither the sympathy nor respect he had expected—merely puzzlement.

"What happened?" she asked. "You stick your fingers in a power socket?"

Marvid had his powerbody spread its pincer arms. "Hardly. Barduun wanted to play pain stakes," he said. "And Captain Solo agreed. What can I say? I thought it would be fun to see Solo suffer."

Savara's brows arched. "You let Barduun play sabacc?" she asked. "With *you*?"

"Why wouldn't we?" Craitheus demanded. "He's our employee."

"He's your *mistake*," Savara retorted. "You should never have sent him through the gate with me. He nearly got us both killed."

"And yet you returned him to us alive," Marvid said.

"*Before* he went barvy," Savara pointed out. "Besides, you needed to see him. You should know what will happen if you go in there yourselves."

"Your concern is noted," Craitheus said. "And so is your fear that, once we have acquired the Force for ourselves, you will no longer be needed."

Savara merely rolled her eyes and turned to Marvid, but she was clearly seeking support where none would be found. Marvid and Craitheus had discussed the gate many times, and they were in complete agreement. Whatever had happened to Barduun inside the artifact, it had bestowed on him the ability to use the Force. And, now that they realized it was possible, the Qrephs were determined to have the Force for themselves. The emperor Palpatine had been a mental gnat compared to them, but he had also been a Force-user—and that had been enough for him to subjugate the galaxy.

So the brothers were determined to go through the gate—when they were ready. First they needed to determine the cause of Barduun's insanity and to learn more about what had happened inside the artifact. Unfortunately, given Barduun's mad ramblings and Savara's absolute refusal to discuss the subject, neither task was proving easy. And because only a Force-user could open the gate, they would need to take along a Force-user they could confidently control—and even Marvid realized that Savara did not qualify in that regard. Still, the Qrephs *would* be going through the gate . . . just as soon as they had identified all the risks and minimized the unknowns.

When Marvid's only reply to her appeal was a pointed silence, Savara's expression turned petulant. "Fine. Let me know when you're ready, and I'll dump you through the gate myself." She let her gaze drop to Marvid's inflamed fingertips, then added, "Maybe you'll have better luck in there than you did in your sabacc game."

"The game was a calculated risk," Marvid said. He knew that Savara's insolence was deliberate, a tactic designed to irritate Craitheus and make Marvid treat her as an equal, but he couldn't help feeling defensive. She just had that effect on him. "Solo's stress levels weren't rising high enough to accurately map his mind."

"That's because he's a better sabacc player than you are," Savara said. "I'm surprised he doesn't *own* Base Prime by now."

"And I'm surprised we continue to tolerate your insolence," Craitheus retorted. "Now, if you're done wasting our time, where are the bodies?"

"We'd like to show them to Captain Solo before he dies," Marvid added. "Especially Princess Leia's. That will generate some interesting stress peaks."

"There aren't any bodies," Savara said. "Or body parts. The crash on the *Ormni* didn't produce any."

Craitheus expressed his frustration by loudly extending his powerbody into a more upright configuration. Marvid merely settled onto the floor, remaining in his nonthreatening, semi-seated shape.

"Pity, but you aren't to blame," Marvid said. "We knew there was a chance their corpses would be incinerated in such a fiery crash."

"You're missing the point," Savara said. "There were never any corpses. Luke Skywalker is alive. So is Leia Solo."

"Impossible," Craitheus hissed. "We saw them crash."

"We kept a record of it," Marvid added. "We studied it on the trip from the *Ormni*. There was no possibility of survival."

"The temperatures reached three thousand degrees," Craitheus said. "No one could have escaped that."

"*Jedi* could," Savara said. "And they did."

"My dear, you *must* try to mitigate your awe of the Jedi." Marvid paused, then added, "The explosion when they struck the *Ormni*—"

"Was a concussion missile penetrating the hull," Savara interrupted. "And the inferno that followed was their fusion core blowing—after they abandoned ship. I am not in *awe* of the Jedi. I know what they can do."

Marvid began to feel nauseous.

Craitheus scoffed. "I assume you found evidence that led you to such an implausible conclusion?"

"Of course," Savara said.

"And what *is* that evidence?" Craitheus asked, clearly still more annoyed than alarmed. "Would it be too much to hope for something more tangible than your opinions and feelings?"

"Not at all," Savara replied. "How about the trail of bodies they left during their escape? Is that tangible enough for you?"

"Escape?" Marvid had to have his powerbody inject him with a dose of stomach calmer. "You're certain?"

"If Skywalker and his sister were still aboard the *Ormni*," Savara asked, "would I be here?"

"Well, you *do* make a point at every opportunity of telling us how dangerous Skywalker is," Craitheus said, "so coming here would appear to be the smart move."

"The smart move would be to leave and let you handle them on your own," Savara countered. "But that would mean abandoning Base Prime."

"You led them *here*?" Craitheus demanded.

"Of course not," Savara said. "But they captured Dena Yus. And even if she doesn't know how to *find* Base Prime, she knows it exists. That's all the Jedi will need."

Marvid glanced at his brother. I TOLD YOU THE MANDA-LORIANS WERE A MISTAKE. THEY DID NOTHING BUT ATTRACT JEDI ATTENTION.

Craitheus looked away. WE HAD TO PROTECT OUR IN-VESTMENT. CALRISSIAN WASN'T GIVING UP.

"Did you hear what I said?" Savara demanded. "They have Dena Yus. They're going to find Base Prime—any time now."

"Then shouldn't you be stopping them?" Craitheus asked.

"That's *Luke Skywalker* out there," Savara said. "I wouldn't have a chance. Not alone."

"But you think we could win *here*?" Marvid asked, growing hopeful. "Together?"

Savara shook her head. "*I* can win here," she said. "You don't understand how Jedi fight, and you have no concept of the power of the Force."

"So, of course, you want command of our security force," Craitheus surmised. "Otherwise we are on our own."

A half smirk came to Savara's face. "Well, you still have Mirta Gev, if you'd rather trust your lives to a buckethead."

"You may wish to reconsider that statement." Marvid was pleased to see the flash of surprise that his ire brought to her face. He might be fond of the girl, but she was still an employee, and it was always wise to remind one's underlings of their place. "You know how we feel about ultimatums."

"It's a strategy, not an ultimatum," Savara said, only slightly chastened. "And it's a fact. Gev can't win this fight. If you leave her in command, Han Solo is as good as free—and you two are as good as dead."

"And yet *you* are the one who let them escape from the *Ormni* in the first place," Craitheus pointed out. To Marvid, he transmitted, YOU KNOW WHAT SHE WANTS.

OF COURSE, Marvid replied. BASE PRIME, GALACTIC SYNDICATED, THE GATE—EVERYTHING WE HAVE. THAT IS WHAT MAKES HER SPECIAL.

IT MAKES HER A *THREAT*, Craitheus objected. I CALCULATE A 52 PERCENT CHANCE THAT SHE LET THE JEDI ESCAPE AND DELIBERATELY LED THEM HERE TO FORCE OUR HAND.

WHICH MAKES HER A MORE CUNNING COMMANDER THAN MIRTA GEV, Marvid countered. To Savara, he said, "The Mandalorians will never take orders from you. You would need to work through Gev."

"Gev is a soldier," Savara said. "She understands the chain of command—as long as Craitheus makes it clear who's running things."

DO YOU THINK I HAVE A BLEEDING CEREBRUM? Craitheus transmitted. I SEE WHAT YOU ARE PLANNING. I SEE HOW YOU DOTE ON THE GIRL.

I HAVE NEVER PUT SAVARA AHEAD OF OUR PARTNERSHIP, Marvid shot back. YOU, ON THE OTHER HAND, WERE TEMPTED BY CALRISSIAN'S PLOY.

THERE IS A DIFFERENCE BETWEEN ANALYZING AND ACCEPTING, Craitheus replied. YOU WOULD HAVE DONE THE SAME.

"Do we have a deal or not?" Savara demanded. "I need time to organize our defenses here—or to slip away, if you two are determined to get yourselves killed."

Marvid continued to glare at his brother. WE NEED HER TO HANDLE THE JEDI.

Craitheus let his chin drop in acknowledgment. BUT WE CANNOT GIVE HER COMMAND OF THE NARGONS. SHE IS AMBITIOUS, AND IF SHE COMMANDS THE NARGONS—

SHE WILL TAKE EVERYTHING, Marvid finished. SHE IS DANGEROUS THAT WAY.

THEN WE UNDERSTAND EACH OTHER, Craitheus said.

Marvid spun his powerbody toward the exit. "Very well, Lady Raine." He used a manipulator arm to motion Savara after him. "Come along. We'll give Mirta Gev the unhappy news together."

Instead of following, Savara turned toward Craitheus. "And you're in agreement?" she asked. "*I* am in command of Base Prime's defense?"

"Oh, complete agreement." Craitheus gave her a sly smile. "What other choice have you left us?"

Twenty

The way Han saw the game now, the problem was Ditto's eye. She was afraid the pain of having it burned—even if it was only a simulated burn—would leave it blind. So, after Gev refused to allow Han's string bet, Ditto had called Barduun's bet of a broken nose and hoped the next chip-card would save her.

It hadn't, and now she was sitting on a twelve-card hand, facing a very painful session with the torture droid. If Ditto's score wasn't a bomb-out already, it soon would be. Meanwhile, Barduun was sitting next to her, drinking in all that fear she was pouring into the Force.

"The bet's to you, Solo," Gev reminded him. Her finger was poised over the zapper button, ready to give him another brain jolt if he tried to cheat again. "We checking it around?"

"Not this time."

As Han spoke, he was watching Barduun, looking for the dusky tell that would suggest the fiend was worried.

It wasn't there.

So Barduun had a pretty decent score, and Han had absolute zero. The smart play would be to bet small and keep the hand going, hoping Barduun would make a mistake or suffer a bad card shift.

But the Qrephs were out of the game, which meant they were thinking about something other than Han

Solo. And *that* had to change. Han needed to do something to set them off, to keep their minds on *him* instead of on the Jedi coming for them.

Han turned toward Gev. "*Now* I bet death, and I call the—" He stopped when Gev's finger started to descend toward the button, then smiled and said, "Oh . . . that's right. I can't do that yet."

"Cute, Solo," Gev said. "I should scramble your brains for trying to call the hand out of sequence."

Han shrugged. "As long as the death bet stands." He paused, trying to think of a way to scare Ditto into folding, then finally decided he had no choice but to cheat by announcing his intention to end the hand. "I can always call the hand after—"

Gev's finger came down, and the probe needles in his head unleashed a blast of crackling pain. He slumped in his chair, shuddering and half paralyzed, until Ohali Soroc's red Duros eyes grew even larger and rounder than usual.

"Stop!" Ohali said. "It is no fault of Captain Solo's if you have fallen for the Qrephs' false promises."

Good, Han thought. Ohali understood his plan.

Gev glared at Ohali, then released the button. "This has nothing to do with the Qrephs," she said. "Solo was cheating *again.*"

"You punish Captain Solo for speaking out of turn," Ohali said. "Yet you work for the Qrephs when you know they will renege on their promises."

"They've paid me so far," Gev said.

"Sure, while th-th-they . . . still need you," Han said, beginning to recover from the jolt. If he could make Gev really angry, she might forget about Ohali long enough for the Duros to disable the brain-zapper button. "But you're a karking fool if you actually believe they can get rid of that nanokiller."

But Gev wouldn't take the bait. She shook her head, then turned to Ditto. "The bet is to you."

"I have to withdraw." Ditto gathered her chip-cards and sent them spinning into the discard pile, her shoulders slumping as she contemplated her losses. "When Captain Solo calls the hand, I'll bomb out."

Han quickly turned to Barduun. "What about you?" He racked his brain trying to recall the Mandalorian word for *coward*. If he couldn't get Gev to bite, maybe Barduun would take a swing at him. "You have the guts to call—or are you just another of Gev's *hut'uuns*?"

Seemingly unfazed, Barduun studied Han for a moment, then shook his head. "Jhonus Raam folds."

"I *knew* you'd fold!" Han let out a whoop, then flipped his chip-cards over, revealing his score of absolute zero. "Look at that, fool!"

Usually, there was no faster way for a gambler to get punched than to gloat over a big bluff. But Barduun wasn't falling for it. He shot Han a knowing sneer.

"They would not have let you risk a coma, anyway," Barduun replied, using the Force to return his own chip-cards to Gev. "The chiefs are not finished mapping your mind."

By then the torture droid was standing behind Ditto, waiting for her to turn around so he could collect her bets. Ditto was pretending not to notice, staring straight ahead and clearly frightened. Deciding the key to making Barduun mad would be to deny his appetite for fear, Han waved the droid away.

"It's okay," he said. "She doesn't have to pay. I don't want her pain."

Ditto looked up, her blue brow raised in hope. "You are forgiving my debt?"

"Sure thing." Han glanced at Barduun and was pleased to see an angry glower directed his way. "Pain isn't really my thing. Besides, no one wants to keep playing."

"*I* do," Barduun said.

Han shrugged. "Suit yourself, but I'm done." He looked across the table at Gev. "Barduun doesn't have to pay, either. I just want—"

"*No.*"

To Han's surprise, the objection came not from Barduun but from the doorway behind him. Two pairs of heavy feet pounded across the floor, then a huge green arm stretched over his shoulder to point at Ditto.

"The game continues," said a gravelly Nargon voice. "Those are the orders we have."

Han twisted around and found both Nargons standing two meters behind him. Their blaster rifles were still holstered at their knees, but he knew better than to attack. Leia had been hard-pressed to bring down just *one* of the things, and she had been using a lightsaber. All Han had going for him was that nobody expected him to be crazy enough to try something.

But crazy was better than giving up. He glanced across the table and nodded to Ohali—and saw Mirta Gev reaching for the brain-zapper button again.

"Don't even think . . ." Gev let the threat trail off when her hand suddenly reversed directions and rose beyond reach of the button. "What the *brix*?"

For an instant, Han thought Ohali had used the Force to keep him from being zapped. But she looked just as confused as Han did, and it was Barduun's hand that he saw gesturing in Gev's direction.

Gev seemed to figure it out at the same time Han did. "Barduun, what the *hell* are you doing?"

Barduun glanced in Han's direction. *Go.*

Whether the voice had sounded in his ears or only in his head, Han could not tell—and he didn't care. He slid out of his chair and down onto the floor, a hundred sharp stings stabbing his head as the probe needles tore free. In the next moment, he was sitting on his rump, surrounded by ankles and knees, with ribbons of bright color dancing through his vision and sweet birdsong chiming in his ears.

That couldn't be good.

Gev's muffled voice sounded through the tabletop. "Don't just stand there, you finheads!" Her hands appeared beneath the table, reaching down toward her ankle. "Stop them!"

Of course. Gev's dealer outfit didn't include a sidearm, and when it came to weapons, Mandalorians never went "naked." Forcing himself to spin around, Han leaned back and reached over his head, hooking his hands behind Gev's ankles. She cried out in alarm and kicked at him, but Han was already pulling, dragging her out of her chair. As she tried to twist away, her head struck the table with a satisfying thump. Then her hands withdrew, grabbing at the arms of her chair.

A pair of loud crashes shook the room as someone—either Ohali or Barduun—Force-hurled the Nargons back toward the door. Han turned his head and spotted four scaly legs—all he could see of the guards from beneath the table—bouncing off the far wall. Their green hands quickly dropped into view, reaching for the blaster rifles in their holsters.

Han clutched Gev's ankles as tightly as he could with one hand, then rolled to his belly and used his free hand to push up her pant leg.

She kicked him in the head, and he smelled Leia's perfume.

Han held tight and shook the effect off. The next time he had a bunch of probe needles stuck in his brain, he would try to find a better way to get them out. His hand reached Gev's calf and felt two heavy neolene straps, then it found a small sheath hanging on her shin.

Gev kicked him again, even harder, and the birdsong in Han's head became a cacophony of cockpit damage alarms. He slipped a slender hilt out of the sheath and found himself armed with a vibroknife. He activated the blade and immediately sank it into the leg that had been assaulting him.

Gev screamed and began to kick at Han with her other foot. He blocked with his free arm, then saw her hand shooting down toward her knee, clutching at her pant leg as she tried to reach her second weapon.

Han slashed the vibroknife up, down, then up again and felt a neolene strap come apart. Gev landed a knife-hand strike that snapped Han's head to the side and had him tasting salt. But a palm-sized holster was already dropping out of her shredded pant leg into a warm cascade of blood. Han snatched the weapon and retreated from her flailing feet, then unsnapped the keeper strap and withdrew a powerful little MandalTech W202 hold-out blaster.

By then the perfume smell was beginning to seem more like sweat, and the chiming in his ears had given way to the screech and sizzle of blaster fire. Han released the W202's safety catch, then raised his hand—only to find himself looking at the bottom of Gev's chair as she toppled backward to spare herself a bolt through her stomach.

There was a reason Mandalorians made good mercenaries: quick reflexes and even quicker thinking. Han fired into the bottom of the chair anyway—and nearly lost an ear when one of the underpowered bolts ricocheted back.

Even with a slashed-up leg, Gev would be back in the fight soon. From what Han could see, the Nargons were directing most of their fire toward Barduun's end of the table. Han rolled the other way and began to crawl.

He had gone about two arm lengths when a thunderous crack shook the room. Everything strobed blue, and the floor shuddered beneath his hands and knees. For an instant he thought his brain had blown its main breaker—then he realized that the blaster rifles had stopped screeching.

He glanced toward the door and found both Nargons pinned against the wall. Their heavy tails were slamming the floor in mad convulsions, and their legs were dancing beneath crooked lines of Force lightning.

"Get their blasters!" Barduun boomed.

Han scrambled from beneath the table. Barduun stood at the other end, both arms extended as he continued to blast the Nargons with Force lightning.

Han blinked, hard—but he felt pretty sure he wasn't hallucinating. A Mandalorian, spraying Force lightning.

"Their blasters!" Barduun repeated.

"Uh, sure thing, pal." Han eyed the long green fingers still wrapped around the stocks of the blaster rifles, then tucked Gev's holdout blaster into his waistband and started forward with the vibroknife. "Got it covered."

Ohali Soroc pulled him back with the Force. "Allow me."

He turned to find the Duros raising a hand toward the nearest Nargon. She tore the Nargon's weapon free and floated it over to Han. He tucked the vibroknife into his waistband alongside the holdout blaster and took the rifle, then turned to keep an eye on the back of the room.

Ditto still sat in her chair, a look of shock on her face and a smoking crater in her forehead. Gev was nowhere to be seen, but a blood smear on the floor led toward the wet bar on the adjacent wall.

"Forget Gev," Barduun said, still blasting the Nargons with Force lightning—and starting to sound tired. As soon as Ohali had the second blaster rifle in hand, Barduun began to back toward an iris hatch in the room's rear corner. "This way."

Han pointed his blaster rifle toward the main door, next to the two Nargons. "Isn't *that* the way out?"

"Did Jhonus Raam offer you a choice?" Barduun reached the rear hatch and looked toward the control panel, then used the Force to enter an access code. "Come along or die. *That* is your choice."

Barduun lowered his hands, and the Force lightning sizzled out. The two Nargons immediately began to stumble forward—slow and shaky, but not so shaky that Han felt like trying to dodge past them. Hoping a heavy blaster rifle would do something against the reptiloids, he opened fire.

The bolts bounced off, but they were more effective than his pistol had been at the Red Ronto. At least these weapons *singed* the scales.

The Nargons' tails began to swish back and forth, and their gait grew steadier.

"Uh, maybe we'd better go with the big guy after all," Han said.

"Agreed." Ohali was already backing toward the hatch. "For now."

Han joined her, and they each raised a rifle to target a Nargon. By the time they had backed through the hatchway into the corridor beyond, both reptiloids had huge scorch circles on their torsos. And both reptiloids were continuing to advance.

Han dropped his aim to the knees and was relieved to see two bolts penetrate. The Nargon kept coming, but at least there were a couple of spurts of blue blood.

Barduun reached for the control panel on their side of the hatch, and both Nargons hurled themselves forward. Han switched to firing at the head and managed to shave the skull crest off his target. Ohali put a bolt through the eye of hers, and Han saw the reptiloid go limp—just before the iris hatch closed around its outstretched arm.

The hatch gave a mechanical wheeze and continued

to contract around the Nargon's muscular forearm. The scales shattered with a series of loud pops, then the hatch leaves sliced through its flesh clear down to the vanalloy.

"*Blast!*" Barduun cursed. He pointed at the control panel. "Kill it. Maybe that will give us enough time."

Han blew the panel cover off with a couple of blaster bolts. "Enough time for what, exactly?"

When Barduun did not answer immediately, Han passed his rifle to Ohali and began to sort through control-panel wires, using his vibroknife to strip insulation and reroute circuits.

"Enough time for *what*?" he demanded again.

"To free the princess," Barduun called back. By the sound of his voice, he was already ten meters down the corridor behind them. "Jhonus Raam is her only hope!"

Han turned to Ohali. "Princess?"

Ohali shrugged. "Who knows?"

Han finished jamming the hatch, then retrieved his blaster rifle and turned to survey the corridor. On one side, a floor-to-ceiling transparisteel wall overlooked an empty courtyard. On the opposite side stood five large air locks and not much else. Barduun was at the third air lock, holding the hatch open and looking impatient.

"I don't like this," Han said quietly. "Any idea where we are?"

Ohali pointed to the air locks. "Those open into the fabrication labs, where the Qrephs create the Nargons and the . . . copies, I suppose."

"Like Ditto?"

Ohali hesitated, then said, "Yes . . . among others."

Han turned and looked out across the courtyard. On the far side sat a large arch-roofed hangar. It couldn't be more than a hundred meters distant, but Han had stood on the surface of enough airless moons to recognize a hard vacuum when he saw one.

There was no easy way across the courtyard. If they wanted to reach the hangar, they would have to fight back through the room they had just left, then work their way through the barracks annex.

Still looking out across the courtyard, Han asked Ohali, "I don't suppose there's an underground tunnel or something that can get us from here to over there."

"Afraid not," Ohali said. "As far as I can tell, this monolith doesn't seem to have an underground *anything*."

Han's gaze snapped back toward the Duros. *"Monolith?"* he repeated. "Then this is—"

"Mortis?" Ohali shook her head. "It may be a Celestial monolith, but it's not Mortis—at least, I hope it isn't."

Han frowned. "Why's that?"

Ohali made a point of not looking in Barduun's direction. "Because whatever Barduun has become," she said, "I'm pretty sure it was the monolith that did it to him."

A sinister laugh echoed down the corridor from the third air lock, and Han looked over to see Barduun sneering at them in contempt.

"There is no escape now, Captain Solo," Barduun said. He extended a hand, and Han suddenly found himself being dragged down the corridor. "We are in this to the end, the three of us."

Twenty-one

Like all of the repeater beacons the *Millennium Falcon* had located in the Bubble, the one ahead was an immense, bulging cylinder pocked by conical transceiver dishes. The *Falcon*'s approach had triggered its automatic hazard strobe, and now, every two seconds, a brilliant silver flash lit vast blue banks of plasma rolling in on it from either side. Luke thought the resulting navigation lane was probably a kilometer wide and a million kilometers high.

But this time the *Falcon* wasn't the only vessel in the abyss. When the hazard strobe went dark, a tiny blue halo appeared to each side of the beacon and grew larger before Luke's eyes. The tactical display was so filled with plasma static that it did not show the two craft at all, but Luke had flown in enough space battles to recognize oncoming starfighters when he saw them—a pair of Mandalorian Bes'uliiks, most likely. This deep in the Bubble, there was not much else they *could* be.

"*There,*" Omad said, pointing through the forward viewport. Still seated behind the pilot's yoke, he had called everyone to the flight deck just a few moments earlier. "You see them? They launched from the beacon's service deck, right after the strobe activated."

"We see them," Leia said, slipping into the copilot's chair. "Are you sure those are the only two?"

"Of course," Omad replied. "The beacon's service deck is too small to hold more than two Bessies."

"There could be more on patrol," Tahiri suggested. The first to reach the flight deck, she was wedged against the tug captain's left shoulder. "And how do you know they're Bessies?"

Omad looked up at her and flashed a dazzling smile. "Trust me," he said. "There are no more on patrol, and those two are Bes'uliiks."

Tahiri arched her brow. "Because . . ."

"Because what good would it be to fly a patrol route through this stuff?" Omad asked. "The plasma is so thick you can't locate your own cannon tips. And who else would be hanging around out here? Only the Qrephs and their Mandos, guarding the final approach to Base Prime."

"The final approach?" Leia asked hopefully. "Are you sure?"

Omad nodded. "I'm sure." He flashed another grin. "But if you need another day to plan, we could always turn—"

"Don't even think about turning back," Leia interrupted. She hooked her thumb toward the access corridor. "Tahiri, you and Ben get back there and take the laser cannons. Lando, get those YVHs ready. Omad, you prep the dropsuits."

"Me?" Omad asked. "I don't know anything about Jedi equipment. Besides, I'm the pilot."

Lando spoke from the back of the flight deck. "Sorry, friend—you're a great pilot, but you're no Jedi." He stepped aside so Ben and Tahiri could run for the cannon turrets. "Come on—I'll show you how to prep dropsuits. They work like those vac shells your prospecting crews use to blast samples."

As Omad relinquished the yoke, Luke motioned Leia toward the pilot's seat. She stayed put.

"You take pilot," Leia said, strapping herself in. "I'll handle the missiles."

"Leia," Luke said patiently. "I know you're worried about Han, but you can't—"

"Quit worrying about me," Leia protested. "I'm not going Dark Leia on you. It's just that our missile-loader has been sticking lately, and—"

"Gotcha." Luke slipped into the pilot's seat, then strapped himself in and took the helm. "It's better to have someone who knows the kinks handling the loader."

By then the approaching haloes had swelled to the size of Luke's thumbnail, which meant the *Falcon* was well within their attack range. He glanced down at the tactical display, but it continued to show only static. He was guessing that, with Rift plasma all around, the Mandalorian displays looked just as useless.

"Artoo, let me know the instant they have a target-lock on us," Luke said. "Leia, try to hail them. It probably won't do any good, but—"

"I know, I know. We can't launch an unprovoked attack," Leia finished, reaching for the comm set. Her voice dropped to a wispy mutter. "Even if they *are* Mandalorians."

She stopped short of hailing the vessel when R2-D2 let out an alert whistle. Lock alarms began to scream throughout the ship, then a series of deep whumps rolled through the *Falcon* as Ben and Tahiri test-fired their weapons in response.

An instant later, two tiny red dots appeared in front of the lead Bes'uliik and rapidly began to grow larger— a pair of rocket engines, propelling missiles toward the *Falcon*.

"Okay, *now* we've been provoked," Luke said. "Take them out."

The launch doors clunked open, and a slender white cylinder drifted out past the viewport. It quickly ignited, then shot forward on a pillar of orange flame. Neither Bes'uliik took evasive action—probably because their own astromechs were reporting that the *Falcon* had not even attempted to achieve a target-lock on them. The Mandalorian pilots were no doubt chuckling into their comm mics, assuming that the *Falcon*'s gunner had simply panicked and launched a wild shot without remembering to get a target-lock.

Never assume.

Luke glanced over at Leia. She had closed her eyes and was raising her hands, reaching out in the Force to locate their foes. The *Falcon*'s missile began to drift toward the rear Bes'uliik—the one that *hadn't* launched its own missiles yet—and still the pilot maintained his course.

By then the two Mandalorian missiles had become flickering circles of fire the size of Luke's fists. Too close.

Luke toggled the intercom. "Anytime back there."

"Just waiting for the order, Dad."

Eight streaks of color lanced out from the *Falcon*'s laser cannons, and the enemy missiles vanished in boiling balls of flame.

That made the Mandalorian pilots reevaluate. The lead Bes'uliik rolled to port and disappeared into the plasma. His wingman launched all four of his missiles, then opened fire with his laser cannon and went into an evasive gyre—which did nothing at all to prevent Leia from guiding her own missile into him.

Usually, when one of the *Falcon*'s concussion missiles struck a starfighter, the only thing left of the target was a ball of flame and shrapnel. But Bes'uliik hulls were made of beskar, an iron so tough that even lightsabers could not cut it. Instead of obliterating the craft, the detonation merely punched a hole through both walls of its fuselage. The Bes'uliik continued to spiral up the lane, more or less on its original course. But now its cannons had gone silent, and it was bleeding smoke and flame into the starless void.

The *Falcon*'s laser cannons chugged steadily as Ben and Tahiri opened fire again. The first two missiles erupted into flame almost instantly. But the second set kept coming, approaching so fast that the *Falcon*'s turrets couldn't swing around fast enough to track the targets.

Tahiri's voice came over the intercom. "A little help up there!"

Luke immediately turned toward the oncoming missiles and rolled the *Falcon* up on edge. The fiery circles of efflux expanded to a meter across—then finally diverged, one silver cylinder streaking beneath the *Falcon*'s belly and the other passing across her back.

Luke clenched his jaw and waited for the whump–jolt of a proximity detonation. He heard only Ben and Tahiri gasping over the intercom, then the pounding squeal of their laser cannons discharging.

"Got mine," Tahiri said.

"Show-off." The rising screech of a prolonged burst followed, then Ben announced, "Got it. We're clear."

Luke rolled the *Falcon* back down and steered toward the repeater beacon.

"*No,*" Leia said. She began to power down the sensor and communications equipment. "We're going after that Bessie."

"Leia, you know we can't," Luke said. "That pilot bugged out."

"A Mandalorian? Bugging out that easy?" Leia shook her head and took the navigation computer off-line. "Think about it, Luke. With all this plasma, there's only one sure way to deliver a message."

"In person," Luke said, feeling a little foolish. "Those Bes'uliiks weren't guards—they were lookouts."

Leia nodded. "If we can catch the one that just left, we can follow him straight back to Base Prime—"

"And hit the Qrephs *before* they know we're coming."

Luke swung the *Falcon* into the plasma bank, doing his best to follow the same vector as the fleeing Bes'uliik. He found himself flying blind, with nothing ahead but a swirling blue glow, so vast and deep that he lost all sense of distance and direction.

"Whoa, Dad!" Ben called. "Where'd the lake come from?"

"Jokes . . . later," Luke said, taking a breath to calm himself. "Busy now."

He began to open himself more fully to the Force, extending his awareness ahead, reaching out to search . . . He found the Bes'uliik crew—a pair of tense, focused presences—just ahead and a little to port. He swung the *Falcon* into line behind them, shoved the throttles forward, and then it really *did* feel like he was flying through a lake.

The viewport became a solid wall of blue, and an eerie silence fell over the flight deck. All sensation of movement ceased, and Luke realized that even R2-D2 had gone quiet. He glanced back to find the droid's processor light frozen in mid-blink, his logic display caught midway between one readout and another. Luke shifted his gaze to Leia and found her eyes fixed on him, unmoving as glass yet still alert and alive, frozen in blue amber.

A heartbeat later, the Mandalorian presences were *there,* so close that Luke felt as if he were on top of them. The bright-hot disks of twin ion engines appeared in front of the *Falcon* and swelled larger, then Luke sensed another presence ahead—a dark, ancient presence that seemed to be reaching into him even as he reached for it.

A cold ache came to his chest. His breath grew short, and he felt his body's warmth oozing from his old wound.

"Luke!"

Leia grabbed his shoulder. She shook him, hard, and he saw that they had caught the Bes'uliik—that the *Falcon* was about to fly straight up its thrust nozzles.

"Luke, are you trying to get us—"

"Open fire!" Luke ordered. "Take them out *now*!"

Two torrents of cannon bolts converged on the Bes'uliik, so quickly that it seemed Ben and Tahiri had opened fire before Luke gave the order. No matter. The starfighter exploded from the inside out, its hatches and access panels tumbling away on boiling pillars of flame, its canopy flashing orange before it disintegrated into a spray of molten beads. Luke slammed the yoke forward, diving beneath the fireball into the blue miasma beyond.

Once he felt certain they had cleared the explosion, Luke pulled the throttles back and exhaled in relief—then felt a cold wave of agony spreading through his chest.

"Luke, have you gone spacesick?" Leia demanded. "Without that Bessie, we can't find Base Prime!"

"Finding Base Prime isn't going to be a problem," Luke said. He took another breath, this time more gingerly, then reached under his robe and massaged the scar tissue over his old wound. "I'm pretty sure it just found *us*."

Twenty-two

Han had not gone three steps before he heard loud banging behind him. When he stopped to look, the dead Nargon's crushed arm was still protruding from the hatch he had just short-circuited, but now it was waving back and forth. For a moment, he feared the thing had somehow reanimated. Then the big green appendage began to jerk up and down, and he realized someone was on the other side, trying to use the arm to pry open the hatch.

"*Captain Solo,*" Barduun called impatiently.

Han felt himself being Force-dragged down the corridor, and he turned to see Barduun's hand raised in his direction.

"Hurry," Barduun continued. "We have little time."

"Hey, take it easy, will you?" Han started to walk on his own again. "I was just checking my work."

Barduun and Ohali had already entered the number-three air lock. Han stepped in after them. Barduun used the Force to seal the outer hatch, then he activated the cycle. Instead of the distant thrum of an air compressor, Han heard the clunk of tiny doors overhead, and when he craned his neck back, he saw a dozen spray nozzles descending from the ceiling.

Barduun gripped Han's neck and tipped his head forward. "Eyes closed," he commanded. "You must be ready to shoot straight, and we are about to be sanitized. The sterilizing agent will blur your vision."

"Shooting straight is always good," Han said. The nozzles began to hiss, and he closed his eyes as the air grew acrid. "So, what am I shooting?"

"Anything that gets in the way," Barduun replied. "You will find many targets."

"And what *is* our way?" Ohali asked. "Because, unless you know a secret route to the hangar, we can't escape through here."

Barduun responded with a booming, sinister laugh. "*Escape?* It is not escape that Han Solo desires. It is revenge—and Jhonus Raam will give it to him."

"Revenge?" Han had a feeling he knew what Barduun was hinting at, and he didn't like it. "Revenge for what, exactly?"

Barduun chuckled. "You know. The Qrephs told you."

"Look, if you're saying Leia is dead, forget it. Jedi don't die that easy." It was the same thing Han had been telling himself since the Qrephs bragged about ambushing her and Luke on the *Ormni*—and it was beginning to sound old, even to him. "In case you haven't noticed, the Qrephs are liars."

"Jhonus Raam felt no deception in their words." Barduun's voice shifted toward Ohali. "Perhaps Jedi Soroc felt something different?"

Ohali hesitated before answering—and a black hole opened in Han's gut.

"*No.*" Eyes clamped shut, he spun back toward the corridor—not sure *why*, exactly, just knowing that he needed to go back and kill something. "They really got Luke and Leia?"

The nozzles stopped hissing. A whir sounded overhead, and the purple glow of a disinfection lamp shone through his closed eyelids. Ohali laid her hand on Han's shoulder. He could feel her touch growing warm and soft as she called on the Force, trying to soothe him.

"What Barduun and I felt only suggests what the Qrephs *believed*," she said. "They could easily have been mistaken."

Han knew better than that. A Columi lie? *Sure.* But make a mistake? *Not real likely.*

He shook his head. "Columi don't make that kind of mistake."

The purple glow faded, and Han opened his eyes. Ohali was standing between him and Barduun, her blaster rifle held at port arms across her chest. The emitter nozzle might not have been *aimed* at Barduun's head, but it was pointed in that direction.

"*Everybody* makes mistakes, Captain Solo," Ohali said. "You must believe that. If you give up on Leia now, the Qrephs have already won."

As much as Han *wanted* to believe the Duros, he wasn't sure he could do it anymore. The Qrephs had outplayed him too many times. They had shaved his head and stuck probes in his brain, and they had shocked him until he had a permanent headache and a tremor in his left hand.

But that was nothing compared to this, to taking Leia.

"If you think I'm giving up," Han said, "you're dead wrong." Now he wanted blood—purple *Columi* blood. "I'm not giving up. In fact, I'm just getting started."

"Captain Solo!" Ohali hit Han in the gut with the butt of her blaster rifle. "Han! You *must* see what Barduun is doing."

"Yeah, I see." Han glanced over at Barduun, who was watching the exchange with a confident smirk. "He's using me to settle his score with the Qrephs. So what?"

"He's using you to feed his dark-side power," she said. "Don't you see that? He needs your rage."

Han scowled. "Fine," he said. "I hope he puts it to

good use. As long as the Qrephs pay, I'm good with that."

The inner hatch hissed open, revealing the lab beyond. Roughly twelve meters square, the room was divided into half a dozen aisles, each lined with a row of tall, upright vats resembling bacta tanks. The sides of the vats were opaque, but the front panels were curved and transparent.

"The Nargons will be after us again soon," Barduun said. "And, this time, more will come."

Motioning his companions to follow, Barduun left the air lock and started toward the left wall of the lab. Ohali blocked Han's way. He rolled his eyes and gently pushed her aside, then stepped past her.

"Captain Solo, please don't do this," she said to his back. "You may be happy to die here . . . but *I* am not."

Her plea hit home. Han realized he was doing it again—running off half-cocked, not thinking about the consequences to himself or anyone else. If he wanted to beat the Qrephs, he had to stay sharp; he needed to think.

Finally Han nodded. "Whatever happens, don't let me get in your way." He glanced back at her. "If you see a chance to run, you take it."

"Without you? Captain—"

Han raised a hand to stop her. "Look, one of us has to take a shot at stopping these guys now, before things *really* get out of hand. That's me." He pointed at himself. "And one of us needs to get back to the Jedi Council to report." He pointed at her. "That's you."

Ohali studied him for a moment, then dipped her chin. "As you wish, Captain Solo," she said. "But I would feel better if *you*—"

"Then we have a plan," Han said, cutting her off. "Now all I have to do is figure a way to make it work."

He turned to survey the lab, looking for ways he could

use it to draw the Columi into a trap—and survive long enough to take them out.

Lit in bright-blue tones, the facility had a cold, sterile feel. Han counted five aisles lined with eight vats each—forty in all. Like bacta tanks, each stood vertically and had a clearplas front. Instead of bacta, however, the tank was filled with a green viscous liquid that was so cloudy and thick that the occupant could barely be seen.

Barduun's gravelly voice rumbled out from a distant corner. "Over here, Captain Solo. *This* you will want to see."

"Give me a few minutes," Han called back. It was impossible to see what Barduun was doing, and given the fiend's sadistic nature, Han wasn't sure he wanted to know. "I'm going to disable this air lock."

"I will give you *two* minutes," Barduun replied. "No more."

Han heard a whir in an aisle to his right, and he and Ohali stepped over to look. A pair of bipedal, slender-faced laboratory droids was moving from vat to vat, monitoring the readouts and vital signs. More droids were crawling overhead—big spidery things that ticked through a gleaming maze of feeder pipes and filter lines.

And both kinds of droids were taking too much interest in Han and Ohali. Several of the spidery droids had scurried over to peer down from the edge of a boxy air duct, while one of the slender laboratory droids had stepped away from his duties and was coming up the aisle to meet them.

"Great," Han muttered quietly. The last thing they needed was an audience. "Any idea what the setup is in here?"

"Unfortunately, yes," Ohali said softly. Ignoring the droid coming toward them, she pulled Han into the next aisle over. "I was brought here several times, when the

Qrephs were just beginning to experiment with Force-sensitive biots."

Han raised his brow. "You mean like Ditto?"

"Precisely. As you have seen, they have some way to go before perfecting the technique. Force sensitivity seems to interfere with the mental development of biots." She led him about halfway down the aisle and pointed to a vat. "But they keep trying."

Peering inside, Han could just make out a blurry blue form matching Ohali's size and build. She leaned her blaster rifle against the vat, then touched a control pad on the front panel. The interior lit up, revealing a half-formed Duros. Its flesh appeared to be growing—or maybe *coalescing*—over a naked vanalloy skeleton.

The thing's eyes popped open, and it began to paddle its arms, using its still fleshless hands to bring itself closer to the clearplas panel. The facial features were incomplete, and there was a long bulge forming along one cheekbone. Even so, Han knew that when the thing was finished, it would look more or less like Ohali.

"Still having a few problems, I see," Han whispered. He pointed at the bulge along her cheek. "Will that go away?"

The answer came from a cheery synthetic voice in the aisle behind them. "It's quite unlikely."

Han turned to see a slender-faced lab droid coming toward them. It was probably the one they had ignored earlier, but it was hard to be sure. They all looked identical.

"They rarely do," the droid continued. Its gaze shifted toward the vat in front of them. "In all likelihood, it will fail its next quality-control inspection."

"What happens then?" Han asked, hoping to hold the droid's attention until he could locate its primary circuit breaker. "Do you just recycle her?"

The droid tipped its head forward in a sort of nod.

"Exactly. We are a highly efficient facility." It stopped three paces away, then said, "Please state your authorization code and your reason for visiting. Do you have instructions for me?"

"Sure, I've got instructions," Han said. He brought his blaster rifle up, pointing the emitter nozzle at the droid's head. "They're right here."

The droid drew its slender head back and retreated two steps. "You are not authorized to carry a weapon. Please put that away before I contact—"

Han pulled the trigger, sending a bolt straight through the droid's vocabulator and out the back of its head. It stumbled a couple more steps, then clanged to the floor in a sputtering heap. A storm of ticking and rattling broke out overhead as dozens of spidery droids retreated deeper into the maze of pipes and vents.

"Was that necessary?" Ohali asked. "I'm sure the Qrephs *already* know where we are."

"Let's hope so." Han began to fire into the feeder pipes and control panels, trying to cause as much destruction as possible. "Now we just need to get their circuits burning."

Ohali reluctantly retrieved her blaster rifle. "Because?"

"Because angry beings make mistakes," Han said. "And for my plan to work, the Qrephs have to start making mistakes."

Ohali wrinkled her blue brow. "Care to fill me in?"

"Captain *Solo*!" Barduun's voice interrupted. "It does not sound like you are disabling an air lock."

Han ignored him and quickly outlined his plan to Ohali.

"Ah." The Duros picked up her own weapon and began to fire into the overhead maze of pipes and ducts. "*Now* I understand."

Two seconds later, they were standing in a rancid-smelling shower of green unfiltered vat goo, with control pads and power cables sparking on both sides of the aisle. Han heard something slosh behind him and spun to find two skinny droids fleeing toward the far end of the aisle. He put a bolt through each of their torsos. Ohali fired three bolts toward the ceiling, and three spidery droids splashed onto the flooded floor beside them.

Good. The droids were the key. For Han's plan to work, they had to eliminate them.

"Captain Solo?" Barduun called again. "Exactly what are you doing?"

Knowing it would not be long before the Nargons and Mandalorians began to arrive, Han ignored Barduun—and motioned for Ohali to follow. They quickly moved into the next aisle, where they repeated what they had just done, then moved on to the next, where they eliminated two more laboratory droids. Han worked his way up the aisle, destroying control pads, while Ohali continued to fire into the maze overhead.

Every once in a while, one of the biots would awaken and come to the clearplas panel to watch. The biots weren't sentient beings—not yet. But they weren't droids, either. They were sad monsters whom the Qrephs had created to serve them and die in misery, and as Han passed by, he found himself wondering whether he was doing the biots any favors by leaving them to their fates. Most had deformities that would doom them anyway. The others would never be given a chance to leave Base Prime alive—not if Han had his way.

He and Ohali were about halfway up the next aisle when a familiar face pressed itself to the clearplas. With brown hair, brown eyes, and a remarkably handsome chin, it was the same face Han had seen in the mirror every morning—about thirty years ago.

Han stopped and stepped closer to the vat. The biot furrowed its brow and pressed its fingertip against the clearplas, pointing at Han's chest. Then it turned to study its reflection in the opaque wall that separated its vat from the adjacent one. It looked back to Han, then pressed the finger to its own chest.

Han couldn't decide whether he should blast the thing or set it free.

"It's very unsettling, I know," Ohali said. Following Han's plan, she picked up a short length of filter line from the debris in the aisle. "The first time I saw one of my Dittos, I wasn't sure whether to protect her or destroy her."

Before Han could say that destroying them was an act of kindness, Barduun's voice boomed out from the next aisle.

"Han Solo, it is time! Come to me now."

Han caught Ohali's eye. "We'd better do this fast." He checked the aisle and, when he saw no droids, nodded toward the vat. "Ready?"

Ohali blew into the filter line to make sure it was clear, then nodded.

"If you are determined." She used the Force to hide her blaster rifle atop an overhead duct, then turned toward the vat containing Han's replica. She reached up. "Can you give me a boost?"

"Sure." Han set his blaster aside, then pulled Gev's vibroknife from his waistband. "But take this, in case Freaky Boy gives you any trouble in there."

Han passed the weapon to Ohali, then cupped his hands to give her a boost. She used the Force to lift the lid on the tank, then scrambled up into the vat. A moment later, Han saw the tip of the filter line poking up above the green liquid. Then Ohali appeared in the front panel, just long enough to give him a thumbs-up.

The biot just looked confused.

A muffled crump rolled through the room, and Han realized he had finally run out of time. He retrieved his blaster rifle and started toward the front of the lab, desperately trying to figure out how he could get past the Nargons to take a shot at the Qrephs.

"Not that way, Han Solo!" Barduun's voice came from behind him, at the end of the aisle. "If you want revenge, you must come with Jhonus Raam."

Han felt himself start backward *before* he turned around. He considered opening fire on Barduun but decided it would be unwise to start blasting his allies before he'd killed the Qrephs—no matter how much those allies scared him.

"Jhonus Raam does not see Jedi Soroc," Barduun said. "Where is Jedi Soroc?"

"Um, she didn't care for the company," Han said, taking his time turning around. He wasn't sure how closely Barduun's use of the Force mirrored that of a Jedi, but he knew that a Jedi's ability to sense lies was one part "feeling"—and one part reading a liar's face. He kept his eyes averted and chose his words carefully. "Maybe she took off."

"Took off *where*?"

Han shrugged. "What am I, her handler? Look, *I'm* here to get the Qrephs. If you're not interested . . ."

Han let his sentence go unfinished as he completed his turn—and saw Barduun's new companion. "Where in the karking void did *she* come from?"

Barduun sneered. "Is that not obvious?"

She was a young Leia—a stunning biot replica complete with long brown hair and big brown eyes. Her belted smock reminded Han of the white gown Leia had been wearing the first time he saw her, and the biot's head was even cocked at the same haughty angle. But where Leia's eyes were intelligent and appraising, the biot's were vacant. And where Leia exuded confidence and determination, the biot looked nervous and bewildered.

Even so, the sight of her made Han's heart ache.

"Uh . . . thanks for thinking of me, pal," Han said, unable to take his eyes off the biot. "But you're crazy if you think a few kilos of vanalloy and vat-grown flesh could ever replace my wife."

The biot slipped behind Barduun, then peered out from behind his huge biceps.

"*This* Leia is not for you," Barduun said. "She is *Jhonus Raam's* princess."

Han studied the empty-eyed biot for a moment, trying not to imagine what Barduun had in mind. "Well, you'd better put her back," he said. "She's not done yet."

Barduun's face grew dusky. "She is not," he agreed. "But that will soon change. Jhonus Raam knows a secret."

He raised both hands in Han's direction.

"All right, all right—I'm coming," Han said, starting forward again. "No need to get huf—"

Instead of feeling the usual Force tug, Han was surprised to see tiny blue sparks at the end of Barduun's fingers. He dived, but it wasn't quite fast enough. A hot sheet of Force lightning crackled past above his back, just centimeters from his head. The air grew acrid with the smell of the dark side, and Han went flash-blind.

He landed in spilled vat fluid, then spun onto his back so he could bring his blaster out of the sour-smelling goo and open fire. He couldn't see, but that didn't stop him. He sprayed bolts down the aisle in Barduun's direction.

Barduun roared in pain, and the crackle of lightning suddenly stopped. Han did not—he kept moving, sliding along the wet floor under his own momentum.

When he heard heavy steps behind him and the screeching of Nargon blasters, he realized his mistake. He swung his own rifle back toward the front of the lab and opened fire. His vision returned—just in time to see a dozen of his bolts ricocheting off the chests of three charging Nargons.

Then Han felt himself being grabbed in the Force again. Barduun pulled him down the aisle backward and dragged him behind the last vat in the row. Han's little misunderstanding about the Force lightning had left a smoking blaster hole in Barduun's thigh, but Barduun was standing on the leg anyway. He swung Han around behind him.

"Jhonus Raam is on *your* side." Barduun used the Force to stand Han on his feet, between himself and the wide-eyed Leia doll. "Try to remember."

"Sorry for the, uh, confusion," Han said. "I thought you were sore because I didn't like your girlfriend."

Han stepped past the biot—who gasped in fear as he passed—and peered up the adjacent aisle. He didn't see much, just a wall of green scales spraying blue bolts in his direction.

Han pulled back, then cringed as the Nargons' bolts ricocheted off the rear wall and came flying in for a second try.

Barduun was already spinning past, outstretched palms turned toward the three finheads. "Go!" he ordered, putting the Force behind his voice. Blaster bolts began to bounce off his palms. "Take Jhonus Raam's princess."

Han cradled his blaster rifle under his arm, then grabbed the biot's wrist with his free hand.

"Where am I taking her?" Not wanting to sound *too* awed by Barduun's Force powers, Han did his best to sound casual. "The hatch on the—"

"Back wall," Barduun finished. "Jhonus Raam has entered the access code."

Barduun lowered one hand, then waved it up the aisle. Half a dozen biot vats ripped free of their mountings and went sailing into the charging Nargons.

"*Go,*" Barduun repeated. "Jhonus Raam will catch up."

Han raced off, more or less dragging the Leia biot behind him. Another blast of Force lightning shook the room. When Han looked back, Barduun was deflecting blaster bolts with one palm and spraying waves of Force lightning with the other.

Clearly, Jhonus Raam was no stranger to the Force.

A dozen steps later, Han and the "princess" reached two hatches in the back corner of the lab. True to Barduun's word, one of the status lights read UNSECURED. Han released the biot's wrist long enough to hit OPEN, then was surprised to reach back and not find her waiting. Han turned to see her backing away.

He caught her by the wrist. "Are you *trying* to get killed? Come here."

The hatch rasped open an instant later, and Han pulled her through, entering a tunnel-like corridor with an arched ceiling. It curved away in both directions, as though part of a circular hallway. A quick glance revealed no other hatches, but the curvature of the passage was so sharp that he could see only five meters in either direction.

The hatch rasped closed again.

The status light changed to SECURED.

A synthetic voice cackled from an overhead speaker. "You have entered a *most-restricted* area."

A hidden panel above the hatch controls slid open, revealing a biometric sensor pad.

"Present your access authorization now."

Han stared at the pad, trying to think of a way to fool the security system—and unable to do more than curse Barduun for forgetting to give them the override code.

A series of clunks sounded from the apex of the arched ceiling, and Han looked up to see pivot-mounted blaster cannons dropping out of a series of hidden doors.

"Present access authorization *now*."

And that was when Barduun's princess asked, "You don't have access authorization, do you?"

Han looked over. "You can talk?"

She cocked her head first in one direction, then in the other. "Of course I can talk," she finally said. "Jhonus Raam taught me."

"Jhonus Raam." Han pinched his eyes shut. "It figures."

He gave up trying to think of a way to fool the sensor pad and simply stabbed the OPEN button on the control panel.

Nothing.

A soft hum came from the ceiling as the blaster cannons began to power up.

"I know you, don't I?" The princess biot blinked her brown eyes. "Are you . . . my father?"

"Your *father*?" Han blurted. "Great. Just what I want in my head at a time like this."

"A time like what?" the biot asked.

A chorus of soft whirs filled the corridor as the blaster cannons began to track their movement.

"Intruder eradication commences in fifteen seconds," the voice warned. "Present access authorization immediately."

Han glanced up, then said, "A time like *that*." He pointed at the blaster cannons. "We're about to die."

"We're not going to die," the biot said. "Jhonus Raam would not let us."

"Yeah?" Han waved his hand around the corridor— drawing a soft whir from the blaster cannons as they tracked his movement. "Then *where* is he?"

The biot's eyes shifted away from Han, but only briefly. "Some rescue. You're not much in the courage department, are you?"

Han let his jaw drop, dumbfounded. "Okay, Creepy Leia—keep it down so I can concentrate."

He turned back to the hatch. He thought about blasting the sensor pad or the controls but decided that was just what the Qrephs would expect from an intruder: panic. And panic was always the fastest way to get killed—especially when dealing with Columi.

"I *do* know you, Han Solo," the biot continued. "Are you *sure* you are not my father—"

"You're a biot," Han replied. "You don't have a father."

"Of course I do. My genes come from *somewhere*." The biot stepped closer. "And *you* know *me*. I feel it."

"Look, sister, I don't care what you feel . . ." Han paused, realizing what the biot had just said. "When you say you can feel it, do you mean . . . *Please* tell me you mean *feel it* in the Force."

The biot smiled. "Jhonus Raam says I am strong in the Force. He has been teaching me."

"Good." Han dropped his blaster rifle on the floor, then turned her toward the hatch and pointed at the OPEN button on the control panel. "Can you reach out to the other side of the hatch and push that button?"

"Of course I can," she said.

The voice said, "Eradication begins in . . . *ten* seconds."

Han had to stop himself from shaking the biot. "Then do it!"

She closed her eyes.

Eight seconds, seven seconds . . .

The hatch opened to the sound of blaster fire. Before they could step through it, Barduun backed across the threshold, deflecting blaster bolts with one hand and hurtling Force lightning with the other. He was laughing so hard his shoulders shook.

When he spoke, it was in the biot's feminine voice. "Captain Solo, are *you* my father?" The hatch rasped closed. His laughter boomed through the corridor, then he spoke again in the biot's voice. "You're not much in the courage department, are you?"

"That was *you*?" Han looked back to Creepy Leia, whose face had returned to the same vacant expression as before. "How? *Why?*"

"The Force, Captain Solo." Barduun lowered his arms, then turned away from the now-sealed hatch. "Always the Force."

Of course, the *Force*. The fight in the lab must have been exhausting, even for Barduun. To stay strong, he had needed to feed on Han's fear.

What kind of dark-side fiend *was* he?

The synthetic voice said, "Eradication begins in . . . *five* seconds."

Barduun took his Leia biot by the arm and stepped across the corridor to the opposite wall—no, *through* the opposite wall.

A holograph.

Four seconds, three seconds . . .

"Come along, Captain Solo," Barduun called. "And don't touch that sensor pad. Touch *nothing*. With these Columi, everything is a trick."

Han snatched his blaster rifle and leapt across the corridor, passing through the holographic wall just as the count inside his head reached one.

"Access granted," the voice said.

Han found himself on a ring-shaped balcony, looking down on a three-meter circle of smooth black stone—Base Prime's natural surface, he guessed. There was a gap in the balcony railing, large enough for a person—or a powerbody—to use. And that was about it. Aside from the security he'd just faced—the blaster cannons and the one-way holographic wall—the little round chamber seemed entirely unremarkable.

Still holding the hand of his "princess," Barduun

stepped into the gap in the railing, then turned back to Han and extended a hand.

"Come along, Captain Solo," he said. "You cannot enter without the Force."

"In a second," Han said. He had no intention of stepping into the black circle of stone. "I have a few questions."

Barduun rolled his eyes. "The only important question is this: do you want vengeance?"

"That depends on the cost." Han nodded toward the circle. "What happens if I go in there with you?"

"You will receive what you desire," Barduun replied. "The power to destroy the Qrephs."

"Power like yours?"

That was the *last* thing Han wanted, and he was pretty sure Leia—the real Leia—would have told him the same thing, had she been able to. There was no *natural* way Barduun could have developed Force sensitivity at his age. And even if *that* impossibility had happened, there was no way Barduun had learned to handle dark-side powers the way he did—not in a few short weeks. Something else was going on here—something that scared Han more than death.

"Will I learn to use Force lightning?" Han asked. "To turn blaster bolts with my palms?"

"All that and more." Barduun extended his hand again, and Han felt himself being drawn toward the dark circle. "Now, *come along*, Captain."

Han pointed the blaster rifle at Barduun's chest. "You go ahead. I'll wait for the Qrephs here." He glanced through the one-way holographic wall toward the hatches on the far side of the security ring. "All things considered, this looks like a pretty good place to hole up."

Barduun continued to draw him across the balcony. "Without the power to destroy the Nargons, this is only a place to die," he said. "You must come with me. It is the only way to win."

"Why do you care whether I die or win?" Han demanded. "What do you get out of the deal?"

"You are not the only one the Qrephs have wronged," Barduun said. "I only want what—"

Han squeezed the trigger and held it down—only to see Barduun's hand shift positions at the last instant and send the bolts screaming back toward him.

Han had been expecting that. He was already diving through the holographic wall, into the outer security ring, rolling over his shoulder and spraying fire blindly toward Barduun. He heard the biot cry out and thump to the floor.

The synthetic voice spoke from above. "Present your authorization code now."

Han found himself flying through the holographic wall again, his chest aching as an infuriated Barduun held him in the Force. He glimpsed biot Leia on the floor with a smoking hole in her head and her eyes open wide. Then he was hanging upside down in Barduun's crushing Force grasp, his blaster rifle clattering to the floor.

Barduun wrapped an arm around Han's legs, then turned back toward the stone circle. Three steps to go.

Han reached into his waistband, drawing the holdout blaster he had taken from Mirta Gev. He pressed the nozzle into Barduun's thigh wound.

Barduun took a step.

Han squeezed the holdout blaster's trigger, firing an energy bolt into the same hole. Barduun's knee buckled and he almost fell, lurching another step toward the circle. Han twisted around, pushing the holdout blaster up between his body and Barduun's.

Barduun staggered another step forward. Han pulled the trigger again and felt himself falling—onto dark, hard stone.

Barduun was stumbling backward, away from Han, onto the balcony. His chin tipped up, revealing the smoky hole where Han's bolt had entered.

Han fired again, burning a small hole through Barduun's breast.

Barduun stumbled back one more step, then tumbled through the holographic wall into the security ring.

The synthetic voice said, "Present your authorization code now."

Han crawled across the stone, then clambered onto the balcony. Barduun wasn't moving, but Han didn't feel like taking chances. He braced his arm on the floor, taking aim through the one-way holograph at the biometric sensor pad on the far side of the security ring.

He opened fire and hit it on the third try.

"Authorization revoked," the voice announced.

A dozen doors clunked open, and a dozen blaster cannons descended from the ceiling. They turned their emitter nozzles toward Barduun's prone figure, and he vanished into a storm of smoke and light.

Twenty-three

Vestara was rushing past the barracks when three thundering booms shook all of Base Prime. She feared for an instant that Solo had improvised a mega-explosive from something in the biot lab, but she didn't see how. There hadn't been time, and the latest reports had him at the gate. Then the sound of secondary detonations began to roll up the corridor behind her, and she realized that at least two of the initial blasts had come from the other direction—from the main hangar.

A determined presence began to search the Force, reaching out from somewhere above Base Prime. An instant later, another explosion came, this time closer and sharper. Another boom followed from somewhere far away, and then a string of blasts seemed to erupt simultaneously in nearly every corner of the sprawling facility.

Marvid and Craitheus floated up the corridor beside Vestara. Even in the broad corridor, it was a tight fit, and she found herself rubbing shoulders with their vanalloy powerbodies.

"It appears the Jedi arrived sooner than expected," Craitheus snarled. "Considering Solo's escape, I find the timing highly suspicious. Perhaps you lured us away from the sabacc game so you could put us in harm's way."

"Right—and risk my own neck?" Vestara countered.

"I wouldn't start hunting for traitors yet. This is just what Jedi *do*—arrive at the worst possible moment."

"That's an understatement," Marvid complained. "I've received the damage report from the hangar. Our fighter squadron was hit before any of them could scramble."

Vestara stifled a groan. The miasma surrounding Base Prime was impenetrable to sensors, so it was ineffective and dangerous to fly a regular patrol. But with the Jedi coming, the moment she'd returned to the base she told the squadron commander to launch his Bes'uliiks anyway. Of course, he had insisted on following the chain of command, and that took time—time they didn't have, as it turned out.

Hoping there might be some way to salvage a few starfighters, Vestara asked, "What's the status in the hangar?" She knew Marvid and Craitheus were monitoring communications through their powerbodies.

"The crews were running for their craft when the second missile took down the shields," Marvid said. He spread his pincer arms. "When the third missile breached the hangar, they were carried away in the decompression wave."

"What about the shields in the rest of the base?" Vestara asked, hoping that all the booms and bangs she was hearing were not shields going down. "Still holding?"

"Not for long," Craitheus replied. "They're already down in several places. The Jedi must be hitting us with a dozen craft."

Vestara shook her head. "Not likely," she said. "They haven't had time to bring extra Jedi into the Rift—and Leia Solo wouldn't twiddle her thumbs waiting for backup. It's the *Falcon* out there and maybe one or two escorts. That's all they need."

Craitheus looked doubtful, but he glanced away without arguing the point. "Let's just get back to the lounge," he said. "You may relieve Gev as we discussed."

The walls began to reverberate to the crump of discharging turbolasers—gunners defending Base Prime. That did not mean they actually had targets in sight. In a battle like this, the Mandalorians would be doing everything possible just to slow the enemy down.

Vestara rounded a corner and spotted thirty Nargons lining the corridor ahead. Some were watching the ceiling, and many were twitching their tails, but all were holding their blaster rifles across their chests.

Vestara slowed and turned to Marvid. "What's this?"

"Our personal security detail," he answered quickly. "With Han Solo on the loose, one can't be too careful."

"That's a lot of bodyguards," Vestara said. "You sure it's only Solo you're worried about?"

"Obviously *not*," Craitheus snapped. "As you've noted, the Jedi are here. Now, if you're done wasting time, I suggest we keep moving."

They reached the Nargons, and two of the bodyguards fell in behind Vestara, while the rest followed the Qrephs. Keeping one eye over her shoulder, Vestara led everyone to the makeshift sabacc lounge.

As she stepped inside, she glanced out the viewport. A steady stream of turbolaser bolts was stabbing up from Base Prime, flashing against the blue miasma. The barrage was unlikely to stop Skywalker or his sister, but it *would* heighten the general fear level, which would make it easier for Vestara to seize control.

And judging by what she saw in the lounge, she *needed* to take control. The walls of the lounge were dotted with burn scars, and the floor was painted with blood. Two biots—one a Nargon, the other a Soroc replica— lay dead on the far side of the sabacc table. The air reeked of detonite and charred flesh, and the security hatch at the back of the room had been blown, creating a small jagged hole.

Mirta Gev was sitting atop the table, snapping orders into a handheld comlink. She was still dressed in her bloodied sabacc dealer's uniform, with her pant leg slit open and her leg extended in front of her. A 2-1B surgical droid was working on a hideous gash that stretched from her ankle past her knee.

With the Qrephs and the Nargons crowding into the room behind her, Vestara strode confidently to the table. When Gev ignored her, she used the Force to deactivate the comlink.

Gev continued to bark orders for another moment, then seemed to realize what had happened. She turned to Vestara and scowled.

"Go away, little girl." Gev clicked the comlink active again. "I'm assessing the situation."

"*Here* is the situation." Vestara used the Force to yank the comlink from Gev's hand. "You take orders from me now. If you do it well, you might even survive."

Gev's brow shot up. "Take orders from *you*?" She shook her head. "Never going to happen."

"It *will* happen," Craitheus said, floating up next to Vestara. "Under the terms of your contract, we may delegate command as we see fit."

"And this *is* your mess," Marvid added. "First, you led the Jedi to the *Ormni*, then you let Solo escape. It's as if the *Jedi* were paying you."

Vestara saw the resentment flare in Gev's eyes and began to worry the Mandalorian might be ready to take her troops home and tell everyone *else* to go suck void. And that could not be allowed—not in the middle of a Jedi assault.

Vestara turned to Marvid and shook her head in counterfeit exasperation. "That's not entirely fair," she said. "The Jedi didn't follow a tracking beacon to Base

Prime." She glanced at Gev. Judging by the Mandalorian's look of surprise—and perhaps even gratitude—the ploy was working. "At least, not a beacon that *Mirta* missed."

"If you're suggesting the *Aurel Moon* led the Jedi here, that's impossible," Craitheus said. "Even if our maintenance droids *had* missed a tracking beacon, it would be impossible to follow it through the Bubble. The plasma here is too thick."

Vestara shook her head. "Your love of technology blinds you. The Jedi have *other* means of tracking their prey." She passed Gev's comlink back to her. "But, Mirta, Marvid and Craitheus are right about one thing—your contract lets them put me in charge. Will you honor the terms?"

Gev shrugged, refusing to commit, then turned to Craitheus. "If I do this, I want to *see* the nanokiller lab."

"I'm afraid that's not safe for you," Craitheus replied, lying so smoothly that Vestara barely sensed the cloying deception in his Force aura. "If even one molecule of the sample has escaped into our lab—"

"So she'll send Thorsteg later," Vestara said. She saw no need to mention the dishonesty she had sensed—not yet. If she was going to set a trap for Luke Skywalker and his sister, she needed to get her forces deployed. "And Gev's contract says nothing about fighting Jedi. Everyone on her team gets a million-credit bonus. If we succeed, Gev's personal fee is doubled."

The crumping of the turbolasers grew more urgent, and the plasma beyond the viewport grew orange with short-range burst attacks.

"Agreed," Craitheus said quickly.

Mirta Gev narrowed her eyes but nodded.

An instant later, the tiny, fork-nosed silhouette of the *Millennium Falcon* appeared in the miasma, weaving and dodging past boiling blossoms of fire.

"Commander Gev," Vestara said. "Have your people disperse their Nargon squads throughout the base. Hold there until the Jedi penetrate the facility."

Gev acknowledged the order with a curt nod, then activated her comlink.

Craitheus was less agreeable. "You're not much of a tactician, Lady Raine." Like everyone else in the room, he was watching the *Falcon* as it careened through the forest of turbolaser fire. "You're anticipating a bombing run, but they're coming to *rescue* Solo. They won't risk his life with such an indiscriminate assault."

A carpet bombing was the *last* thing Vestara expected— and it took an act of will to ignore the insult. She was not ready to eliminate both Columi, but it would make her happy to see Craitheus die in battle, provided the Nargons didn't hold *her* responsible. By design, the reptiloids were fiercely loyal to the Qrephs. If she hoped to ever claim the brothers' empire for herself, she could not risk the Nargons' vengeance.

Outside the viewport, two dark specks dropped from the *Falcon*'s belly and began to descend. As they adjusted their trajectory, they steered toward the barracks area.

"Dropsuits," Vestara announced. She turned back to Mirta Gev. "Once the Jedi have penetrated the base, have all forces converge on the laboratory wing."

"You're drawing the enemy into a trap." Gev's tone was approving. "Where?"

"The gate," Vestara said, pleased that Gev was responding to her directly. "The security ring should confuse them just long enough to give us an advantage, and there are three entrances, so we can hit them from multiple sides."

Gev nodded. "Good."

As Gev relayed the order in Mando'a, Vestara turned to see four more specks descending from the *Falcon*.

Her stomach went hollow. That made *six* dropsuits—six Jedi.

It didn't make sense.

"Using the gate is an excellent idea," Marvid said. "We know Han Solo is hiding in that area, so you *could* have a useful hostage. But how will you lure the Jedi into your trap?"

"Not *me*, Marvid." Vestara turned back to the viewport, where the *Falcon* was still approaching. The dropsuits now resembled six bulky, big-shouldered silhouettes. "*You* will."

"You intend to use *us* as bait?" Craitheus demanded. "You must be mad!"

"Mad or desperate." As Vestara spoke, she watched one of the jumpers vanish into a turbolaser blossom—then come out on the other side, tumbling and glowing but still in one piece. "Either way, it's *you* the Jedi are here to hunt. If you don't want to draw them into the gate, name your spot. That's where we'll set the trap."

Marvid hesitated. "The gate is fine."

Beyond the viewport, the six silhouettes sprouted gouts of white flame and spiraled toward the base in wild helices. Their arms began to swing back and forth, flashing and flaring as they sprayed miniature missiles at Base Prime's turbolaser emplacements.

Miniature missiles?

Vestara extended her Force awareness toward the nearest silhouette. She felt neither fear nor excitement; only cold, empty danger.

"Correction," she said. "Those aren't dropsuits. They're battle droids."

A string of small explosions rocked the base as the miniature missiles struck their targets. The payloads weren't large, but the missiles were well aimed. They took out the turbolasers' emitter tips and forced feedback explosions, and the defensive fire quickly dwindled to almost nothing. The *Falcon* wheeled into a powered descent, and four new silhouettes dropped from its belly.

The newcomers appeared less bulky than the battle droids, and they weren't spraying anything. Vestara extended her Force awareness in their direction—and sensed four angry Jedi, bristling at her touch.

And one of them felt all too familiar . . .

Ben Skywalker.

Vestara began to reexamine her priorities. Her chance of winning this fight had just plummeted. Defeating Luke Skywalker and Leia Solo would be challenging enough, even with two hundred Nargons and twenty Mandos at her disposal. *Ben* Skywalker was a different problem. He knew how Vestara thought and what she felt—because he knew *Vestara* better than anyone did.

And, unlike his father, Ben would be hunting *her*, his former lover, with far more intensity than he felt for the Qrephs. Vestara knew Ben would not stop until either she or he was dead—or she was beyond his reach. The smart thing now would be to cut her losses and run.

But Vestara had nowhere to run. Her time with the Jedi had made Vestara Khai a pariah among her own people. She did not dare return to the Lost Tribe until she had enough power to rule them, and she could never win that power by doing the *smart thing*.

Vestara motioned the Qrephs toward the blown hatch at the back of the lounge. "You two, go."

The Qrephs wasted no time, rushing to the exit so quickly they toppled the 2-1B, who was just finishing up Gev's dressing. The Mandalorian pushed off the table to test her leg.

And four sharp bangs rang through the ceiling. A breach alarm sounded over the intercom, and automatic hatches started to slam shut throughout the base.

The shriek-and-thud of several different firefights began to echo through the corridors. The Nargon bodyguards hesitated, then turned toward the Columi. Vestara stepped in front of the mob and extended an arm.

"Those of you to this side, hold here to protect the Qrephs," she said, indicating ten Nargons. "The rest of you, go with Marvid and Craitheus."

To her relief, the Nargons obeyed—as quickly as they could, anyway. Her orders called for twenty huge reptiloids to squeeze through a small blown-out hatch, one by one, and that took time.

Too much time.

A loud thump sounded outside the lounge, beyond the main entrance, and a Mandalorian officer went tumbling past the doorway with a smoking hole in his chest. Vestara used the Force to hit the control pad and secure the door, then snapped the lightsaber off her belt and spun toward the blown hatch.

The last ten bodyguards were still awaiting their turn to squeeze through. Vestara and Gev used the delay to place the rear guard. Gev ordered two Nargons to take cover behind the wet bar, and Vestara used the Force to create a shield for three others by tipping the heavy table on edge.

All the while, the muffled din beyond the entry grew progressively louder. The shrieking of blaster rifles rose in pitch, and the battle droids' cannons became a pounding *thump-thump-thump*, as steady as a heartbeat.

Finally, the last of the Qrephs' bodyguards escaped through the rear hatch, allowing Gev and Vestara to follow. Vestara sent Gev out first, then reminded the rear guard that they were fighting to protect the Qrephs—their creators. "No one gets past this room!" she commanded, knowing full well that she was asking the impossible.

By the time Vestara had stepped through the hatch, Gev was already limping down the corridor after the Qrephs. It was difficult to see the two Columi ahead of the green mob, but the whole mass appeared to be stopped in front of the third air lock—the one that led through the biot lab to the gate.

"Marvid?" Vestara called. "What's the problem? Just open it!"

"We *are* trying," his voice replied. "But the attack has activated breach protocol."

An emergency-response system, breach protocol prevented the labs from being accessed if a pressure imbalance was detected anywhere in Base Prime. Vestara pointed to the large sliding door at the far end of the corridor.

"We'll go through your residence!" she called. "We have to move!"

A deafening blast shook the lounge behind her. Vestara stepped back to the hatch and peered into the room. Through the smoke and chaos, she could barely make out the red eyes of a YVH battle droid glowing out of a jagged hole in the opposite wall. It tipped its dark head forward and stepped through. The droid's heavy armor was immediately pocked by blaster fire, but its cannon arm continued to blaze, blasting the table apart and dropping one Nargon after another.

"Charge him!" Vestara yelled to the survivors, using the Force to augment her voice. "Rip his circuits—"

The droid's arm swung in her direction, and she barely managed to withdraw before a cannon bolt sizzled past her head. Deciding there was no time for a counterattack, she turned and started up the corridor, where Gev, the Qrephs, and the Nargon bodyguards were *still* gathered around the third air lock.

And no one seemed to be entering the lab.

She hurried toward the mob. To her left, the white glow of propulsion jets lit the transparisteel wall opposite the labs. She glanced out and saw two battle droids dropping into the courtyard. Four smaller figures were angling down behind them, drifting over the still-glowing ruins of the hangar to join the droids. All four wore the armored drop-suits of the Jedi Order—and all four were pointing heavy assault weapons in her direction.

Too fast.

The Jedi were coming too fast—before Vestara had a chance to set her trap. Using the Force to shove Nargons aside, she pushed through the mob toward Gev and the Qrephs.

As she moved, she reached out for *Ship,* calling to him in the Force.

Be ready. Be close.

Lady Khai, am I not always ready? came *Ship*'s reply. *Am I not always close?*

When Vestara reached the third air lock, she found Craitheus resting his powerbody on the floor, with his interface arm plugged into a droid socket. Meanwhile, Marvid was hovering beside him, studying strings of code on the control panel's display.

And just twenty meters away, at the far end of the corridor, was the sliding door that provided access to the Qrephs' private wing. The door's status light glowed red for secured, but, unlike the entry to the lab, it had not been sealed by breach protocol. By comparison, it would be child's play to open.

"We're out of time!" Vestara used the Force to pull Craitheus away from the air lock and spin him toward the sliding door. "We'll go through your residence!"

"We will *not,*" Craitheus answered. His voice was a bit muted, because Vestara kept him facing the door and would not let his powerbody turn around. "We gave you command of the Mandalorians, Lady Raine—not *us.*"

Vestera ignored the objection and, using the Force to shove Craitheus ahead of her, started toward the residential wing. As she moved, she kept an eye on the courtyard. The Jedi and their battle droids were hovering just above the monolith's surface, preparing a breach assault. Half their team seemed focused on the ruins of the hangar and the adjoining barracks. The other half—two Jedi and a YVH—were steadily advancing on the transparisteel wall. Judging by their silhouettes and the relative size of their Jedi dropsuits, the advancing pair was a male and a female. They carried a black two-meter rectangle stretched between them, and the YVH followed, partially obscured by the barrier.

The rectangle, Vestara knew, was a breach blanket. Void jumpers and Jedi used them to breach hijacked ships without causing explosive decompression. The invaders would need about ten seconds to reach the wall and attach the device. A couple of seconds after that, the corridor would be filled with Jedi and battle droids.

Twelve seconds. Vestara grimaced. Twelve seconds wasn't even enough time to reach *Ship*.

The soft whir of a powerbody drew Vestara's attention, and she turned to find Marvid blocking her path.

"Savara, stop." He pointed at the lightsaber hanging from her belt. "The lab walls are not thick. Perhaps you could use that trophy of yours to cut—"

"Are you spacesick?" Vestara gestured toward the viewport. "Can't you see what's coming for us?"

"Of course we can," Craitheus said, breaking free of her Force grasp and spinning back toward her. "We can *also* see that we outnumber them three-to-one. Show some courage, Lady Raine. Perhaps it's time to make your stand against the Jedi."

Vestara frowned. When Columi talked about courage—especially someone else's—they were definitely up to something. She snapped the lightsaber off her belt and started toward the residence.

"I am *going* through that door," she said.

Even before she had finished speaking, a string of cannon thuds sounded behind her. The Nargons returned fire, and when Vestara glanced back, the corridor was filled with screaming bolts and flying body parts—all of them green and smoking. Beyond the debris, a figure was emerging from the lounge—the YVH battle droid. His glowing eyes were two red dots, staring straight down the passage toward Vestara.

A heartbeat later, a dazzling light filled the corridor as the breach blanket detonated. A tall rectangle of transparisteel flew across the passage and smashed into the opposite wall. Vestara's ears started to ring, and Nargons flew through the air like storm debris. Some were missing appendages or had smoking wounds. Others were simply tumbling, looking confused and *still* spraying blaster fire in every direction.

Vestara spun toward the sliding door and saw Gev diving through behind the Columi. Vestara Force-launched herself toward the opening—and felt a cold shiver race down her spine. Igniting her lightsaber in midair, she twisted around and instantly found herself batting energy bolts aside. The male Jedi was steadily advancing, firing his blaster with one hand and Force-hurling Nargons aside with the other.

She cleared the threshold and landed on her back, two meters inside the Qrephs' residence. The Jedi's faceplate was rising into his helmet, and she glimpsed his red hair, his blue eyes—and a handsome jaw clenched in determination.

Ben Skywalker.

His gaze met hers, then he stopped and cupped his blaster with both hands. When Vestara saw the emitter tip drop, she knew he was aiming at her feet—and her lightsaber was in no position to defend them. She started to roll away, but it wouldn't be fast enough. The door was closing too slowly, her position was too vulnerable . . .

She spotted Craitheus hovering to one side of the door. As the first bolt screamed, she grabbed him in the Force and *pulled*. She heard the screech of two more bolts, then the sliding door thumped shut.

The screaming did not stop.

Craitheus's powerbody dropped to the floor so hard that the larmalstone cracked. The screaming continued, as shrill as a leaking pressure line.

Maybe it *was* a leaking pressure line.

Vestara rolled to her feet and found Marvid hovering about three meters away, his Columi face an enigmatic mask, his huge dark eyes tracking her every move. But his weapons arms were pointed at the door instead of at her, and there was no anger or hatred in his Force aura, only shock and grudging admiration.

She glanced back at Craitheus. His little mouth was still agape, but the odd screaming had grown fainter. Now it was only a high-pitched whine.

A tremendous boom shook the durasteel door. A red-glowing bulge appeared on its surface where a cannon bolt had struck the other side.

Vestara started toward Marvid. "I'm so sorry," she said. "I just reacted by instinct."

"You did what was necessary," Marvid replied. He pointed toward his brother's powerbody. "Bring him."

He turned and started down a chromalloy hall, heading in the general direction of the gate. A second cannon bolt struck the door, and this time a small split appeared. Vestara used the Force to lift Craitheus off the floor, then glanced over at Gev, who was now armed with a blaster rifle she had claimed from a dead Nargon somewhere along the way.

"You heard the bighead," Gev said. She motioned Vestara down the hall. "You did what you had to."

Marvid led them through a series of three doors—securing each one behind them—then finally stopped in a white workshop filled with tools and spare parts for Columi powerbodies. He pointed to a clamping pedestal on the far side of the room, between a doorway and a row of tall shelves.

"Put him there."

Vestara lowered the powerbody onto the pedestal. Craitheus continued to whine, and she leaned in for a closer look. He had taken three hits: one in his powerbody, just above his shoulder, and the other two in his own body—one in his torso, and the other in his cranium. His eyes were closed, and the wounds were too charred for Vestara to make any guesses about the damage. But it looked bad.

"Craitheus?" she said. "Can you hear me?"

If the Columi understood her, his face showed no hint of it.

A tremendous bang sounded from the foyer, and Vestara felt the floor jump beneath her feet.

"We don't have much time," Gev said. She was standing beside the entry to the workshop, watching the screen of an internal security monitor. "I don't think they're even bothering to cut through the doors. They're just blowing them."

"Don't worry, this won't take long," said a female voice—a *very* familiar female voice, which sounded a lot like Vestara herself.

Vestara spun around to find a human woman—well, *mostly* human—standing in the corner. Roughly Vestara's own height, she had a familiar build and an all-too-familiar face with big brown eyes.

Really big brown eyes, beneath a cranium that was twice the size of a normal human's.

"*Marvid?*" Vestara asked, too stunned to tear her gaze away from her . . . well, her replica. "What the hell?"

"Isn't she remarkable?" Marvid replied, drifting behind Vestara. "I added a few of Mama's genes to improve her intellect, but otherwise she's based on you."

The biot looked at Vestara. "You're pretty," she said, "but you're redun—"

"You made a *biot* of me?" Vestara interrupted.

Marvid's tone grew soothing. "Naturally," he said, still behind her. "You should be flattered. It shows what I think of you."

Then he opened fire.

The first bolt hit Vestara in the right ankle. The second destroyed her left knee. She couldn't tell exactly where the third bolt went; by then, she felt nothing but the pain below her thighs.

She found herself on the floor, with no memory of falling. She was simply on the larmalstone, watching her lightsaber fly into the biot's outstretched hand. She screamed at Marvid, "You blasted me?"

"And *you* used my brother for a shield." Marvid pointed a control arm toward Craitheus. Activated by remote, the powerbody rose off its pedestal and floated toward him. "I'm willing to call that even."

"*Even?*" Vestara replied. "Craitheus was going to sell you out!"

"He *considered* it, but only briefly," Marvid corrected. "You, on the other hand . . . Well, you and I both know it was only a matter of time before you tired of me, or I of you. It's better to end things now."

Another boom sounded from the direction of the foyer, this time a little closer. Vestara called out for *Ship*, urging him to hurry, then watched Marvid lead her biot and his brother's powerbody toward a doorway on the far side of the room. She could not believe how he had betrayed her—or that he had taken her completely by surprise. Under the circumstances, she had *no* chance of stopping the Jedi.

Unfortunately, escape was almost as unlikely. *Ship* couldn't evacuate her from the middle of the Qrephs' residence. She had to get to an exterior wall, to find a suitable extraction point—and she could no longer accomplish that on her own.

"Marvid, wait!" Vestara called. "I forgive you for making the biot. I can live with that."

Marvid raised a pincer arm and waved without turning around. "Goodbye, Savara."

Gev remained standing at the door, watching the security display above the control pad.

"I'd blast him *for* you," she said. "But I still have that nanokiller problem to fix."

"You know better, Gev." Vestara's pain had grown so bad that she was starting to worry about hallucinations. She wasn't positive that Gev was actually still there—maybe she only *needed* Gev to be there. "The Qrephs were leading you on."

Gev's eyes grew hard. "Says you."

"Look, I understand," Vestara said. "Desperation plays tricks on your mind. But I've personally explored just about every corner and turn of this base—and I'll bet you have, too. If the Qrephs were working on a cure for your nanokiller, that lab would have to be *here*, in their private wing. Have you seen anything like that? *Anywhere?*"

Gev sighed, then shook her head.

"That's what I thought," Vestara said.

The Mandalorian glanced at the security display. "I'd wish you luck with the Jedi," she said, "but we both know it won't do you any good." She turned to limp after Marvid, no doubt determined to see him die first—and as painfully as possible.

Vestara caught hold of Gev with the Force. "Wait," she said. "Wouldn't you rather live to fight again? Tell your people to bug out, and let's leave Marvid to the Jedi."

Gev turned her head and cocked a brow. "You can get us out of here?"

Vestara closed her eyes, then reached out for *Ship* . . . and felt him waiting about thirty meters away, somewhere beyond the walls of the Qrephs' residence.

"I can." Vestara pointed in *Ship*'s direction. "As long as *you* can carry me."

Twenty-four

Marvid rounded the corner to find a spidery cleaning droid moving down the corridor ahead of him, also fleeing the battle in the main part of the residence. Its reservoir orb was dribbling blue solvent, and he found himself fighting a sudden urge to blast the droid for damaging the floor.

Of course, that would only have spilled even *more* solvent onto the delicate larmalstone, and Marvid was surprised to realize how much the stress of the Jedi attack had affected his judgment. Twice already he had caught himself pursuing such faulty lines of thought, and once he had actually considered simply abandoning his poor wounded brother.

Fortunately, Columi did not suffer such mental lapses for long. Marvid had narrowed his options to two. He could go to the residence hangar and attempt to escape in the blastboat that he and Craitheus kept for just these sorts of emergencies. Or he could use his biot, Savara Two, and flee through the gate.

The considerations for each option were numerous, but the ultimate decision hung on a few likelihoods. If he fled in the blastboat, Craitheus would certainly die, Base Prime would be lost, Marvid would be hunted by Jedi for the rest of his life, and Han Solo would live.

If Marvid fled through the gate—well, he didn't really

know what would happen. But the Jedi would be forced to follow him into the same dark-side nexus that had driven Barduun mad—and under those circumstances, Marvid's superior intellect would prove decisive. With luck, he might even be able to eliminate the entire strike team and keep Base Prime secure. Besides, with Solo still trapped inside the gate chamber, Marvid would have a chance to kill him on the way through.

That made the choice easy.

As Marvid and his two companions began to overtake the droid, it quickly moved to the wall and drew its tangle of arms in tight. Marvid was still leading his brother's powerbody by remote control, and the droid glanced briefly in Craitheus's direction before looking back to Marvid.

"Are we evacuating?" it asked. "Should I proceed to the hangar?"

"No need for that," Marvid said. He moved to the opposite wall and led Craitheus past the droid. "It's just a little Jedi problem. I'm on my way to take care of it now."

"You are? I am relieved to—"

The droid's reply ended in the *snap-hiss* of an igniting lightsaber. A head clunked to the floor, then more pieces began to drop as the lightsaber groaned and growled.

Marvid stopped to look back and found Savara Two hopping around the droid, hacking it apart with wild, frenzied attacks.

"Two!" he barked. "What *are* you doing?"

Two brought the blade down in a fierce strike, slicing the reservoir orb apart and unleashing a flood of cleaning solvent.

"I'm practicing," she said, "for the Jedi."

"Then stop it," Marvid said, trying to hide his dismay. In most ways, Two was a great disappointment to him. But at least the biot succeeded where it really counted—she had the Force. He started down the corridor again. "Anyway, you're not ready to fight Jedi yet."

"I *feel* ready," Two said. She Force-sprang to his side, then began to whirl the lightsaber in a pretty red circle. "I'm ready to die for you, Marvid."

"I would rather you didn't," Marvid said. His gaze was already fixed on a chromalloy vestibule ahead, where a pair of gleaming hatches hung on opposite walls. "You're more use to me alive."

"But I *would* fight them for you, Marvid." Two reached over and stroked Marvid's cranium. "I'd do anything for you."

Marvid kept his eye on the glowing lightsaber, still ignited in her other hand. Like all of the third-generation biots based on Force-users, Two had impaired mental function. Craitheus believed that their technological core interacted with the Force to corrupt the development of their minds. Marvid suspected the monolith itself was causing the problem—an opinion Savara Raine had shared with him—but he was unsure how to counter it.

When Marvid did not reply to the biot's profession of loyalty, she grew desperate and stepped in front of his powerbody. "Did you hear me, Marvid?" she asked. "I love you *that* much—enough to die for you."

Marvid stopped, keeping a wary eye on the whirling blade in her hand. "I know," he said. "I made you that way."

Two gave him her sweetest smile. "I'm glad you did." She whipped her lightsaber through the air in a mock attack. "But you should have let me kill that bonebag Savara. She didn't deserve you."

A sharp *bang-clang* echoed around the corner behind them, and Marvid knew the Jedi were catching up. He chose his next words carefully.

"Savara Raine is more useful to us alive. The Jedi will need to blame *someone* when Luke Skywalker dies—

and I'd rather it not be me." He used a pincer arm to motion Two toward the vestibule ahead. "Now, let's hurry. The Jedi mustn't catch us here."

"You go," Two said. "I can hold them off."

"Not yet." Marvid nudged her forward. "I need you with me."

Two smiled. "You *do*?"

"Yes, so I can pass through the gate," Marvid said. "I don't have the Force, remember?"

"I remember."

Two Force-leapt all the way to the hatch, then turned to face him. She began to whirl her lightsaber again, looking confused.

"But won't the gate make us mad?" she asked. "The *others* went mad."

Marvid struggled to remain patient. "The others weren't Columi."

Savara Two looked uncertain. "But I'm only *part* Columi," she said. "A very small part."

"That's true," Marvid said, catching up to her. "But you did say you would do *anything* for me."

The battle was building to a new ferocity. Han could feel that in the growing rumble beneath his feet, hear it in the rising screech of wall-muted blaster fights. Every once in a while he thought he could hear yelling voices, sometimes even catch the muffled sizzle of a striking lightsaber. It was still too early to know *whom* he was hearing, but he was starting to hope that Ohali had been right—that Leia and her brother *had* survived the ambush and had finally come.

Unfortunately, there wasn't much Han could do to find out. He was completely safe as long as he stayed on the durasteel balcony. But the instant he stepped through the holographic wall that surrounded it, the cannon doors retracted and a synthetic voice started to ask for nonexistent authorization codes. Even so, there were three hatches on the outer rim of the security ring, and he had risked his life many times by trying everything he could think of to open them all.

That was the trouble with Columi traps. The longer you were stuck in one, the more insidious they grew.

Half afraid that the battle sounds he was hearing were just a new twist on the Qrephs' torture games, Han grabbed his blaster rifle and went to stand across from the noisiest hatch. Through the one-way holograph, the hatch had a blue tint that made it look like a holograph itself. Near the control pad, there was a carbon star where he had fired a dozen bolts at it earlier.

Knowing that the pinging of a blaster bolt would carry through the battle din far better than his voice, Han fired a bolt into the door.

"Hey, Leia!" he yelled. "Is that you out there?"

He fired into the door again . . . and the holographic wall dissolved.

A synthetic voice spoke from the ceiling. "Access denied."

"*What?*" Han yelled. It didn't make any sense. He had fired at the doors dozens of times, and nothing like that had happened. "Wait, hold on . . ."

Out in the security ring, doors clunked open. Blaster cannons began to descend from the arched ceiling and pivot toward the balcony.

Han turned and hurled himself over the railing. He came down hard on his blaster rifle and felt his breath leave. The cannons roared, and ricochets boiled across the stone circle toward him. He saw darkness ahead and scrambled to shelter beneath the balcony, then lay there in the shadows, aching and gasping and cursing the entire Columi species.

How long the barrage lasted, Han could not guess. It

felt like an eternity, but he was still struggling to fill his aching lungs when the rain of cannon bolts finally stopped. A strange stillness fell over the chamber, and for a second he lay beneath the balcony, listening to his ears ring.

Then the battle din grew abruptly sharper as a hatch door opened, and Han grew aware of an unwelcome emptiness in his hands. He looked out from under the balcony and found his blaster rifle lying in plain view out on the stone circle—exactly where he had left it in his scramble to escape the automatic cannons.

The bottom half of the handgrip had been blown apart. Otherwise, the weapon still *looked* functional.

The hatch closed again, and a familiar whir sounded from the security ring. From his position, Han couldn't see who had arrived—but he knew that sound.

Powerbodies.

Staying on all fours so he could not be spotted from the security ring, Han scrambled out and started for his blaster rifle. He just hoped it still worked, because now that he had his shot at the Qrephs, he was *going* to take it.

As he moved, a female voice spoke near the hatch. "*There's* a body."

Han was astonished to recognize the voice. It sounded like Vestara Khai—a lot like Vestara Khai—except it was not quite so cold and confident.

"Keep looking," Marvid replied. "That's Barduun."

Han glanced up to see if he could identify the woman, but the far edge of the balcony continued to block his view of the security ring.

"There's another body," the voice said. "This one's a she, and she's a biot."

Creepy Leia.

Han reached the blaster rifle. He snatched it on the go and scrambled the rest of the way across the circle.

"I don't care about *those* bodies," said Marvid. "We

need to find Solo. The security cannons should have torn him apart when I dropped the holograph."

Fuming, Han ducked back under the balcony. Marvid had *known* he was trapped in here. He and Craitheus had probably been toying with him the entire time, watching on some hidden surveillance cam and laughing at Han's efforts to escape.

The whirring stopped at the edge of the balcony. "He's not out here," Marvid said. "Take a look inside the stasis circle."

"The stasis circle?"

Marvid sighed. "The circle of black stone."

"Oh, *that* stasis circle."

"And search *under* the balcony," Marvid added. "If Solo survived, he will be there."

Okay, so maybe Han was only *one* step ahead. But he still had a shot—and he was going to take it.

"And remember not to step into the stasis circle yet," Marvid continued, "not until I'm waiting and I give the order."

"I won't, Marvid." A pair of small feet stepped on the balcony and began to cross toward the railing. "I'm not going anywhere without you."

The battle din outside the hatch was continuing to build as the fighting drew closer. Marvid would have to make his move soon—whatever that move *was*. Han began to belly-crawl, trying to move into position to attack from behind as the Columi entered the stasis circle.

"Oh, wait."

The small feet turned and began to trail behind Han—then abruptly grew silent.

"I found him!"

The *snap-hiss* of an igniting lightsaber sounded from the same spot as the voice. Han cursed under his breath. He might not know *who* she was, but he had a pretty good idea *what* she was.

A biot—and, like Ditto, she could use the Force.

Han rolled away, just in time to avoid being split down the center as the droning lightsaber slashed through the balcony. He started to bring his blaster tip up—then thought about the ricochets and rolled again. The blade came again, this time so hard that the tip struck the stone beneath the balcony and bounced back up.

Han spun his legs around ninety degrees, gambling that any biot inexperienced enough to put that much power behind a lightsaber attack would not be thinking much about strike patterns.

As expected, the third attack came down perpendicular to the first two. Now she had cut three sides of a square. Hoping for the fourth, he rolled back the other way—and that was when the Solo luck finally returned.

A tremendous bang shook the chamber, followed instantly by the clang of a blown hatch hitting something metal—like a powerbody, maybe. Han rolled back the way he had come, but the biot's mind was no longer on him.

"Marvid!" she screamed. "Marvid, I'll save—"

Her cry was drowned out by two short bursts of cannon fire. A dozen meters to the right, a three-meter section of railing dropped onto the stasis circle, both ends still glowing. An instant later, a pair of powerbodies shot through the gap and dropped to the dark stone.

Han was already blasting. The first three bolts ricocheted off the armored chassis of the lead powerbody, which promptly spun around. Strapped into it was the half-dead form of Craitheus Qreph, a blaster burn through his huge cranium, another through his tiny torso. But the Columi's condition didn't stop his powerbody from leveling a launching tube in Han's direction.

Continuing to fire, Han rolled, paused . . . saw the orange streak of a mini-rocket flash past, then rolled again and felt the heat of a small detonation behind him.

Han fired again, rolled again—and narrowly escaped being killed when the biot's lightsaber came slashing through the balcony. The second powerbody spun around, pointing its launching arm in his direction, and Marvid's amplified voice boomed across the stasis circle.

"Forget Solo!" he ordered. "Come to me *now*."

Han faked a roll, then cringed away when Marvid fell for the feint and sent a mini-rocket streaking past. Han aimed for the launcher arm—only to have a bigheaded, giant-eyed version of Vestara Khai drop down to block his shot. She thumbed off her lightsaber and made a sweeping gesture with her hands.

Han felt a Force nudge—not much, but enough to deflect his aim. A string of bolts shot across the stasis circle and vanished beneath the balcony. He rolled again just to be safe, then brought his blaster rifle back toward his targets, who were suddenly nothing but shadows, shimmering above a chromalloy shaft so deep it might have plunged all the way to the Galactic Core.

Han managed to squeeze off three quick bolts, but he had no idea whether he hit anyone. All he caught was a glimpse of Marvid's silhouette, raising a pincer arm in a rude farewell. A curtain of silver radiance rose to engulf the three figures, then an amplified voice said, "You lose, Solo. I win."

The radiance slowly sparkled into nothingness, and when it was gone, so were the Qrephs and their biot.

Marvid's parting words only made Han's jets burn that much hotter. The Columi might have gotten away for the moment, but this wasn't over yet—not even close. Amid the screeching blaster bolts and booming blaster cannons out in the corridor, he could hear the oscillating drone of whirling lightsabers.

And voices. Familiar voices.

Still holding his blaster rifle, Han crawled from beneath the balcony.

"Han?"

That voice was familiar and female, and it made Han's heart jump.

"Han, are you in here?" Leia called. He could tell she was using the Force to search for him, because her steps were starting to ring across the balcony, moving toward the edge where he had been hiding. "Han, are you—"

"Down here!" Han called.

He rose and turned to find Leia racing across the balcony. With half her hair missing, a combat vac suit splattered in blue Nargon blood, and a comlink headset worn over a face still red with healing burns, she looked about the way Han felt—and she was *still* the prettiest woman Han had ever seen.

Behind her, a single YVH stood out in the security ring, one red eye studying the arched ceiling. Luke was still out in the corridor, just beyond the blown hatch, one hand using his lightsaber to bat blaster bolts aside, the other gesturing to someone Han could not see.

A synthetic voice said, "Access denied."

Leia cocked her head, turning to look toward the sound, and Han's heart leapt into his throat.

"Leia, down here!" Han yelled, reaching toward her. *"Now!"*

Leia was already vaulting over the rail. Han caught her by the hand—and felt the stone go instantly soft. He looked down and saw the stasis circle turning translucent beneath their feet.

"Better comm Luke, if you can." As Han spoke, a deep, vine-draped pit opened beneath their feet. "Tell him we're going after the Qrephs."

The mound of dead Nargons began to shudder again. Ben watched in amazement as two more of the huge reptiloids appeared, crawling out of a body pile so huge it clogged the corridor. The Nargons were met by a hail of YVH cannon bolts, and they quickly fell as motionless as their fellows.

Their Mandalorian officers had bugged out about five minutes earlier, and the Nargon security force had instantly become more of a nuisance than a danger. And there lay the true peril, Ben knew. Faced with such a mindless foe, it would be easy to grow complacent.

Or to simply run out of power cells.

Ben sensed a presence behind him, then glanced back to find his father approaching.

"I'm going after Han and Leia," Luke said. Instead of attempting to shout above the battle noise, he used the throat mic to transmit his voice over the strike team's comm net. "I think they went inside the monolith."

"They *what*?" asked Tahiri. She was kneeling behind one of their surviving battle droids, placing some charges that would slow down a Nargon charge—if the reptiloids ever figured a way to get past the pile of bodies. "Was that part of the plan?"

"It was unexpected," Luke admitted. "But they're following the Qrephs, and the Qrephs killed thirty thousand people at Sarnus alone. We can't let that pair escape inside the monolith."

"Yeah, that could be bad." Ben shot a glance toward the hatch through which the Qrephs had fled. They had just lost a battle droid taking out the automatic security system, and he wasn't eager to add his father to the casualty list. "Be careful in there."

"I think the YVH cleared the way for me," Luke said. "I'm more concerned about the situation here."

"We'll be okay, Dad," Ben said. "We have this under control."

"I know you do," Luke said. "But stay in touch with the *Falcon* in case you need to evacuate—"

"And keep an eye on our other approaches," Ben interrupted. "And pay attention to our danger sense, because this still smells like a trap. I *said* we have it, Dad."

An expression that was equal parts pride and love came to Luke's face, and that was when Ben realized there was something his father was not telling him.

"Now you're scaring me," Ben said. "What's wrong?"

Luke smiled. "Nothing's wrong." He clapped a hand on Ben's shoulder, then turned toward the hatch. "And that's a very good feeling right now."

Twenty-five

Luke hung suspended in a whirling column of starflies that died—suddenly and all at once—then sank, dimming, into the darkness below. For an eternity, he floated motionless in the silent gloom, alone with his thoughts and the icy ache of his old wound. He found himself wondering whether he would ever see Ben again, wondering many things: how he would find Han and Leia, what the pain in his wound foretold, whether the Qrephs had stumbled across Mortis after all.

The dark side swirled all around him—a hot, nettling breeze that burned his eyes and made him feel queasy. Something rustled nearby, unseen, and the air grew solid beneath his feet. Ebony shapes began to coalesce into tall stone pillars, which broadened at their bases and tops into the floor and ceiling of a vast, dank-smelling catacomb.

In the distance Luke saw a pair of tiny golden haloes, located side by side and gradually shrinking and growing dim. He started after them, then ignited his lightsaber to see by and sent a thousand shadows whispering away. As he moved, the shadows began to glide across the floors and slide off pillars and hiss in behind him, always creeping in closer. Occasionally he paused to listen for words, but each time he stopped, the hissing faded to silence. Once, he turned to look and thought he glimpsed a dozen pale eyes watching him from beneath a line of dusky brows. But the shadows rustled back into the darkness so quickly he could not be certain whether they were real or imagined.

After a few dozen steps, a golden radiance began to light the surrounding area. He looked down and discovered that his entire body had begun to glow—except where Abeloth had reached into his chest. There, Luke had a dark hole the size of his fist.

He continued toward the distant haloes, hoping they might be Han and Leia. The two radiances appeared to be moving away, so Luke walked faster. The last of the shadows fell from the pillars, and the pillars turned white, then developed a papery bark and became tree trunks. When Luke looked up, he discovered an immense green forest canopy where moments before there had been cavern ceiling.

After a few seconds, or hours—who could say?—the still-distant haloes grew larger and brighter as he began to gain on them. A mob of dark, amorphous masses appeared, trailing the two lights—and closing in fast. Luke deactivated his lightsaber and hung it from his equipment harness, then cupped his hands around his mouth to call out . . . and heard another lightsaber snap to life, directly behind him.

"A Mandalorian Force-user?" Leia asked. "That's . . . rare."

She was walking next to Han, passing through an open colonnade of vast proportions, with white pillars that rose a hundred meters into a sky of swirling blue haze. Vines were spiraling up the pillars literally before their eyes, flocks of brightly colored birds were swooping about their heads, and she was holding Han's glowing, translucent hand and feeling happier than she had in a long time. They might be trying to hunt down a pair of super-genius mass murderers who wanted them dead, but at least they were doing it together. As long as they had that, they had everything.

Han shook his head. "You're missing the point," he said. "Barduun was some sort of accident. He wasn't *born* Force-sensitive, and he wasn't one of their biot experiments. He was a normal guy who couldn't use the Force at all—until *after* the Qrephs sent him in here. It's like something got into him."

"Are you suggesting he was possessed?" Leia asked. She knew of other cases where a dark-side spirit had taken control of another being, but none that had involved a space–time-warping gate whose function she could barely fathom. "That's a possibility, I suppose. But I don't think we should leap to any conclusions."

"Who's leaping?" Han asked. He waved his arm back toward the catacombs, which they had left some time ago. "You saw those shadows. Didn't it seem like they were trying to get a little too friendly?"

"Maybe," Leia said. "Okay, let's assume you're right and they *were* dark-side spirits." She turned to look back over her shoulder. "Are you saying the Qrephs came in here because they actually *want* to be possessed?"

The entrance to the catacombs was no longer visible behind them. Instead, the vine-wrapped pillars in the distance had given way to white tree trunks and, above that area of the colonnade, the sky had changed into a rich green canopy. A distant figure—her brother, Luke, she thought—stood amid the trees, pivoting away.

Gliding through the forest, approaching the figure from three different sides, were a trio of dark, amorphous masses—banks of shadow that seemed to slip through the woods like an inky black fog.

"The Qrephs are pretty arrogant," Han continued, apparently unaware of what was happening behind them.

"Maybe they think they can outsmart a few dark-side spirits."

Finally Han turned to look back, too, and just then a crimson lightsaber ignited within the middle shadow.

Luke pivoted and sprang, launching himself into a series of cartwheels that sent him rolling through the forest like a wheel. His attacker emerged from the shadows, wild-eyed and fierce. She was a grotesque caricature of Vestara Khai, with huge brown eyes and a big oval head like a Columi's. She came kicking and chopping, all anger and no skill.

Still cartwheeling, Luke flicked his palm up. The Force rushed into him with wild, burning fierceness, then he unleashed a blast of energy so powerful it blew the flesh off her vanalloy skeleton—*that* was a surprise—and she tumbled away in pieces, her crimson blade tracing spirals through the darkness.

Luke's shoulder glanced off a tree. He hit the ground, off balance and disoriented, a little unnerved by the raw power he had just unleashed. The Force had swept into him with pure unshaped potential, and he had killed with it—more out of surprise than necessity.

Too easy . . . too tempting.

He heard the whir of a powerbody to his left and sensed danger to his right. He snapped the lightsaber off his harness and rolled over his shoulder, and the forest exploded into cannon fire from both directions. He whirled, trusting his hands to the Force, and began to send bolts pinging into the shadows that he now saw drifting in from his flanks. Once, he heard the crump of a bursting blaster-gas reservoir. Twice, he heard the *thud-hiss* of energy striking flesh. But every time he tried to dance out of harm's way, the attacks intensified and forced him back into the crossfire.

It was not good to be a luminous being fighting shadows.

Then metal projectiles began to plink off stone, and Luke realized his attackers—the Qrephs, presumably, hiding inside their shadow clouds—had been attempting to wear him down with their first assault, hoping to catch him by surprise when they switched to a new tactic.

And their strategy had worked.

Luke hurled a blast of Force energy into the shadow cloud on his right, heard a powerbody drone and wood crackle. But the attacks continued from the left, and a string of sharp impacts climbed up his back—metal slugs flattening themselves against his vac-suit armor. The last one punched through and buried itself deep beneath his shoulder blade.

Luke's sword arm fell limp, and his guard went down. He sprang into an arcing Force dive. Two more slugs caught him in the neck and sent him spinning, and he crashed into a smooth white tree trunk.

He landed in a heap at the foot of the tree, a curtain of pain and darkness already falling in around him.

Han spotted Luke lying at the base of an immense tree trunk, his face distorted by pain. While Han's body was still glowing brightly, Luke's had faded to a pale sheen, and a river of blood was pouring from two holes in his neck.

Han rushed to Luke's side. "Hey there, buddy," he said, kneeling. "Don't you wor—"

He stopped short when he saw the eyes. They were peering out at him from the wounds in Luke's neck—big yellow eyes with slit pupils, trying in vain to blink away the blood.

Han set his blaster rifle aside, then opened the thigh pocket on Luke's vac suit and pulled out the medkit.

"You're going to be just fine," he continued. Better not to mention the yellow eyes. "Trust me."

Luke finally seemed to register Han's presence and managed a weak smile, then his gaze drifted left and the smile faded.

"Luke, stay with me, pal." Han fumbled the kit open and searched for the big bacta bandage. "This is nothing. Remember Hoth? Hey, this is nothing, you hear me, Luke?" He found the bandage and ripped open the sterile wrapper. "Luke?"

Leia, who had been advancing on Han's flank, arrived behind him. "Han, trouble!"

Han slapped the bandage over Luke's neck wound, then traded the medkit for his blaster rifle and turned. Leia was now two steps to his left, looking over his head. She was holding her droning lightsaber in one hand and whipping the other hand forward in a pushing gesture, and Han heard something heavy go crashing through the forest behind him.

But there was something behind *her*, too—a bank of shadow slipping through the trees and heading toward them. Han heard the hum of a blaster cannon powering up.

"Go!" Han said. "I've got the one behind you."

"Okay!" Leia called, racing past. "Be careful!"

As if *that* was going to happen.

Hoping to draw fire away from Luke, Han was already springing off at an angle. He sent two blaster bolts screaming into the darkness, then dived into a somersault just before a stream of cannon fire answered his attack. He rolled into the shadow bank, came up, and found himself facing the blocky silhouette of an approaching powerbody.

Han fired again. The powerbody pivoted and began to advance sidelong. Still firing, Han charged, listening to his bolts ping off the powerbody's armor. The gaping mouth of a launch tube swung toward him.

Han feigned a dive to his right. The launch tube swung in that direction and sent a mini-rocket streaking into the ground. Han dodged and rolled over his shoulder, then came up to find the powerbody swinging back so it could bring all its weapons to bear.

Again, Han opened fire. This time he was close enough to see that Luke—or someone—had already reduced the powerbody to a pitted, charred, vapor-leaking wreck. Meanwhile, its pilot—Craitheus Qreph—looked even worse. In fact, Han had never seen blaster wounds so bizarre. A blue tumor was pulsing out of the hole in the Columi's head, and thick, fleshy lips surrounded the gaping holes in his abdomen. One of his arms had been blasted off entirely, and he seemed to be growing a tail to replace it.

But the powerbody's cannon arm was still working. As it swung in Han's direction, he continued to fire and sank two more bolts into Craitheus's huge cranium.

The Columi returned fire—*after* he was hit, with the smoke still rising from two fresh holes in his head.

Impossible.

Han's leg went numb and flew out from beneath him. Then his entire gut erupted in fiery pain, and he felt himself being spun away.

Automatic fire. It had to be, because Craitheus *had* to be dead.

Han kept firing anyway, twisting around as he fell, putting bolt after bolt into the powerbody and the big-head's brain. He wasn't taking any chances—not when Leia would be the Columi's next target.

The muted boom of an exploding actuating motor rolled through the forest. Han hit the ground, awash

with pain—as if a womp rat were clawing out his guts—
and the acrid fumes of burning chemicals filled his nostrils.

An eyeblink later, Craitheus's powerbody crashed into
a tree and exploded a second time. Mini-rockets began
to shoot through the forest, tearing boughs from the
trees and setting off a chain of distant detonations.

Now Craitheus was dead.

Han turned toward the sound of the second explosion
and saw a powerbody lying wrecked and burning at the
base of a splintered tree.

He *had* to be.

Leia advanced, spinning and leaping. Her body bent and
pivoted as she sidestepped shrieking mini-rockets and
ducked hissing fléchettes, and her lightsaber wove a bas-
ket of color as she batted cannon bolts back toward her
shadow-cloaked attacker. She was one with the Force,
her luminous golden body an eddy whirling in its wild
current, her entire being a maelstrom of cold resolve and
focused rage, of a single all-consuming purpose: to kill.

Marvid had managed to right his powerbody after her
latest blast of Force energy, and he was backing away
from her in a crooked flight that left half his cannon
bolts flying wild. An internal power cell just above his
shoulder had exploded, leaving a jagged hole in the armored cover plate and coating half of Marvid's head
and body in corrosive chemicals. The resulting burns
looked truly awful, with large diamond-shaped blisters
that were healing into copper-colored lizard scales before Leia's eyes.

She was gaining on him fast, and they both knew it
was only a matter of heartbeats before she closed the
distance. She danced past a string of fléchettes, batted a
cannon bolt aside, and Force-leapt across the last five

meters. Then she was on him, her lightsaber angling down toward his head.

A pair of tremendous booms shook the trees behind her, and Leia felt a terrible ripping in the Force as Han dropped. A cold wave of stunned disbelief boiled through her, and she must have hesitated, because suddenly Marvid was extending a new arm, pressing its rounded end against her abdomen. Deep inside the Qreph's power-body, a low hum began to build.

"You lose, Jedi," Marvid said. "I—"

Leia was already pivoting, sliding along the mysterious arm and bringing her lightsaber down on Marvid's collarbone. The blade crackled, filling the air with blood and smoke and sparks as it sliced down through vanalloy and flesh.

The low hum became a thrum. The front half of Leia's vac suit simply melted away, and the skin on her abdomen began to blister and char. She turned to dive away, and her insides exploded into a volcano of boiling pain.

Han lay on the forest floor, groaning in agony, for hours, days, maybe even a week. He had a char hole in his gut the size of a Wookiee's fist, and his leg was one big fiery ache from the knee up. From the knee down, he felt only a cold throbbing numbness that would have scared him to death—had he not been pretty sure he was already dead.

Because nobody could take this much pain for this long and live through it.

But it *couldn't* have been that long. Han could still hear Marvid wailing as Leia's lightsaber growled and sparked its way through the Columi's powerbody, and he had been listening to exactly the same sounds from the moment he hit the forest floor.

Maybe this was what happened when someone died. Maybe a dead guy's mind simply went into a closed loop, and he spent eternity remembering his last moment in life.

No fair.

That wasn't how Han wanted to spend eternity. He wanted to spend it holding Leia's hand and recalling the good times—their wedding in Cantham House on Coruscant, their honeymoon watching the Corphelion Comets, the births of their children, all those years of living and fighting and loving together . . . everything. *That* was how he wanted to spend eternity—not lying around on some forest floor, groaning his guts out.

The eternal moment ended with a low, reverberating thrum.

Leia screamed and thudded to the ground someplace behind him, then her lightsaber fell silent—and so did she.

Han forced himself to stop groaning and to listen, and he heard an anguished moan in a voice so soft and distorted he could recognize it only as female—and there was only one female it could be. He wanted to call out Leia's name, to hear her tell him that it was somebody *else* moaning and she was fine, but his mouth refused to obey. Every time he opened it to call her name, all that came out was the sound of his own pain.

The radiance began to fade from Han's body, and the shadows started to whisper toward him, coming in closer, eating away at the small ring of light that still surrounded him.

We can help.

The words were so low and wispy that Han could not be sure whether he was really hearing them or just imagining them in the rustle of the shadows around him.

We can save you.

Yeah? Han tried to speak the word aloud . . . and discovered that it was work enough just to think it. *What's it going to cost me?*

The shadows said nothing, but they remained nearby, whispering through the trees, turning the trunks from pale to dark wherever they passed. Han recalled the shadow he had glimpsed during the sabacc game with Barduun and wondered if this was where it had come from, if the Mandalorian had been through the gate before him and been foolish enough to accept what the shadows offered.

Han closed his eyes and listened. He could still hear the woman moaning.

Leia.

He dragged the heel of his uninjured leg across the forest floor and felt himself turn. A good sign. Dead men couldn't turn themselves—at least not outside the monolith.

But in here, who knew? Han was starting to think that time and space were something that existed only *inside* sentient minds. And if *that* was true, maybe it was true of life and death, too. Maybe time and space, life and death, were just the lenses through which sentient minds perceived existence.

Leia continued to moan. Han used his leg to turn himself farther . . . and then his eyes were open and he was looking at Leia, a luminous being curled into a fetal position, rocking back and forth and moaning in agony. A few meters beyond her lay Marvid, a smoking heap of powerbody and flesh, motionless and cloaked in shadow. And Han could see Luke, too, still slumped at the base of the tree where he had fallen, but holding his head up and glowing with a deep golden light.

Han's gaze went back to Leia. He wanted to end her anguish even more than his own—would suffer *his* anguish for eternity, as long as hers finally ended.

We can help her.

The shadows came whispering in again, this time so close that they had completely eaten the ring of light that surrounded him, so close that they seemed to be drawing the radiance out of his own body.

We can save her.

Han didn't ask what it would cost, because he didn't want to know. He would give almost anything to save Leia—his sight, his hearing, his sanity, his life, his spirit—whatever it was that made him Han Solo.

But Han had lived around Force-users since the day he'd met Luke on Tatooine, and that was long enough to understand the temptations of the dark side. If he asked for Leia's life, he wouldn't be saving her—he would be condemning them *all*. That was how the dark side worked. It seduced and promised, and sometimes it even delivered. But the cost? The cost was always too much. The dark side took everything a person was—and a big piece of who his loved ones were, too. Han and Leia had learned *that* when Jacen fell to the dark side. The entire Solo family had paid the price—especially Jacen's twin sister, Jaina, who had been forced to hunt him down and put an end to his reign of terror.

Go away.

Han felt as though he had nearly spoken the words, and the rustling shadows did retreat—but only an arm's length. The shadows were patient. They knew that eternity was a long time to listen to the suffering of a loved one, so they would wait. Han's mind would change . . . eventually.

In no time at all.

"Go . . . *away*." This time, Han *did* manage to speak aloud, and the shadows whispered away, back into the forest.

In their wake, they left a swirling cloud of smoke and the rising crackle of fire. A yellow curtain of flame had appeared in the narrow space between Leia and Marvid, still only centimeters high but rapidly climbing.

Han pushed himself to a seated position. The effort sent waves of agony coursing through him, and he quickly grew weak and began to tremble.

But he didn't allow himself to collapse—*couldn't* allow himself to collapse until Leia and Luke were safe. He pointed toward the rising wall of flame.

"Hey, Leia! Luke!" His voice was not exactly loud and booming—but it was audible. "Get up! Fire!"

Luke staggered to his feet. Leia just uncurled, far enough to look in Han's direction. Then she uncurled some more. Her hands went to her mouth, as though she was trying to yell.

When nothing came out, she gave up and simply pointed.

Han looked over his shoulder and saw a meter-high wall of flame behind him, rising in front of Craitheus's wrecked powerbody. Han tried to stand . . . and collapsed, exhausted and in pain. He looked back toward Leia and found her shining more brightly than ever and already lurching to her feet. What had become of Marvid, there was no telling. The flames behind Leia had risen to two meters, and they were too bright to see through.

Acrid smoke began to curl down out of the trees, filling Han's lungs and belly. He coughed and let his head drop, nearly passing out from the pain.

A second passed, or perhaps it was an eternity, then a pair of golden figures emerged from the smoke, so dazzling it hurt Han's eyes to look at them. He stared anyway. They were Luke and Leia, healed by the Force and looking stronger—and more powerful—than ever.

Leia came to his side. Through the radiance, Han could see that her vac suit had been melted away around her midsection, revealing a large swath of pebbly skin that looked almost like armor. She knelt at his side and slipped her hand beneath his head, and his agony began to fade.

"Han," she said. "I told you to be careful."

"Look . . . who's talking," Han answered, struggling to breathe. "I'm not the one . . . who looks like . . . she walked into a hot fusion core."

"Always the smart guy."

Smiling, Leia leaned down to kiss him, and Han felt his strength begin to return. She always had that effect on him.

Luke cleared his throat. "Sorry to interrupt, but we need to move on." He used the Force to create a path through the wall of flame, then motioned for them to follow and started forward. "This fight isn't over—and if we give the Qrephs a chance to regroup, it's only going to get harder."

"*Regroup?* Are you serious?" Han asked, reaching to retrieve his blaster rifle. "Marvid *might* have made it, but don't waste time worrying about Craitheus. I put half a dozen blaster bolts through his brain, and *then* I blew up his powerbody—with him in it."

"And you were hit by two cannon bolts, while I took a micropulse straight to the belly," Leia said.

Using the Force to lift Han along with her, Leia rose and started after Luke. "What makes you think the Qrephs are any easier to kill in this place than *we* are?"

"The Force is strong in here," Luke added. "*Very* strong. It heals even non-Force-users, and it heals quickly."

"Could have fooled me." Han pointed at the patch of pebbled hide on Leia's abdomen. "If you call that healed—"

"And it's raw," Luke interrupted. He gestured at

Han's wounds. "Which means that in here, the Force doesn't always heal according to form."

Han was almost afraid to look. When he did, he saw that the cannon shot to his belly had scorched away most of his thin lab tunic and burned a hole deep into his abdomen. And now the hole was covered by a translucent membrane that did not look much like skin. But at least the bottom half of his leg, visible below the singed-off knee of his trousers, appeared sort of normal. It was the right size and shape, but so hairy it could have belonged to a Wookiee.

"The Force gets confused?" Han asked, still looking at his leg. "Really?"

"Not confused," Luke clarified. "It's just . . . raw and unformed, I think. And it's unimaginably powerful. In here, we're literally made of the Force—and that makes *us* more powerful, too." His eyes dropped to Han's abdomen. "And a bit unformed."

Han studied his wound for a moment, then shrugged. Being "a bit unformed" was better than being dead.

At least, he hoped it was.

They passed through the gap in the flame curtain, which Luke had just opened. As they emerged on the other side, they entered a fire-charred landscape dotted with narrow basalt spires that rose impossibly high. A carpet of golden lichen covered the rocky ground, mounding into knee-high masses that changed before their eyes into thorny yellow bushes that shot up into tall barrel-shaped cacti. And passing between the two most distant cacti, but still close enough that Han could make out their huge round heads wobbling atop their tiny bodies, were the figures of two Columi.

Walking.

Not floating in powerbodies, but walking on their tiny bowed legs, waddling across the desert like a pair of potbellied nerf herders.

Leia lowered Han's feet to the ground, then slowly began to release her Force grasp. "Can you stand?"

Han tested his balance and, finding that he was strong enough to keep it, took a couple of wobbly steps.

"I'll be fine." He released his blaster's trigger safety. "Let's go."

He was not happy to feel Luke's hand on his shoulder, pulling him back. "Sorry, Han. You're going to be the reserve on this mission."

"*Reserve?*" Han shook his head. "I might be a little slow getting in there, but you're not having this fight without me."

Leia stepped in front of him. "Han, we have no choice," she said. "You can't use the Force."

Han scowled. "Yeah, well, neither can the Qrephs."

"They can now," Luke said. "When the shadows offered help, the Qrephs didn't refuse."

"We have to stop them here, *before* they escape." Leia touched Han's cheek, then added, "And there's only one way to do that inside this monolith—the same way Luke destroyed their Vestara biot. By using the Force."

"Yeah? Well, I did some pretty serious damage to Craitheus earlier," Han protested. "That's got to be worth something."

"But you didn't kill him," Luke said. "Not permanently. The best thing you can do for us now is to follow as fast as you can, then stand in reserve. We may need you to cover our retreat."

Han's heart began to sink, but they were right, and he knew it. Craitheus had returned from near-death twice now, and, as far as Han could tell, Han and the Jedi ought to be dead themselves.

He let out a sigh, then nodded. "Yeah, I get it," he said. "Go on. I'll catch up and be ready to cover a retreat."

Leia rose up on her toes and kissed him, long and hard. "Goodbye, Han," she said. "I love you."

Before Han could answer, she pulled back and turned away, then ignited her lightsaber and started to run. Luke did the same, and together they raced away across the blossoming desert. Han started after them, gaining strength with every step.

"You, too, Leia," he whispered. "I love you, too."

Luke charged across the desert forever, Leia at his side. They had opened themselves to the Force completely, and it was pouring into them from all sides, raw and potent and unformed, neither dark nor light until it entered them and they made it so. It devoured them as it sustained them, filled them with a boiling storm of power their bodies could not long sustain.

The Qrephs were a few hundred meters ahead, a pair of dark specks racing up a flower-carpeted gulch toward a distant circle of radiance. The shimmering shape would have looked like a pond, except that it stood vertical to the ground and was located at the base of a distant basalt spire.

"Luke, that has to be the gate," Leia said. "We can't let them reach it."

"Agreed," Luke said. Leia had repeated what Han told her about Barduun, so Luke understood that if the Qrephs were allowed to escape, they would become not only Force-users but insane Force-users, imbued with a darkness that he did not yet understand. "We stop them now. *Reach*."

As Luke spoke, he was reaching out. He quickly found the Qrephs, a pair of dark, oily presences burning cold in the Force. He began to pull, and then he and Leia were *there*, in the shadow of the looming spire, spinning and whirling across the flower-carpeted gulch, catching forks of Force lightning on their lightsabers, dancing ever closer to the two Columi.

A dark blast of Force energy caught Leia square in the chest. She staggered and started to fall backward—then put a hand down and pushed off, came up leaping, and went into a Force flip that carried her to within a dozen paces of their quarry.

What happened next, Luke only felt: the invisible hand of the Force clamping down on his throat. His vision narrowed instantly. The blood to his brain had been choked off. Five seconds, he thought. Five seconds until he lost consciousness.

Maybe less.

He reached out in the Force, trying to find the Qreph who was attacking him—trying to find *either* Qreph—but he was too dizzy already. His hearing started to fade, his vision narrowed to nothing.

Three seconds. Maybe.

Luke launched himself into a Force leap, whirling his blade through a Jedi attack pattern, whipping his feet back and forth in blind snap kicks and targetless heel strikes. His hearing faded to silence, and he felt himself starting to drop . . . then the ground came up beneath his feet and his knees buckled.

Desperate to locate his attacker, Luke reached out in all directions and *pulled,* grabbing at every being he could sense. He felt a jolt of surprise from Leia and let her loose. He found the Qrephs just ahead, standing well apart, two beings full of fear and anger and hatred. He pulled harder and felt them slide toward him, their fear blazing into panic and their anger deepening to rage.

The Force grasp slipped free, and the blood came roaring back into Luke's head. His hearing returned first, and he heard Leia a few meters to his right, her lightsaber growling and hissing as she blocked a fork of Force lightning.

Then the crackle of more lightning sounded nearby, this time coming from high on the bank of the gulch. Luke tried to bring his lightsaber around to catch the attack, but his reflexes were still too shaky. The fork took him dead center, and every muscle in his body clamped down.

Luke ignored the pain and *pushed,* then felt the Force lightning slide away as his attacker staggered back. He leapt up—or, rather, *tried* to leap up—and managed to regain his feet.

His vision had cleared, and he could see the Qrephs twenty paces ahead, fighting from opposite sides of the gulch. Craitheus had sprouted half a dozen horny spikes where Han had peppered his head with blaster bolts, and he was halfway up the right bank, hurling dark blasts of Force energy toward a steadily advancing Leia. Marvid was on the opposite side of the wash, half covered in diamond-shaped lizard scales and still struggling to recover from Luke's Force push.

Neither Columi was standing on his crooked legs so much as levitating above them. Their gray noseless faces had turned dark and spectral, with a sinister glint of yellow shining in the depths of their huge eyes, and when their hands moved, it was with an eerie grace that made their slender little arms look more like tentacles than actual limbs.

Clearly the two Jedi were no longer fighting Marvid and Craitheus Qreph. They were battling something far worse, something Luke did not yet understand— manifestations of pure dark-side hatred, perhaps, or even ancient dark-lord apparitions desperate to return to the world of the living.

And access to that world stood less than fifty meters

away, via a circle of shimmering light too bright to see through.

Luke reactivated his blade and began to advance alongside his sister, pivoting and dodging, slipping past Force blasts and deflecting one fork of Force lightning after another.

The Qrephs were retreating as fast as the Jedi were advancing. The gate stood thirty meters away, then twenty-five . . . and Luke and Leia were not closing the distance.

A booming laugh rolled down the wash. "Jedi *fools*." Marvid's voice had grown deep and baleful. "You cannot win. We have the Force now, too."

Actually, Luke thought it more likely that the Force had *them,* but he did not say so. The time for talking was past.

Ten meters.

To his left, Luke noticed a boulder resting atop the rim of the gulch. He sent it tumbling toward Marvid's head.

The Columi's hands quickly fluttered up and hurled the boulder back toward him. By then Luke was overflowing with the Force. He felt as if he were burning from the inside out, being incinerated by the raw power flowing into him and through him. He launched himself over the boulder.

"*Now,* Leia!" Luke turned a hand toward Marvid and poured himself into a fierce blast of Force energy. "We end this now!"

The impact sent Marvid tumbling, head throbbing and chest aching. Skywalker's attack should have killed him—he knew that. He could feel the fractures in his skull, feel how his eyes were bulging from their sockets. But the laws of biology were not the same inside the monolith. Here, the Force sustained all things, rejuvenated them and made them strong.

Even Columi.

So, instead of dying, Marvid went flying into his brother, and together they tumbled through the desert thorn brush, their thin limbs flailing out of control, their big heads banging into the ground time after time.

Then they stopped. The shadow spirits inside them began to call on the Force, drawing it into their battered bodies, using it to mend their fractured bones and heal their bleeding organs. Then he and his brother rose, standing on their own thin legs.

It made Marvid feel primitive and brutish, alive in a way he had never before experienced. Like an animal— like a vicious, hungry animal that knew only appetite and fear and rage.

Craitheus stepped next to him. "Can you feel it, Marvid?" he asked, turning back toward the basalt spire where the gate was located. "The power?"

"I feel it," Marvid replied, also turning. Skywalker and his sister were about twenty meters away, Skywalker circling toward their left while the Solo woman moved to block their path to the gate. "The Force is ours. The *galaxy* is ours."

"The galaxy is ours," Craitheus agreed. "*After* we kill Skywalker."

The shadows did not like that idea. Marvid was seized by a sudden desire to rush the Solo woman, to blow her out of his path with Force lightning and flee through the portal before Skywalker could stop them. He ignored the urge. The shadows were responding only to their own fear, trying to escape the immediate danger so they could flee into the galaxy and sate their appetites.

But Marvid knew better. He was smarter. For Craitheus and him to achieve real power in the galaxy, Skywalker and his sister had to die—now, inside the monolith.

Marvid started back toward the spire. "We'll feint an attack at the gate," he said, "then whirl on Skywalker and take him by surprise."

"Excellent," Craitheus said. "We take them one at a time. With Skywalker gone, the Solo woman won't stand a chance."

The desire to attack the Solo woman grew more urgent. *Rush her now,* the shadows urged. Marvid ignored them and stepped to his brother's side. The primitive instincts of the shadows were no match for the strength of Columi minds.

Han raced after Leia and Luke, keeping up as best he could—which was not at all. He watched their silhouettes spinning up the yellow gulch far ahead of him, bouncing off the tall cacti and the dark basalt spires, growing constantly brighter and larger. He felt strong enough to fight again, but no matter how fast he ran, he could never catch them.

How could he? They had the Force, and he didn't.

The two Jedi had become golden balls of lightning, dancing back and forth between the rumbling darkness of the two Qreph brothers. The fight became a battle, the battle a war, and the war a conflagration—an endless storm of thunder and blood that raged across the yellow desert for all eternity.

Luke saw the Columi turn toward Leia and the gate, then he extended his free hand, grabbing them both in the invisible grasp of the Force. He jerked them back in his direction and they came flying, launching themselves straight at him—fully in control. He saw them spinning around in midair, their hands rising to attack, and realized he had fallen for a ploy.

Luke released his hold. Too late.

The Columi were already spraying streams of dark-side energy at him, hammering him with a torrent of cold, pummeling power. Luke staggered and almost went down, caught one stream on his lightsaber, and had the weapon torn from his grasp. He began to stumble back, fighting to keep his balance and bring up his own hands.

The Qrephs landed four paces in front of him, their huge eyes growing even larger, their small chins dropping. They had underestimated his strength, Luke guessed. They had expected him to fall quickly, and he had surprised them. Craitheus drew his arms back, readying another attack.

And then Leia was leaping in behind the Columi, one hand holding her lightsaber and the other hitting Craitheus with a wave of energy so fierce it became a yellow torrent of flame. Marvid stumbled away from his brother in shock, giving Luke the half second he needed to turn his palm forward and loose his own blast of golden energy.

Marvid swung his hand over to block, and the two streams of opposing energy met. The Columi's flesh melted into smoke and his bones dissolved into ashes, and Luke glimpsed a shadow tumbling away on the shock wave. Then a searing agony washed over him as the wave of Force energy took him, too—at once burning his body and healing it, devouring him and renewing him.

Luke hung in that last moment, caught between death and life, for an eternity. He was at the end of his life and at its beginning, drowning in agony and filled with bliss, and he began to see that *this* was the essential nature of the Force. The Force was life, and life was growth, and nothing grew that did not change.

And change was destruction.

That was why the dark side existed. Life bore death, death nourished life, destruction came before rejuvenation. And pain came before healing. The dark side was as necessary to life as the light side was. Without it, verdant worlds would stagnate, galactic empires would rule forever.

Luke saw all that and more, saw that conflict was as necessary to progress as was harmony, that suffering was as essential to wisdom as was joy. Perhaps there was no pure good, no absolute evil. There was only life, only change and growth, suffering and joy . . . death and rebirth.

There was only the Force.

Han saw Luke and Leia come together, trapping the Qrephs between them, no more than twenty paces from the shimmering gate. He heard the swishing roar of the Force's power being loosed, and then he saw only light—a stabbing golden brilliance that made his eyes hurt and his ears ring. It flashed through him in a blast of searing heat that stole his breath and filled his entire body with a fiery ache.

Then the spire dropped, its severed base striking the ground with a deafening bang. The dark column stood swaying for a moment, then finally toppled, crashing down so hard it made the ground jump and thunder boil through the air.

A curtain of dust billowed up to roll across the desert, and Han found himself running through a gray haze, lost and alone and yelling for Leia.

Twenty-six

As the dust settled from the air, the desert became a forest of tree ferns and giant club mosses. Where the spire had fallen, a hole in the haze opened into a blue liquid sky. It appeared watery and still, and Han felt as though he were looking up through the bottom of a lake. He could see a tall mountain rising along one shore, and every once in a while he thought he saw a face ripple past, as huge as a cloud.

Then the haze closed in again, and Han remained alone. He began to rush through the fungi forest, calling for his lost wife and his best friend, searching for the spot where they vanished—where they had no doubt sacrificed themselves to stop yet another evil from entering the galaxy.

And for what?

Luke and Leia had spent their entire lives fighting *why*? To defend a government that had turned its back on the Jedi Order? To bring peace to a galaxy that valued it too little and would never have it? Han shook his head.

No.

Luke and Leia had devoted their lives to one thing: fighting the power of the dark side. It was that simple. Wherever the dark side rose, whenever the Sith had dared show themselves—there Luke and Leia had rushed, never hesitating, never flinching. It had been their destiny to shepherd the galaxy into a new era of hope, and not once had they shrunk from that calling.

Now that destiny would pass to someone else.

Because Luke and Leia were gone. Han understood that. They had become one with the Force, and Han expected that he would be joining them soon.

He wasn't sad or frightened, or even sorry. He just wanted to hold Leia's hand one more time, to look into her brown eyes and see her smile again.

Then it occurred to Han that he might be dead already. Or dead *again*. Or still dead. In this place, it was hard to know.

He stopped walking and turned in a circle, searching for some sign of Leia or Luke—for some hint that he would not spend eternity without them.

He saw nothing but green fronds and ivory pillars streaked with brown, smelled nothing but the muskiness of the forest, heard nothing but the shadows whispering around him, offering to help, aching to devour him.

Han dropped to his knees. "Ah, Leia," he said. "I wish I could have gone with you."

Leia drifted in agony and ecstasy, nowhere and everywhere, an amorphous mass of self-awareness bound together by will and desire. She saw her body below, a whirling ball of golden radiance still tumbling across the desert, so hot that, in its wake, it left a trail of flaming thorn brush.

Her enemies—she could no longer recall their names—had disintegrated into smoke and ash. But her brother's body stood about twenty meters from her own, still reeling and so bright she could barely look at him.

Leia could not recall *his* name, either. She knew she should remember, but she could feel herself dissolving into the Force, becoming one with it. And in this strange place, as *she* vanished, so did her past, and her treasured memories grew impossible to hold.

That frightened her. It shouldn't have, she knew. Becoming one with the Force was the fate of every Jedi who served it. But she could not help feeling there was something she had left undone—something that should not be forgotten. Someone she could not abandon. Not yet.

But *who*?

She was finding it difficult to bind her own essence together, to recall even her own identity, let alone someone else's.

Then a familiar voice spoke her name, and she remembered.

Han.

A sudden silence fell over the forest, and Han saw the shadows flee through the undergrowth. There was a golden radiance ahead, shining through fungi and ferns, changing them before his eyes into the neatly ordered trees of a Coruscanti strolling wood.

"Leia?" Han rose and started forward. "Leia?"

And then he saw her, a golden glowing figure running down the path with outstretched arms, so radiant and bright it hurt his eyes to look upon her. He met her halfway and swept her up into a flying hug. Leia kissed him hard on the lips, and he felt the Force flowing into him, filling him with warmth and life and joy.

They held the kiss for an instant, or perhaps it was a day, then Han set her feet on the ground and stepped back to look at her. She was Leia—but not as he had last seen her. She was the Leia of their youth, brown eyes shining with a fervor not yet tempered by the loss of her two sons and the deaths of more close friends than Han could bear to recall.

After a moment, the joy in Leia's face changed to concern. "Han, what happened to you?" she asked. "Was it the carbon-freezing?"

"Carbon-freezing? What carbon-freezing?"

"You don't remember?" Leia asked. "Vader laid a trap on Cloud City. He froze you in carbonite—"

"And you told me you loved me," Han finished. "How could I forget?"

Leia's only reply was a look of confusion.

"You remember that, right?" Han was getting worried. "You *said* it: *I love you.*"

"Of course I remember," Leia said. "But that's the last thing I remember . . . and now you look so old. I didn't think carbon-freezing did that to people."

Han would have laughed if he hadn't been so frightened. "It's not the carbon-freezing, sweetheart."

He didn't understand what had happened to Leia's memory—to *her*—but there wasn't much about this place that he did understand. He was just going to have to work with it and hope for the best.

"For a while," Han continued, "I was a wall decoration hanging in Jabba's palace. Then you rescued me. Do you remember that?"

"Yes." A gleam of anger came to Leia's eyes. "Jabba put me in that blasted slave outfit, and I strangled him with my own chain. And you knocked Boba Fett into the sarlacc pit. Is that right?"

Han grinned. "Right."

"What happened after that?"

"Well, the emperor lured us into an ambush on Endor," Han said, watching in delight as every word brought a new glimmer of recognition to her eyes. "But we turned that around, remember? In the end, it was Palpatine who died."

"And there was a celebration," Leia recalled. "With Ewoks—hundreds of them."

"Right again," Han said.

He went on to tell her about everything they had done together—founding the New Republic and defeating the remnants of the Empire for good, getting married and having babies, the decision to raise their children as Jedi. As he spoke, the young Leia of his past began to mature before his eyes, growing ever more beautiful but also wiser, and even more open and compassionate.

Then Han reached the era of the alien Yuuzhan Vong invasion of the galaxy. He paused, uncertain that he wanted to put Leia through the torment of those years again. But it was already too late. Her memories were flooding back without any prompting from him. He could only watch as the deaths of Chewbacca and Anakin etched her face with sorrow—and as the anguish of Jacen's fall to the dark side stole the light from her eyes.

When the sadness did not fade, Han took her hand. "Before Jacen became Darth Caedus, he gave us a granddaughter," he prompted. "Her name is—"

"Allana," Leia finished. "She's the heir to the Hapes Consortium, and she lives with her mother, Tenel Ka. But that feels almost like a dream to me."

"Allana is real," Han assured her. "And she's a great kid. What else do you remember?"

Leia gave Han a wry smile, no doubt aware that he was trying to avoid lingering on the most painful parts of their shared life. "I remember the Lost Tribe of Sith and their invasion of Coruscant," she said. "And I remember Jaina's wedding."

Han smiled. Leia was coming back to him—even if he wasn't quite sure what that meant in this place. "What about now?" he asked. "Do you remember where we are? And how we got here?"

Leia's eyes grew hard. "I remember, Han. Sarnus, the Blue Star, Base Prime," she said. "I remember all of it."

Han was relieved. "What about the Qrephs?"

"They're the least of our problems," Leia said. "They're dead."

Han wanted to believe her, but after seeing the Columi return before, he didn't feel like taking chances. "You sure? Because they've been pretty hard to kill."

Leia paused and seemed to shudder a bit but nodded. "I'm sure. The Qrephs are gone—just like I would have been, if you hadn't called me back so quickly."

Han frowned. "So *quickly*?" He didn't understand. "Leia, you were gone so long I thought I had lost you for good."

Leia looked confused. "Han, I didn't go anywhere. I fought the Qrephs, then I came straight back, as soon as I heard you call."

Han shook his head in bewilderment. "I don't know how to explain it," he said. "You were gone . . . and it felt like I was looking for you forever."

Leia glanced around the strolling wood, her eyes widening as though she was seeing their surroundings for the first time. She took Han's hand, and her voice grew somber.

"Han, am I dead?" she asked. "Are *we* dead?"

Han wasn't sure how to answer.

For one thing, he didn't know. And if it hadn't occurred to Leia that she might be dead before now, he didn't want to break the news in the wrong way. She might dissolve into the Force right there. Or she might vanish into . . . well, wherever she went *last* time and doom him to an eternity of searching.

"*Han?*" Leia's voice had grown urgent. "I don't like it when you spend that much time thinking. It's dangerous."

"Take it easy, will you?" Han scratched his head for a

moment. "All I know is, you vanished in a big golden flash—at least that's what *I* saw. It looked like someone set off a baradium bomb."

Leia considered this, then said, "So we're dead."

"*Maybe* we're dead," Han corrected.

"*Probably.*" Leia glanced around the garden again, and Han hoped she might be thinking that it wasn't such a bad place to spend eternity together. Instead, she asked, "What about Luke? Did he make it?"

No sooner had she spoken Luke's name than a luminous sphere appeared in the strolling wood. As it approached them, it began to resolve into the shape of a man.

"I'm here," Luke said, joining them.

Unlike Leia when she returned, he actually looked a little older than before the explosion, and perhaps a bit wiser and more at peace with himself. The wounds in his throat had closed, and Han saw no sign of the freakish eyes that had been inside the holes earlier. Recalling his own deformities, he glanced down and was relieved to discover that the membrane covering his belly wound looked almost like burned skin now, and his injured leg was no longer quite so hairy.

When neither Solo was quick to respond, Luke asked, "Is this a private party or something?"

"Sorry," Han said, returning his gaze to Luke. "We were hoping you made it out of here, that's all. Leia thinks we're dead."

Leia cocked her luminous brow. "And you *don't*?"

Han shrugged, then shot her one of his best lopsided grins. "Hey, as long as we're together—"

"We aren't the ones who died," Luke interrupted. "That was the Qrephs."

Han waited for an explanation. When none came, he finally asked, "Says who?"

Luke smiled. "I do. When Leia and I destroyed the

Qrephs' bodies, we set their shadows adrift," he said. "And without living bodies, the Qrephs can't invite the shadows to return. Trust me, the galaxy is rid of Marvid and Craitheus Qreph—forever."

"I can buy that," Leia said. "But what makes you so sure *we* are still alive?"

Luke spread his hands. "To tell you the truth, I'm not a hundred percent certain," he said. "But since we *do* have bodies, and Han seems to be returning to normal . . ."

"The odds are on our side," Han agreed. He glanced around the garden, searching for some hint of an exit portal. "At least until we starve to death—or go crazy in here."

"That's not going to happen," Luke said. "Follow me."

Luke turned and started down the path. His bright figure drove the shadows deep into the woods as he passed.

Han looked over at Leia, then asked, "You think he actually has a clue where he's going?"

Leia shrugged. "Who can say?" she asked. "But unless *you* have a plan—"

"Are you kidding?" Han asked. "My plan is, follow the Grand Master."

Luke led them down a twisting path that seemed to turn back on itself repeatedly, crossing and recrossing identical intersections so many times that Han started to think they were lost. Still, the terrain did not change. The trees remained relatively small and neatly ordered, and the shadows continued to retreat ever deeper into the woods, until they no longer intruded at all.

After they had been walking for a while, Luke's pace began to slow, and he spoke in a tone that sounded more melancholy than relieved. "We're almost there."

"Then don't sound so glum about it," Han said. "It'll be good to get back."

"It will be good to leave *here*," Luke allowed. "But we can never go back, not truly."

"No," Leia agreed. She and Luke shared a knowing look, which vanished almost before Han caught it, then she added, "Not to the way things were."

"Whoa . . . *guys*." Han didn't like the turn the conversation was taking. "This place didn't change us *that* much."

"But it *did* change us," Luke said. "If only because it opened our eyes to something that's been happening for a while now."

"Opened our eyes to *what*?" Han demanded. "And if you say I'm getting old, someone's going to get blasted."

Leia smiled. "It's not about age, Han." Her eyes filled with joy and sadness and contentment, with longing and acceptance. "It's about stepping back for a while."

Han scowled. "Who needs to step back?"

"I do," Leia said. She took his hand. "*We* do. We've spent a lifetime battling to make the galaxy a better place. But life is about more than fighting, Han. There needs to be time for rest and love and happiness."

"Exactly," Luke said. "Life is like the Force. It needs balance."

"The *Force* needs us to take a rest?" Han scoffed. "That's what you're telling me?"

"More or less." Luke paused and looked into the trees for a moment, then said, "Maybe there was a time we had to keep fighting because there were so few of us. But the Jedi Order is strong now, and we have to let others take the lead, so it can grow even stronger."

Han hesitated. "Well, I guess I *could* use a break, as long as it's good for the Order." He actually liked the idea of some downtime with Leia, but it also scared him. He turned to face her. "What if we get bored?"

"We *won't*." Leia squeezed his hand, and the light in her eyes turned racy. "Trust me."

Han responded with an enthusiastic smirk. "In that case," he said, "count me in."

"Hold on, you two," Luke said, laughing. "Let me get us out of here first."

Luke led them a few steps farther, then stopped in the middle of the trail and turned to Han.

"Ready?" he asked.

"You bet," Han said. He looked around and saw nothing but more trees. "But, uh, ready for what?"

"To go back," Luke said. "This is it."

"The gate?" Leia asked.

"Exactly," Luke said. "Can't you feel it?"

Leia closed her eyes, then tipped her head back. "I can," she said, smiling. "Lando is there, and Ben."

"Where?" Han looked up and saw only a patch of gray sky through the canopy of neatly ordered trees. "I don't see anything."

"Don't *see*, Han," Luke said. "*Feel.*"

"I'll try," Han said. "But without the Force—"

"You don't need the Force in here," Luke said. "But there is no *try*, Han. There is only doing."

Han rolled his eyes and muttered, "Easy for you *Jedi* to say."

Still, he closed his eyes and began to focus on feeling the open sky. To his surprise, he experienced a sense of peace . . . which quickly blossomed into full-blown contentment.

He heard Lando's voice somewhere above, asking, "Are you sure you felt your father reaching out for you? I don't see anything."

"Hey, Lando!" Han called. "Down here!"

He opened his eyes and saw that the terrain had shifted under their feet. Now they were standing in a small courtyard with black stone paving and a dry fountain in the center. About five meters above their heads, peering down from among the branches along the edge of the courtyard, was the smiling face of Lando Calrissian.

"Han, old buddy," Lando called, "is that you?"

Ben's face appeared beside Lando's. "Dad?"

Luke stepped to Han's side, opposite Leia, and grabbed Han's arm. "It's time," he said. "Let's go."

"You don't have to ask me twice," Han said.

He took Leia's hand and squeezed it tight, and together they all started forward. As they advanced, the fountain suddenly began to jet water, and the surrounding trees rustled in the wind. Han felt every cell in his body start to sizzle, then his stomach dropped as though he were riding the fastest turbolift in the galaxy, shooting up into the sky.

The next thing he knew, all three of them were back on Base Prime, walking across the stasis circle toward the balcony, where Lando and Ben stood at the railing, staring at them in openmouthed surprise.

Han exchanged relieved glances with Luke and Leia. "Man," he said, pulling them over to the balcony. "*That* was a trip."

Lando and Ben stooped down to reach beneath the railing and pull everyone to safety.

"Welcome back!" Lando cried. He wrapped one arm around Han and the other around Leia, crushing them in a perfect imitation of a Wookiee hug. "You two really had me worried this time."

"Uh, thank you, Lando," Leia said, trying—and failing—to extract herself from his hug. "We were a little worried ourselves."

"Is everyone okay?" Lando finally let go and stepped back to inspect them. A concerned look came to his face, and he asked, "You *do* know you're glowing, don't you?"

Han looked down and saw that Lando was right. His skin was still shining with the same golden light that had permeated him inside the monolith. But at least his body looked right again—or close enough. His injured leg was completely normal, and the only sign of his belly wound was what looked like an old burn scar.

"Yeah, and glowing isn't the half of it," Han said. "Maybe we should head for the *Falcon*'s medbay and get the heck off this monolith."

Han looked up to find Lando studying the scar on his stomach with an expression of bewilderment.

"Hey," Han said. "Didn't anyone ever tell you it's rude to stare?"

"Uh, sorry," Lando said. "But that burn scar looks at *least* a year old, and you've only been gone a few hours. What the blazes *happened* in there?"

"Long story," Leia said, taking him by the arm. "We'll tell you all about it back on the *Falcon*."

"Which can't be soon enough for me," Ben put in. "We're done here. We've recovered all the data from this place that we're ever going to get—though I don't know how *anyone* will ever make sense of it. This stuff is way above my head."

"We'll worry about that later," Luke said. "First I want to be sure nobody *ever* uses this base—or these labs—again."

"The charges are already set," Ben replied. "And we placed the thermal detonators in the gate. Once they go off, it will be impossible to tell there was ever anything here."

"And we have quite a few concussion missiles left," Lando added. "By the time we leave, the only thing left of Base Prime is going to be its heat signature."

"Good," Leia said. "But we can't stop there. We also need to prevent anyone from using the monolith again."

"You mean anyone like *Vestara*," Ben said.

"I mean *anyone*," Leia said. "Which means we have to stop them from finding it. Maybe we should save a few missiles and take out the repeater beacons inside the Bubble."

Han cocked a brow. "The Bubble?"

"The Bubble of the Lost," Leia explained. "I'll explain more about it later, but it's enough to say the Bubble is the reason the monolith is so hard to find."

"Right, and the harder it is to navigate the blasted thing, the better," Lando said. "Taking out the repeater beacons is a good idea. And Omad has some thoughts on an early-warning system we can deploy around the perimeter."

Luke nodded his approval. "Good. We can talk about that on the way out." He turned back to Ben. "Now, what's the situation with our team? Everybody all right?"

"Affirmative," Ben said. "We lost all but one of Lando's battle droids, but Base Prime has been cleared and secured. Omad and Tahiri are both aboard the *Falcon,* taking care of Ohali—and keeping an eye on Dena Yus."

"Dena is still alive?" Leia asked. "I didn't think she was going to make it."

"She found the formula for her enzymes." Ben turned to Luke. "But I'm not so sure that's a good thing. How do we handle someone who helped kill thirty thousand miners? She has to answer for that."

Luke considered this a moment, then nodded. "She does, but what that means isn't something to be decided right now." He paused and looked around. "Not here. Why don't you and Tahiri take her back to the Jedi Council? They can pass judgment."

"What do you mean, *they*?" Ben asked. "Aren't you coming back with us?"

Luke shook his head. "Not for a while." He started

across the balcony, motioning for the others to follow. "I need some time."

"Time?" Ben's voice grew worried. "For what?"

"For myself." Luke paused and rested a hand on Ben's shoulder. "I've been leading the Jedi for forty years, son. I think it's time for a change."

Ben looked as if he thought his father had gone mad. "A *change*? What's wrong?"

Luke laughed. "Ben, stop worrying. I'm fine."

They'd reached the security ring. Han started to cross toward the hatch that led into the biot lab.

"Whoa!" Ben used the Force to pull Han's hand away from the control. "You don't want to open that. The automatic filtration and nourishment systems were destroyed during the assault, so it's pretty ripe in there."

Han thought of the dozens of biots he had seen inside the lab, and he didn't know whether to feel relieved or sad. Mostly he was glad that the monsters who had created them would never have a chance to build another one.

"We'll go through the residence," Ben said, pointing toward a blown hatch about a quarter of the way around the security ring. "It smells a whole lot better."

Ben led the group into a chromalloy corridor that Han had not traveled before. The bodies had all been cleared away, but the halls were so pocked and battle-scarred that it was a wonder the walls were still standing.

As they advanced up the passage, Ben fell in beside his father.

"So, Dad, if you're not coming back, what do I tell the Masters about this place?" he asked. "Is it the Mortis Monolith?"

Luke shook his head. "The truth is, I don't know. But if Mortis was *ever* here, I don't think it is anymore," he said. "The Force inside the monolith was too raw, and there was no hint of Balance."

"Any sign of the Ones?" Ben asked. "Or that Anakin and Obi-Wan were there?"

Again, Luke shook his head. "Nothing," he said. "In fact, I don't even think we should assume that this is the same monolith Anakin and Obi-Wan visited."

Han frowned. "Come on," he said. "How many monoliths can there be?"

"Who knows?" Luke asked. "The galaxy is a vast place. There could be dozens of monoliths, or thousands . . . or just the one. The point is, we have no way of knowing—and it really doesn't matter, because Mortis isn't here. At least, not now."

"Fair enough," Han said. "But if this *isn't* Mortis, then what is it?"

Luke shrugged. "You saw what the Qrephs were using this place for," he said. "After that, I'm not sure any mortal *should* know what this place is."

"Nice dodge," Leia said. "But the question remains, Luke. Do *you* know what it is?"

Luke met her gaze and smiled. "I'm still mortal, Leia," he said. "The monolith didn't change that."

Epilogue

With a lone Twi'lek onstage singing light-and-easy raboa tunes to a handful of listeners, the Red Ronto seemed almost sleepy compared to Leia's last visit. A furry-faced Bothan sat alone in the far corner, blowing hookah smoke into a filtration vent in the wall. A gang of hangar mechanics nursed drinks after a midafternoon shift change. Even the bartender looked relaxed, leaning against his pipe-swaddled swill dispenser with all four arms folded across his chest.

At the moment, there was no place Leia would rather be. She and Han were sitting in the same booth where they had first met Omad Kaeg nearly three months ago. Omad was here again, too, crowded around the table with Tahiri, Ohali, Ben, Luke, and—best of all—Jaina and Jag. They were all joking and laughing and paying no attention at all to the curious glances from the cantina's other patrons. And Lando was just returning from the bar, carrying their second bottle of Corellian Reserve.

"So, are you *sure* Mirta Gev got away?" Han was asking no one in particular. "She couldn't have been moving very fast. I cut up her leg pretty bad."

"What can I say?" Tahiri replied. She was sitting between Jaina and Omad. "Ben and I covered every centimeter of Base Prime while we were setting the demolition charges. Gev wasn't there."

"I'm betting she escaped with Vestara," said Ben, who was sitting next to his father. "I saw both of them retreating into the Qrephs' residence right after we breached the wall. After that, there was no sign of them."

"*Great,*" Han muttered. "A Mandalorian teaming up with a Sith. Now they both qualify for blast on sight."

"Maybe," Leia said. She laid her hand on Han's knee and gave it a squeeze to calm his nerves. "But that's not going to be *our* problem. Remember?"

The storm clouds drained from Han's face, and he flashed his most endearing cockeyed grin.

"Of course I remember," he said. "It's the best plan ever: you, me, and the *Falcon,* with all the time in the Void and about a thousand galactic wonders to see. How could I forget?"

"You're really going to do it?" Lando asked, opening the Reserve and starting to pour another round. "Han and Leia Solo, *retire*?"

Leia felt Han tense up again, just a little, and she gave his knee another squeeze. So far, he had been doing a good job of pretending the torture sessions on Base Prime were "no big deal." But she knew he was hurting, both inside and out, and he needed time to recover.

As a matter of fact, so did *she.* If the journey into the monolith had taught her anything, it was how incredible Han truly was. For over four decades, he had been keeping up with her and the rest of the Jedi *without the Force.* But he couldn't do that forever. No one could. Sooner or later, Han would start to slow down. And before that happened, the Solos deserved some time alone—like normal people. She let Lando's question hang for a moment, until all eyes at the table began to turn toward her.

"Well, *retire* might be overstating it," she said. "But we're definitely taking a leave."

"As long as you stay in touch," Jagged Fel said, "and do a better job of it than you did out here. Jaina was sick with worry when you didn't report back for so long."

"Don't exaggerate." Jaina punched him lightly in the shoulder. "I wasn't *sick*."

Jag grinned. "Not once we decided to come investigate," he said. "But before that . . ."

"Well, I am very glad you came," Omad said to them both. "It will be good to have your help setting the new security beacons around the Bubble. It's not exactly my area of expertise."

"It's our pleasure, Omad," Jaina said. "And it's as much for the Jedi's sake as the Rift's. Besides, after all the help you gave Luke and my parents, it's the least we could do."

"It was nothing," Omad said, giving a dismissive wave. "And I owed your parents for backing *me* up against Scarn and his Nargons."

Lando finished pouring, then picked up his own glass and turned to Luke.

"How about you, Grand Master?" he asked. "Are you still planning to have Ben and Tahiri take Dena back to the Jedi Council?"

Luke nodded. "As long as you and the miners' cooperative still agree," he said. "She needs to atone for her crimes somehow, but just what that means is a difficult question. The Council will have the wisdom to find an answer."

"And, in the meantime, Master Cilghal will get a chance to study a living biot up close," Tahiri added. "I don't think we should assume that all the Qrephs' biot spies are going to die off. Some may have found a way to fabricate their own enzymes. Life will out, after all."

"I agree," Ohali said. "It's even possible that some of

the biots don't need enzymes. The Qrephs were always experimenting."

"Good points," Luke said. "Be sure to mention them in your briefing to the Council."

"We will," Ohali said.

Lando started to lift his glass for a toast, but Ben raised a hand to stop him.

"Wait. You're still dodging the big question, Dad," Ben said. "If you're not coming back with us, then where *are* you going?"

Luke's expression remained patient. "I thought I explained that."

Ben rolled his eyes. "A *retreat*, Dad? *Really?*" He shook his head. "I'm not buying it. If you think you can go after Vestara Khai without me—"

"I'm *not*," Luke interrupted. "I just need some time away."

Ben scowled, still doubtful. "And what about the Jedi?" he asked. "How do you expect the Order to get along without its Grand Master?"

Leia saw Luke's gaze flicker from Ben to Tahiri and Jaina, then to Ohali and herself—from the youngest generation of modern Jedi to the eldest—and she felt the calm that came to him in the Force. Luke had done his work well. The Jedi Order was strong and vigorous. The time had come for him to step out of the way, to let his creation grow into something larger than himself.

After a moment, Luke looked back to his son.

"Ben, I've been away for months now. You've read the same Council reports that I have. Did you see anything to suggest that the Jedi Order can't get along without me for a while?"

Ben furrowed his brow. "Well, no," he said. "But . . . I still don't understand it. You aren't going all *Yoda* on me, are you?"

Luke chuckled. *"Going Yoda?"* he repeated. "Would that be so bad?"

Ben thought about that, then shrugged. "Only if you expect me to visit you in a swamp," he said. "Otherwise, I guess I'll deal with it."

Luke grinned and clasped his son's shoulder. "In that case, I'll be sure to avoid swamps. Now, how about we let Lando make his toast?"

Ben smiled and picked up his glass. "Sure thing." He turned to Lando. "Sorry to hold things up."

Lando returned the smile. "No worries, Ben. Nobody gets between me and my Corellian Reserve."

He started to raise his glass again—then Ohali asked, "What about you, Lando? Are *you* going to retire?"

Lando's eyes widened in mock horror. "Me? Not in *this* lifetime. I do intend to go home and see Tendra and Chance, but I'll be back to rebuild the Sarnus Refinery."

He raised his glass again, then looked around the table. "Now?"

Leia nodded and raised her glass, as did everyone else.

"Thank you." Lando held his glass out toward the center of the table, then said, "To good friends."

There followed a moment of silence. Jaina frowned. "That's *it*?" she asked. "After all that buildup, that's your big toast?"

Lando put a hand on his chest, feigning injury. "I thought it was simple and eloquent." Then he winked at her. "How about this: to good friends, good times, and new journeys."

They all extended their arms and clinked glasses.

"To new journeys," Luke repeated. "And may the Force be with us all."

Read on for an excerpt from
Star Wars: Kenobi
by John Jackson Miller
Published by Century

"It's time for you to go home, sir."

Wyle Ulbreck woke up and looked at his empty glass. "What's that you say?"

The green-skinned bartender prodded the old human on the shoulder. "I said it's time for you to go home, Master Ulbreck. You've had enough."

"That ain't what I meant," Ulbreck said, rubbing the crust from his bloodshot eyes. "You called me 'sir.' And then 'Master.'" He leered suspiciously at the barkeep. "Are you an organic—or a *droid*?"

The bartender sighed and shrugged. "*This* again? I told you when you asked earlier. My eyes are large and red because I'm a Duros. I called you what I did because I'm polite. And I'm polite because I'm not some old moisture farmer, deranged from too many years out in the—"

"Because," the white-whiskered man interrupted, "I don't do business with no droids. Droids are thieves, the lot of them."

"Why would a droid steal?"

"T'give to other droids," Ulbreck said. He shook his head. The bartender was clearly an idiot.

"What would—" the bartender started to ask. "Never mind," he said instead. He reached for a bottle and re-filled the old farmer's glass. "I'm going to stop talking to you now. Drink up."

Ulbreck did exactly that.

To Ulbreck's mind, there was one thing wrong with the galaxy: people. People and droids. Well, those were two things—but then again, wasn't it wrong to limit what was wrong with the galaxy to just one thing? How fair was that? That was how the old farmer's thinking tended to go, even when he was sober. In sixty standard years of moisture farming, Ulbreck had formed one theory about life after another. But he'd spent enough of the early years working alone—odd, how not even his farmhands wanted to be around him—that all his notions had piled up, unspoken.

That was what visits to town were for: opportunities for Ulbreck to share the wisdom of a lifetime. When he wasn't getting robbed by diabolical droids pretending to be green bartenders.

They weren't supposed to allow droids inside Junix's Joint—that was what the ancient sign outside the Anchorhead bar said. Junix, whoever he was, was long since dead and buried in the sands of Tatooine, but his bar still stood: a dimly lit dive where the cigarra smoke barely covered the stink of farmers who'd been in the desert all day. Ulbreck seldom visited the place, preferring an oasis establishment closer to home. But having traveled to Anchorhead to chew out a vaporator parts supplier, he'd stopped in to fill his canteen.

Now, half a dozen lum ales later, Ulbreck began thinking about home. His wife was waiting for him there, and he knew he had better go. Then again, his wife was waiting for him there, and that was reason enough for him to stay. He and Magda had had a horrible fight that morning over whatever it was they'd fought about the night before. Ulbreck couldn't remember what that was now, and it pleased him.

Still, he was an important man, with many underlings

who would steal him blind if he was away too long. Through a haze, Ulbreck looked to the chrono on the wall. There were numbers there, and some of them were upside down. And dancing. Ulbreck scowled. He was no fan of dancing. Ears buzzing, he slid off the bar stool, intent on giving the digits a piece of his mind.

That was when the floor attacked him. A swift, scurrilous advance, intent on striking him in the head when he wasn't looking.

It would have succeeded, had the hand not caught him.

"Careful, there," said the hand's owner.

Bleary-eyed, Ulbreck looked up the arm and into the hooded face of his rescuer. Blue eyes looked back at him from beneath sandy-colored eyebrows.

"I don't know you," Ulbreck said.

"Yes," the bearded human responded, helping the old farmer back onto the stool. Then he moved a few paces away to get the bartender's attention.

The brown-cloaked man had something in his other arm, Ulbreck now saw—a bundle of some kind. Alerted, Ulbreck looked around to see whether his own bundle was missing before remembering that he never had a bundle.

"This isn't a nursery," the bartender told the newcomer, although Ulbreck couldn't figure out why.

"I just need some directions," the hooded man responded.

Ulbreck knew many directions. He'd lived long enough on Tatooine to visit lots of places, and while he hated most of them and would never go back, he prided himself on knowing the best shortcuts to them. Certain that his directions would be better than those provided by a droid pretending to be a Duros, Ulbreck moved to intervene.

This time, he caught the railing himself.

Ulbreck looked back warily at the glass on the bar. "That drink ain't right," he said to the bartender. "You're—you're . . ."

The newcomer interjected cautiously, "You mean to say they're watering the ale?"

The bartender looked at the hooded guest and smirked. "Sure, we *always* add the scarcest thing on Tatooine to our drinks. We rake in the credits that way."

"Ain't what I mean," Ulbreck said, trying to focus. "You've done slipped somethin' in this drink to put me out. So you can take my money. I know you city types."

The bartender shook his bald head and looked behind him to his similarly hairless wife, who was washing up at the sink. "Close it up, Yoona. We've been found out." He looked to the hooded stranger. "We've been piling customers' bodies in the back room for years—but I guess that's all over now," he said jokingly.

"I won't tell a soul," the newcomer said, smiling. "In exchange for directions. And a bit of blue milk, if you have it."

Ulbreck was puzzling through that exchange when the bartender's expression changed to one of concern. The old farmer turned to see several young humans entering through the arched doorway, cursing and laughing. Through his haze, Ulbreck recognized the drunken rowdies.

The two in their twenties were brother and sister Mullen and Veeka Gault, hellion spawn of Ulbreck's greatest competitor out west, Orrin Gault. And their cronies were here, too. Zedd Grobbo, the big menace who could outlift a loader droid; and, at just a little over half his size, young Jabe Calwell, son of one of Ulbreck's neighbors.

"Get that kid out of here," the bartender yelled when

he saw the teenage tagalong. "Like I told the other guy, the day care's around the block."

At the reference, Ulbreck heard catcalls from the young punks—and he noticed his savior turning to face the wall with his bundle, away from the troublemakers. Veeka Gault shoved past Ulbreck and grabbed a bottle from behind the bar. She paid the Duros with an obscene gesture.

Her fellow hooligans had moved on to a helpless victim: Yoona, the bartender's wife. Catching the startled Duros woman with a pile of empties on her tray, Zedd spun her around for sport, causing mugs to fly in all directions. One struck the shaggy head of a patron at a nearby table.

The Wookiee rose to register his towering disapproval. So did Ulbreck, who had disliked several generations of Gaults, and didn't mind helping to put this generation in its place. He staggered to a table near the group and prepared to raise his objections. But the Wookiee had precedence, and Ulbreck felt the table he was leaning against falling anyway, so he decided to check things out from the floor. He heard a scuffling sound and only vaguely registered the arrival of the bartender's wife, who scuttled into cover beside him.

The Wookiee backhanded Zedd, sending him across the room—and into the table of some people Ulbreck was pretty sure *were* thieves, even though they weren't droids. He'd eyed the green-skinned, long-snouted Rodians all afternoon and evening, wondering when they'd harass him. He knew henchmen for Jabba the Hutt when he saw them. Now, their table upended, the thugs moved—chairs overturning as they shot to their feet and reached for their guns.

"No blasters!" Ulbreck heard the bartender yell as customers stampeded for the exit. The call didn't do a bit of good. Trapped between advancing attackers, the Gaults, who had drawn their pistols when the Wookiee struck their comrade, began firing back at the Rodians. Young Jabe might have fired his weapon, too, Ulbreck saw, had the Wookiee not lifted him from the floor. The titan held the howling boy aloft, about to hurl him into a wall.

The bearded newcomer knelt beside Ulbreck against the bar and leaned across him toward the bartender's wife. "Take care of this," the man said, placing his bundle in her hands. Then he dashed into the fray.

Ulbreck returned his attention to the bar fight. Above him, the Wookiee threw Jabe at the wall. But somehow, boy and wall never met; as Ulbreck craned his neck to see, Jabe's flailing body flew in an unnatural curve through the air and landed behind the bar.

Stunned, Ulbreck looked to see if Yoona had seen the same thing. But she was frozen in terror, eyes squeezed shut. Then a blaster shot struck the floor near them. She opened her eyes. With a scream, she shoved the bundle into Ulbreck's hands and crawled away.

Ulbreck turned his own frightened eyes back to the brawl, expecting to see the Wookiee beating Jabe to a pulp. He saw, instead, the hooded man—holding Jabe's blaster and pointing it at the ceiling. The man fired once at the lightglobe suspended overhead. A second later, Junix's Joint was in darkness.

But not silence. There was the Wookiee's howl. The blaster shots. The shattered glass. And then there was the strange humming sound, even louder than the one in Ulbreck's ears. Ulbreck feared to peer around the edge of the table shielding his body. But when he did, he could make out the silhouette of the hooded man, lit by a wash of blue light—and stray blaster bolts of orange, ricocheting harmlessly into the wall. Dark figures advanced—the criminal Rodians?—but they fell away, screaming, as the human advanced.

Ulbreck slid back behind the table, trembling.

When quiet finally came, all Ulbreck could hear was a gentle rustling inside the blanket on his lap. Fumbling for the utility light he carried in his pocket, Ulbreck activated it and looked down at the bundle he was holding.

A tiny baby with a wisp of blond hair gurgled at him.

"Hello," Ulbreck said, not knowing what else to say.

The infant cooed.

The bearded man appeared at Ulbreck's side. Lit from below by the portable light, he looked kindly—and not at all fatigued by whatever he had just done. "Thank you," he said, taking the child back. Starting to rise, he paused. "Excuse me. Do you know the way to the Lars homestead?"

Ulbreck scratched his beard. "Well, now, there's four or five ways to get there. Let me think of the best way to describe it—"

"Never mind," the man replied. "I'll find it myself." He and the child disappeared into the darkness.

Ulbreck rose now, turning the light onto the room around him.

There was no-good Mullen Gault, being revived by his no-good sister, as Jabe limped toward the open doorway. Ulbreck could just make out the Wookiee outside, evidently chasing after Zedd. The bartender was in the back, consoling his wife.

Jabba's thugs lay dead on the floor.

The old farmer slumped back down again. What had happened in here? Had the stranger really taken on the toughs alone? Ulbreck didn't remember seeing him with a weapon. And what about Jabe, who'd seemed to hang in the air before he dropped behind the bar? And what was that blasted flashing blue light?

Ulbreck shook his aching head, and the room spun a little. No, truth was, he just couldn't trust his besotted eyes. No one would risk his neck against Jabba's toughs. And no one would bring a baby to a bar fight. No decent person, anyway. Certainly not some hero type.

"People are just no good," Ulbreck said to no one. Then he went to sleep.

Meditation

The package is delivered.

I hope you can read my thoughts, Master Qui-Gon: I haven't heard your voice since that day on Polis Massa, when Master Yoda told me I could commune with you through the Force. You'll remember that we decided I should take Anakin's son to his relatives for safekeeping. That mission is now accomplished.

It feels so strange, being here, at this place and in this circumstance. Years ago, we removed one child from Tatooine, thinking him to be the galaxy's greatest hope. Now I have returned one—with the same goal in mind. I hope it goes better this time. Because the path to this moment has been filled with pain. For the whole galaxy, for my friends—and for me.

I still can't believe the Jedi Order is gone—and the Republic, corrupted and in the hands of Palpatine. And Anakin, corrupted as well. The holovids I saw of him slaughtering the Jedi younglings in the Temple still haunt my dreams . . . and shatter my heart into pieces, over and over again.

But after the horror of children's deaths, a child may bring hope, as well. It's as I said: the delivery is made. I'm standing on a ridge with my riding beast—a Tatooine eopie—looking back at the Lars homestead. Owen and Beru Lars are outside, holding the child. The last chapter is finished: a new one has begun.

I'll look for a place nearby, though if I hang around too long, I half expect Owen will want me to move someplace else, farther away. There may be wisdom in that. I seem to attract trouble, even in such a remote place as this. There was some mischief yesterday at Anchorhead—and before that, some trouble in one of the spaceports I passed through. None of it was really about me, thankfully, or why I'm here. But I can't afford to react to things as Obi-Wan Kenobi anymore. I won't be able to turn on my lightsaber without screaming "Jedi Knight" to everyone around. Even on Tatooine, I expect someone knows what that is!

So this will be it. From here on out, as long as it takes, I'm minding my own business and staying out of trouble. I can't play Jedi for this world and help save the other worlds at the same time. Isolation is the answer.

The city—even a village like Anchorhead—runs at too fast a pace. Out on the periphery, though, should be another story. I can already feel time moving at a different pace—to the rhythm of the desert.

Yes, I expect things will be slower. I'll be far from anywhere, and alone, with nothing but my regrets to keep me company.

If only there were a place to hide from those.